ENTRAPMENT

GREG PRADO

Titanite Books

Contributors:
Editor, Tawdra Kandle
Cover Design, Glencora Martinez

ISBN: 9781707408436

To Devyn, who believed in me and my dreams
before they'd manifested as a reality.

ENTRAPMENT

ONE

ALICE TRUDEAU SAT TAPPING HER FOOT ANXIOUSLY. SHE sliced open a vacuum-sealed container of cigarettes and fumbled with the packaging as she eagerly plugged one into her lips.

I know I'm supposed to wait 'til we are there, but it's just—this isn't my life, she thought.

Alice possessed a sort of refined beauty. She was skinny and tall. Her walnut-colored hair fell just beneath her shoulders. It was straight as an arrow. Her white blouse was neatly pressed. Her clingy black pencil skirt was short enough to be interesting, but long enough to cover all the important parts. Why had she chosen to wear this outfit? Alice uncomfortably shifted in her seat. The first few hours of travel were almost manageable, but by midnight, she wished for sweatpants.

Alice tried to maintain her face, despite almost all aspects of her life falling to bits. Image was everything for the head of the household. She could not allow cracks to show on the surface of her visage. Doing so would just cast blood in the water for sharks who were all too eager to devour the fortune that lay firmly in her control now. So, Alice sat in her seat on this train, uncomfortable and anxious. She tried to breathe as best as she could but found herself gasping every time she looked forward to her new charges.

A pair of blonde children sat in front of her. James and Eleanor Wortz were nine and eighteen respectively, and right now, the pair looked almost giddy. They were in Alice's care, but they most definitely did not belong to her.

Fucking Jack, she thought, with a twitch in her eye. *I'm not a mom. This isn't me. Why did he have to—*

"Aunt Alice, look!" James piped up.

The boy pointed out the window at a serpentine ice cavern the train was passing through. The wheels clicked as they crossed a steel bridge which stretched over a mammoth gap in the ice cap. The air pocket was two to three hundred meters across and snaked out in various directions almost endlessly. They had already been traveling for three hours underground.

We must be close now, Alice thought, rolling her eyes. She was completely immune to the resplendent beauty surrounding this modern marvel of technology as it continued to dip deeper into the ice cap.

"Blue Life" was scrawled across almost every surface in the lavish train. The branding was gaudy and distasteful. The light blue cursive font whose letters all flowed into each other curved into a circling flourish at the end. Alice Trudeau was not *that* kind of rich, she liked to think. She tried to differentiate herself from the others on the passenger car by how she treated the ordinals. She always thanked them for their service. She tried to slip credit chits to them whenever possible. She was almost a humanitarian.

The ordinals were a group of people enslaved in everything but name. They'd come to Mars searching for a better life. Upon arrival, they'd found rental prices that always seemed to perfectly match their annual salaries. They fell further into debt, all the while trying to stay afloat. Often, twelve were assigned to a room.

This was, of course, incomprehensible to Alice. She was just trying to survive minute-to-minute.

"How much longer is this train ride?" Eleanor moaned.

Alice considered lighting the cigarette in her mouth. There was hardly any danger down here. She was burning an exhaustible air supply, but this was an exceptional situation. She ripped the white stick from her mouth and tried to hide it from Eleanor's view.

"Soon, love," Alice tried to sound less than annoyed for her niece's benefit. "Right around the corner, I'm sure."

A moment later, the train was swallowed by the glistening blue-white tunnel again. It looked like it would scrape the sides of the vehicle at any moment. Alice knew this was hardly likely, especially with explicit care that was taken in the production of the train, but she couldn't help fiddling nervously with the nicotine-laced tobacco in her fingers. It had been eight years. She had almost forgotten what the taste was going to be.

Alice was looking forward to the beach, the crisp open air, and the luxurious speakeasy atmosphere with libations of every kind at their resort destination. She honestly doubted it was going to be a good place to bring children, but she wasn't exactly off to a fantastic start with the guardianship, anyway. This was a once-in-a-lifetime opportunity. She had, of course, heard the rumors about the grandeur of The Arbor.

Everyone had.

Alice had almost jumped out of her skin when she'd read the initial correspondence. Blue Life, the conglomerate her father used to work for, had written with condolences on the death of her brother. A certificate had been enclosed for seven nights at the *exclusive* ice lodge at the pole. It had sounded like a fairy tale: Alexis Fox had done the impossible. He had done what others might never have even considered. He made spending seven nights under two-kilometers of the polar ice cap sound not only intriguing, but scintillating.

Eleanor sat with her mid-back-length strawberry blonde hair curled lightly over her shoulders. She was slumped in her own row, with her arm braced against the window. Satellite reception couldn't pierce the ice. As someone who was so used to getting the news, updates, and communications from Mars and Earth, she was really struggling to entertain herself during the first few hours of her trip. She had no idea how she was going to survive a week down there. She figured the Lodge had to have a relay connection to the outside world. There was simply no way those important people would be disconnected from their money for that long. She guessed the Ordinals working there would probably want to talk to their families, too. *Do they have to pay for their calls?* she wondered. *Are they even allowed to make calls?*

She huffed and glanced down at her transparent phone display. With a button press, it lit and displayed a hologram projection of the time that seemed to hover above the sheet of glass. 11:42 PM shone brightly, illuminating the dim train cabin.

In front of her, a man groaned and began to stir at the light.

There was someone in front of her? Eleanor hadn't even seen him get on. He must have been sleeping for the entire ride. Despite this, it appeared that his slumber was nearing its end. She saw a messy head of black hair peek above the wrapped leather seat directly in front of her. He looked young—ish . . . maybe twenty-four? Eleanor *was* eighteen now. She was an adult. In fact, she had been one for several months. She didn't need to ask her aunt's permission for anything.

Was that too old, she wondered? Eleanor had never met a boy she didn't like. She hardly expected this trend to radically change now, especially when she had a week to kill all alone.

"Eleanor!" James' face popped through the armrest beside her.

"Jesus!" she exclaimed. "What do you want?"

"I'm bored," he said before drifting off in thought for a few seconds.

Eleanor grunted and looked back toward the little red x in the corner of her phone. She thought that maybe her sheer force of will could push radio waves through miles of ice.

"Want to play a game!" He wasn't asking her a question, he was telling her what they were going to do. *He* wanted to play a game, and made it clear this was what was happening. "Let's do I spy."

This should be fun, she sighed in resignation.

"Fine. I'll go first," she said, her eyes searching the cabin.

The locomotive was a throwback to the early rail era of the 19th century. Faux wood paneling lined the walls in a convincingly printed pattern that almost looked like mahogany. There was carpet along the floor in an oriental diamond pattern. The mauves and verdant greens twisted in and around each other as they snaked up the narrow corridor between the sets of double seats. Her eyes drifted to the roof of the car where she saw hanging lamps with frosted glass and fire-like glow emanating from them. They bathed the passenger car in an intimate luminescence that encouraged sleep and curiosity.

Finally, her eyes rested on it.

"I spy something peach," she spoke confidently.

James looked around eagerly like a cat searching for a butterfly. His eyes combed the luxurious compartment for what his sister's gaze might have fallen upon.

"Is it the carpet?" he asked.

"No!" she returned.

He continued looking. Despite a variety of shades in the train car, James struggled to figure out his sister's discovery. He stood up out of his seat and peered down the open cabin. He saw the recently restless man with black hair two rows ahead of him, an older man in a black tuxedo at the end of the car, and an ostrich head at the back wall, peeking from a trophy mount beside the exit door.

"Is it the ostrich?" he wondered, staring at the pinkish neck.

"You got it," she breathed in an unimpressed whisper. Eleanor was trying to sneak a glance between the seats to observe more of the black-haired man's bulging arm. A single vein ran down his tricep out of his short sleeved button-down. She subconsciously raised her eyebrows in interest as he reached upward for a stretch, linking his fingers together and rising from his seated position.

He was gorgeous, sporting tanned skin that must have been hard to maintain on Mars. The button-down brushed gunmetal shirt was just slightly tight in all the right places. He wore a a pair of neatly pressed khakis that had wrinkles running down the backside. *What a backside it is,* she thought to herself.

"Eleanor, it's my turn!" James piped up.

"In a minute," she returned absently.

"How far out are we?" The man's smooth voice cracked as he leaned over and cricked his neck to the side. He looked over Eleanor's doe-eyes to ask Ms. Trudeau.

"Oh, I'm not sure." Alice almost stumbled with her words as she was yanked from her daydream about cigarettes. "Perhaps another hour or so?"

The man nodded heartily and glanced around the car to find it empty except for the children and Alice. "I guess we're the only ones who were damned fool enough to hop on the first plane out," he chuckled lightly to himself as he flattened the creases in his shirt and rested his elbows on the top of his seat to talk to Alice.

Eleanor was speechless as the well-built man leaned over her. He talked like some early movie star and looked the part as well. His accent let her know that he was American. She wasn't usually fond of men from the United States. They were so self-righteous and proud. This gentleman hardly appeared to be any exception to the rule, but by God—she could see herself forgiving all sorts of malfeasances for him.

"Yeah, it's been a bad few months," Alice said, knowing that she had just invited follow-up questions. "This vacation is going to be really good for all of us."

The man nodded and seemed to think to himself for a moment. "Do they even allow children at the lodge?"

Alice let out a single "Hah!" as she leaned back and looked out her window. "I don't really have much choice here. . ." she continued.

Eleanor broke her transfixed gaze on the black-haired man to glance back toward Alice. She probably didn't mean that the way it sounded, but it stung nonetheless.

". . .that is to say, they need it as much as I do. When their parents—" The words caught in Alice's mouth. She noticed Eleanor's scowl through the seat cushions and paused.

The black-haired man noticed the awkward exchange and moved into the aisle quickly. He took a few large steps back toward Alice and threw himself down beside her without being invited or welcomed.

On the contrary, Eleanor seemed to pierce her aunt's soul as her glare intensified. It was one thing to hint at the fact that she was an orphan now, but quite another to stand between Eleanor and an attractive man.

Alice finally had to look away to force the tense situation to abate. She found herself face-to-face with the American at an all-too-personal proximity. She leaned back against the windowsill to give herself some room. This was neither the time nor the place for a new fling, and she quite familiar with the fact that her romantic decision making was among the worst.

"I'm Winston Graham," he said, thrusting a well-worked hand forward to again invade Alice's personal space.

"Alice Trudeau," she spoke softly, hesitantly offering her palm to the extremely handsome man. "It's a pleasure to meet you."

She had always been taught to be proper and polite in social interactions. Although her family had emigrated to Mars from Great Britain, they were hardly about to leave proper United Kingdom culture behind on their home planet. Alice had only lived without her mother for a couple of years. She had finally gotten her independence. Now, she had kids.

"I assure you, the pleasure is all mine," Winston returned.

Eleanor exhaled sharply and looked at James, who was sitting rather dumbfounded as a silent observer at all the levels of the conversation unfolding before him.

"James!" she barked.

"What?" he returned, confused by her frustrated tone.

"It's your turn," she muttered through clenched teeth.

The children continued to chat as the train clicked onward.

"So, Alice, have you been to The Arbor before?" Winston asked.

"No, this is my first time. I'm very excited to see it. Like I said, it's been so long since I had time to relax. This stuff with the estate has dragged on for months and months. It is odd to think that almost a year ago, I lost my brother," Alice's sentence drifted off toward the end. She blinked absently to try to whip herself back to reality.

"I'm sorry," Winston placed a rough hand over hers.

"No, it's fine," Alice assured him. She was so used to saying it that she had almost begun to believe it. "Mother always told me I was the strong one. I just didn't believe her. I still don't."

Alice's life had spiraled out of control over the last two years. Her father had died when she was fourteen, leaving her mother as the primary caregiver for most of her teenage years. They'd moved to Mars for a fresh start. Jack, her brother, had had a job lined up, and it had seemed like the most sensible thing to keep the family together. They had the means and absolutely nothing tying them to Earth anymore. Life had been so happy and carefree for a while, then Alice's mother had died of a brain hemorrhage. It was instantaneous. Alice had been so enjoying her work that she hadn't really bothered to keep a strong connection to her family. She regretted that more every day.

"I believe it," Winston nodded. "You're tough, I can tell. I work as head of security at the peacekeeper plant. I know the ones who have what it takes to cause damage and the ones who are all talk. You, Alice, I would not want to cross."

A grin managed to creep its way across her face.

"Well, that is sweet of you to say," Alice replied, lowering her gaze slightly and trying not to shake her head in disagreement. "I just didn't see any of this coming. I mean, first my mum, then my brother gets—"

Winston had an intense stare. He was riveted by her tale. Alice knew that look well. Her tale of woe and sadness often had proved entertainment for her "friends." They devoured the details like wolves, ever hungrier for the goriest tidbits. She was tired of being murder porn for bored heiresses.

"You know what?" Alice stopped herself. "Let's talk about you. You said you worked in security?"

Winston sat up a little bit taller, entirely proud of himself. The one reliable standby when conversing with the ultra-rich was the predictability of how easily they could be distracted to talk about themselves.

"Yes ma'am!" He smiled. "I work with the best in the business, keeping our factory line safe. There has been more than one nasty character try to break into our facility, thinking they can rewire the robots or something. We have successfully shut down all attempts thus far with *extreme* prejudice."

"Wow," Alice pretended to be fascinated by his minimally interesting life. "That's quite interesting. So how many assaults have there been?"

"Well, Mr. Fox doesn't like me to discuss the specifics," he frowned. "Let's just say there has been plenty of action, and I know how to handle myself."

Mr. Fox? Now there was someone she wanted to learn more about. He lived a notoriously cloistered life. He was a man of business and did that one thing well. Eccentric was the most fitting word to describe him. Although he had led Jones Computing and Networking for ten years now, no paparazzi photos of him had ever been released as far as Alice was aware. He teleconferenced most of the time, or so people said, and had been quoted many times as saying he never wanted his family to be a part of his business. He was keen on keeping them out of the public eye as much as possible. With the wealth that had been amassed by the sale of peacekeepers, he could do that and then some. This was especially true because Fox also owned Centurion, the broadcasting network of Mars. He was able to effortlessly scrub all mentions of himself outside of JCN thanks to a "minimally invasive" AI construct that had been tasked with keeping his family out of the news.

"You've worked with Mr. Fox?" Alice almost spat.

Winston chuckled and nodded. "Yeah, department heads get to conference directly with him every quarter or so. I've actually met him once. That's why I'm here!"

Winston pulled out a letter from his pocket. It was the most immaculate cursive scrolling Alice had ever seen, and she had been forced to take calligraphy as a child.

Mr. Winston Graham,

Your exemplary service in the line of duty has been observed and will be rewarded henceforth. To begin, you are invited to join me at my personal lodge in the tunnels of Blue Life water processing. I have created something truly extraordinary there and see fit to share it with just a few lucky souls every year. If you find this proposition amenable, you will find your tickets enclosed for one week of your choosing. Please provide sufficient notice so that I might be in attendance to welcome you.

Sincerely,

Alexis Fox

"He's going to welcome you *personally?*" Alice was shocked, and her voice didn't hide that.

"That's what the letter says," Winston reiterated. He laughed for a few seconds and then added, "I guess that means he does an excellent job with public relations when I am this excited to see my boss in person."

Winston was hardly alone. Alice was thrilled to be getting the chance to meet Mr. Fox, if only for the insider info she would gain from the experience—not that she had much time for gossip anymore. Her eyes drifted back to the icy walls shooting past her window. She was returning to the dark place now. She couldn't help thinking of Eleanor, standing there in stupefied shock in the entryway as she gazed at a pair of legs at the end of the hallway. Her mother's body lay across the threshold of the master bedroom.

The police had said that it was a robbery gone bad. That was equal parts oversimplification and understatement. Jack was so short-sighted. Someone must have known that he kept a reserve of platinum under his bed. He didn't trust the banks on Mars. He said everything was a little too chummy. Maybe if he had placed more confidence in the burgeoning financial system, he would still be alive.

At some point, Alice drifted off to sleep.

She was jolted awake by a surprising announcement.

"I'm Alexis Fox..."

TWO

AS THOUGH A BUCKET OF ICE WATER HAD BEEN TOSSED haphazardly in her lap, Alice awoke with a start and sat bolt upright. She looked with bleary eyes around a dimmed cabin. The lights had been taken down to almost nothing except for a bright outline which she could hardly make out walking down the narrow hall.

". . .and I have a question for you. Do you yearn to breathe free?"

The vague silhouette of a man in his late fifties continued to move confidently at a snail's pace down the aisle. The projection was incredibly vivid, although it was monochrome in varying shades of three-dimensional white and grey. His arms would occasionally brush against a leather seat and stretch themselves in an inhuman glow over the material before reforming again.

Alice had worked with this technology before. She was a city planner on Mars, in charge of two settlements that were just beginning to find their footing. With the rise of automation, Earth had become an inhospitable job environment. What had once been a sci-fi fantasy, colonization of a foreign world, changed to become a bastion of hope for the unemployed billions. Their home planet was dreadfully overcrowded, over-polluted, and had a definite bias against those less fortunate. Mars had that same prejudice too, but it was hardly sold that way to the huddled masses.

"Wow," James whispered. "That's wicked."

The boy looked up with wonder into the apparition before him as though a spirit had appeared in their midst. Light trumpets were blowing a patriotic tune as accompaniment to the man's continuing monologue.

"The United Mars government will tell you that it's a crime to waste. They say recycling and reuse are a Martian's responsibility. I would posit another argument. Our communal styles of living have all but erased the individual and his right to enjoyment of the self. When I advanced the idea of constructing a lodge underneath two miles of water-ice, some laughed and called it impossible. I will tell you this: I have never served as jester to anyone."

He spoke with such wanton confidence that Eleanor found herself enraptured. Even the self-assured Mr. Graham sat back in his chair to get a better look at the towering phantom. He stood almost seven feet high. His hair was parted to the right, and his suit looked elegant even in projected profile.

"I am a man of industry but I desired to return to a world before the advent of the technology into which we have all been born. I craved a world without phones buzzing in our pockets. I wished for a world nestled securely in humanity's glistening golden age. I gave birth to an oasis.

"I created: The Arbor."

The pitch-black cabin was suddenly bathed in light as the train emerged from its tunnel and the passengers got their first real view of the lodge that they had all heard so much about. Alexis Fox's image disappeared to give the full striking effect he clearly desired.

Eleanor's eyes widened in disbelief as she stood to her feet to get a better view.

The train was about a hundred feet above an impossibly large mansion surrounded by a towering dome of ice, like a snow-globe. The canopy was still another fifty feet above their heads and rose to a narrow vent at the ceiling in the middle of a glassy blue paradise.

The home itself, if Arbor was to be called that, was modeled on the height of 1920s opulence. Its apricot-painted exterior stretched upward for two stories. The Spanish tile roof was dotted at either end by a pair of conical turret accents.

Eleanor and James almost pushed each other over as they scrambled to the opposite benches from their resting positions to stare downward at the breathtaking sight.

"It has a *beach*?" Eleanor's voice cracked with excitement.

Even Alice walked mesmerized across the walkway and kneeled on the cushioned leather to raise her view ever so slightly. She felt Winston walk up uncomfortably close behind her to join in their enchanted viewing.

The palatial estate had at least five bedrooms that Alice could count on the side of building that was currently facing her. She guessed there were at least twelve living spaces, including the almost guaranteed Ordinal quarters. Eleanor was right. A long white-sand beach sat at the end of a gratuitously portioned lawn. A tennis court with cherry clay surfacing was placed directly behind the home. Alice struggled to take it all in as the train sped toward another tunnel.

Mr. Fox's voice continued behind them.

"An escape for man and woman alike, The Arbor shatters the shackles of modernity and provides a rarified experience that is to be luxuriated in by all who grace its lavish halls."

"Holy shit," Winston mumbled.

"You can say that again!" James piped up without breaking his gaze with the mansion.

"James," Alice halfheartedly chastised, her stare also transfixed.

"I invite you to this distinctive experience," Mr. Fox's booming voice added. "I challenge you to expand your horizons. I am delighted to be the first to welcome you to my paradise. Revel in your time here, and return to your world entirely changed by mine."

Less than a minute after the view had emerged, it disappeared all at once. They were again surrounded by now-glistening ice. The air was clearly above freezing temperatures at the lodge, how far above freezing remained to be seen.

Alice began to toy with the cigarette she had almost forgotten that she'd palmed.

"I've been waiting for that, too," Winston smiled, producing a lighter from his pocket. "I'm so goddamn tired of being told it will clog carbon scrubbers. Sometimes I just want to have a smoke."

Eleanor looked over her seat at the silvery box as he clicked it and produced a cobalt jet of flame. She looked to Alice, waiting for her response.

Alice was uncomfortable and entirely uncertain. On the one hand, she wasn't Eleanor's mother. On the other, if she didn't provide an example for her only remaining family, who would?

"Oh, that's all right, Mr. Graham. I think I'll wait until after dinner." She gave a polite nod and returned the cigarette to its opened carton.

"Suit yourself, I suppose." Winston wasn't about to let his excitement fizzle as he raised a stick to his mouth and gave a long drag that seemed to last for hours in Alice's mind. She watched without trying to seem like she was undressing the wrappings of paper with her eyes.

A moment later, the steward moved to their side. He seemed uncertain but reached to tap Winston on the shoulder.

"I'm so sorry, sir," he began. "But you'll need to wait until we reach mansion grounds to smoke."

Winston let a puff escape the side of his mouth in the direction of the poor suited man.

"Fuck off," Winston groaned.

"Sir—" the ordinal began, but stopped himself. "I do hope you enjoy your stay."

Eleanor knew the rich had a disdainful attitude toward the ordinals. They thought themselves above the poor, and why shouldn't they? Ordinals literally lived below their feet in hollowed out longhouses underground. The construction method was cheaper than living on the surface, if you didn't mind the mildew and lack of windows. Several families crowded into a bunkhouse in one long room that had a pair of bathrooms at the end and a single kitchen halfway down the row of beds. Life was far from luxurious for those less fortunate.

Alice furrowed her brow at Winston and almost wanted to say something, but hesitated as the train's brakes caused the cabin to slightly shift. She tried not to think about the fact that she had two pairs of eyes watching every little move she made. How would she ever live up to Jack and Cara's example? She was a poor imitation of perfection, and an unworthy substitute. Still, Alice was absolutely resolute in her determination to provide the best life she could for these children. If only she could communicate that to them.

The steel sang as the rolling mechanical behemoth came to a slow screeching halt. The brake calipers released with a hiss, and the suited ordinal moved to open the exterior cabin door. He immediately turned to a closet they had hardly noticed and began retrieving floor-length overcoats. There were a pair of fur-adorned ones for the ladies, and navy-blue suit coats for the gentlemen. The chill was evident as fresh air began to flood the cabin.

Eleanor shivered at the frigid atmosphere and was the first to stride forward and retrieve her coat. It looked custom-tailored. The ordinal handed hers over with a confident grin. She slipped it over her shoulders and marveled as it hugged tightly to her curves as though it had been measured for her. That seemed impossible. James followed quickly on her heels and eagerly snatched for the miniature men's coat that lay beside a much larger one that was clearly intended for Mr. Graham.

Alice tilted her head in slight disbelief. She was breathing free and unrestricted air for the first time in what felt like eons. Her feet began to move on their own toward the front of the train. She'd known that the experience would be unique when she'd accepted the invitation, but she wasn't expecting anything of this magnitude.

The fur felt warm against her skin. It was softer than she could have imagined. She had felt faux-fur before that was often incredibly convincing and had she never experienced this coat she would have known no different, but this was *real*. It was beyond luxurious, it was extravagant. The entire experience would have left a sour taste in her mouth on any other day, but now, she had been swept up into the magic. Alice was entirely breathless on this journey. If nothing else, it had served as a worthy distraction from the droning on of what had become her day-to-day life.

James was the first to disembark down the shining brass steps that the ordinal had extended to the ground. His eyes scanned the station in near-disbelief. A shimmering scarlet carpet extended from the train about a hundred feet ending at a rounded disc that he assumed was a door of some sort. James had no idea how it was to open, and he hardly cared at the moment. The train arrival area was no more than a hundred feet long, but he was able to see the

tunnel continuing beyond the icy platform. As he glanced down
the welcoming area, he saw another pair of red carpets, both con-
verging in a trident toward that same round nickel-colored door.

Maybe more people are coming? he thought.

James took his first step onto the frozen platform and shivered although the coat was keeping him quite warm. He reached
down to brush his hand against the ice, almost to verify its status,
and patted it contentedly as his hand moistened on the surface. It
was freezing in the cavern, obviously. He wondered what it would
feel like after that nickel portal rolled its way open.

As James continued down the path, he paused. A clicking
noise startled him, and a projection illuminated in an arch above
him. He had never seen projections used like this. It was always
for entertainment purposes, not for illusions. It looked as though
he was really walking under a pearlescent archway.

"Let go"

He walked farther and a second archway lit above him.

"Of your troubles"

A curious grin turned into a large smile as he walked closer
to the door.

"And embrace"

He almost ran to the door with adolescent excitement as a
final sign completed the phrase.

"The Arbor"

Winston Graham stepped from the train just after Eleanor.
He straightened his suit coat and took a deep breath as the chilled
air filled his lungs. It burned ever so slightly, but he was too en-
amored to care. The sight was stunning. Cobalt flood lights illuminated the walls of the cavern a deep and mysterious blue. The
towering ceiling sat fifty to sixty feet above their heads. There was
no obvious ventilation, but there must have been a good deal of
air pushed into the cave from some unseen filtration system. He

knew that they had passed an airlock door on their way into this station. The rushing air would have been difficult for a man to walk against, but a train had a massive amount of momentum to push through the pressure differences in the harsh Martian atmosphere. He knew that there were at least three storage tanks behind the passenger cars for the water-ice they were mining.

Blue Life was Mars' only provider of fresh water that wasn't produced by the recyclers. As the population boomed, some of the residents turned up their noses at drinking their own filtered refuse, even if it were almost identical to the mined water at the molecular level. The pure recycled water was used for agricultural purposes and for the ordinals down below. They were not exactly in a position to argue. He drew out a final puff of his cigarette and then stomped it out on the ice beside the carpet.

He had always been surrounded by beautiful things, but this was a level of splendor that he had never seen matched. He drank in the atmosphere, and although the cold was uncomfortable, he longed to feel the fresh air on his skin again. He shrugged the coat from his shoulders and let his arms expose themselves to the chill as his hair stood on end. They would be warm again soon enough. He wanted to enjoy this.

"My man, if you could?" Winston called as he tossed his coat back toward the train haphazardly. The ordinal managed to keep the thin line of his lips slightly angled upward as he bowed slightly, then briskly hopped to the carpet to grab the navy overgarment.

Alice moved to grab the coat for the man, but he quickly dipped in front of her.

"Beggin' your pardon, ma'am," he softly interjected as he retrieved it and returned to the train without another word. He shook his head slightly as he pulled the cabin door shut.

"Thank you!" she called a second too late.

Alice was very much a product of her two worlds. She

worked so closely with ordinals that she felt some familiarity and compassion toward them, but at the same time, she hesitated to be *too* empathetic. The wealthy were vindictive and even cruel at times. If she made herself seem less like she belonged, they might begin to view her as *one of them.* Ordinarily, this would not have concerned her, but she was the head of her family now. If she threw away their clout, her niece and nephew might have a much harder life and an even more challenging time being accepted into the higher workforce.

After she stepped a few paces farther, the train hissed and began to roll again down the tracks. The passenger cars crawled by and were followed by dozens of cylindrical storage containers for the water that would be mined down the line. Despite the fanciful nature of the visitor compartments, the train served a definite purpose other than ferry.

She caught up with Winston and continued to bathe in the atmosphere of the frozen terminal as she whispered almost reverently.

"I can't believe Fox built this here," she said.

"It would have been impossible for him to build it anywhere *but* here," Winston quickly retorted.

"And why is that?" Alice almost sniped.

"Think about it. The ice creates a bubble for the air held inside it. If it were built anywhere else on Mars, Mr. Fox would have had to construct an impossibly large dome, provide the raw materials, and then finance the mansion. At least here, the habitat was already created by mining efforts," Winston finished, confident that he had solved the mystery of the Arbor.

Up ahead, James reached his hand out to touch the circular door. Before he could make contact, the disc spun and separated into little pieces like a camera's iris. It retreated into the frame and revealed a small room that he assumed was the elevator.

The elevator had a round opening at each side with a precisely cut brass molding surrounding it. There were no buttons. There were no indicators. There was just a bare metal room with a peculiar being standing in the back righthand corner of the twelve foot by twelve- foot space.

The thing was an android of some sort. He wore a tuxedo and looked to be a man in almost every way except his face. There was no face. There was simply a glossy black curved oval in the shape of a head. He had on Oxford dress shoes, neatly pressed slacks, and velveteen white gloves, but Eleanor's eyes kept being pulled back to its lack of a face.

"That's fucking weird," she whispered to herself.

"What?" James called from a few feet in front of her as he stepped fearlessly inside.

"I said, that thing is weird," she grunted as she paused just outside the elevator door.

"If you would step inside." The android made a gesture with his gloved hand for her to move toward him. He didn't move his torso. He simply rotated his hand and pointed to the floor in front of him.

"Oh no." Eleanor whipped around to face Alice. "No way am I getting in there with that thing."

Alice looked around the stark elevator and smiled at the boy who was already rocking on his heels with excitement to see the wonderland that awaited below. He tapped his fingers eagerly against the chrome handrail and started to thump his foot.

"Well, Eleanor, the train just left," Alice said with a shrug. "You're either coming down with us or sitting here to freeze in the station for two days while the train loads up down the line."

"Come now, darling." Winston patted Eleanor's head as he strode inside the portal. He turned back around to face her and smiled as he waved her inside.

"Sure, Winston," Eleanor dizzily replied as she seemed to float into the confines of the sterile environment.

Alice hesitated before she walked inside. The elevator didn't fit with the rest of the experience. It seemed massively overbuilt. It was beyond sturdy. She wondered if it had been used for the mining operation that was here before the mansion, but it looked new. Something about the crisp appearance of the varying shades of silver and the perfectly still android made her shiver.

She finally joined the others, and the iris closed behind her almost instantly. Lights illuminated the room from cross-like fixtures in miniscule gaps between plates of metal. It looked decidedly modern. It just didn't fit the mansion, the train, the decor, or the man. She had a bad feeling. It was like something was pulling her back toward the train, but she fought the urge. Alice could feel the walls closing around her. She tried to smile for the kids.

Alice wasn't built to suffer through the trauma she had endured for these few years. She had wanted for nothing as a child. She had the tendency to make bad decisions and liked to run at the slightest sign of trouble. She wasn't ready for her mother to die. She wasn't prepared for her brother and sister-in-law to be murdered in cold blood. She couldn't fill their shoes. She certainly wasn't able to provide emotional support to a pair of young minds who needed guidance now more than ever.

Alice focused on evening her breathing. She thought back to what her therapist had said. Inhale for five seconds, hold it for two, exhale for seven seconds. Pause naturally. Let the bad thoughts pass like a ship in the night. When they come back, just let them slip back out again. Don't dwell.

She had her eyes closed for a few moments before a mechanical voice spoke again.

"My name is Silas, and I will be your steward for the

duration of your stay." The robot seemed to try to give all the gestures of a human butler as he opened his palms in a sign of fealty.

"I get a robot servant?" James spoke first.

"I am the steward for all of The Arbor," Silas returned neutrally. "I serve you and all of the other guests."

"There are no ordinals here?" Winston asked.

"No, sir," Silas answered. "Only the ones who are invited, the same as you."

Winston's face contorted as though he had bitten into a lemon.

"You *invite* ordinals here?" he clarified. "As *guests?*"

"Yes sir," Silas confirmed, his robotic voice containing no emotion. "Mr. Fox has guests of many different backgrounds here. Anyone can be invited to the Arbor. They are all given the same welcome."

"That's pretty cool," Eleanor said. "I never really understood why they have to be slaves everywhere."

Winston scoffed and was about to begin a volley of arguments when the back door of the elevator slid open. The white light of the room was mixed with the yellowish daylight color flooding through the door. It was bright, like a sunny day.

As a city planner, Alice knew the difference between faux brick print and laid brick. That said, the walkway was the most convincing forgery of red brick she had ever seen. The weathering was right. It even seemed to have the blackish mildew stains that always found its way between cracks in the porous material. She was more attracted to the grass. It was real.

"My God." She almost hopped from the doorway and dropped to her knees in the soft dirt. She ran her hands through the rich soil and wiry plant. It wasn't a grass, per se. Scientists had genetically modified plants with various algae blooms to create heartier breeds, which could survive in an environment with minimal atmosphere and harsh conditions. Whether it was a dust storm, flooding rain, blistering heat, or paralyzing frost, these amazing plants could not only survive, but thrive. They worked tirelessly to terraform the surface of the planet one hectare at a time. It seemed like this algal grass was what provided the oxygen supply to the Arbor.

"I haven't seen real grass since I was a little girl." Eleanor smiled and joined Alice on the lawn.

Alice wouldn't ruin the illusion created by the industrious Mr. Fox for her.

"Me neither." Alice smiled and nudged her niece. "This place is like paradise."

Winston hadn't stopped to revel in the little things. He was already halfway down the path to the mansion, and James was wandering aimlessly just behind him. He seemed so carefree and had nothing in his arms. It was strange for Alice to travel to a new destination without any luggage, but the instructions on the invitation had been clear.

Guests were allowed one bag each. That bag would be picked up by courier at the train station and delivered to the room just after guest check-in. This was another detail that seemed to bite at her. Why couldn't they just bring a carry-on? It was hardly the norm for people of means to carry their own bags, but the fact that it was prohibited was a strange thing to specify.

The air was crisp inside the dome. Temperatures seemed to hover in the low fifties. It was cold enough to require a jacket, but much more pleasant than the frigid reception terminal. The walls of the dome were moist as the air melted the massive mountain of ice above it at what must have been a snail's pace.

Alice knew it would be a very long time before the ice gave way. She guessed it would take hundreds of years, assuming no one did anything to stop the melting. The water dripped down along the sides into a horseshoe shaped lake which placed the mansion on a bit of a peninsula. The pathway wound down the narrow stretch of land toward the stunning peach building. It had a cream facade which came up to a pair of Gothic pointed architectural features on the second floor. A trio of decorative windows that resembled French doors sat facing the guests who were walking down the path. She saw a delicious-looking spread of hors d'oeuvres sprawled across a titanic table. Alice seriously considered going there first and skipping the check-in after what had been a fifteen-hour journey from their home between the flight and the train ride. She was starving. She hadn't been able to convince herself to eat along the way.

Without pausing to wait for the rest of the attendees, Winston pushed his way through a massive oak door. The wood was real and looked almost ancient. Black iron bindings ran along the face of the weathered entryway. Stained glass accents of emerald green, exotic purple, and canary yellow flanked the doorway in small circular accents along both sides of the framing. He grabbed the hammered brass handle and turned it hard. The hinges cracked and creaked slightly as it opened.

Silas had somehow reached the entryway before Mr. Graham and took the door from his hand as it opened.

"After you, sir." He motioned for Winston to enter the ornate room.

The entryway had natural stone tiling in a wide path down the middle of the room. The greys of the slate were surrounded by a tan grouting. The walls were a stucco, a soft Spanish orange that had been expertly smoothed. It looked as though it had been finished by hand. A dark mahogany reception desk sat directly in front of Winston. To his left, a group of guests were gathered silently in a huddle. They were just on the other side of an open, doorless entryway. Their eyes combed his frame, trying to figure him out.

"Fuck!" a young man exclaimed in a whisper.

He was immediately slapped on the chest by an older man standing beside him.

"Shut up, you're going to ruin it for all of us!" a woman whispered.

Winston tilted his head, curious and wondering. He didn't give it much thought before moving forward to the massive reception desk. A humanoid shape emerged from a nearby doorway and stopped at the rear of the desk. The android looked almost the same as Silas but had a pearly white globular head opposite his ebony colored counterpart.

"Sorry for the delay, sir!" The faceless man spoke. "Welcome to the Arbor."

"Thank you—" Winston paused uncomfortably.

"Timothy," the robot returned.

"Thanks, Timothy," Winston let his shoulders shrug slightly. He tried to let the tension drain after sleeping in such an uncomfortable position for so long.

"Your room key, sir." The robot passed a brass key to Winston. The number 7 was bolded in elevated golden typeface on a small wooden tag. Winston played with the key and gave a grin at the primitiveness of it all.

James was the next to enter the room. The same huddled mass of people let out whispered curses before speaking up softly.

"A kid? You can't be serious!" a man gasped.

James glanced at the group that was almost comically pressed to the doorframe. The four people continued to whisper with looks on their faces that James couldn't quite make sense of. There might have been disappointment, fear, anxiety, and anger, but James was more focused on finding his way to the food to worry himself much on the issue.

Eleanor came in on his heels and cast a curious glance on the people gathered to her left. Her eyes wandered up to spy Winston shuffling his way up a staircase that snaked around the wall of the round room. She wished at that moment she was a little older. Eleanor had just turned eighteen, but sometimes felt like she was still a child. She was told by everyone around her that she was an *old soul*. Eleanor knew that was what people said when they wanted to call someone an awkward loser without being mean.

She felt lucky to be where she was. She knew there were many underprivileged people all around her, but her last grade school years had been awkward. She should have been looking at colleges. Luckily, on Mars there was just one university—online school.

Sighing, she bit her lip slightly as Mr. Graham disappeared from view. She knew Winston was out of reach, but like the many colleges she wished for, a girl could dream.

As Alice moved into the reception area, something just felt strange. It was bright and roomy, like a hotel should be, but something wasn't sitting right with her. She felt a tugging in her gut. It was nerves. It had *always* been nerves. She hadn't been right since Jack had died. Seeing him like that seemed to change something within her in a permanent and unfixable way. She almost drifted through life now, unmoored and afraid. She checked her door locks multiple times before bed. She'd had the most advanced alarm system money could buy installed professionally inside her home. But despite these things, Alice still felt uneasy. She would jolt awake most nights in a cold sweat. The slightest croaking of the air recycler would send her tumbling into an anxiety attack. She slept with a stun gun under her pillow. Nothing seemed to bring her relief.

Why are all those eyes peering at me? Alice wondered. She shuddered a bit. *It's just your nerves, girl. Get ahold of yourself. You've not had a proper sleep in weeks. You need this.*

Suddenly, one of the sets of eyes widened ever so slightly and darted straight for her. Alice stepped back and reached to her side where she always kept her miniscule container of mace. She was ready to strike.

"Oh! My! God!" A woman almost shrieked, pacing her words awkwardly apart like a row of soldiers. "Alice Trudeau, how *are* you, darling?"

Alice let out a sigh as her estranged friend half-ran toward her.

"Hey, Rose," Alice smiled. "I'm surviving, dear."

Rose Grayson opened her arms for a hug without asking, flinging them around Alice's neck. Rose was always one to over-ex-aggerate her movements. Alice had often thought of her as a bit of a show-pony. That said, it was strange to see her again. The two of them had been positively inseparable before the issue with *Mark*. Alice pulled her mind away from him. That was not the way to repair what was already a tenuous reunion.

"Alice, we simply must catch up before I go. Care to pop over to the snacks? I'm a bit peckish, and I can smell the cake from here," Rose finished, bouncing on the arches of her feet and rock-ing slightly.

"Yeah, that sounds lovely," Alice began. "Let me get Eleanor and James set up with their room, and then we can dip in before I completely lose consciousness."

"Eleanor?" Rose paused. "James?"

"My niece and nephew," Alice clarified. "You don't remember them? I know they were just little when you last saw them. They have grown so m—"

"*Why would you bring them here, Alice?*" Rose screamed out hoarsely.

Alice was taken aback. She had not expected to see Rose in the first place, but this was entirely staggering. Eleanor and James looked back at Rose, who had made them feel like unwanted toys. James' constantly sunny disposition had become distinctly clouded in a single disquieting moment. The room was hushed. A feather falling to the cold stone floor would have sounded much like a cymbal clattering at that particular second.

"Rose, I didn't even know you would be here." Alice softly tried to explain. "If this is about Mar—"

"No, *no!*" Rose shook her head emphatically, almost distantly. "It is not about him."

Rose stood staring at her ex-friend as though the cogs in her mind were jammed up.

"You see, there aren't supposed to be children here!" Rose laughed awkwardly. "No children allowed, I'm afraid. They are going to be kicked out, darling."

Alice had a slew of emotions shooting past her. She had no right to bark back to Rose, but the woman was acting hysterical, even for Rose. If this was some kind of punishment for what Alice had done, then Rose shouldn't be taking it out on the family. What had they done to deserve that sort of mistreatment?

"Rose," Alice's words were clipped. "We are here, and we are planning to stay. These children have been through a lot, you see. Did you hear about—Jack?"

Rose rolled her eyes.

"Of course, I heard about Jack, Alice!" Rose groaned. "I am just trying to save us both some heartbreak when they say that the children must leave. Let's go check, shall we?"

Rose marched with a great deal of pompous righteousness to the reception desk where Timothy was silently awaiting the next query he could resolve. Alice followed with some hesitation, pondering exactly what to say as she approached.

Rose had a gracious frame. She was short but curvy. Even though she did not look it now, her body had always attracted men to the pair of women. Rose would bat her eyes and giggle to a waiting crowd of suitors. During their college years, there was a new lover in Rose's bed every night. Occasionally, she would toss a scrap Alice's way like a gracious master to a hungry hound. Rose had always been the center of attention. Apparently, her stay at the Arbor was no exception.

"Timothy, dear," Rose cleared her throat and snapped impatiently. "What is your policy on children at the resort?"

Timothy was unmoving and stoic. He looked as though he had not heard Rose so she began to repeat her inquiry.

"Timothy!" she insisted, her voice growing louder. "Please tell me what—"

"The children have been accounted for, per Ms. Trudeau's reservation," he replied, shifting slightly to look at Rose with faceless attention.

"No, no. That cannot be right. There is an entire bar in there stuffed full of whiskeys, vodkas, and even absinthe!" Rose chuckled nervously and glanced at Alice as if looking for agreement. "This place is debauchery incarnate. People have *sex*, and not just in the rooms!"

Rose continued to berate Timothy while Alice turned to Eleanor and James.

"*I'm sorry*," she mouthed as Rose's shrill voice modulated up and down with varying degrees of emotion. "*I'll get our room.*"

"If we could just—" Alice pushed past Rose to address the android. "If we could just get our room keys, we can sort out the situation in a tic. Let's just get them away from the disagreement. It's upsetting James."

Timothy grabbed another set of keys from the rack behind the desk. The numbers 4 and 6 were emblazoned in raised golden print.

"The rooms are not adjoining," Timothy explained, "But you will be next to the children."

Alice took the keys and turned to hand one to Eleanor. Her wrist was caught from behind. She glanced back to see a manic expression on Rose's face as she gripped her hand around Alice's wrist. Her knuckles quickly whitened as her fingers closed like a vise around Alice's delicate frame. Alice tried to pull away, but Rose only stared. Her eyes were wild. Her calm and holier-than-thou demeanor had been traded for one of desperation. She tugged Alice roughly like a misbehaving child as her breath began to quiver.

"Alice, listen to me," she whispered. "If our friendship ever meant anything to you, you will send those children away *now*."

"Rose, you're starting to scare me." Alice continued to pull back but was recoiled every time.

"Ha ha ha!" Rose manically chuckled. "No need to be afraid, love!"

Alice stepped backward this time and put her weight behind her arm. She yanked back but only served to pull Rose face to face with her.

"Rose, please. I don't understand. Let me go!" Alice started to panic inside but tried to put on a brave face for the children. James and Eleanor were staring, awestruck. Their minds struggled to take in what was happening. James scooted closer to his sister, who put an arm around him.

Rose continued in an overwrought whisper.

"Alice. You need to put them on the next train. Promise me," Rose pleaded. "*Promise me!*"

"Okay, all right. I promise they will go on the next train," Alice agreed. "Now will you please—"

Her wrist was released as soon as she acquiesced to Rose.

"Lovely, darling!" Rose said, resuming her overly cheery tone at full volume. "Well, I will see you in a few minutes for cocktails, right?"

Alice stared at Rose; her mouth agape as she turned away from the almost-bipolar woman.

"Yes, well . . . let me just unpack, and maybe you'll see me," Alice replied.

"Oh, wonderful!" Rose called as Alice ushered the children quickly toward the stairs. "It's a date then, love!"

"Aunt Alice," James piped up as he started the climb up the ornate stone steps. "What was up with—"

"Not now, dear." Alice continued to press firmly against his back to urge him up the stairs. "Let's just get to the room."

Alice almost jogged up the flawless marble stairs as she tried to leave all memory of that interaction behind. What had been excitement at first had turned to something else. They would leave in the morning with the first train.

THREE

O N THE OTHER SIDE OF THE WORLD, WILLIAM RUTGER, M.D. and his wife, Amelia, boarded a winged shuttle along with a handful of other passengers. Dr. Rutger was a professor at Oxford University. He had been pleasantly surprised by the invitation he'd received from a professor who used to work alongside him. A week at Fox's exclusive resort sounded a bit too cushy for him, but that said, he had heard that digital devices were not allowed at the lodge.

Dr. Rutger was not entirely enthralled with the digital invasion that had been pervading everyday life more and more. He had been born when computers could be held in the hand, not implanted under skin. He hated that advertisements seemed to converse directly with him everywhere he went. It was enough that they could talk. It was worse that they had access to his personal data, like some unsolicited assault on privacy.

"A week apart from technology," he muttered to his wife. "Sounds positively delightful to me."

"I don't understand your stalwart aversion to all things digital," Amelia whispered to her elderly husband. "It is my understanding that the march of time is going to continue long after we are dead. Our choice is to resist the tide and entrench ourselves in the past, or to try our damnedest to seem less out of touch than we really are."

William frowned and shook his head. He hardly felt the same naivete that his wife held dear. They were going to be part of the old guard, regardless of their efforts to the contrary.

"You may be right, but I quite like my trench of antiquated behavior. I'm loath to leave those ways behind me." Dr. Rutger wore a hardly noticeable grin as he stepped into the narrow cabin. Despite two hundred years in the skies, humanity had still never managed to prioritize comfort over fiscal responsibility. He took a deep breath of the air from the tunnel behind him and began to wobble his way down the carpeted walkway.

The aged man roughly stomped upon the foot of Mark Reese. Mark howled quietly as William gave a thoroughly unenthusiastic apology.

Mark had been rehearsing for weeks in preparation for his trip. *Mr. Jonathan Hulsey. Charmed.* He tried to sound convincing in his head. The facade was an important one if he was to be successful in his mission.

"Mr. Jonathan Hulsey. Charmed," he repeated quietly as he sat lonesome in his row.

Mark was one of the few investigative reporters on the planet, which sounded quite odd in his mind. He tried to cast light on shadowed secrets without getting himself killed. This sometimes proved to be more of an arduous task than he first expected. Witnesses and sources tended to disappear before any colossal revelations could be uncovered. This time, he had a bit of a dangerous idea. He would assume the identity of the source. Jonathan Hulsey had been invited to The Arbor at the planet's south pole. Luckily, this guest was within Mark's sphere of influence.

Mark was average in many ways. He was about as tall as most men. He was a bit more handsome than many. He had brunette hair that was invaded by grey. His voice was smooth and low. Each sentence sounded as though it had been thoroughly ironed out before exiting his lips, because it had. Mark thought about what he said before speaking. This fact alone meant that the slippery Mark Reese was able to charm many simply by reading the situation and reacting accordingly.

"Jonathan," he repeated softly under the hum of the idling engines. "Lovely to meet you."

He quieted his mind and leaned back into his business-class seat. He opened his jaw wide to try to stretch his clenched muscles. The joints cracked and popped like a cement mixer as he tried to release tension. He placed a hand to the side of his face and rubbed his flaring jowls. TMJ had always been an issue for Mr. Reese, now Mr. Hulsey. He cocked his neck slowly to one side and then the other. He had to act *relaxed*. No one was ever this nervous going on holiday. They were loose. They were calm. They were at ease.

All of these words perfectly described Evelyn Fox as she stumbled her way onto the jet. She braced her arm against the walls of the plane as she tried to stabilize herself. She giggled slightly and pursed her lips in mock embarrassment. Evelyn was hardly one to regret her actions at any time. She moved through life at an unrelenting and unforgiving pace. When she worked, she dutifully toiled. When Evelyn played, she flung herself headlong at the adventure and wholly freed herself of inhibitions.

Having already taken the initiative to enjoy some libations, Evelyn was confident that the journey would pass quickly. She eyed the few remaining seats on the small shuttle. One was next to a lithe, athletic man. He looked to be ethnic, she thought. Was that the way she should refer to him? She was long past giving more than a single thought to political correctness. Regardless of this, he was already asleep and hunched well into the real estate of the seat next to him. She could wake him but thought better of it, looking elsewhere for a more comfortable ride.

Another man looked positively disquieting. He had a far-off gaze that seemed to pierce the exterior of the hull and settle far off beyond the distant horizon. His face was worn and wrinkled. Every crease seemed to tell a different tale of woe and heartbreak that Evelyn was none too eager to discover. His salt and pepper hair was slightly tangled. It had been brushed, just not within the last few hours. There had been some attempt at managing the crisscrossed puffed dome that sat on his head, but it clearly had a mind of its own. Again, this seemed a bit more than Evelyn wanted to deal with in her current state.

Finally, her eyes rested on a delightfully handsome man in his forties. He had side-slicked brown hair. His hazel eyes seemed polite but nervous. His chiseled frame indicated that he could be a *lot* of fun for her. A sly grin began to inch its way across her loosened face as she considered the possibility.

Evelyn was in her early thirties, but she simply adored the pleasures that life could offer. She did not let them control her, but she allowed herself to indulge whenever she traveled to her father's resort. The Arbor had seemed like a bit of a garish concept to her, but she'd reconsidered the first time she went to visit. It had spirits, it had spirited young people, and it had enough of a pleasant atmosphere that all inhibitions seemed to evaporate from the attendees' minds. Evelyn was often one to take advantage of this and grasped the reins of her sexuality firmly when she decided to visit the ornate abode.

"You will do *just* fine," she whispered lustfully.

She sauntered toward the man as she bumped seat after seat with her uneven gait. She steadied herself with each step and finally seemed to attract his attention as she plopped down beside him.

"God, I'm so ready for this." Her American accent had a tinge of refinement in its intonation, despite her current inebriation. "Is it your first time?"

Mark cleared his throat slightly and turned to face the lovely girl. She was delightfully proportioned and *just* Mark's type.

But he had a job to do. He didn't have time for this. Did he? His persona offered a certain degree of anonymity that he was not often afforded. A minor transponder transplant meant that he now was registered as Mr. Jonathan Hulsey. Some minimally invasive prosthetic implants meant that his face even looked like Jonathan's. He wore the man's clothes and cologne. He tried to convince himself that he *was* Jonathan Hulsey. If he couldn't act convincingly, then his assignment would be over before it began. Maybe a distraction would prove to be beneficial to his full embrace of the character. She did look to be a fun diversion. He finally spoke, after staring for what would have been an uncomfortably long time with any other stranger.

"Yes, it is," he answered. "I'm quite looking forward to the experience."

"Me, too," she replied. Her eyes seemed to dance over his body. "I'm here for a great time. Are you ready for it?"

"Hah, yeah," Mark gulped, trying to fully immerse his mind in the character he was now playing. "I am thinking it isn't your first time?"

"No, sweetheart, that ship sailed *long* ago," she said as her lips ever so slightly rolled together in anticipation. "What do they call you, handsome devil?"

Holy hell, Mark thought. *I need to keep my head about me with this one.*

"Jonathan Hulsey." Mark introduced himself as he had practiced ad-nauseum. "It's a pleasure to meet you."

"Evelyn Fox," she smiled. "F. O. X." She giggled. "I'm sure the pleasure will be shared, Mr. Hulsey."

Across the row sat Omario Richards. He was an ordinal success story, someone who'd clawed his way from the undercities of
Earth and rose to fame through his merits alone. They weren't
technically called ordinals on Earth, except when certain well-off
citizens were upset. Then the term was flung around as a modern
slur. Racism didn't exist anymore, or so Omario was told by friends
and coworkers.

"*How do you feel as a true success story coming from exotic island
life?*" he'd once been asked. Had he lived an exotic life? It certainly
didn't feel that way when his mother had worked three jobs just to
provide a few scant morsels for her four children. Was it a *tropical
paradise* when Hurricane Sophia had eradicated eighty percent of
his beloved Jamaica? Was his life truly idyllic as he'd tried not to
listen to hushed whispers referring not only to his socioeconomic
status, but how his "kind" were naturally more athletic?

Omario rolled his shoulders back. He was above that now.
He did not have to concern himself about how people treated him.
That wasn't to say he didn't still feel the pang of hurt when he
campaigned for charities to assist his island and was told that their
infrastructure had been a mess before the storm, and they *really*
should have fixed that first, as though the disaster had somehow
been their own fault. Jamaica had been hit by winds of 175 miles
per hour for days as the storm lingered. Anything in the Sophia's
path had been annihilated, from the weakest wooden shacks to the
strongest government buildings. No method of construction could
withstand power like that.

Despite this, Omario did his best to live in peace. He'd gotten his family out and improved the lives of those he could. What
more was he to do?

Football had been his sport since he was five. He had first been
noticed in middle school. His coaches had called him a natural,
and it was not an exaggeration. Omario was equal parts lightning

bolt and juggernaut on the pitch. A born striker, he had a full football scholarship from the day he turned 16. Schools chomped at the bit to recruit him. Major League Soccer was a logical step, and he'd dominated there as well. There were those who criticized his technique. Many said he was too confident. Others were disappointed by his lack of team faithfulness, but none questioned his raw talent.

This trip would be a much-needed relief for Omario, whose club had just finished the season at a win ratio of 57%. It was respectable, sure enough, but hardly a red-letter league year. He had never been to Mars before arriving on the previous day. Maybe he would just be able to be a man at a hotel, not "O.R. Lightning," as the announcers called him. He enjoyed the fame, true enough, but sometimes he just wished for a quiet retreat to the serenity he'd known as a boy.

Just in front of Mr. Richards sat Peter Corgrave. He was an investigator for the family of an actor from Earth who had disappeared after a job on Mars. A man in his forties, Wade Gomez had written home that he was safe, but that he had decided to stay on Mars as the job situation was so much improved. Wade was unmarried, but he'd brought groceries to his mother on a weekly basis. She found it impossible to believe that he would desert her. They had been so close. Correspondence had entirely dried up, and although that was a common occurrence, a job was a job to Peter.

The strangest thing was, Wade's mother was right. He could find no trace of Wade Gomez anywhere in colonial records for the three cities he had visited. No one had an entry of him arriving or leaving. While ordinals were treated like slaves, masters usually tried to keep track of their property. It was entirely possible that he'd had an "accident" that his employer did not want to cover, but he had no family or next of kin on the planet. A death would have been cheap, while covering it up would have been costly.

Peter had a single lead that he had not explored. Wade had been hired for a job while he resided on Earth that specified his needing to purchase early 20th century period clothing. While on Mars, Peter had seen an ad for The Arbor and happened to notice the theme. It was serendipitous that he was able to arrange for a temporary stay with the Blue Life Corporation. They wanted to be sure their name was clear in the matter. In their defense, they were entirely transparent with regards to the investigation. They provided him all employment logs and noted his absence. That said, they were willing to provide two nights at company expense to clear their name. The last thing Blue Life wanted was bad publicity.

The company showed no concern for the man, only their own good name. Peter was hardly surprised or bothered. A life of crime investigation had led him to the understanding that all people were fundamentally vindictive survivalists. Even those who appeared to go the extra mile were almost always doing so to further their own well-being. There was no good, no evil, just people. Wade wasn't different, but he deserved a chance at survival as much as the next person. It was Peter's job to ensure he got that opportunity.

A couple of nights in paradise ain't bad, Peter thought. New York City had been his home since birth. He was plain. He'd made efforts to look unremarkable. If he blended, he could get the information he needed without being noticed. He was good at being invisible. Despite his age, he was quick, he was quiet, and he had a reputation for results.

Peter hardly minded sitting alone. He enjoyed the solitude when the whole of his life was spent surrounded by the throngs of innumerable residents in the world's second most populous city. This was his first time traveling to Mars. To go from a city with over ten million residents to a planet with a total of just under a million people was alien. He was not able to think clearly without the constant droning hum of background noise that penetrated every nook and cranny of New York. It was near silent everywhere he went on Mars. The whine of the engines aboard the shuttle was comforting. He closed his eyes and allowed himself a dose of sleep.

Dr. Rutger was jolted from his slumber as the wheels of the plane touched down for landing. He hadn't remembered falling asleep and blinked in surprise. The cabin lights were dimmed, and his wife was looking out the tiny circular porthole.

"I don't suppose there is much to see," his voice croaked.

"Absolutely nothing but red dirt," Mark added from behind the pair.

"Yes, but we passed a large dust storm an hour back," Amelia said. "You don't think that would affect the resort at all, do you?"

Evelyn Fox chuckled. "We're more than a mile under ice. Unless the storm has drilling equipment, we'll be all right."

"I meant the air filtration system," Amelia said, crossing her arms across her chest. "I'm not foolish. And you are . . .?"

"Evelyn Fox," she replied. Behind her Mark mouthed, "F O X," *spelling out her name with a sarcastic glint in his eye.*

"You must be Alex's girl," William observed as he stretched his neck from side to side.

"Yes, I am," Evelyn confirmed. "Would you like to ask me all the questions people usually bombard me with?"

"No, no. I'm sure that is none of my business," Dr. Rutger answered. "I'm a physician. I can understand the desire for confidentiality. Quite honestly, I used to have patients eager to provide me with an autobiography that I had absolutely no interest in hearing. My thirst for gossip never developed, I suppose."

"Well, thank God for that," Evelyn smiled. "You all are actually lucky. My father only visits the lodge once per year. He is there this week. The mystery will be solved for you by dinnertime tonight. You will be meeting the prestigious Alexis Fox."

Evelyn's voice held a note of mockery as she finished. There seemed to be more than a hint of resentment of her father's stardom and mystery. It hardly could have been easy for her as a girl to have everyone asking questions she had been trained not to answer. It might have been enough to push even the most stable of individuals to drink. Considering her well-known business acumen, it was understandable that sometimes she had to find relief in unhealthy outlets.

"What brings you here, sir?" William asked, turning to face Mark.

"Oh, same as most I would suppose," he responded. "I hate to admit it, but I was gifted a free week by my friend Viola."

"I can say the same," William grinned slightly. "There is nothing wrong with frugality, young man. What is your name?"

"Mr. Jonathan Hulsey," Mark said, thrusting his hand awkwardly over the seat. Dr. Rutger seemed to be taken aback by the enthusiastic handshake but met his grip anyway.

The craft finally rolled to a stop, and the docking clamp closed around the exterior hatch with a disquieting snap. A moment later, an ordinal near the front of the plane opened the door for the passengers. The melting pot of personalities wobbled their way out of the twelve-seat plane. The jetway had a glass roof to provide scenic views as they exited. The creeping ice began just a few hundred feet from the runway. The terminal looked small, but the train had already arrived and would function as little more than a transitional link in the chain.

Evelyn Fox had no intention of slowing down as she moved from the stark red cement terminal to the next transition tunnel. She gave the butler a nod as she entered the train car and made an immediate left through a door which required her retinal scan.

Mark Reese followed her into the tunnel but turned right to the passenger section.

"Jonathan!" Evelyn called.

Mark continued to walk and found an open seat on the beautifully decorated train. He began to stow a small briefcase under his seat and heard Evelyn call again.

"*Jonathan!*" she repeated.

Shit. I forgot, he thought. "Yes, Evelyn?" he finally replied.

"You'll find this cabin is much more comfortable!" Evelyn grinned. "Home-cooked food, lounge chairs, chess . . . a bed."

Her singular use of the word *bed* piqued Mark's interest.

"All right, I suppose. That sounds more interesting than sitting in a narrow seat for six hours," Mark said, standing to his feet.

"You *suppose?*" she teased. "If you aren't enthused about the prospect, I'm sure I could find company who would be."

"Why, Ms. Fox, it would be my honor to devastate you in a game or two," Mark prodded back.

"You can try, Mr. Hulsey." Evelyn traced a hand along Mark's shoulder as he joined her at the entryway to her room. "I think you'll find I'm full of surprises."

Her car was sleek. The décor was entirely different from the passenger car he had been in before. Large glass windows ran down both sides of the train with minimal steel supports bridging the gaps in long panes of glass. The design was austere but classy. A black table was encircled by four white stools. A crystal chess board sat in the middle, with frosted white and mirrored glass squares. Evelyn tossed her jacket onto a stainless-steel coat rack, revealing her tight pink tank top underneath. A pair of black form-fitting khakis looked as though they had been painted onto her café au lait colored body. Jet black hair was pulled into a ponytail behind her that bobbed as she walked. She stopped in front of a small kitchenette that stood a few feet before the king-sized bed that took up almost half of the room. A black comforter lay over white sheets, with a pair of red-sham covered pillows leaning against what looked to be the most comfortable pillows he'd ever seen. As fun as Evelyn seemed, it had been quite some time since he had slept in bedding that exquisite.

"Can I get you a drink before I deliver your ass-kicking?" Evelyn called as she bent down to open what Mark assumed was a liquor cabinet. She retrieved a crystal decanter of brown fluid and placed it on a drink tray.

"Bourbon?" Mark asked.

"Thirty-five-year Kentucky import," Evelyn affirmed as she pulled the top from the container and breathed deeply. "It's one of my indulgences. It costs more to buy and fly in than a ticket to the resort, but the smooth burn—"

Her voice quieted as she poured herself a glass and gave a tight swirl of her wrist to make the amber liquid whirl around the walls of the cup. She sipped slower than Mark would have expected. She savored the whiskey as it drained slowly into her waiting mouth. She stopped short of downing the entire glass, but only just.

"*Tell me* you can resist this," Evelyn moaned.

Mark shrugged his shoulders and opened his palms as he walked to sit at the chess table. "I really, quite wish I could."

Mark found his resolve evaporating along with his dignity as the stunning woman poured another glass for him. She grabbed the tray from the bar along with the bottle and set it down beside the chess board as she sat opposite him.

Evelyn pulled a black case off the wall and set it down in front of her. She released the clasp fastener to reveal a superb set of carved marble chess pieces. One side was deep coagulated red stone with mossy green lines of mineral running through it. The other was bright white, with flecks of gold interwoven in vines around the pieces like a net. This was not an amateur's chess set.

"So, is this your set?" Mark asked.

"Ouch!" She held a hand against her breast. "What, is this too finely crafted to be a girl's chess set?"

"No not at all, it is just—impeccable," Mark explained as he reached across the table to analyze the pieces closer.

"Yes, these were a gift from Father." Evelyn leaned back in her chair and had a small sip of whiskey. "Cheers!" She held her glass out toward Mark.

Mark's glass met hers before he drank a generous sip of the smoothest bourbon that had ever touched his lips. He grunted in approval and then enjoyed another sip before setting it down.

"Oh, that's amazing. . ." Mark breathed, staring at the fluid before continuing. ". . . Nectar of the gods."

"Thank you!" Evelyn returned, tracing the edge of her chess set. "Anyway, I think Dad wanted another boy, but he never outright told me so. He always loved chess, and that was one thing we could really bond over. He was a member of Mensa, you know. Father won chess championship after championship when he was in high school back on Earth. He always helped me learn from my losses. He'd say exactly how he beat me. He pushed me to do better." Evelyn paused for a moment to reflect on her words and sipped her drink.

"That sounds like a lot of pressure," Mark said as he pushed the beautiful velvet case back to her.

"Oh, God, you have no idea!" She laughed with a bounce as she gulped the remainder of her drink and slammed it back to the table. "Be a gentleman." She smiled and pointed to her cup.

Mark took this instruction without needing further coaxing and filled her cup more than halfway. He topped his off before returning the bottle to its seat on the tray.

"Trying to get me drunk, Jonathan?" Her low and powerful voice dragged slightly, making her sound like a young Katherine

Hepburn. She took another hearty sip and continued. "It's hardly necessary, but patience is a virtue."

"Evelyn, I can take some of yours if it's a bit too much." Mark tried to offer an unnecessary compromise.

"Too much? Hah!" Evelyn's mood continued to improve as the alcohol began to take effect again. "Believe it or not, Jon, I actually have much more trouble with small glasses. They're harder to track. I lose count far too easily. At least with a full cup, I know exactly how much farther I can push myself before I lose any necessary motor ability."

"That's an interesting way of putting it, Evelyn." Mark smiled and drank. "I usually count small glasses."

Evelyn nodded, lost in thought. "You know, that reminds me of a chess story!"

Evelyn was so full of life. She exuded confidence, intelligence, power, and beauty. It wasn't often Mark found himself intimidated by a younger woman, but Evelyn was a force he had never experienced before.

"So, my father and I were playing chess—which must be impossible to imagine—when he asked me what I thought of the ant," Evelyn began. "I said it appeared to be a pest but was often helpful in things like decomposition of dead organics, aeration of soil, and cleaning of messes that most aren't willing to tackle."

"How old were you, Evelyn?" Mark asked.

"Twelve," she flatly answered. "And it's rude to interrupt. I'll continue."

"*Twelve*," Mark marveled. He remembered his favorite cartoon from when he was that age. He'd hardly given much thought to soil aeration or decomposition as a pre-teen, nor did he have any idea that ants had a thing to do with it.

"He says, '*Evelyn, it is of paramount importance that one does not underestimate the power of the ant.*'" She deepened her voice and sharpened her accent to match her father's, and Mark couldn't help but find himself enthralled. "My father moved pawn after pawn into these large wedges all over the board, the analogy clear enough. They were structured so that no one pawn could be caught easily without ensnaring its attacker in a trap. I moved as best I could, but it was hopeless at that point. Father's skill was far beyond my own. He said, '*Each ant on its own is weak and easily toppled, but a colony is a formidable force. They can decimate animal populations in Africa, ravage crops all over America, and overwhelm entire islands when they are introduced as a foreign invader. Evelyn, you will often find yourself wanting to make large movements, plays for power, but learn from the microscopic ant. It kills nothing quickly, but when given time and a multitude of moves, it can be unstoppable.* And then he knocked over my king and declared a loud *checkmate,* as though I should have seen it coming ages ago."

Mark shook his head. "I can't imagine saying that to a twelve-year-old."

"Oh, please," Evelyn scoffed. "I was *hardly* a typical twelve-year-old and now I'm far from a typical thirty-one-year old."

"That much is sure," Mark agreed.

"The lesson really did mean a lot to me, though. It taught me the peril of impatience." Evelyn began to distribute chess pieces for their game. What Mark once held as a fair degree of confidence in his skills was dwindling to little more than a glimmer of hope.

"Go easy on me?" Mark grinned.

"Never, darling," Evelyn breathily replied.

Mark had an *aha* moment a few moves in when he realized that she'd left her knight open in a play for board center control. His pawn took her piece, and she let out a mockingly pained cry. Two moves later, her queen forced his king into checkmate.

"Jonathan, it's like you weren't even trying!" She tried to stifle a laugh. "I'm sorry. I'm sorry. I shouldn't tease. It wasn't fair of me to play you with limited information."

"What do you mean, *limited?*" He prodded for more elucidation.

"Oh, sweetheart, I was ranked in the top five grandmasters among women for three years," she bragged. "After that, I won."

"And did you rank after that?" Mark asked.

"No, dear. I thought it best to quit while I was ahead," Evelyn stood from the table and moved the tray of liquor back to its nesting on the counter. "Besides, I had a company to help run."

"*Run?*" Mark's curiosity was transparent.

"Yes, Jonathan. I'm the Chief Operating Officer at Jones Computing," Evelyn said.

"*Really?*" Mark stood from his seat and walked closer to her. "Well, you were right."

"In what way?" Evelyn bit her lip slightly as she took a step closer to Mark, leaving no room for a sheet of paper.

"You are—" Mark moved his palm across her cheek and drifted down her neck. ". . .full of surprises."

In a smooth and rapid movement, Evelyn lifted her shirt above her head and shrugged her bra to the floor. Her hands unfastened his belt nimbly as he moved his grip to her hips and tugged roughly.

"Easy there, tiger," she breathed. "You can pull on those all you want, but they won't budge. I can help with that."

She moved to unbutton her pants, but Mark grabbed her waistband and flicked the button aside as he slipped his hand lower.

"You're doing what I say tonight," Mark informed as he finally removed her remaining clothes.

"Ooh, not many men have the balls to boss me around," Evelyn moaned. "And that's after you heard about my position."

"Let's work on my position now," Mark laughed as he tossed her roughly over the bed.

FOUR

ALICE TRIED IN VAIN TO LULL HERSELF TO SLEEP. SHE WAS extremely intelligent, and that meant it was her job to worry on behalf of everyone who pondered less than she did. The memory of what had happened the night before had been seared into her mind like a brand. There was a bruise forming in a ring around her forearm where Rose had clamped down a few hours before. She rubbed it slightly as she examined the tender yellows giving way to dark green and blue.

The unmetered horror was unforgettable. She tried to put it from her mind. She tried to breathe deep and clear her thoughts but found them returning frequently.

9AM train, she thought as she glanced at her watch. The antique was a Jaeger LeCoulture. It had been her mother's. Its delicate silver was accented by a ring of gold around the dial and an ornamental mother of pearl face.

Alice longed for her mother's courageous spirit. Strength of character was the gift she most needed and yet found herself most definitely lacking. Her spine was pushed tight by her clenched muscles along the length of her body.

She stared up at the ceiling. It had a cream-colored molding trim around a repeating floral pattern in the stucco. The room would have been lit by sconces on the walls if she had not been laying in the dark.

"Jason, lights!" she called.

She sat in silence for a moment, forgetting where she was. *Right, no Jason,* she thought as she threw her legs over the side of the bed. Her black nightgown draped across her milky thighs in the light peeking from the window as she sat up. She tossed the drapery aside and looked outside. The room was lit a pleasant pinkish yellow to imitate a sunrise. Any other time, she would be excited to play tennis, or swim, but today, she just wanted to get the children to safety.

The room was papered with a beautiful forested floral print. The furniture was period Victorian and appeared genuine. She brushed the nightstand with her fingers and marveled at what it must have cost to import. The doors had brazen handles and locking plates. They were painted the color of French-vanilla ice cream. Her bed was well-cushioned and had a delightful spring to it. If she had been able to sleep, it would have been a good rest. The room was large and had a sitting room attached to the bedroom with a fireplace, a couch, and a small door to a balcony she had not seen before.

In an ideal world, the room would have been perfect for a week of relaxation.

She decided to wake the children. She had never unpacked, and she'd instructed Eleanor to keep their suitcases closed as well. Alice dressed in a peach-colored blouse with tiny pearl buttons and a pair of straight-legged white pants. She opted to put on only the most minimal amount of makeup and tossed her hair slightly so it looked less like she had just rolled out of bed. The bags under her eyes could hardly be hidden. Alice's anxiety was stretched over her face.

She walked into the hallway and was struck by the beauty of the polished stone tile floor in the faux sunlight. The marble had dots of red peppered throughout the design, and the tile had been polished to a brilliant finish. Light crept in through a window at the far end of the hallway, illuminating the entire passageway. She walked next door and turned the key to the children's room.

When she opened the door, the lights were out, and their coats were neatly folded atop the two rolling suitcases. Eleanor was well-ordered, just like Alice. She kept James in line as much as could be expected. That might have been the reason that arguments between the two women were so frequent and intense. Both could see their own pristine reflection in each other's eyes.

"Eleanor, love, it's time to go. We have an hour before we need to be at the platform," Alice softly spoke.

Eleanor's eyes opened slowly, and she nodded as her arms raised above her head. Alice was more than a little envious of her niece's effortless beauty even while the girl still retained the family brilliance. She looked as though she had snuck to the bathroom to apply makeup before Alice had entered, which hardly seemed likely.

Despite this, Alice knew she herself was desirable in her own way. Mark certainly seemed to like her.

"James," Eleanor said. "Wake up. We have to leave in twenty."

James let out a yawn which transformed into speech halfway through it.

"Oh, I don't know. So Rose is crazy. Can't we stay?" he frowned.

"James, you know I want to as well, but it's too dangerous," Eleanor answered. "It's all a bit too odd for me to justify. That look in her eyes. . ."

Eleanor shivered unconsciously as her sentence drifted off. James hopped up from bed in his blue sateen pajamas, his bare feet patting along the floor. He ducked into the bathroom and slammed the heavy door shut behind him.

"It's not easy being the villain, hmm?" Alice said.

"I wasn't trying to be a monster," Eleanor huffed as she moved to the mirror and began fixing her hair.

"The level mind never is. We just see things that other people don't have the sense to preoccupy themselves with. It's a cruel gift, I'm afraid." Alice sighed and rubbed a hand over Eleanor's shoulder. "You are lucky. I'm clever but quite plain. You are just so—beautiful."

Eleanor scrunched her hair together in dissatisfaction with her hands as she let the tangled reddish mess fall to her back. Her pale freckled skin seemed a whiter shade of alabaster than she remembered when she examined it in the mirror.

"I don't *feel* beautiful right now," Eleanor returned gruffly. She grabbed a hairband from her nightstand and pulled the usually luscious curls into a ponytail. "But we are going home anyway, so what do I care?"

Alice tried to comfort the girl as Eleanor threw a fresh tank top over her sports bra. "I'm so sorry," she began. Eleanor had seemed okay about leaving when James was in the room but her true mood had begun to show. "I don't know what got into Rose, but she was so serious about the whole thing."

"Maybe—" Eleanor pushed past Alice and unzipped her suitcase while it was still standing. She fumbled around blindly in the bag as she continued. "Maybe it wasn't what got into her, but more who got into you. She could be punishing us for your—"

Eleanor looked both ways to make sure James hadn't slipped back out of the bathroom.

"Your *fuckup!*" Eleanor harshly whispered.

The words cut Alice like glass. She opened her mouth to respond but was wordless. Alice had no idea Eleanor knew about what had happened with Mark. How could she have known about the affair?

"Eleanor, I don't think it's appropriate for you—" Alice began.

"Just save it," Eleanor interrupted as she pulled a pair of yoga pants from her bag and zipped it again. "We are doing the right thing and going home because I know it is the most responsible thing to do. If it is just some cruel prank, then I guess Rose gets her kicks."

Alice clenched her jaw tightly. There was no way to have this conversation here. There was no time to discuss her poor decisions with Eleanor. She wasn't even entirely sure she could explain herself if given the chance. James popped out of the bathroom in a blue T-shirt and black sweatpants. He looked entirely ridiculous as he threw his dress coat over his shoulders and straightened it.

"Well let's go—I guess. Eleanor, do you need to go to the bathroom?" James said.

"No, nutter," Eleanor answered. "I'll have plenty of time on the train."

Alice looked down at her watch as she opened the door. 8 AM sharp. They would wait for their transportation at the platform. The Arbor made her entirely too nervous. The children bobbed down their bright staircase ahead of them as Timothy prepared a set of five keys on the reception desk beneath her. Alice crossed the lobby and dropped her key along the same line of prepared rooms.

"Checking out," Alice flatly declared.

"Checking out, ma'am? I have you down for a week," Timothy replied.

"Yes, I'm aware. There have been some—" Alice looked at the pair of impatient children who were less than enthused to be leaving, before returning to Timothy's faceless gaze. "Extenuating circumstances."

"Well, I'm dreadfully sorry to hear that," Timothy said in an insincere empathetic tone that he had undoubtedly been programmed with. "You'll be departing tomorrow then?"

Tomorrow? Alice thought.

"No, we're leaving on the 9 AM train," Alice corrected. "Today."

"But, Ms. Trudeau, the clock just rang 9," Timothy pointed to a grandfather clock encased in glass just into the reception foyer she had never attended.

The hour was clearly pointing to the IX on the Roman numeral face of the clock.

"No, it's 8*am!*" Alice screeched, pointing to her watch.

"I'm so sorry madam, but that is mainland time. The pole is in a different—" Timothy started before Alice darted from the desk.

"Go!" Alice ordered, sprinting in the lobby with her bag flailing behind her in tow.

The children sprang to action and threw the massive door open. Cold wind blew into the warm lobby and Alice realized she was still holding her jacket in her arms. There was no time for comfort. They *had* to make that train.

The trio ran with their belongings banging into every possible surface along the walkway. The wheels hardly touched the ground as they bounced along the brick. Alice felt tears well as the cold breeze blew harshly against her face. The hiss of the train coming to a stop echoed through the cavern.

"Shit!" Alice cursed as she flew closer and closer to the waiting elevator door.

The portal opened, and Rose's familiar form sullenly walked from the room.

"Hold the elevator!" Alice shouted, trying to catch her breath as she breezed past the distraught woman.

"*Why* aren't you all on that platform?" Rose pleaded, sounding nauseated.

"Mainland time!" Alice answered as she made a controlled crash into the opposite end of the elevator.

Eleanor and James flew in behind her, and Rose hammered the raised section on the elevator door's edge. With a curse muttered under Alice's breath, they rushed past Silas, who she hadn't noticed before.

"Something wrong, ma'am?" he queried.

"Fuck!" Alice tapped her foot loudly as the elevator doors slowly closed and rotated shut. "Can't this thing go any faster?"

Silas turned to face her, but the words of her questions didn't seem to make sense to him.

"I'm sorry, but I don't understand that question. Is there something I can help you with?" Silas clapped his white gloved hands together in a praying stance.

Alice rotated to face the door that would open when they reached the top. She almost hyperventilated as the portal finally began to rotate. It seemed to creep inch by inch as it entered the open position.

"Come on," Eleanor groaned. "*Come on!*" she repeated with vigor.

The doors finally began to spread and Alice squeezed through as soon as she possibly could.

"No, no, no," she mouthed as she raced toward the train. The steward shut the door as she noticed six figures observing her from the red carpet. "Wait, *stop!*" she screamed.

"Alice?" Mark murmured in disbelief as he stared for a moment.

"Stop them!" Alice shrieked shrilly.

"Sir!" Mark called as he waved his arms. "Open the d—"

The train had already begun to slide along the track.

Alice showed no sign of slowing as she crossed the four arches she had entered underneath.

"Please!" she begged as she stumbled on a crease in the carpet. "Stop!"

Despite Mark's plaintive gesticulation and shouts, the train moved farther and farther until it slipped out of sight.

The crowd was silent, except for Alice's sobbing. She had fallen to the floor just after the fork in the carpet. Her bag was still sliding along the ice from where she had let it go as she tripped.

Everyone stared at each other in wonderment.

The children, who had been more disappointed than anxious just a few moments ago, were gasping for frozen air as their chests heaved. Their faces were ones of devastation. Even James, who had been so brave and determined to stay, looked mortified. They were all stoic, frozen in more ways than one.

Alice continued to weep as she folded her arms over the back of her skull. She huddled on the floor. She had failed them.

Mark jogged to her side and threw his coat over her bare shoulders. She was shivering.

"Alice, are you all right? What are you doing here?" Mark asked.

Alice sniffed and tried to compose herself. What was she doing here? What was *he* doing here?

"Mark, I—" she whispered.

"Jonathan," he quietly corrected. "*Jonathan Hulsey*," he stressed in a whisper, turning his back to the group he had entered with.

"What?" She blinked rapidly, trying to clear her vision as she finally raised her head.

"On assignment. I'll explain later. Please play along," he said in a soft voice as his eyes begged her cooperation.

Alice seemed hesitant to ignore anything those eyes told her to do.

"Right." She coughed slightly as she rose to her feet. "Nice to see you again, *Jonathan*."

"*Really?*" Eleanor groused and threw up her hands in disgust behind Alice. She began to walk back toward the elevator.

"Where are you going, El?" James whispered, in the spirit of the mood.

"One, don't call me that," Eleanor answered, "And two, back to the lodge. We're going to have to wait for the next train, and I'm not going to sit here freezing my arse off."

James looked toward Alice but decided to follow Eleanor like a lost puppy. He jogged with his suitcase and caught up to her in short order. Meanwhile, a bit of a crowd had begun to gather around Alice.

"You all right, dear?" Amelia Rutger spoke first.

"I have been better," Alice answered, trying to straighten her clothes for the impeccably dressed new arrivals. "Alice Trudeau."

Even in an emergent situation, Alice's manners were hardcoded.

The group stood a few steps back from Ms. Trudeau and Mr. Reese, unsure what to make of the spectacle they had just witnessed. Evelyn closed the gap after a momentary pause.

"Evelyn Fox." She offered a polite grin and shot her hand forward.

"It's a pleasure." Alice nodded as she met her grip for a handshake. It was firm, crushing, really, and cold.

"I simply *must* hear more about how the two of you know each other." Evelyn chuckled lightly and slid suspicious eyes toward Mark. "Jonathan and I *really* got acquainted on the ride over, and I feel this is an interesting chapter I've yet to read."

I bet you got to know each other intimately, Alice thought. The shameful flush in Mark's cheeks was present for more reasons than the intensely cold air surrounding them.

"Well, there is no point standing about in the cold," William growled as he moved through the hubbub. "Come along then!"

Alice knew he was right. She had already failed to do her duty as a guardian. There was no sense in freezing to death on top of it all. She trudged back toward the elevator with a defeated slump in her shoulders.

"You look like you could use a drink," Omario added as he lit a cigarette and brought it to his mouth. His voice was baritone and silky. His accent made each word flow smoothly into the next.

Alice's eyes widened with desire at the sight of the cancerous white stick.

"You want one?" He spoke through the side of his mouth as he blew out a cloud of white smoke.

"Meet me at the bar in ten minutes, and I will definitely take you up on that." Alice let her head fall and tugged the coat tighter around her chest. The terminal felt even colder than she had re-membered it.

FIVE

U PON RE-ENTERING THE ESTATE, ELEANOR RAN UP THE STAIRS
to her room. She violently flung her case against the luggage
holder and opened it. She retrieved a blue and white speckled
one-piece that she had bought specifically for this occasion. James
entered the room just as she walked to the bathroom.

"Are we going swimming? It's pretty cold!" he said.

"You can do whatever you want. We are trapped here now, like
it or not. *I* am going swimming," she said firmly.

James flipped his suitcase on its side in the middle of the floor.
He tossed clothes in a heap as he dug for a pair of brown woolen
slippers, red swimming goggles, and his bright blue swimming trunks.
He grabbed a shower cap from the sink outside of the bathroom
while he waited for Eleanor.

She walked out wearing a coverup over her suit and glanced at
all the accoutrements in James' full arms.

"What is—" she started. "Why do you have a shower cap?"

James looked down at the rubbery cover and shrugged.

"I thought you wore it while you swam!" he insisted before
tossing it to the floor.

Eleanor knew she couldn't ditch James with a clear conscience, but he really pushed the word embarrassing to a new level.

"Do you *really* plan to wear those slippers down to the beach? They're going to get sand all along the inside." Eleanor tried to sound sympathetic but came off as annoyed.

James' smile sunk. "I don't have to come if you would rather be alone."

Eleanor tipped her head to the side and furrowed her brow. She walked toward her brother and reached out a fist a few inches from his chest. "Don't be daft. We're a team, right? You and me. We must stick together. We are each other's only family now."

"We have Aunt Alice, too!" James' wide grin returned as he pounded his fist against hers.

"I suppose," Eleanor shrugged. "Now, go get changed!"

The siblings passed Alice on their way back downstairs.

"You're going swimming?" Alice wondered in disbelief. "It's fifty-five degrees out there!"

"Don't worry about us!" Eleanor dropped a hand on Alice's shoulder. "I've brought our coats for afterward, and I promise we'll sit for an hour by the fireplace when we get back. Is that alright?"

Alice shook her head and opened her mouth slightly to speak. She could list all the many reasons why they should stay in the house, but she needed to pick her battles.

"Of course, darling," Alice laughed softly. "One hour getting warm by the fire. I'll hold you to it."

"Thanks, Aunt Alice!" James hopped slightly as he wobbled down the stairs in his slippers.

Alice stared in disbelief at his peculiar outfit, but simply yelled, "Stay together! Be careful! Back in *one* hour!"

"We will!" he answered from the lobby as he shuffled after his sister.

Alice re-applied her makeup when she got upstairs. She ran a straightener along her messy and tangled hair as she brushed it. She looked distressed after fleeing the mansion like a bat out of hell. It was not like her to do things without thinking. She was always responsible. She had to hold it together for her niece and nephew. Alice twisted the hands of her watch one hour forward. She would not be caught unaware again. She considered changing her blouse but, in the end, simply tucked it back into her waistband and grabbed a decorative belt from her suitcase. She observed herself in the mirror.

Alice wore a maroon shade of lipstick that glistened slightly. She pursed her lips and blotted the excess on a napkin. She was finally ready to face everyone downstairs.

She descended from the second floor wearing a pair of black pumps that she had retrieved on her way out the door. Her heels clicked as they met the cold polished marble. She could see into the lounge before she entered. The man who had invited her for a cigarette was sitting at the bar within view. A cherry bar top ran above eight green leather stools with brazen foot rests. The barkeep was Silas, with the addition of a white waist-high apron. The floor was an almost ebony-colored hardwood.

The walls were adorned with a green crisscross pattern and gold filigree accents. The ceiling had gorgeous oak beams exposed with black bracketing. A few tables sat in front of the bar, but most were empty. Dr. and Mrs. Rutger sat at the far end of the room by a window that overlooked the front lawn. Rose Grayson sat at the end of the bar. She had a pair of empty glasses in front of her and a third in her hand that she was absentmindedly sipping.

Girl must have worked fast, Alice thought. *It's only been half an hour.*

"Oy!" Omario Richards called to her. "I saved you a seat!"

Alice nodded and walked across the empty lobby to her reserved section. She scooted as far away from Rose as she could manage.

"Thanks, Mr.—" Alice let her sentence drag.

"Richards," he answered. "Omario Richards."

"Well, Mr. Richards, thank you for meeting me. I'm quite a mess, and I was supposed to be gone on that train." Alice sighed as she signaled Silas to come to her.

"Silas, I'll have a gin and tonic, please," she ordered.

"Right away, ma'am," Silas returned with a faux Brooklyn accent.

Alice and Omario looked at each other before entirely breaking their icy façade and relaxing into a small fit of laughter.

"They made him, 'talk like a fuckin' New York bartender?'" Omario said in a poor imitation of Silas' accent.

"It's so foolish!" Alice added. "He's a *robot*! Why would they waste time programming that into him?"

Rose slammed her empty glass down at the other end of the bar.

"Au—then—ticity," she snipped, aiming at no one in particular as she stared straight forward. "Glad to see you're already having fun, Alice and—"

"Oma—" he began.

"I really don't care," Rose interrupted. She raised a finger and tapped her glass so hard that it pinged and began to roll sideways. It came to rest at the lip of the bar.

"Right." Alice breathed in deeply. She didn't respond to Rose before turning back to Omario. "So, what do you do?"

"You mean, you really don't know?" Omario seemed surprised that anyone wouldn't be familiar with him on a first name basis.

Alice gave a pair of awkward chuckles. "Should I?"

"Omario Richards?" he repeated. "Number 12 on Team England? We just won the cup?"

"Ohh!" Alice pointed to him. "You're a footballer!"

"Right, yeah," he affirmed. "You still have no idea who I am, do you?"

"Sorry, no," Alice smiled as she took a sip of the drink Silas had just slid down to her waiting hand. "I'm apologize, I don't really follow sports especially with my work on Mars. Congratulations, though!"

"Oh, it's fine, miss—" Omario paused. "You know I just realized you never told me your name."

"Oh no!" Alice paused mid-drink and lowered her cup to the bar. "My name is—"

"Alice Trudeau!" Rose shouted as she lowered a fourth glass. "Part-time architect, part-time parent, part-time scholar, *full*-time slag."

There it was. Alice had wondered how long Rose would be able to maintain civility.

"Rose." Alice leapt to her feet and cautiously walked across the bar to stand behind the still-stoic Ms. Grayson. "Can we talk about this later? I am sure you have a lot to say, and I completely understand."

"You *understand?*" Rose seethed. She spun around to face Alice but slightly overshot. She slammed her left knee into the bar. "Fuck! Goddamnit, that hurt!"

Alice moved to help her friend but hesitated given the circumstances. Her jolting motion was noticed by Ms. Grayson.

"Don't!" Rose growled. "Don't you fucking touch me."

"I'm sorry, I know. That's why I backed off." Alice put her palms up and took a step back. "Rose, I think we should talk about this. It's been two years. I fucked up. I take full responsibility for that. You didn't deserve—"

"Oh, well, then all *must* be forgiven then!" Rose laughed. "Hear that, everyone? Alice is *sorry* she fucked my husband! What a saint."

Alice glanced around the room at the faces staring back at her. There was a mixture of disapproval, annoyance with the situation, and sadness.

"Okay, Rose, can we talk about this somewhere else? I'd rather talk in a space where we can work through some of this. You are my friend, and I can't even begin to say how sorry I am," Alice said. "If not for us, then for the kids. They still laugh that you call yourself Aunt Rose, but we really are—"

"No, Alice. I do not want to *talk about this somewhere else*," Rose declared. "I don't want to talk to you anywhere. I wasn't supposed to see you here. None of this has gone like I wanted it to."

As she completed her sentence, Rose dropped off the barstool. She was more than a little unsteady as she walked back out of the lobby. Before Alice knew it, Omario was by her side with a cigarette sticking out of a pair of fingers. She snatched it before he even had a chance to officially offer. She put it between her lips and lowered her mouth to meet a lighter that he had produced.

The blue jet of flame engulfed the tip of her cigarette. She breathed in deeply and watched in wonder as the end began to glow. Her lungs were filled with a familiar burning warmth as the smoke filled her. She coughed slightly as she released an opaque cloud of dense ecstasy.

"Oh, fuck yes," she whispered hotly.

"Looked like you needed it," Omario said.

"Oh, that is an understatement," Alice sighed. "It's been eight years. God, I know I can't go back to them, but this could have been *such* a wonderful week."

Omario smiled for a moment, but his face soon changed to one of confusion.

"What do you mean, 'could have been?' Why were you trying to get to that train so urgently?" Omario wondered.

Alice debated. Should she tell Omario or not? After a moment of deliberating, she went back to her original seat. She gulped down the half of her drink that remained and patted the stool next to her. Omario walked back down the bar, and Alice waved down Silas.

"Another, please!" she said with a wave.

At the back of the house, Mark sat in the library with Evelyn.

"—and you were still married?" she queried, folding her arms and placing a book about bowhunting back on the shelf. "The scandal of it all, Jonathan. You seemed like such a boy scout."

"Unfortunately, yes," Mark returned. "I know I should have divorced that *vapid* cunt first, but Alice was there and just as— God, I don't even know. I had just gotten out of a very bad relationship when I met Rose. She was so beautiful, she was rich, and she was a devil in bed. I thought I could overlook the other factors. I thought we would work on them together. I know I should have just—"

"Jonathan!" Evelyn interrupted. "I'm never one to judge. God knows, I have done the same for far less noble reasons. I was just surprised *you* had it in within yourself. You have nothing to apologize for, dear."

Jonathan rose from a ruby velvet bench he had been sitting on. The cushioned ripples were held in place by buttons all along its length. The library was longer than it was wide. A pair of shelves faced each other and stretched eight feet high. Ladders on rollers were free to move across the library's length. It was clearly not an ill-used room. The books appeared to have been loved for a lifetime. The titles painted a vivid picture of the man who collected them. He had books on statistics, game theory, differential calculus, and more advanced theorems that he hadn't even heard of. Fox had collected first editions of Rand, Darwin, Dickens, and some extremely weathered copies of works by Shakespeare.

"This can't be—a first edition print," Mark sounded awestruck. He gingerly began to slide the book from its placement on the shelf. *Shakespeare's Comedy of: The Tempest,* was written in black and red lettering on the front cover. It was sheathed by a thin plastic sleeve. He looked at the zipper seal and turned to Evelyn for permission. "May I?"

"Ha! Darling, do I look like the sort to stand on tradition and protectionism?" Evelyn answered. "By all means."

He eagerly but carefully unclasped the seal inch by inch. Without thinking much about it, he lowered his nose to smell the binding.

"I know it's weird," Mark laughed at himself. "Old books just have this delectable aroma that can't be reproduced in our modern world."

"Oh, don't be ridiculous." Evelyn raised a side of her lips and leaned in to sniff the book after Mark. "It's something with the paper and the bindings as they age. The scent is positively intoxicating. It's what's kept me reading all these years."

Mark traced a finger along the pages. The 1908 copy illustrated by Dulac cracked threateningly as he tried to open it.

"I'd better not," Mark decided and began to slide the book back into its protective shell.

"I suppose Father might be a bit cross if you destroyed a text worth 200,000 credits," Evelyn said.

"Jesus." Mark jolted as he carefully placed it back in its home on the shelf. "How many of these have you read?"

"Hmm." Evelyn placed a finger on her chin and began pointing as she counted in her head. She moved up and down the room and finally stopped. "Seventy-two, I believe? Seventy-two shelves worth. I used to read by the shelf, just to keep myself straight."

"Shelves?" Mark repeated. "You are quite an incredible woman."

"Stop, Jonathan," Evelyn insisted playfully. "You'll make me blush. Worse, you're getting quite smitten already. We should be keeping this light, what with your ex-wife upstairs and your mistress downstairs."

"You've got a point," Mark groaned, rubbing the back of his head. "They were really the last people I wanted to run into here."

"Yes," Evelyn acknowledged as she turned to face Mark and ran a finger around his chest. "The awkwardness must be exacerbated by the fact that you're fucking a gorgeous heiress who flaunts her sexuality as a method of intimidation."

Mark grinned but seemed otherwise distracted as he walked toward the wall-length window at the end of the long library. "Yes, I'm starting to realize that she is quite a pistol."

Evelyn joined him at the window but kept a healthier distance this time. "It's damned freezing out there. Who the hell is swimming?"

Her gaze fell on the beach just past the tennis court. Eleanor was wading at shin depth in the crystalline and serene water. James wore his goggles and stood at the edge of the beach. He seemed hesitant to force more than a toe in at a time.

"El!" James called. "It's like I'm walking into ice-water. I don't want to swim in this!"

Eleanor pretended to enjoy the frigid liquid that lapped gently at her knees. Every time it rose higher, goosebumps forced their way farther from her skin. She tried earnestly not to cross her arms over her chest as a breeze whipped past her. The air was in the fifties, but the water felt like it was at most in the upper forties. She would be forced to retreat soon enough.

"Oh, c-c'mon James! Don't be a tosser!" Her voice trembled slightly despite her stalwart stubbornness.

He took a step forward with renewed determination and doused his right foot into ankle-deep water.

"Holy Jesus!" James screamed and retreated back to the significantly warmer sand. He threw on his slippers and wrapped himself in a towel.

"C—coward!" Eleanor called to him as she wished for the coverup she had come down to the beach in.

Deeper in the water, about thirty feet out, a burst of mist exploded upward. Eleanor almost jumped from her skin as arm after arm shot from the water and made its way toward her.

"What the hell?" she whispered as she began to take long backward steps out of the water.

"Eleanor! Get out of there!" James shouted.

She did as he'd said, moving faster and faster until she saw Winston Graham toss his hair as he rose from the depths. She stood frozen as the chiseled man began to take long strides toward the beach. He didn't appear to see her at first but quickly diverted from his path when his eyes rested on Eleanor.

"Have we met?" Winston asked as he wiped his dripping face with a free hand.

Eleanor's jaw hung open. She knew it rude to stare. She couldn't help herself.

"I don't think so." Her voice shook. "Not officially? I sat behind you on the train in."

Winston shuffled a hand through his hair as he leaned to the side. He tried to dry off as he continued speaking. "No, no. I think I would have remembered *you* sitting behind me."

Eleanor's face flushed a deep pink. Her instinct was to look away and cover herself as she realized it wasn't her mind Winston was interested in.

"Um, yes. I definitely was." Eleanor spoke with a bit more hesitation now. "Aren't you cold?"

Winston brushed his shining body with his hands, trying to get the remaining liquid off. "Not while I was under. Quite refreshing. Now I'm feeling the chill a bit more."

Eleanor laughed nervously. She began to move back toward James while maintaining eye contact with the man. She was beyond attracted to him, but there was something strange about the way he looked at her. "Well, I'm freezing. I think I better get a towel around me."

"Oh, that's a shame," Winston took a pair of steps and closed the gap between them almost instantly. "We wouldn't cover Botticelli's *Venus* with anything that might obscure her nude beauty."

Eleanor kept moving. She winced slightly as she stepped on a shard of rock and fell back. Her ass dropped into the water, and she let out a loud cry.

"Shit!" she exclaimed.

Winston lowered a hand to help her up. Eleanor thought twice but accepted the assistance as the chill penetrated her body to the core.

"How'd you like to meet me in my room for a drink in a few minutes?" he asked. "We could get you out of those wet clothes and warm up—together."

"Holy hell," Eleanor whispered and turned from his uncomfortably hot stare. "Actually, I really need to get my brother back to the room now. He must be frozen solid!"

She walked a bit faster. Despite her feelings toward Winston, she was most definitely unprepared for what he was offering. Part of her was flattered, but another was disgusted. She knew how old she *looked*. Eleanor was aware of the fact that she was eighteen, but she doubted that anyone else would have guessed that.

"If you change your mind, you know where to find me!" Winston called as their distance continued to widen. He walked back to his things which Eleanor hadn't noticed in a pile about fifty feet from their towels.

Eleanor reached her brother a few moments later. He was still huddled in a ball like an armadillo made of terry cloth. As she retrieved her coverup and towels from the pile, James looked up to her in frustration.

"That's my warmth fort!" he growled.

"All right, well, I'm cold too, and I need to cover up," Eleanor returned.

"Oh, don't worry about it. If we get to go back by the fire, I'll be happy," James said.

Eleanor nodded and waved for him to take the lead. James walked in the most peculiar stride.

"You look like a fabric bigfoot!" Eleanor laughed. James turned back to face her as he continued to step toward the house. He raised his arms above his head and contorted his hands. He roared as they reached the back door of the home.

James lead the way to the common room, goggles in hand. Just inside, Rose Grayson sat warming herself by the fire. Eleanor caught the back of James' arm to stop him and made part of his towel monstrosity drop away.

"Hey!" James yelped.

Eleanor shushed him, but Rose heard the commotion. Her full body was illuminated from behind as she turned to face the children. "James and Ellie!"

"Back, let's back up," Eleanor whispered out the side of her jaw.

"James, you're quite grown!" Rose cried, extending her arms as she began to rapidly approach scantily clad pair. "Ellie! You look right shaggable! God, I'm so fucking old. Could I borrow your ass and tits for tonight? I promise I'll return them in the morning, but it's been so long."

James walked backward but soon was entangled in the mess of towels he had just dropped.

"Bloody hell!" He tipped sideways but caught himself before the floor. In a flash, he moved to the pile of towels and scooped them up. The cloth piled to chin height on the boy.

"Now, James, listen!" Rose slurred her words. "Just because I'm the *cool* aunt doesn't mean I won't report you to the proper authorities for—shitting—pornography."

James stared back in utter confundity.

"No—no. Profanity!" Rose corrected with an obnoxiously loud giggle.

Eleanor flattened her smile into a line and glanced subtly to James to head back out of the room.

"No, no! You children can't go anywhere yet!" Rose demanded as she tiptoed quickly around the siblings to prevent their egress from the shadowy room. What seemed inviting a moment ago now felt like the river Styx, dragging them to oblivion. The red floral walls once looked like art. Now they closed in like chains.

Eleanor was terrified of two things. She despised sharks and was mortified by awkward social interactions. Ocean-predators had been left behind on Earth, so she was left with her biggest fear on The Red Planet. Rose pulled her in close as they moved right in front of the fire.

"So, Ellie, how is school? Staying out of trouble?" Rose asked.

"Uh, huh, Yeah, well, I go to online school, so there isn't much of an undesirable crowd to fall in with," Eleanor coughed and elbowed her little brother to encourage a quick escape.

James had dropped to his knees and was warming his body by the fire when she cleared her throat for a second time. He seemed to be relishing in warmth above their current conversational difficulties.

"Oh, well, that's right!" Rose exclaimed. "James how 'bout it? How's your family life? You are getting along with *this one* all right?"

Rose bent over in cawing laughter at what seemed like the funniest of jokes to her.

"Well, yeah! I don't have a lot of family to get in disagreements with anymore, so it's more peaceful. I miss our big family, though."

Eleanor felt a shot to her heart. She always focused on how to get by without Mum but was reminded of her sibling's quieter struggles as he so casually suggested their family size had been reduced.

"James," she whispered. Eleanor looked to him with the heartbreak that she hadn't felt since the funeral.

"Oh, darling, that's simply *dreadful*. I didn't mean to bring up painful memories!" Rose dropped to a cushion on the floor as she began to shake her head with her palms covering her face. "I don't know how I didn't think of it! I forgot your mum and— Oh I shouldn't be talking about that. Oh, bloody hell I've cocked it up again. I didn't think of it! I didn't think of you. Oh, God. I didn't think of you. Why didn't I think of you?" she almost wailed to herself.

As Rose dropped her hold on the two, they both pulled away. The children quietly slipped backward and prayed for silence.

"God damn it," Rose sniffled. "Why didn't I? How could I forget?"

The woman lowered her shoulder down to the floor as the children began to run from the living room. They flashed up the stairs as their plastic soles slapped against the steps. James was fully sprinting as they reached the top walkway.

"Open the door! Oh, my God!" he grunted.

They both fell into the room as she turned the key.

"That was *so* creepy! Blegh!" Eleanor shouted as she slammed her back into the inside panel of her door.

James hopped with high knees, seemingly trying to shake off the cooties left by "Aunt Rose." He flailed his arms in comic circles like an itchy gorilla.

"Why did she wig out so much when she talked to me? It was too weird!" he fussed.

Eleanor grabbed a change of clothes and disappeared into the bathroom. James shook his shoulders one more time before slipping under the covers of his comfy bed. He pulled the sheet tight to his body and tried to put the image of Rose from his mind for the second time.

SIX

JAMES WAS AWOKEN BY A MAN'S VOICE. IT WAS SILAS, WHO sounded like he was in the corner of the room.

"Dinner will be served in one hour at 6 PM," he declared from a speaker that had been painted to match the room's decor.

On the other side of the wall, Amelia Rutger shoved her husband's shoulder. He was seated at their window reading in an armchair. The man huffed slightly and replied to his wife.

"I wasn't sleeping," he announced.

"No, dear, of course not. You were awoken by Silas' intrusion." His wife grinned as she finished unpacking their suitcases into the armoire. She shut the drawers and brought him a cup of water. "Time for your medication, dear."

He took the pills from one of her hands and gulped them down with the water he had been delivered. "Bloody pointless, this whole thing. I'm pumping my body full of chemicals to buy myself another year, maybe two?"

"A year with a wife who loves you, yes," Amelia replied. "Is that too much for me to ask?"

William grasped his wife's empty hand. She'd stood by him

through eight years of medical school, fifteen years of practice, and twenty-two years of teaching. It was only right that she should be by his side as he marched toward the end of his life.

"Hmm, well, I suppose a bit of pain is worth it if I am to spend these last days with you," William surrendered. "Let's enjoy this time. We are not guaranteed a single second, so this might be the last time we—"

"No, no. I will deal with that moment when it comes. I'll not have you providing me previews." Amelia shook her head and went to slip on a pair of cream flats with lacy trim. "Join your girl for a brief libation before dinner?"

William stood up. He grabbed his black suit coat from a hanger in the closet. He buttoned it while looking in the mirror. Modern medicine had brought a relief from the pain but had not produced an effective solution for his ailment. Cystic Fibrosis was a genetic disorder that William had effectively managed for the majority of his life. As he aged, it had taken a turn for the worse. His choices were to spend most of his life attached to oxygen generating machines and complex lung cleaners, or he could live what little time he had left with suppressants and pain relievers.

He wasn't about to die attached to life-giving monstrosities like some Frankenstein. He was better than that. He was going to go out with a bang. He resolved to travel the worlds, both of them, with his wife of over fifty years.

"Are you quite ready to go?" Amelia asked from their open doorway. "It is rude to keep a lady waiting."

They walked arm-in-arm down the stairwell and moved to the same table they'd occupied a few hours earlier. William pulled out a seat for Amelia, and she gave an acknowledging nod to him in thanks.

Alice Trudeau, apparently finished with playing mother for the day, was seated across from them at a table having a lively conversation with Omario Richards.

". . . have they really tried to get their team off the ground, though?" Alice asked.

"They have, and they even went to the cup a few times. Arsenal was just able to offer so much more money right from the start. Jamaica didn't even bid. I've been with them for three seasons now," Omario replied.

"Money. Money always does the talking doesn't it, Omario?" Alice coughed slightly as she put out a cigarette on the tray in front of her.

"It's not just money. I love my island, but I saw this as a chance to make a better life for my family. You don't understand what it is like to live as someone who has never been—"

"Black?" Alice finished.

Omario chuckled. He shook his head and stared down at his drink which he swirled. Alice would never have said something like that when she was sober. He had seen how composed she was at the start of their meal. That said, his blood boiled a bit.

"Wow, no. Definitely not where I was going with that," Omario corrected. "But, let's talk about it in a minute. I was going to say poor. People say money can't buy happiness. I say, try going to bed hungry for a few months straight with no air conditioning, and then tell me you wouldn't be happier with a soft pillow and a cool hotel room."

"Omario, I'm sorry. I really shouldn't have—" Alice tried.

"No, nonsense!" Omario laughed and sipped his drink again. "A pretty little white girl comes and talks to me about possibly dragging the race card into the equation, but she's drunk. I wish that was the most offensive thing I'd ever had said to me about my race. You were just curious. Well, let's talk. How many times have you been stopped by a police officer?"

Leo was black. Her first husband was taken far too soon. Alice thought that mentioning him *might* send the wrong message about what her intentions were with the apparently famous football player. Plus, it was a bit of a mood killer to mention a man being struck down in the prime of his life.

"Uhh," Alice thought aloud. "Maybe twice? Once when I was in Egypt, and then when they found Jack."

"Right then." Omario let no time elapse from the end of her sentences and the start of his own. "I am famous now. I thought the harassment would finally drop off a bit, and it did, but I still get those uncertain looks from London police. They walk over to me with suspicion, and then figure out who I am after they see my license. I'm popular now, but not famous enough to be allowed a berth when I'm walking down the street with a woman," he sighed. "It's just life, I know that. I've come to accept that I have to work for what I get. It doesn't mean I don't get burned when I see a mate get busted with 5g of coke and get a slap on the wrist and a warning. If I had so much as a joint on me, I'd be taken to lockup at minimum and sent upriver at worst."

Alice wanted to argue with his words. She wished to tell him that he was being obscene, but something rang true about his statements. When she left the dorm with Leo Trudeau during her college years, she could remember the suspicious looks friends gave them. She had strangers walk up to the pair and ask Alice if she was all right, their eyes whipping back and forth between the two of them. It had seemed silly at the time, but she knew that it meant something more.

"I'm sorry. I can understand how that must frustrate you," Alice apologized.

"Alice." He smiled. "I don't think you've ever done anything to me that warrants an apology. I just wanted you to understand that I had a lot of things influence my decisions as I got into sports."

As their conversation ended, Evelyn Fox entered the lounge, followed closely by Mark.

"Silas!" she called as she surveyed the room.

"Yes, ma'am?" he answered from behind the bar.

"Let's put these three tables together. I think it could be fun for us all to get to know each other a bit better! Make it a table for ten," she ordered.

Silas dropped the rag he had been holding and quickly moved to the dining area. He first took the chairs away from their respective tables and then began to scoot them into one long dining table. He asked William and Amelia to move over, and they obliged. William angrily murmured something about robots and knowing their place under his breath. After that, Silas moved to Alice's table. Her eyes hadn't left the pair who had just entered the room.

"Mr. Richards, Ms. Trudeau, won't you join our other guests at the center of the room?" Silas queried with a gesture toward the newly formed dining party.

Omario looked to Alice. She seemed hesitant to move.

"Silas, thanks for the offer, mate, but I think we would—" he started.

"We'll move," Alice interrupted.

"You *sure*?" Omario asked, trying to give her an out.

"No, I'm positive!" Alice smiled, trying to sound unbothered by the situation.

Omario shrugged. He took his seat next to William Rutger, sitting directly across from Alice. Evelyn squeezed herself into the seat on the other side of Alice. Mark had a regretful look on his face as he lowered himself into the seat diagonally across from the uncomfortable woman.

"So, Alice, what is it that you do?" Evelyn posed the first question to her neighbor.

"I'm in city management," she replied. "I work under Mayor Dretch in Villanova."

"Oh, my! You're the one heading those new project developments, right? What is it, Saronga, Saluta?"

"Yes, I'm the planner for two new settlements that have been gaining pioneers quickly. Their names are Corsicana and Saratoga. The farmers there have really been showing some promise. I'm trying to plan it out well to accommodate for population increases and—"

"Dust storms, I hope?" Evelyn poked.

She was referring to the failed settlement at Edgemere. The people there had gotten a real foothold. They were thriving. Then, a dust storm had swallowed the entire Martian atmosphere. Larger settlements were able to clean out particulate buildup that resulted as it raged on, but Edgemere had been less fortunate. All four hundred and seventeen residents were found dead the week after the storm when rescue ships were able to approach. They had to unearth the docking port from eight feet of piled sand. The colony had spent weeks preparing, but they'd failed to account for what might happen if the dust storm dragged on for over two months, which it had.

"Well, that was a bit before my time," Alice said. "But all new settlements are built with storm protections guaranteed for at least 6 months of activity, which there has never been in recorded history."

"Ugly business that was." Evelyn shuddered. "I can't help but imagine what it must have smelled like for those first responders."

Alice knew all too well that the smell of death wasn't dignified. There was no proper way to die. She knew that a body expelled all piss, shit, vomit, and blood, in her brother's case, upon an individual's passing. Even though Jack and Cara had been found only twelve short hours after their murder, the rusty odor had been heinous.

She recalled what it had been like to enter their bedroom.

Jack had been face down on the floor. A gunshot wound had entered just above his spine and shards of the hollow-point shell had ripped out between his eyes. It had been an execution. There was an awful amount of blood. It had dripped down the steel paneling of their habitation like a scene from a slasher film.

Cara seemed to have been caught unaware. She'd fallen midstride with a shot through her windpipe and neck. Another bullet-hole was discovered just behind her temple by investigators. Alice knew that this was because the first shot wouldn't have killed her instantly. She probably screamed and gurgled as the life drained from her dying body. The shot to the head might have been mercy, but more likely it had been to stop the unpleasant gasping and pleading.

Alice felt a bit dizzy again. The room seemed to quiet, but she heard her own name being called.

"Alice, you all right?" Omario asked.

"Oh, fine. Sorry, I just got distracted with something else," she muttered absently.

"I hope it wasn't anything I said, Alice." Evelyn held a hand to her neck and bowed her head slightly.

It was at that moment Alice decided that she was not at all charmed by Ms. Fox.

"No, Evelyn, don't you worry a bit about it," Alice almost hissed. "Thank you for the lovely evening, Omario. I better head up and get ready for dinner."

Omario gave an awkward wave, his face showing real concern. "*Sorry,*" he mouthed, not even sure what had just transpired between the two women.

Alice jogged up the steps to her room. She tried to think calming thoughts. She tried to breathe, but all she wanted to do was cry. Why was she still so bothered by death? Why couldn't she face the issue without clamming up and tumbling into a fit of hysteria?

She turned the key to her room and slammed the door shut behind her. She stripped off her clothes and yanked open the shower door. She turned the water on full blast and let the icy spray flow over her. She shivered at first, but warmth spread over her as the temperature adjusted. She wanted to calm down. She needed to put on a brave face for Eleanor and James.

A few minutes later she dried herself and rifled through her suitcase to find a pair of black dress slacks, a beige button-down top, and a pair of shining gold teardrop earrings. She pulled her watch around her wrist and looked at the time. It was just past 5:40 in the evening. She exited her room and knocked on the children's door. Eleanor was dressed in a similar outfit, except that her blouse was pink.

"Great minds!" Alice smiled, motioning between herself and Eleanor.

Eleanor forced a grin but was mostly annoyed that she had to share a look with her aunt. Why did Alice constantly have to point out their similarities?

"I suppose," Eleanor acknowledged. "James, are you ready to go?"

"Oh, yeah!" he loudly announced. James slid into view in a white button-down shirt with a bright red clip-on tie. He was still tucking his shirt into his waistband as he ran to the door. His black-socks glided over the glassy stone tiling.

"Get your shoes," Alice instructed. The boy doubled back and returned with a pair of black sneakers in his hand.

"Those are your dress shoes?" Eleanor groaned.

"What? They're shiny! I thought they would be good for dressy occasions or adventures alike!" James tried to justify.

"Just put them on, James." Alice shook her head and looked at Eleanor. For the briefest of moments, the women understood each other and sympathized.

As soon as the boy had finished preparing himself, the trio exited the room and began walking downstairs.

"I'm excited!" James interjected. "Do you think Mr. Fox will be there? I bet he's ugly. Maybe he has huge warts or powder-white skin! Maybe that's why he stays so far away from everyone."

Alice laughed softly. She opened her mouth to discredit the notion but realized that she had no idea *why* Mr. Fox was so reclusive. As they continued down the stairway, a thundering of footsteps made the three of them turn around. Peter Corgrave, the detective Alice had yet to be introduced to, was gaining on them rapidly as he came down the stairs.

His pace slowed as he neared the other guests.

"Oh, you'll have to excuse my manners," he grunted. "I've been sleeping, and I only just realized the time."

But Peter was lying. He had not been sleeping at all. Peter Corgrave had been reviewing the connections he had already deduced. There was clearly some sort of preexisting relationship between Jonathan Hulsey and Ms. Trudeau. Her fit at missing the train seemed to give credence to the private detective's supposition that he was on the right track for where Mr. Gomez had gone missing. He wasn't sure exactly what precipitated her frustration, but she was clearly upset to be staying at The Arbor another night. There were indeed odd happenings at Fox's magnificent lodge. Peter's only question was how dear Mr. Gomez had been involved. He looked on Ms. Trudeau sadly. Her weeping reminded him of the war.

Peter had been responsible for evacuation of civilians during mainland European bombing. Transports had been required to be wheels up fifteen minutes prior to ballistic bombardment by enemy forces. They had been able to save so many lives that would have been otherwise lost, but there was something soul-crushing about lying in the face of someone who was about to die.

"*The next transport will be about five minutes behind this one. Please step back!*" he would say.

They would often fight their way forward, in which case sonic repulsors would pound them backward into the ground. Worse were the fathers who would hold their children high into the air in some desperate plea to save them.

His commanding officer's orders had been clear. *Take off fifteen minutes before ICBM impact. No excuses. Five hundred civilians saved are better than none.*

Peter had known that his CO was right. It was no easier with that realization to condemn the waiting thousands to death. He had been just a boy then, but he remembered the sleepless nights that followed.

What had Alice heard to make her so desperate to cut the vacation short before it had even begun?

Peter knew that Evelyn was here by her own volition. He further understood that she was one of two who had not been invited. He was the other.

An invite-only resort hardly seemed to be a self-sustaining business model. That said, he doubted the great Alexis Fox exactly needed the money. It seemed the resort was not open more than twice per year. He learned it stayed open for periods of three to four weeks, and then would shut down. The company blamed winter freezes for the inconsistent schedule, but it was one of the many red flags that had already showcased themselves to Mr. Corgrave.

Another curious situation was the extension of Ms. Rose Grayson's stay. Every other guest of the resort had checked out at the end of their week-long visit except Rose. Why had she stayed? This was a question he intended to have answered during their meal.

The group of four people finished their trip down the

stairwell in silence. They entered a dimly lit dining room that was attached to the bar by a pair of double doors which had been thrown open in anticipation of the guests. There were a pair of silver candelabra on the blood-red tablecloth. Twelve seats had place settings in front of them. Fine China plates with pewter scroll along their edge were placed carefully.

At the far end of the table, exactly opposite the door, sat a tall man. More than his stature was large. His presence was dominating. His echoing voice filled the narrow room whenever he spoke. His laughter boomed like a thunderclap when his daughter leaned close.

Alexis Fox's unmistakable silhouette was illuminated from behind by a roaring fireplace. His head turned to face the entering guests as they arrived.

SEVEN

"**A**HH, MORE NEW FACES!" FOX SAID AS HE CLAPPED his hands together eagerly. "Timothy, announce our new friends, please!"

The white-faced Android moved from his hardly visible position at the rear corner of the room.

"Inspector Peter Corgrave!" Timothy loudly declared.

Mr. Corgrave gave a small wave and walked down the room past Amelia and William Rutger to a seat with a small note card in front of it. He sat to the left of Alexis Fox, directly across from Evelyn Fox.

"We appreciate your attendance and will of course provide you with any information you might need in relation to the disappearance of Mr. Gomez," Mr. Fox declared as he shook Peter Corgrave's hand with a paralyzing strength.

"Ms. Alice Trudeau and her charges, Eleanor and James Wortz!" Timothy again called.

"Ahh, Ms. Trudeau. It is truly a rare pleasure to meet you. Firstly, allow me to extend to you the sincerest of condolences. The loss of a loved one is always horrendous, but to lose a family so suddenly . . . I am awestruck by your resolve and competence in managing such a difficult situation." Mr. Fox finished his thought and moved down the table to pull out the chair for Alice. He shook her hand as she sat and continued more quietly. "You are a remarkable woman. If there is anything my staff or I can do to make your stay more pleasurable, please let me know."

Alice blushed. She didn't like having the spotlight so focused on her.

"Thank you, Mr. Fox," she managed to whisper.

"Call me Alex. Please." Mr. Fox gave another warm smile before he walked back to the head of the room.

"Who are we still waiting on, Timothy?" Evelyn asked.

"Mr. Graham and Ms. Grayson have not yet arrived," he replied.

A pair of empty seats sat at the entrance side of the dining room.

"Well, I do despise repeating myself." Alex sighed in frustration. "He will simply have to catch up when he arrives."

"Shall we begin, then?" Evelyn asked.

Alex Fox snapped his fingers. "Timothy, bring in the first course."

A carefully prepared salad was delivered plate by plate by Silas and Timothy, who darted back and forth from the servants' door. A pair of halved strawberries sat atop a bed of mixed greens. Black balsamic drizzle zigzagged across cashews and gorgonzola crumbles. Alice's mouth watered. She had snacked at the bar but hadn't eaten properly since the previous afternoon. She counted to ten in her head before daintily retrieving her salad fork. Two seats down, James was already on large mouthful number three.

"*James!*" Eleanor whispered with a nudge.

"I like that one!" Alex laughed. "Everyone else so concerned with demeanor and decorum while this little one sates his needs."

James gave a peculiar smile to his sister as he whispered a reply through a full mouth, "*He* likes me!"

Eleanor sighed and ate her salad with less enthusiasm than
her brother. The delicious mix hit her palate like a freight train.

"Oh. my God," she whispered.

"I'd hazard a guess it has been quite some time since you had
freshly cooked food?" Alex asked.

"Well, we have had cooked food, but these are real strawberries," Eleanor gasped.

"Yes," Alex nodded. "The soil here is extremely rich. We have
a greenhouse in the basement. It doesn't produce enough food for
large-scale production but plenty for a few guests several times
per year. The curry we will be having momentarily is made with
chickens raised in a chamber beside our grow-house. We are almost entirely self-sufficient here."

"That's amazing," Amelia interjected. "I would assume the refuse from the livestock is used to fertilize the soil?"

Alex guffawed. "Well, Mrs. Rutger, you don't hesitate to describe the machinations behind a sausage factory, do you? Yes, we
also make our own fertilizer."

James paused and surveyed his next bite. The hesitation
was momentary as he continued to shovel salad into his waiting
gullet.

"Well, I have never chained myself by political correctness!"
Amelia said as she lifted her glass for a drink.

"That is a trait I am sure we share." Alex raised his own glass
and drank after her.

The dining party turned to face the double doors as loud
footsteps grew closer and closer. Winston Graham slid into the
dining room and hopped into his chair in one motion.

"Eating already?" he wondered.

Evelyn wrinkled her nose.

"My father's time is far more valuable than yours, insect," she snapped.

"Evelyn," Alex quietly spoke. "A queen must show dignity if she is to be respected."

She nodded, but Mark could see her fists tensing and releasing under the table.

"I am curious as to Ms. Grayson's whereabouts," Alex mused.

"Probably passed out in the common room," Eleanor whispered to James.

"Where did you say?" Alex asked, looking directly at Eleanor.

"Oh, I was just—" she stammered. "The last place we saw her was in the common room."

"Ah, good girl," Alex approved. "Timothy, please see if Ms. Grayson remains in the common room. Maybe she can still make the main course."

Timothy nodded and left the room forthwith. Everyone waited for several minutes as forks began to scrape at almost empty plates.

The android finally returned.

"Ms. Grayson is not downstairs or in her room," Timothy announced. "Would you like me to check the grounds?"

"Oh, nonsense." Alex shook his head. "Just bring out the main course, and we will locate Ms. Grayson later."

As the robots began delivering full plates of Tikka Masala, the room was filled with a strong aroma of roasted vegetables, chicken, and spicy potatoes. The chef had clearly taken a few liberties in his interpretation of the dish, but the scent was delightful.

Alice's mother had always said the surest sign of a well-prepared meal was silence after it was served. The room was still and quiet except for the occasional gulp of wine as the guests filled themselves to the brim. James was, unsurprisingly, the first to finish.

In the entryway, the grandfather clock gonged out seven long chimes.

"Oh, that was incredible. I haven't eaten something that good in—well—ever!" Eleanor sighed in complete satisfaction.

Alex coughed deeply as he laughed. He brought a napkin to his face and cleared his throat. "Must have been too good to stop eating myself!" he exclaimed.

His coughing fit continued for a few more moments, but he eventually collected himself.

"Father, are you all right?" Evelyn asked.

"Fine, dear," he reassured. "Must have just gone down the wrong way."

William Rutger's eyes were immediately drawn to the blood which stained Mr. Fox's white napkin as he set it back down in his lap. A tiny splash of bluish red was visible beneath his left earlobe.

"Mr. Fox, I don't believe you are all right," William spoke. "I am a doctor, if you will let me—"

The lights all went out in the room.

"*What the bloody hell?*" Omario shouted.

"El?" James whispered.

"William, what is going on?" Amelia grabbed for her husband's arm in the darkness.

An awful scratching filled the dining room. It sounded as though it was being produced from nothing, as though a malicious specter had begun to haunt the dining hall. Then, it stopped.

"Welcome to *my* Arbor," a low, awful voice called.

"Who is that?" Alice screamed.

"You are here because I have desired it to be so," the scratchy demonic voice continued. "You are here because you are to be my prey."

"All right! That's it!" Omario shouted. He clicked his lighter in his hand and produced a small flame. It was hardly enough to see his own face, but he felt like he had a slight bit more control now.

"You will all be tested over the next few days. You will be tried. You will learn things about each other you never knew before. You will be hunted."

"What the fuck is this?" Eleanor whimpered.

"Listen for the gong of the clock. That signal will initiate each new hunt. I will pursue relentlessly. One of you will die. At each passing, a single loud bell will peal out. From the moment of each death, you will have another few hours until I begin again."

James shook his head. "No, this isn't right. I don't want to be here anymore. El, I don't want to stay here anymore!"

The voice continued.

"You may run, you may forge alliances, you may fight, but make no mistake—one life will be claimed every time those bells chime. The methods will vary, but I have seen fit to leave you all a little clue at the end of the dining room. Perhaps it is worth a look."

"*You* will be hunted by my father and me," Evelyn shouted indignantly. "You will be the one to die!"

"To my first victim, I wish you an expedient death. To my other contenders, fight with everything inside you. Good luck."

A moment later, all the lights flashed on to their full brightness.

An uproar flooded the dining room.

"What the hell do you think this is, Mr. Fox?" William seethed.

"Call a train for us to get out of here!" Eleanor screamed.

"Aunt Alice, I'm scared!" James said.

"Now listen here!" Alex Fox shouted as he continued to cough. "I had no part in any of this!"

William watched in horror. Mr. Fox' fingertips were stained

a deep maroon. What had been a tiny splotch of blue had spread down his neck in darkness and up onto his face. When he coughed again, his hand was covered in bright red blood.

Alex began to gasp. He tried for breath but found none. Each cough spurted more blood onto the tablecloth in front of him. Red lines began to spread in the whites of his eyes. He coughed again and turned to vomit a stream of purple sick onto the tile behind his chair.

"Daddy!" Evelyn screeched. She raced to his side, but he shoved her away as he fell to the floor. Blood began to freely flow from his nose as his head met the ground. The coughing ceased.

William jumped from his seat first. He grabbed the man's wrist and checked for a pulse.

"Dear me," he whispered. The doctor dropped the wrist to the ground. "He's dead."

Evelyn let out a guttural cry as she buried her face deep in Mark's chest.

"What happened?" Alice asked.

William moved to answer but was interrupted by a loud twang. The clock outside the room let out a piercing gong and the room was effectively silenced.

"It was just like he said," Winston mumbled. "Just like that fucking voice said!"

"I'm calling for help!" Peter declared. "Where's the phone?"

"One in the kitchen," Evelyn said, running a hand over her father's body. "Was it some kind of poison?"

William examined the body. He noted the splotching up the arms and neck. Profuse blood loss. Vomit intermingled with blood.

"I have never seen this used, but it looks like—arsenic," the doctor announced. "Acute arsenic poisoning. I have never heard of it progressing this quickly before, though. Usually arsenic poisoning is slow. A tiny dose in food over weeks will make these symptoms occur over a longer period. This had to have been a massive dose. The salts would have been obvious in food, unless—"

His eyes rested on Mr. Fox's plate of curry.

"Unless you had a dish that was significantly spiced to mask the flavor," he finished.

"Guys, look!" James pointed at the mantle behind Mr. Fox's seat. What had been unnoticeable in the dimly lit room now stuck out. A clock.

"Look at that," Mark wondered aloud. "It has one hand. It's pointing to a skull."

The clock had ten markings along the edge of its dial.

"That is the symbol for hazardous substances!" Evelyn announced.

"This is a clock depicting how we are going to die," Alice absently moaned. "First was poison, second looks like a bear trap, third is a set of crosshairs, fourth is—what?"

A pair of triangles with circular openings at the top and spikes just beneath that were at the fourth position.

"Never mind that," Mark said. "Is that an angel at position five?"

"The next looks to be a set of pills?" Eleanor added.

"A—pill?" William repeated.

"After the angel, it's some kind of road?" Amelia speculated. A pair of wavy lines were curving down a path.

"Final position is a deformed head, with a sword through its skull," Winston said.

"This is madness!" Evelyn shouted. "We need to get out of here, and I know just how to do it."

"Phone is dead," Peter sighed as he re-entered the room. "Can't say I'm surprised."

"Father has—" Evelyn paused. "Father had an emergency transponder in his office. It was meant for just an occasion like this."

"Maybe not exactly like this," Winston quipped.

"Shit!" Evelyn cursed. "It uses a retinal scanner. I tried to get into it once. I thought he would eventually trust me with—"

She took a moment and turned from the crowd of people. A second later, she was back to her determined self.

"That is our best shot for getting out of here," Evelyn finished.

"I will see what I can do," Peter said, "because eyes are not going to work in the scanner."

Catastrophic hemorrhaging leaked blood from every nook and cranny in Alexis Fox, including his eyes. The once lively set of irises were flooded with an almost black color now.

The group's talking was interrupted by a sound at the rear of the room. The single hand of the clock had ticked one position forward. If the voice was to be believed, they had approximately twelve hours.

"No, I don't want to be here anymore! I don't like this!" James' voice trembled as he spoke.

He flew from the room. His tiny footfalls could be heard skittering up the steps in the lobby a moment later.

Alice moved to check on him. Eleanor took off ahead of her.

"You need to help them figure out how to get us out of here. I'll get James," she said.

Alice grimaced. She knew she needed to be there for her family, but at that moment, "being there" meant adding her brain-power to the rapidly developing think-tank downstairs. Alice was not sure she was any more able to cope with the situation than he was, but she had to channel her mother. She needed to be stalwart. She needed to focus.

"Okay." Alice let the word fall as she breathed in deeply. She turned back to face her fellow prisoners with an uncommon re-solve. "We should pair off. No one alone. I think we have all seen this movie. We should know what happens when people wander off alone."

"And who put you in charge?" Winston spat from Alice's left.

Alice smoothed one hand over her outfit slightly before turn-ing to face the belligerent man.

"Do you disagree, Mr. Graham?" she asked.

"Of course not, I just—" he said.

"You don't disagree," Alice clarified. "Do you have a better plan, then?"

"No." He spoke through narrowed lips.

"Brilliant," Alice smiled. "Evelyn, is there a weak spot in your father's office? Any windows? We need a backup plan."

"There are two," Evelyn said. "Both are military grade ballis-tic glass with a titanium nanomeshing. You would need a tank to blast through it."

"That's an idea." Alice seemed to become momentarily distracted.

"What?" Mark wondered. "A tank, Alice?"

Alice shushed Mark. Her mind was racing and did not have time to stop and play catch-up with her ex.

"Peter, what do you need for your plan?" Alice asked.

"Access terminal," he replied shortly. "I'm an investigator, so slicing systems is a bit of a specialty."

"Evelyn, can you help with that?" Alice said.

"Oh yes, ma'am," Evelyn returned with a mock salute. She turned to face Mark. "Entertain yourself, Jonathan. I'll be back soon."

Alice could not help rolling her eyes.

"Silas, where do you keep fertilizer for the soil downstairs?" Alice refocused.

"In the basement, Ms. Trudeau," he answered.

"Bring it all upstairs. Bring any granulated plant food or powdered sugar you might have as well. I'll also need lamp oil if you have it," Alice spoke, finishing her laundry list.

Silas rotated to look at Evelyn.

"Oh, do as she says, Silas. I give her full administrative command access. Treat her like you would me," she groaned.

Without a word, Silas left the room, followed closely by Peter and Evelyn.

"*Jonathan,* why don't you document what is happening here? Winston, would you mind pairing up with him for the moment?" Alice asked.

He nodded. Mr. and Mrs. Rutger joined Omario in waiting for their marching orders.

"Omario, we are going to check the elevator. I doubt it is that easy, but it is worth a shot. Dr. Rutger, would you both work to search for medical supplies? We could make bandages from cloth. I trust you might know more about this than me."

"Certainly, love," Amelia responded and walked from the room with her husband.

Upstairs, Eleanor was trying to talk sense into James. She pounded the door of their suite in frustration.

"James! I know you are in there! Let me in, please!" She sounded like a mix of angry and sick.

Only silence echoed back.

"James, please!" she repeated. "We need to be at our best right now! I know you must be scared, but we have to work together."

"I'm *not* scared!" A small voice protested.

He could have fooled Eleanor.

"Okay, then if we are not scared, let's work on finding weapons!" Eleanor tried a different tactic.

"What kind of weapons?" James asked.

"Oh, well, I don't know much about defending myself. I was thinking maybe some candlesticks?" Eleanor baited her brother.

"Candlesticks? There has to be something better than that," he retorted.

"Well, I'll just see what I can find, I guess," Eleanor sighed.

"Wait!" James shouted. He opened the door, and in his tiny hand he held a massive six-inch hunting knife.

"Bloody hell, James!" Eleanor shrunk back slightly. "Where did you get that?"

He sheathed the blade and held it close to his chest.

"You aren't taking it from me!" He scowled at his sister.

"I wouldn't think of messing with you anymore, little one. It seems like you are already familiar with it," Eleanor chuckled.

"*Yeah*," he almost bragged as he slipped the sheath clip over his pant waistband. "I got it after Mom and Dad—I just wanted to feel safe. I ordered it online. I used Aunt Alice's card."

Eleanor smiled widely.

"You're bad, James. Never change."

The boy patted his oversized blade and ran back into the room.

"Do you think curtain pulls could be used as rope?"

Probably not, Eleanor thought. That said, it was a good distraction from the boy's worry.

"Definitely," she nodded. "Let's get all the rope we can find!"

Needing no further encouragement, James clamored his way up onto the windowsill. He drew his knife and sliced the thin string from its nesting at the top of the frame. He saw a figure wandering her way around the tennis court outside. She kept trying to sit on the net but fell sideways repeatedly. Rose Grayson continued to make good use of her time and resources.

"I've heard that animal rawhide like the rug in the common room can be excellent protection against the elements or small projectiles." James added as he rocked his wrist back and forth. "I read it on one of my National Geographic magazines."

"*You're such a nerd,*" Eleanor chuckled softly.

"What?" James loudly asked.

"I'm glad you heard that!" Eleanor replied, suppressing a smile.

Downstairs, Dr. and Mrs. Rutger watched the entire affair as they pulled stuffing from the benches in the library.

"This is good cotton," the doctor mused. "Dense fibers. It will make an excellent sealant if the need arises."

"A painful one, perhaps," Amelia sighed.

"My dear, when the choices presented are bleeding out or having a wad of abrasive cloth shoved into the open wound, most men would see the benefit in the primitive but effective solution," he argued.

"Beggars cannot be choosers, this is true," Amelia agreed. She began to rip the leather binding from the benches as well. The wrapping pulled off in long strips from the edges.

"Clever woman." William patted his wife on the back. "Those will make excellent tourniquet straps."

She grunted against the brass rivets as she continued to pull the leather free.

"One picks up things with a doctor for a husband."

William knew she did a bit more than that. Amelia was perfectly content with her life, but she was tenacious in her search for knowledge. He always tended to be candid when talking with those he viewed as intellectually inferior, but this was never a concern with Amelia. It was part of what attracted him to her all those years ago. She had a quiet kind of brilliance. She'd never let him return his college textbooks at the end of the semester. She read everything in sight, and that included medical journals. William often wondered which of them was the more capable: the doctor who was schooled in medical practices, or the wife who was self-taught.

Amelia draped the pieces of leather over a chair at the front of the room. She sat for a moment and watched Rose just outside their window.

"I do believe she is hiding something," Amelia said.

William joined her at the chair and placed a hand on her shoulder. "With what motive?"

William had his own suspicions, but he wanted to play devil's advocate.

"Well, the way I see it, Rose was here before the rest of us. Every other guest, without exception, left when we arrived. I am not saying that alone constitutes guilt, but her mood has been quite unstable for the entirety of our visit. She has been either openly hostile, or publicly inebriated the whole time."

"Sometimes both," William added.

"Indeed." Amelia stood and looked out of the wide window more closely. "Yes, I am quite resolved in my opinion. That is the drunken gait of a guilty woman."

William took a step closer to the window. He tilted his head a bit before replying. "But do you really think Rose is the one who orchestrated all this? She seems to lack the gumption, if I may say so. She hardly seems the type to mastermind a murder plot."

Amelia pondered this. She tapped her chin and continued to track a drunk and disorderly Rose Grayson.

"I suppose not, but I would argue we lack the evidence to be sure at the moment. Women can be just as conniving as men. Though I will admit, the male sex has a greater tendency toward—delusions of grandeur. The odds are better that the megalomaniac is a man," Amelia agreed. "But I must reiterate, that woman is hiding something. Whether she is a murderer or not has yet to be seen."

She paused momentarily before her stare became one of blank shock. As her inquisitive mind quieted, she began to think on the horrors that had already transpired and those yet to come.

William grabbed the medical supplies from the chair behind him. He placed an arm over his wife, which seemed to jolt her back to reality.

"Come, my dear. We have more work to do before sleep. I do believe we will need the rest."

Just on the other side of the library wall was Alexis Fox's office. Four inches of reinforced concrete separated the captives of the Arbor from safety. The door of the room was oak-covered, but Peter Corgrave had been told it was sheet steel on the inside. Evelyn moved behind the reception desk to a room no bigger than a coat check and slid a panel aside in the wall.

"You wanted a terminal, Mr. Corgrave. Here it is," Evelyn pointed.

A small computer screen was nested under the wallpaper facade. A little keyboard dropped from the panel as the hidden door slid away. As Peter approached the console, he noticed something upsetting.

"There's no network connection?" he groaned.

Evelyn sighed.

"I believe I already told you that my father had an emergency transponder *in his office*. It would stand to reason that the transponder would be the only network access point in the manor, wouldn't it?"

Peter took a breath. It had been many years since he'd attacked a system without using networked tools. He would have to take the long way around. "I can suppress dialogues and create a script to brute force the password, unless you happen to have it?"

Evelyn shook her head. "If I did, I am sure we would be in the office by now."

Peter plugged a small flash drive into the unit. A pair of terminal windows opened on the screen in the foreground in front of the login box.

"This could take a while. If the password was eight characters long, it could take up to four hours for the attack to succeed. If the password was ten characters, it could take a couple of days. If it was twelve or more characters—"

"We will be dead long before it is solved," Evelyn finished. "Well, let's hope my father valued his time enough to shorten his encryption protocols."

Peter agreed. "Crossing my fingers. My attack stick should ring when the password is cracked. It has a small alarm on it."

"That being the case, I am going to get a drink so that I might get a few winks of sleep," Evelyn said. She paused in the doorway. "Coming? Apparently, we are sticking together, so chop, chop."

Evelyn got her drink and walked through the house in a state of stunned disbelief. The reality of the matter had not hit her yet. Her father was dead. She had trained for this moment for years but never expected it to happen this way. She was ready to lead; of this fact she was sure. She did worry about the board. Despite her business acumen and position, she was concerned they would try to give the position to her older brother simply because he had a penis and had lived in the universe a few short years longer than she had. The reality of the situation was embarrassing. Her brother was a self-indulgent imbecile, and yet he was the rightful heir to the power and prestige of the JCN fortune. She needed to reshape the narrative before news got out. Her father had clearly groomed her for this. With any luck, he'd made his intentions known in his will.

Unsurprisingly, Alice found the elevator unresponsive. The doors were two-inch hardened steel. She would have an easier time bringing down the walls of ice than piercing the impregnable barrier. She found her way upstairs and held her nephew, James. Omario opted to sleep on the floor of her room. The children shared her bed. The crew of individuals had spent a limited few hours preparing. They had medical supplies at the ready. Alice knew they would be needed first thing in the morning.

James fell asleep quickly, followed by Omario. Alice and Eleanor both stared at the ceiling, refusing to acknowledge each other's restlessness.

You need to sleep. You will need the rest! Alice thought to herself. She did not feel much like a leader, but she knew that the mantle had been passed to her by default as soon as she began disseminating instructions. She chose to think of it like another management job. It was just like work.

She lied to herself.

EIGHT

ALICE'S PHONE BUZZED AT 6:30 SHARP. THE LAST TIME SHE had checked, it was 3am. She must have gotten a little bit of sleep after all. By the speed of the clock ticking downstairs, she estimated that the group had about twelve hours from the moment of Mr. Fox's untimely demise until the next hazard made itself known.

She got up and stretched expansively. The same sunrise glow that had greeted her the first morning reprised its role as she peered out. But something was different. She squinted to see cords of rope entangled at various points in the yard. There were metal implements facing inward along the tennis court. It reminded her of spike strips police would throw down to catch escaping criminals in old-Earth movies. The realization dawned on her like a wave crashing against a sandcastle.

"Wake up!" she shouted.

Omario and Eleanor sprang to their feet instinctively. James was slower. He had worry in his eyes as he spoke.

"Aunt Alice, what is it?"

"I don't know if the clock accelerated, but something is very wrong outside," Alice breathed, almost afraid of her own words.

Eleanor ran to the window and threw the curtain aside. Light shot in blinding rays across the darkened room.

"Shit," she mouthed almost soundlessly. "James, grab the weapons."

"The what?" Alice wondered as James leapt from bed.

"Weapons, for defending ourselves!" James fired back as though the answer should have been obvious.

"Oh, of course!" Alice chuckled, almost forgetting herself.

James dragged a bedsheet from the closet. A fire-prod, steak knives, and an improvised rope made of towels and sheets tied together were among the many offerings of the display.

"When did you do all this?" Omario asked.

James shrugged. "I wigged out for a bit, but then we spent an hour or so creeping around the house and commandeering means of self-defense."

Alice considered saying something about slinking around the house with a killer on the loose but decided against it.

"Thanks so much for your services, sir," Alice said with a salute.

Omario took the fire poker, Alice took a pair of steak knives, and Eleanor did the same. The four individuals slowly peered their heads out of the room. The mansion looked innocent enough. Eleanor feared what sinister tricks could be sitting just out of view.

Another door opened farther down the hallway. Omario cocked back his metal implement in preparation for a fight. Peter Corgrave gave a small wave. Omario lowered his guard, but only slightly. As Peter left the room, he was followed by Winston Graham.

"Did the two of you have a sleepover, then?" Alice laughed.

"Wasn't it your idea to stay together, Alice?" Winston growled.

She tried to hide her grin. "You're right. That's the safe thing to do. Thank you for taking my advice to heart."

Hearing the commotion in the hallway, Rose Grayson tumbled out of her room in silk pajamas.

"Could you all please just keep it down a bit?" she moaned.

By wonderfully serendipitous coincidence, William and Amelia Rutger exited their room and slammed the door shut loudly behind them. "Are we ready for the day, then?"

Rose stumbled a bit at the reverberating sound of the old couple entering the hallway.

"Fuck me raw," she hissed, holding her head.

"Where the hell have you been?" Alice hissed. "Alexis Fox is dead. We're being hunted. We need to be on our guard if we are to—"

"Oh, dear!" Rose sighed, stretching her arms high over her head. "That sounds—dreadful! What's for breakfast, then?"

"What's for. . ." Alice paused, shaking her head rapidly as though she'd just been pied in the face. "Are you quite mental, then? Rose, there's a killer on the loose!"

"Then I'd better get a head start on my consumption!" Rose nodded, before bopping down the hall to the stairs.

Alice stood dumbfounded at the departure of her once-friend. Rose was crazed beyond anything she had been when they were close. She was hiding something.

"We had better get downstairs soon," William gravely sighed. "If my hypothesis is correct, the next hunt should begin in a half-hour."

As the group made their way downstairs, the smell of freshly grilled bacon filled the air.

"At least it smells like we won't have to worry about breakfast," James whispered as he poked Eleanor, laughing at an already seated Ms. Grayson.

The tense congregation of guests made their way to the same dining room that held such bad memories from the previous night. Alex Fox's body had been cleaned up. Evelyn sat opposite Mark at the front of the room. Mr. Fox's chair was empty, and no one moved to claim it. Everyone seemed hesitant to eat, except Evelyn who ate with decorum, but quickly. Of course, Rose was almost finished her plate before the others sat down. They all watched the two eating woman as though they were ticking time bombs.

"The way I figure it, poison has been used already," Evelyn answered the unasked question. "Our killer seems to be about theatrical production. There is no way, with that knowledge, he would poison the food again. That would be—*predictable*."

James took this as gospel truth and began to eagerly shovel forkfuls of eggs and potato into his mouth. Eleanor shrugged and followed her brother's lead.

"I suppose she's right," Amelia sighed. "And if the food is poisoned, at least the death will be quick and predictable."

The table's occupants looked nervously around at each other. Another hour from now, the odds were good that one of them would be dead. With this unhappy thought, Alice ate with more vigor. The clock's hand was almost on the next marker. She awaited the tick-tock in nervous silence. Her watch read 7 AM. She closed her eyes and awaited the inevitable.

The first peal of the bell made everyone jump from their seats. Each following one caused eyes to twitch and hands to jerk across the room.

"Godspeed everyone," William declared on the fourth ring of the bell.

"Everyone stay with your group," Alice reminded around the sixth bell.

On ring seven, every light in the Arbor was extinguished.

"Damnit!" Peter exclaimed.

Eleanor was the first one to think of using her phone's flashlight. The beam trembled as she raised it to look around the room. Evelyn, Alice, and Peter followed suit.

"Looks like we have our group leaders," Evelyn said.

Alice's head pondered that for a moment before she objected.

"My kids stay with me!" she flatly shouted.

Eleanor couldn't fight her smile.

"I'm hardly a kid, Aunt Alice, but if it will make you feel better, we won't get separated," she promised.

That warm moment was interrupted by a sharp banging noise against the stone wall. The sound of metal clanking to the ground fixed every gaze in the room at the direction from which it originated. When the flashlights caught up to the sound, the culprit was clear.

"Grenade!" Winston screamed as he dove toward the door and disappeared from view.

The other guests followed him. Slim beams of light tried to illuminate their way as they sprinted from the dining room. Rose caught Alice with her shoulder as too many people tried to exit the double-doorway in a split-second. Alice flew sideways into the open door and caught her ribs against the brass handle. She winced as she fell to the unyielding floor, her phone sliding out of reach.

"Aunt Alice!" James screamed, immediately running to her aid.

The boy crouched down to her and pulled with all his might. Alice began to rise a moment later, wincing at the pain in her rib cage. As she straightened, the crew was startled by a pop from inside the dining room, followed by a hissing noise.

"Gas!" Peter shouted. "Get away! That thing could fill the whole downstairs!"

Without knowing exactly what they were being gassed with, Alice had a hard time judging just how far to run. She was unfortunately familiar with the effects of tear gas, after watching the riots when she was a girl. Her mother told her to stay away from the windows, and Alice had, but begrudgingly. She'd wanted to see what was happening below. Even though she'd been just a girl, she'd wondered how the protesters had felt being forced from their homes and then corralled and gassed in the streets. She'd felt for them. She'd wanted to help them. Now, she understood the feeling of being herded so much more clearly.

"We need to be careful!" Alice shouted. "That grenade is not going to be the end of the attack. Stay together!"

Winston, ever one to rebel and work his own way, took the side corridor out and toward the common room. Peter told him to slow down, but it was of little use. In the pale illumination of the flashlight, he didn't see the tripwire as his foot caught it.

A brilliant flash shot through the bottom floor of the mansion, followed by a deafening blast.

Peter's eyes struggled to adjust as his vision swirled. He picked up Alice's phone from the ground and shone it down the hallway. By the condition of the building, he deduced that the grenade was a flashbang, but that wasn't all the tripwire controlled. Winston Graham was bound to the wall by a pair of thick cords. One looped around his chest, and the other entangled his feet.

"Help!" He struggled to cough out the word.

Peter carefully made his way across the lobby. He checked for elevated tiles and stepped thoughtfully.

It was as he took his time that Eleanor noticed the ropes moving. "They're tightening around him!" she screeched.

James, ever gallant, raced toward Mr. Corgrave, hunting knife in hand. He flew down the hallway but came to a sliding stop before he reached Winston. He carefully avoided a slightly raised tile and finally dropped to a seat as he began to saw at the rope holding his legs. Peter stepped over the same tile that had given James pause and began to tug at the rope around Winston's chest.

"We're going to get you out of there. Just hold on!" he reassured the panicking man.

Breaths came short and shallow for Mr. Graham. He began to hyperventilate as he pushed his shoulders out to try for breathing room. A few moments later, James had successfully freed his legs.

"Good work, kid!" Peter patted James on the head. "Now give me the knife and I'll cut away this one.

James hesitated. He didn't want to part with his precious knife, but that rope would be difficult to gain leverage over at its height. He slowly extended the handle of the knife to Mr. Corgrave.

"But you have to swear to give it back! It was my dad's," James fibbed.

"Of course, James," Peter obliged, none the wiser.

Alice, Eleanor, and Omario had started to move carefully toward the three boys. As Eleanor stepped forward, her leg crossed something invisible, and that step made the tiles in the hall before them slide slightly apart. Massive and intimidating spikes rose three feet into the air in front of them across the entire length of the hall.

"James!" Eleanor screamed. The spikes had completely separated them from the boys. Desperately, Eleanor looked for a way around where there was none. Her brain spun for an answer. "We'll move out front to the tennis court and meet you in the back! Stick together! Please be safe!"

"El?" James stared, confounded. He looked up and down the spikes and realized that the polished metal was going to be impossible to cross for both parties. "Don't leave me!"

Tears welled in his sister's eyes. She should have been right beside him. She should have grabbed him when he went to run. Why wasn't she faster? Her heart felt like it had been punched into her stomach. She wanted to vomit, but she put on a brave face for her terrified brother.

"Use your weapons! Keep them safe!" Eleanor turned away to hide a sniff before continuing. "You're the toughest boy I know. Walk slowly and let the men go first!"

Peter was struggling to free Winston from the top binding. He had cut away half of the rope, but it had begun to dig into his skin at the back. He was going to have to cut dangerously close to flesh to completely free the man.

"This might hurt, bud," he warned.

Winston's eyes showed fear, but he had begun to turn purple. He tried to reply, but gasps and creaks were all that left his mouth. Peter was going to need to act fast. He sliced at the remainder of the rope and tried to avoid skin as much as possible. Time was running out. Winston looked like he was slipping from consciousness.

Peter continued the rocking motion of the blade quicker now. Blood flowed from slits where the knife extended beyond his cutting stroke and touched skin. It was dreadfully sharp. Peter wondered why a nine-year-old boy would need such a destructive tool.

Finally, the last few strands were severed, and the tall man dropped to the ground. He gasped for air and coughed. A little sick accompanied his heaving breaths as his lungs readjusted to their full capacity and over-exerted themselves. He prostrated himself on his back for a moment before turning to James.

"Thanks, dude!" he croaked.

James nodded. He turned to Peter and extended a palm.

"Right, kid. Sorry, here it is," Peter said as he passed the knife back to James.

James sheathed it smoothly. It seemed that he must have practiced that by how effortlessly he was able to return it without even looking.

"Not a problem. Just doing my duty." He gave a thumbs up to Winston, and the man returned it with gratitude as best as he could.

Eleanor and Alice breathed a sigh of relief.

"James, we are going to go make our way around," Alice said. "We love you! Stick together!"

"I'll see you soon!" Eleanor called. "Very soon!"

James nodded, but his countenance was one of confusion and fear. He was more scared than he had ever been. He knew he had to be brave. He had to hide his feelings of dread away. Now was the time for courage.

In the entryway, Evelyn, Mark, Amelia, and William had begun to make their way toward the kitchen.

"We can use cloth napkins and liquid antacid to create a sort of mask for ourselves in case we get caught in the gas," William said as he led the way. "I brought the medicine with me, so we will make enough for everyone and try to get back together."

"What's the point?" Evelyn sighed. "Whoever is to die will die assuredly. Our focus should be on our own survival and making sure it isn't one of us."

Amelia gasped. "Young lady, that is a very pessimistic view of our current predicament. There is also the chance that the killer could be defeated by one of us."

Evelyn shook her head. "Not likely. Do you see how much time he had to prepare this place, right under my father's nose? That spike trap was a modification to the structure. Whoever made it must have had access to the building when none of us were around. Such as it is, he is in a much more advantageous position than us right now. In fact, you could easily assume that this was an inside job. It had to be. Someone angered by my father, I'm sure."

"It is possible," William conceded. "But consider this: who would have had access to this place without your father present?"

Evelyn stopped and shone the flashlight on William.

"What are you trying to imply?" she slowly spoke, making sure her offense was made clear.

"Nothing is sure yet, Ms. Fox, but it would be safe to assume that the killer had to throw the gas grenade. I have seen no one new so far. As such, we can possibly deduce that the one who is trying to kill us is someone we know."

Mark was taken aback. "You think it's one of us?"

"It makes sense, does it not?" Amelia agreed with her husband. "We would have most likely seen someone in the house by now if we were not alone. This means it is logical to assume that someone here is not who he—or she—claims to be."

Mark swallowed hard. Keeping his true identity secret seemed even more critical now.

"Let's focus on surviving for the moment," he suggested. "We can talk about who is trying to kill us after the next—"

Mark stopped. He didn't want to say the words he was thinking. *After the next person dies.* He had gathered a respectable amount of evidence from the night before but hardly anything that would establish culpability for the misdeed. Of course, he wanted to know, but he dreaded the thought. William's logic was right. One of the three groups currently traversing the mansion almost certainly had a murderer in their midst.

Back at the reception desk, Alice had finished examining the exit door. There was nothing she could clearly see as a trap, but caution would need to be taken, nonetheless. She took a stance with her left arm extended toward the handle of the door while keeping as much of her body away from the opening as possible. Eleanor was behind her, and Omario stood by her side.

"Let me get it," he demanded. "You get back with the girl.

Don't try arguing either, because you are all they've got. If I die, some Arsenal club fans will be disappointed, but they'll weather the pain."

Alice took a big step back from the door. Omario was right, as morbid as it sounded. She had a duty to protect and be there for her family. She squeezed Omario's arm as he passed her.

"Thanks, you're very brave."

"Right, let's see if it gets me killed," he breathed as he turned the doorknob. The door opened . . . and nothing happened.

"Oh my God, it was nothing after all!" Eleanor smiled.

The door creaked to its full width and made a click. Fear flashed in Omario's eyes. A deafening booming flooded the hall. A puff of smoke shot through the opening and dissipated upward. Everyone was all right. Across the room, the reception desk had not been so lucky.

A massive spray of buckshot stripped the finish off most of the middle of the desk. Splinters of wood sat in a small pile at the base. The structure of the desk remained mostly intact.

"Real mahogany," Alice chuckled.

"Real explosives, too," Omario added as he leaned into the now open doorway to spy the device which caused the explosion.

A small hubcap-sized disc with a domed protrusion sat just in front of the opening. A two-inch hole faced the doorway and was smoking. A wire extended from the base to the far-side of the door, clearly designed to trigger when it was opened. It appeared to be an improvised explosive device of some kind, but he doubted it was the only one that lay in wait for unsuspecting guests.

"You all okay?" James' small voice hollered from across the floor.

"We are fine, love!" Alice called back. "We are making our way around the house now to rendezvous with you."

"All right!" he answered with uncertainty.

The situation was awful. Alice knew her heart would skip with every bang and hiss she heard over the next hour or two in fear that James' luck had run out. *Deep breaths.* She thought. *He is smart. He will be fine.*

Omario slowly walked through the previously trapped door with his weapon held high above his head. He saw only blackness as he called for the flashlight. Alice shone the light ahead and revealed a tangled mess of rope and iron monstrosities. One thing was certain, they would try to stick as close to the perimeter of the house as possible. They did not need to be dragged out into the inky blackness with no light or hope of escape.

It hadn't occurred to Alice until the lights lining the dome went out for the hunt that although it *felt* like daytime, the Arbor was underneath almost two miles of ice. No matter the time of day, without artificial illumination, it was pitch black around them; poignantly reflecting the situation.

Back in the house, Winston rubbed his chest. It felt like there was a rib or two broken, but he would wait to be examined by Dr. Rutger before making any statements to his party. He couldn't afford to show weakness, not now. Doing so might paint him as a weak member of the group. That was not a position he cared to fill with a hunter on the loose. He knew from his time watching wildlife documentaries, lions always targeted the weakest or slowest of the herd first.

He looked down at James. That boy was definitely weaker than him, but would the killer have the gumption to murder a child? Hardly seemed likely. That said, Peter Corgrave, with his gut nursed by what Winston assumed to be years of drinking, would be a much fatter prize than he would. All he needed to do was focus on avoiding the traps and making sure Peter took the lead.

"After you, sir," Winston said more politely than he had ever managed before in his adult life.

"All too kind, aren't you?" Peter sighed. He walked forward, snatching Winston's phone from his hand. "If I'm to lead, I'm doing so with control of a flashlight."

"Fair enough, Pete," Winston obliged.

The men made their way to the back of the house at a snail's pace. They avoided a pair of wires along the way and saw a tile that raised ever so slightly. All things considered; Peter thought the group was doing a good job.

When they reached the back door, which led to the courts and beaches, the men stopped.

"What nightmare do you suppose is behind there?" James muttered darkly.

Peter wanted to be assuring, but he knew they also needed to stay vigilant.

"I wish I could tell you with certainty that it was safe, my boy. The best we can do is use care and proceed with caution."

James gulped. He crouched beside the doorway underneath a small window to the outside. He looked over the sill and an idea occurred to him.

"Pass me the flashlight!" He spoke intensely, but in a whisper. As if they needed to hide from someone. "I'll check the door on the other side."

Peter wasted no time in providing the child what he wanted. James directed the light as tightly to the corner of the window as he could.

"Glare is pretty bad, but I don't see anything. It looks totally empty out there."

"That's good," Winston sighed in relief. "That's good, right?"

Peter scratched at his hairline. He thought about it but did not like his conclusion.

"I am hard-pressed to believe our murderous phantom chose to be a philanthropist here. If there is no visible trap outside, that leads me to believe that the trap is—inside the room with us."

"Give me that!" Winston snapped as he took the flashlight from James' hand. He flashed the beam around the short hallway from side-to-side. "I don't see anything, do you?"

Peter shrugged. "I hope I am wrong, but I simply am stating the salient facts. This monster is out for blood, and I doubt he will stop until that thirst is satisfied."

"What a sordid mind you have," Winston growled as he impatiently grabbed the door lever.

"Wait!" Peter ordered a second too late.

Winston flipped the handle down to no effect. No mischievous machinery was heard. No explosions.

"There, Pete, you see?" Winston repeatedly jiggled the handle and pressed against the still-locked deadbolt. "Not a booby-trap, just goddamned locked."

James pushed against the window frame, trying to raise it, but it was also held in place by some hidden mechanism.

"Looks like he is herding us," Peter sighed. "There must be definite paths we need to take."

Slightly defeated, the trio made their way back toward the kitchen. They would need to meet up with Evelyn and her team.

As they reached the end of the hallway, the open doorframe let out a metallic clank. A sheet of steel dropped down from an otherwise invisible nesting and sealed the hall with the locked door at the opposite end.

"Great!" Winston clapped his hands. "Are we supposed to bash through the door?"

"It's solid oak," Peter answered. "It probably has magnetic locks to boot. The door is not going anywhere."

"So we are just supposed to stay in here?" James whined.

As he finished his sentence, the group heard a liquid rushing through the ceiling overhead.

"That's a bad sound," Winston whispered.

The room started to shrink as the ceiling pressed down from above them.

"Run! Get to the window!" Peter screamed.

The men ran to the back of the house they had just came from. Winston tried to lift it as he got there, but Peter pushed him aside when he reached their last hope. He slammed his elbow against the glass plate but had no effect. The pane was made of thick plexiglass.

"My knife has a self-defense ram at the base!" James fumbled to grab the knife from his belt as the plate above them crossed the top boundary of the tall window.

Molding splintered off as it was scraped from the wall. The press left no slack for fixtures or furniture.

Peter took the knife from the boy and flipped the sheath to face him. The spiked bottom of the handle was hardened aluminum. He hoped a few good strikes would be enough. The man battered with everything he had, and cracks flew in every direction on the window.

Winston hammered the pane along with Peter. He doubted its efficacy, but anything was better than waiting as the ceiling dropped to less than five feet high. The men were forced to lower themselves to adjust. A pair of floor lamps along the hall creaked and snapped at their midpoints.

Finally, a hole began to open in the durable window. It looked big enough for James and Peter hefted the boy into his arms and tossed him through without hesitation. James winced as he landed on the wooden deck outside with a painful thud. He watched in horror at what he was sure was the end of both men inside the hall.

Now four feet off the ground, the ceiling continued to descend. Only slightly more than two feet of window was left showing from the outside. The time for care had run out. Winston hopped through next, squeezing his body through the narrow opening and stripping off still more as he pulled through. This gave Peter hope. If he was to survive, he had to jump for it. He tossed the knife through first and then came to a screeching halt at his gut. Winston pulled hard on his arms. James followed suit and did the same.

One inch moved forward, then another as the man cried out. The ceiling had reached his hip and was pushing him against the windowpane. Winston tugged with everything he had. He worked out four times per week. Jogged daily. He was in peak physical condition. He knew he could pull more than the man's shoulders could take, but he had no more leeway to be careful. The young brute stomped a foot up on the exterior wall and pulled harder than he had ever tried before.

Tears flowed down Peter's cheek as lamenting cries were layered over screams. His right shoulder popped from his socket, but his torso finally slipped through the opening. He gave a howl, but also a smile of relief as he pulled his right leg through behind him. His left leg would not move past his shins.

"Fuck!" he bawled in open panic. "Fuck, no!"

Winston resumed the powerful pull and dislocated Peter's left shoulder with an awful snap. His shrieks were inhuman as his shinbone snapped under the enormous pressure. Blood began to flow down the exterior wall as his knee was forced upward against the leverage of the falling ceiling.

"Holy fuck!" Winston shrieked as a sliver of the poor man's tibia was forced upward through his exposed calf as Peter's leg fell back down toward the ground. The bone completely severed now; a flap of skin was all that held Peter's leg aloft.

A moment later, Peter dropped limply to the ground. The screaming had stopped. Peter was unconscious. James retched up his breakfast onto the ground beside him as he shrunk back in horror.

The screams had been clearly heard by all on the grounds

of the Arbor. William Rutger held his satchel of medical supplies tight and moved to the back door of the kitchen toward the
library.

"It sounds like someone will need medical attention. We
need to move quickly," William said. "I haven't heard screams like
that since the war."

"Yes, but we must also move cautiously!" Evelyn warned.
"One never knows what might be—" Her mouth dropped open as
her left foot sank a little further into the tile she had stepped on.

"Evelyn!" Mark called as he jumped across the kitchen prep
table toward her. She slipped just out of reach a few moments before he reached her.

Evelyn fell out of sight instantly. Dr, Rutger moved around
the long steel tables in the center of the kitchen that he could
barely see. The pots and pans lining the walls looked like shadowed spectators watching the gory sights unfold. Mark beat the
man to the other side as he picked up the phone that Evelyn had
dropped. He turned the beam toward the floor and saw a neat
three by three tile hole in the ground that had dropped out. The
panels hung loosely and opened into the unfinished basement of
the house.

"Are you all right, Ms. Fox?" Amelia yelled down first.

Evelyn's jumbled pile of limbs began to straighten itself as she
rolled over onto her back.

"I've had better days!" she answered.

William ran through ideas in his head. Evelyn looked to be
all right for the moment, but she could hardly be left there. He
began searching in drawers almost blindly.

"What are you looking for?" Mark asked.

"Light," William replied curtly as he threw open more cabi-
nets and containers.

Amelia was finally the one to reach onto the island and

retrieve a pair of stick lighters and a butane torch from the center workstation.

"Darling!" She grabbed his attention and tossed the lighter across the room to him.

The aged man moved quicker than Mark would have thought possible as he caught one lighter, then the other. He handed the pair to Mark.

"I would leave you the butane, but I am gravely concerned we will need it for some less pleasant operations," William sighed. "Try to get her out. We will need the flashlight."

"Like hell!" Evelyn protested from below.

"This is *not* the time to squabble!" William barked with a stomp of his foot. "Flashlight, sir! *Now!*"

In the face of such valiant determination, Mark weighed the options and did as he was told. He traded Evelyn's phone for a small lighter.

"Good man, Jonathan. You may have just saved a life. Now get her out of there!" William said as he moved back to the rear door of the kitchen and rushed out of sight with his wife behind him.

"Well, Robin Hood, I hope you are quite pleased with yourself," Evelyn groaned from the darkness.

Mark lit the small flame. It cast an extremely limited amount of illumination to which his eyes began to adjust. He took the other lighter and held it down through the opening blindly.

"It is still about four feet above me," Evelyn said. "Go ahead and drop it. I can see it more clearly than you can see me."

Mark reluctantly dropped his only other source of light down into the abyss of the basement. Almost immediately afterward, he heard the clicking of the trigger, followed by a dimly lit Evelyn scowling up at him.

"Best get comfortable," she moaned. "I don't think I'll move much more from my current position. If he wants me, he can have me. I won't be the one to trigger an assisted suicide."

Mark nodded. He glanced around at the few objects around him that he could make out. "I'm going to try to find something to get you out."

Evelyn nodded and lay back down against the cold clay floor. "You know where I'll be."

Just on the other side of the wall, William was trying his best to navigate the library. He walked purposefully and cautiously. William was no stranger to navigating dangerous terrain. Six years into his medical practice, his beloved Great Britain had been pulled into the third global war. He'd volunteered right away, anxious to defend his homeland.

Sovereign governments of the world had become complacent with peace. The bloated bureaucracies were a result of the prosperity of World War II. They had just over a hundred years before the next global conflict, and it had set a new standard for the carnage of battle.

The alliances were drastically different than before. Countries that had friendly relationships just decades earlier were sending their young men to the fronts of warfare as cannon fodder against one another. The battlefield was so much faster than in years past. Hunter-killer drones could sweep along enemy lines and eliminate an entire battalion in minutes. Tanks were felled by electromagnetic pulse grenades and rendered useless. It was the most confusingly brutal war the world had ever seen because technology had made well-established techniques obsolete.

Dr. Rutger had been trained to look for trip-sensors attached to robotic gun emplacements. A field medic was either good at searching out the tiny glint of an infrared sensor, or he died. When a sensor was spotted, medics were taught to block the beam with newly developed smoke grenades that made visual tracking impossible by all but an organic set of eyes.

At that time, he had been in peak physical shape. His reflexes were unmatched. He'd managed to stay alive. He was one of the few. More life was lost in the Third World War than all other wars in history combined. Between the bombs, the atrocities, the horrific battlefronts, and starvation/exposure, one in seven people alive in 2039 was dead by 2042.

The turning point of the conflict had come with the introduction of peacekeeper mobile weapons platforms. Armored as heavily as tanks, they sported EM-resistant plating that reduced the effectiveness of all but a direct hit from scrambling waves. Their speed was almost unimaginable. They crossed countries, eliminating hostiles with deadly precision. Their turrets were extremely capable anti-personnel weapons, and each robot was equipped with depleted uranium anti-vehicular rounds for a variety of situations including bunker-busting.

The war was over. Jones Computing androids had utterly annihilated both ground and air forces with unmatched efficiency. Unconditional surrender had been provided by the UK and their allied European forces within three months.

Now William held a quart-sized bag of flour in his hand. Amelia trusted her husband but still, she wondered.

"I'm afraid I must ask, what is the flour for, William?"

"The purpose is twofold," William responded. "It can trigger tripwires and sensors from a distance, but more importantly, it can permanently block beam receivers if targeted properly, preventing a second triggering."

Amelia accepted his explanation and put up her fist as an order to pause. She pointed at the floor in front of them at a wire strung between two shelves and running the width of the room. The Rutgers took a few large steps back. William wound up an underhanded pitch and chucked the bundle of flour at the wire. Amazingly, it met its target on the first throw. The wire stretched and pulled from the wall.

There was no time to wonder about the trap's effect. Six steel spikes fired from the horizontal axis of the bookshelf on the right and embedded themselves deeply into the wood wall on the left. The needles were about six inches long and appeared to be fatal by their velocity on expulsion.

"Good eye, Amelia," William complimented. "Let's keep this up. A man needs our help."

William took the lead again and pushed farther into the deep room. As they stepped to the wire previously triggered, William thought he saw a passive sensor a few shelves ahead. He got a couple of feet closer, and his suspicions were confirmed.

The couple again drew back as William poured a new bagful of flour from a sack Amelia had hefted from the kitchen. He tossed the open flour-bomb at the camouflaged sensor and it sprayed outward in a white puff. It covered the shelf entirely.

Suddenly, Amelia heard a slight hissing from the middle of the room from a vent beside the ceiling lamp.

"Gas!" she exclaimed as she brought the sticky bluish soaked napkin to her face.

"These won't work for long!" William's voice was muffled to the point of incoherence. "Make for the door. We need to get it open!"

With the floor space of the library clear, and the room filling with some sinister invisible gas, William and Amelia raced as quickly as their legs allowed. Amelia moved to the right of the door, but William called her over to the left.

"Leather belt, please!" he ordered.

Amelia obliged and pulled a strip of hide from her satchel. William looped the strap once over the handle and extended the length of the leather as far as it could stretch off to the side. He turned the handle slowly and pulled the door open. Their ears were stunned by a deafening shockwave. The couple fell back as the door disintegrated and took a few feet of the opposite wall with it. Their path was clear, and they were safe.

They whipped outside and dropped their bandanas. The path of debris cascaded out in a conical shape from a central charge point. Shrapnel tore into the stone walkway. The ground was singed in a foot-wide rectangular shape beside the doorway.

"Claymore by the looks of it," William mumbled. The high explosive pack had been used due to its efficacy in battle for almost a hundred years before it was retired. When the goal was to absolutely deny entry to an area and cause maximal damage to a soft target, the claymore mine was the weapon of choice. Unlike land mines, they were easy to disarm and relocate by the intended party, while their simplicity made them lightweight and hard to notice.

"How did you know?" Amelia asked in awe. "How did you know to drop to the left instead of the right?"

"Entrapment is always most common on the dominant hand of the target. Over eighty percent of individuals are right-handed. As such, duck to the left when trying to stay out of sight or avoid pitfalls."

The pair dusted off themselves and breathed in the chilled air. Their ears continued to ring loudly, and William guessed they would continue to do so for hours to come.

"Doc!" Winston cried from across the deck. "Over here!"

William made haste and dropped to the side of the now-pale Peter Corgrave. Blood pooled at the site of the injury and spread out into a puddle up to his thighs. He felt the man's wrist and detected an erratic pulse.

"Cut the pants off his leg carefully. We need a sharp blade," William instructed.

Once again, James stretched to grab his trusty hunting knife. He passed it to the doctor.

"Amelia, I trust you can take care with this matter? Avoid touching the serrated—" William tried to instruct.

"I will take care, William. We will need to heat the blade after I have finished with it," Amelia stated without explanation.

"Heating the blade?" Winston repeated. "You aren't going to—burn it."

"We most certainly are," Amelia returned. "A tourniquet is not sufficient to provide pressure to seal both the anterior and posterior tibial arteries. Without cauterization, he will bleed out in minutes. We do not have another option."

"We will also need to disinfect the wound after we cauterize. Infection could be deadly if the bandage is not applied and changed every day," William continued his wife's edict.

Amelia slit the pant leg and pulled it apart, fully exposing the horrid sight. Tangled muscle intertwined with shattered bone a few inches below the knee. This was not going to be an easy fix.

"We'll cauterize first, then clean and dress the wound. Are you ready?" Dr. Rutger asked his counterpart.

Amelia nodded. She held the butane torch at the peak of the blue flame's inner cone. She moved this up and down the first couple of inches on the knife. The knife began to blacken and slightly glow at the tip. In a single motion, he grasped the bubbling vessel and pressed the glowing knife point to it.

James flipped his head away as the artery sizzled. The doctor held it there for a moment before removing the red-hot implement.

"Torch," he shortly instructed.

Amelia brought the still-active flame to the knife and re-applied heat to the tip until it relit an uneven orange. Once again, William touched the knife to the artery on the opposite side of Peter's mangled bone. The bleeding stopped.

Dr. Rutger trimmed flesh and sinew to enable a clean seal for his bandage. Winston stared at the carnage like a bit of bloodied roadkill that he wanted to look away from but just couldn't. The doctor stuffed cotton into the wound and began layering strips of cloth across until it was covered. He finished the bandaging with a leather strip around the calf. It looked surprisingly neat for an emergency operation with improvised medical equipment.

"William, that actually looks professional. How did you do it?" Winston asked.

"I've done more with less before, and in equally stressful situations," William sighed as he cleaned the blood from his hands with rags and vodka. "Now, Mr. Corgrave is not safe here. There is a killer on the loose, and he is easy prey at the moment. He will need to rest in his room for a considerable amount of time. I can watch over him there, and change bandages as needed. Let's retrieve Jonathan and work on getting the patient upstairs."

Winston doubted the doctor's words. He felt cold to think it, but Peter was almost lifeless anyway. What was the point in risking their lives to protect him? He was literally and figuratively a dead weight.

"Is it really worth it, doctor?" Winston argued.

"I'm *sorry?*" Amelia whipped back with a piercing gaze.

"He's as good as dead!" Winston shouted in frustration. "He's going to get us all killed!"

William moved to respond, but Amelia held a palm up.

"Finish cleaning up, dear. I can handle this."

William had learned long ago not to second-guess his wife.

"Mr. Graham." Amelia cleared her throat. "My husband has just performed a very successful surgery on our compatriot. Leaving him in the lurch would be no different than leaving dear James to die. It would be the same as abandoning *you.* I would urge you to reconsider your position as your current stance only wastes time and oxygen that could be used keeping your betters alive."

Winston's face burned. He was not accustomed to being spoken down to.

"*Listen here—*"

"*Not another word!*" William thundered as he turned back to face Winston and the others. "My wife and I risked life and limb traversing traps and hazards in order to help this man. We will not be leaving him here. You may help us, or go your own way, but be assured—if you leave, I will expend no such effort rescuing you in your hour of need."

James' jaw hung open at the exchange. Winston looked to him, almost asking for support. He found none. James tucked his shoulders back and puffed out his chest.

"I think Dr. Rutger said to go get Jonathan," James reiterated.

Winston's chest rose and sank in silence. He felt rage but contained it for the moment.

"Obviously."

Winston finally obeyed orders and walked back into the library. At the front of the home, Alice, Eleanor, and Omario tiptoed around the yard carefully. They avoided rope after rope, making good progress back toward the tennis court.

Then they saw it.

Something was glowing just at the beachhead. A trio of pale green eyes surveyed them. Eleanor felt the blood drain from her face. Her stomach twisted, like it was being wrenched in two.

"What the fuck is that?" she muttered through heaving breaths.

"It's—" Alice searched for possible rational explanations. She wanted to say something. She had to reply. She needed to reply it was nothing. She needed to lie. "I—"

Fabric whistled against itself as her feet were pulled tightly together. Alice cried out as she felt the rope tighten like a noose around her ankles. All at once she fell sideways and dropped her light to the ground in panic. She clawed at the lawn for some sort of grip. She was zipping toward the lights on the beach faster than seemed possible. Darkness swallowed her sight as she watched Eleanor and Omario shrink smaller and smaller.

As quickly as it had started, she stopped. Alice could hear Omario yelling for her, but her eyes were pinned to the thing standing above her. She couldn't see anything but those eyes. The horrible emerald glow rotated slightly to get a different perspective. A hand flipped what seemed to be the scope.

It hit her. *Night vision. They are night vision goggles. But who—* Alice suddenly remembered a salient detail. She had a knife in her belt. She fumbled toward her backside, trying to reach the blade. She could feel it, but in her current position, the darkness was disorienting.

The being cleared its throat.

Before she could think, she was sliding against rough and abrasive sand. Alice suddenly knew the end of this trap.

"No!" she screamed, trying to get enough leverage to grab the blade. "*Fuck!*"

The wind was knocked from her lungs as she hit the water. It was bone-chilling. Her body felt numb within seconds. She relied on her sense of touch as she grabbed the knife from her belt. The frozen temperature and the pressure made her head feel like it was caving in on itself, but she needed to cut loose. She had a pair of children to care for who had already lost almost everything. They were not going to live without her, too. She swiped madly at the rope binding her feet. She sliced low to avoid cutting limbs unnecessarily. She ripped through it quickly and felt her body float freely. The issue now was that her body hung in forty-degree water.

She paddled upward with her hands and kicked with her feet like a mermaid. She saw a light at the water's edge. It seemed to be about twenty feet from her. *How hard could it be to swim twenty feet?*

Her body answered with vengeance. Her arms felt heavier than they had ever been. Her legs locked and refused to kick. The lack of oxygen made her gasp in a breath of icy water. Her vision blurred as she kicked against the sand underwater. She needed air so badly. She would have killed for it.

Her mind betrayed her as she lost consciousness. She returned to a scene she had no desire to revisit.

NINE

"**C**AN YOU DESCRIBE THE ROOM EXACTLY AS YOU SAW it when you entered the home, ma'am?" a deep brutish voice demanded.

"It's exactly the way it was!" She creaked in return, sniffing back tears. "I knew I couldn't touch anything."

"And the girl didn't, either?"

"No!" Alice coughed; she was breathing short shallow breaths. "I pushed her out of the room before she could—"

Alice's voice broke. She recalled how Eleanor had lunged for her mother. She felt the pain in her voice as she screamed that awful shriek. Alice had hit her niece with all the strength in her body to push her from the room, but Eleanor had retaliated with inhuman power. She wanted to get closer. Alice knew she couldn't let her have what she wanted. Even in a crisis, Alice led with her logic.

"I stopped her before she could—hold her mother," Alice finished.

The policeman sketched notes in a tablet as she talked. He nodded, trying to sound considerate as he gathered all the relevant evidence. He reassured her that she had done the right thing. She'd preserved the crime scene, which apparently was going to *"make catching the fucker a lot easier."*

She'd signed statements as Eleanor sat in the corner of the room. Her eyes were empty. She rocked slightly. She looked shell-shocked. Alice had peered at her for an eternity. She was knocked from her trance by the policeman's repeated query.

"Do you have a place to stay?"

She did. She knew who to call. She knew how much Eleanor would hate it. They arrived at the home the next morning.

"Ms. Trudeau, I must say I was surprised to receive your message," the grey-haired man said as he answered the door. "I don't usually answer the door myself, but for you three, I made an exception. This must be Eleanor and James? I'm Lucius Freeman."

"Mr. Freeman, thank you again for putting us up like this. They have to—clean—before we go back to the home." Alice tried to hide her disgust. "When you said you owed me a favor, I didn't mean to collect like this. I thought I'd ask for a Jason, or my own personal robot army."

The words felt awkward leaving her mouth. She didn't know how to converse with someone after a tragedy like what had be-fallen her family. She had to keep her appearances up, but she was unsure how to make sad small talk. She wanted to retch any time she thought of the event, so that topic was off-limits. It led her to act as though nothing was wrong.

Eleanor tapped her foot behind Alice.

"Would you mind terribly if the children put their bags in the guest quarters?" Alice took her hint.

"Of course, it's right down the first hall to your left. Follow that tunnel all the way down. You can't miss it," Lucius replied.

Eleanor muttered a thank-you as she walked past the proper adults and dragged herself into the lavishly decorated home.

"Hear that, James? A tunnel. Cheers," Eleanor grunted.

Lucius Freeman walked toward the living room, seeming to expect that Alice would follow. Alice stepped across the frosted glass floor. The design of the home gravitated toward dramatic angular surfaces. There was nothing soft. There was no love in the place. Black and white themes cut across hard nickel and steel framing. It was tasteful, but impersonal. It was expensive. That was guaranteed.

"Jason, brew some drinks for us. I'm sure Ms. Trudeau has had a long journey," Lucius demanded flatly.

"Of course, sir," a voice replied from nowhere. A click and hiss was heard as a pair of mugs dropped from their rack and were caught by an inhuman arm. The large control unit hung from the ceiling and seemed to move about without any sort of visible propulsion. It seemed strange to see the circular disc slide along without any commands or visible superstructure. Spindly black claws effortlessly moved about the kitchen and performed the duty of making coffee in a seamless motion, adding sugar and cream by other arms while the main-hand held both mugs. The whole thing rotated with two steaming mugs and skittered to the living room to delicately set them on the glass coffee table.

"That's really something else," Alice said with a bit of awe and trepidation in her voice.

"He's incredible, isn't he? A real work of art. My son's creation has made the both of us very rich," Lucius proudly stated. "Jason has single-handedly put the competition out of business. Nothing is even close to the complexity of the algorithms used in his programming. We didn't even patent his coding, because we would have had to disclose the exact makeup. Better to let them try to reverse engineer him. Paul, my son, put protections in place so that Jason produces false code to malicious extractions. He is able to fight hackers on his own."

"It's unreal," Alice breathed. "To think that Jason is analyzing every word we say and learning from each moment."

Lucius laughed as he took a seat on the black couch. He grabbed the coffee on the right and sipped. "Perfect as always, Jason. Just as I like it."

Alice sat down and stared at her steaming mug of tea.

"I never told you how I take it," Alice realized aloud.

Lucius held out a hand to the cup, inviting her to take it. She did and sniffed the brew. It was warm and inviting. It was the only thing enticing about the whole home. She sipped the liquid slowly, and the delicious gourmet fluid danced across her taste buds.

"Oh my God," she muttered. "Two cream, no sugar. How did he know? Most people don't take it that way."

"My heuristics study data from a consolidated online database," Jason answered. "You ordered your coffee this way on May 7, 2102 at a coffee vendor in Villanova," Jason answered. "I trust it is satisfactory. I understand tastes may change from time to time."

"Uh, no. It's great, Jason. Thanks," Alice unevenly returned. She knew her data was public. She knew what she posted was for everyone to see. She did not think of it ever being used this way. What else was out there that she hadn't even imagined? She shuddered at the thought.

Lucius took another drink from his warm beverage before setting it back on its coaster.

"That will be all, Jason, I believe you're making her nervous now."

"Yes, sir," Jason answered before zipping from the room through the same opened doorway they had walked through.

"I didn't want to say this in front of the children, but I must now," Lucius paused. "There are no words to express my sadness at hearing of the brutal murder of Cara and Jack. I can assure you, given our family's closeness, I have my peacekeepers out night and day assisting police in their efforts. If they hear a whisper of the culprit, or catch a glimpse of a suspicious person, I will inform the authorities immediately."

Alice returned her mug to the coaster.

"Thank you, Mr. Freeman. It's really too kind of you to put us up and assist like that."

"It would be villainous of me to do anything else. My actions are those of a concerned friend and citizen. If nothing else, as you mentioned earlier, I owe you a great deal. Were it not for your efforts installing the radiation shielding, my plant would have been cooked by forces I wasn't even aware of prior to your cautionary tale. The timeliness of the whole thing was serendipitous. You protected the plant mere months before the largest solar storm ever recorded. I don't have to tell you what cosmic radiation can do to unprotected circuitry. It would have cost me hundreds of billions of credits in invested technology. You have nothing to thank me for. I am the one in *your* debt."

Alice lowered her gaze slightly. She wasn't used to such high praise.

"It was my pleasure, Mr. Freeman," She grinned, straightening out her white skirt before continuing. "Now, I'm told that the scene should be catalogued and cleaned within a week, which means we will be out of your hair at that point. I can't imagine we will live there long. I'm going to pack our things the moment we get back. I can't stand the thought of it—of sleeping in the same home where—"

Alice's emotions betrayed her again. The pain was so fresh. The wound was raw. She calmed herself and cleared her throat.

"Take your time, dear." Lucius placed a hand on her knee. "You don't have to worry about a thing. You are welcome here as long as you need. I will have Jason pull up properties in the area for you. I'll even have him negotiate with the sellers a bit to get you the best deal possible. If you were to need any help with the financing—"

"Oh no, Mr. Freeman. Thank you for the offer, but between my mother and my brother, I'm afraid I have more funds than places to spend them now."

She was distraught but still level-headed enough to know it was a bad idea to end up beholden to Lucius Freeman. The Chief Information Officer of JCN had a hand in every purse on Mars and ears in still more households. Lucius Freeman was one of the most powerful men on Mars. For now, he was in her debt.

"I'll have him work on that list, then. You've been listening, Jason?" He smiled.

"Yes, Mr. Freeman," Jason answered. "Already finished. Feel free to peruse at your leisure."

"That being the case. . ." Lucius rose from his seat and waved his hand in front of what Alice thought was a wall. The metallic curtains pulled back and revealed a picturesque Martian landscape. It was barren, but stunningly beautiful. Alice stood to admire the view as the wall finished opening.

"Make yourself at home," Lucius finished.

Back inside the Arbor, Mark and Winston carried Peter through the kitchen. Amelia had lashed together some leather straps to hoist Evelyn with the men's assistance. Evelyn seemed minimally grateful to her saviors. She had left a position of relative safety and relaxation for one of much less-certain fate.

The group finally back together, they moved back through the space they had already cleared and approached the grand stairway with caution.

"Let us go first," William demanded as he and his wife took the lead. They were met with little argument after their repeated displays of will. The group of exceptional individuals were far from accustomed to following orders, but they accepted the fact that William had survived all five years of the third world war close to the front lines. He was good at staying alive.

The old couple slowly climbed the stairwell a bit before waving the men and Evelyn forward. There were no traps. There was no appearance of foul play.

"Might he only have trapped the first floor?" Winston guessed.

"I would bet exactly nothing on a killer's kindness," William whispered. "It is all the more important for us to be on our guard."

Was it too much to ask for a moment of grateful relief? Winston groaned in complaint as they reached the top of the stairs.

"Still nothing." William continued to survey the walls, looking for a trigger that was not there.

The group of people walked toward Peter's room, key in hand. It was all too easy.

A clang of steel against stone was heard downstairs as the front door flew open.

"Help!" Omario called. "We need help! Dr. Rutger, anyone?"

William looked to Amelia.

"Evelyn, take this. Get Peter into his room," William said as he passed her a brazen key.

"Yes, that's all right. Go. We can take care of this," she replied.

William and Amelia Rutger ran downstairs, followed by a very worried James.

"Just the four of us, then?" Evelyn said. "Let's get him safely into his room and get the hell out of here."

"What's. . . where am I?" Peter mumbled, trying to open his eyes.

"We are getting you to a place to rest," Mark said. "Just shut your eyes. We'll have you laid up comfy in your bed momentarily."

"I'm not staying here like a sitting duck, that's for sure," Winston contributed grumpily.

"What a shame. I'm sure you were first choice for bodyguard." Evelyn laughed as she turned the key.

Evelyn pushed the door open and felt herself freeze. Standing in front of her was a tall, hooded figure. She had only a microsecond to examine his features before he shoved her backward into the hallway. Evelyn didn't plan to scream. The sound was summoned from the depths of her chest like some malevolent spirit and dragged on for what felt like hours.

A male voice laughed and slammed the door shut.

"Evelyn!" Mark called as his hand banged against the doorknob and tried to turn it.

His attempts were halted by a horrible snapping sound. The banging of stone cascaded down the hallway before them. He flashed the light to see the cause and felt his throat catch. Panels of the floor were rapidly dropping open in a similar manner to the trapdoor in the kitchen, but on a much larger scale. The entire floor was disappearing from underneath them.

"Run!" Winston screamed as he dropped Peter's shoulder and bolted toward the stairs.

Mark stumbled under the weight of the wounded man as the door to the bedroom remained closed before him. Evelyn stumbled backward before turning to run. Mark knew there was no way he could save Peter alone.

"Jonathan, go!" Peter ordered weakly. "You can't help me alone."

"*Goddamnit!*" Mark roared as he finally resolved to drop the helpless man and retreat.

The exchange lasted all of two-seconds, but it stretched out as adrenaline surged through Mark's body. His feet pounded as he raced away from the retreating floor. He reached the stairs just before the final panel dropped.

Mark tried to imagine that the thudding sound was in his head. He tried to ignore the squelch of flesh. He knew there was nothing he could have done, but that didn't prevent the sting of defeat. He wasn't entirely sure of Peter's fate before Amelia screamed from the lobby below.

Two bells chimed loudly a moment later.

Omario saw the mess as he carried Alice toward the common room. Peter lay akimbo across several of the same spikes that had separated the two groups of people earlier. Omario didn't rush to help him. It was clear. Peter Corgrave was dead.

Seconds later, a warm hum filled the room as the power kicked back on. Light bombarded the senses of a group that had become accustomed to the darkness. As though called by some ethereal force, the traps gradually withdrew and reset across the house, as best as they could.

Omario winced as the slender rods of steel withdrew back into the cracks between the rock they had emerged from. Peter lowered to the ground slowly as they sealed themselves invisibly back in their nesting. The damage to furniture and fixtures remained, but The Arbor looked almost entirely normal within a minute.

Mark recoiled slightly at the carnage before him as he reached downstairs.

"Winston, I need you to follow me upstairs. We need to flush out the murderer. We both saw him in that room."

"I suppose I do owe Peter that," Winston agreed. "Besides, I am almost sure we will find nothing. A man like that knows how to disappear."

Omario had no time to waste. He stepped around Peter's

body and raced down the hall to the common room. Alice needed a fireplace, or she would slip into hypothermia momentarily. To his surprise, Rose already sat in the room.

"Ahh, I see you all finally saw fit to remember me," Rose sighed, drink in hand.

"Where were you?" Omario wondered as he gently laid Alice in front of the already burning fire. Rose had wasted no time in her journey to relax.

"Where else?" Rose dryly replied. "I grabbed a drink from the bar. I thought that if I were to die, I should do it quickly. *Mark* didn't even notice me pass. Typical of him to focus on his new fling, I suppose."

"Mark?" Omario wondered aloud as he moved to Alice's side. The other guests of the manor flooded into the room just as he spoke. Mark and Winston followed shortly. Dr. Rutger gave a peculiar look at his statement but still walked straight to Alice's side with his wife.

"Who is Mark?"

Mark stopped dead in the doorway. He thought about running. He considered slipping out the back. He decided it was better to face the issue head on than allow everyone to think he is the murderer.

"Yes, Mark," he finally admitted, stepping forward into the center of the room. "I have been concealing my identity because I was on assignment. My name is—"

"On assignment!" Rose laughed deeply. "You make it sound like you are a mild-mannered newspaper reporter by day and fucking—superMark by night!"

Mark thought better of arguing with her now. "My name is Mark Reese. I'm an investigative journalist for the—"

Evelyn stopped his explanation with a shrill laugh as she stepped forward from the group.

"Well, this *is* a surprise, Mr. *Reese*. When were you going to tell us all?"

"Evelyn, you have every right to be up—" Mark tried to explain.

Evelyn reached out a palm and cupped his testicles before clamping down on them. She squeezed with increasing intensity as she closed the remaining distance between the two of them.

"Was it when my lips were wrapped around your cock? No. Was it when my beloved father was murdered before my eyes? Unfortunately, not."

"Evelyn." His voice came out as a whimper as he crumpled before the small-framed woman. "Please!"

"Were you going to tell us after you watched everyone else die? Inform us after you had a nice, juicy, story about my father's remaining legacy? Or was it all for your own vindictive pleasure?"

She released the man and turned her back to him.

"I suppose I should never have expected anything better of you. I know a parasite when I see one." Evelyn finished as she snatched a decanter of clear liquid from the table next to Rose, who sat agape observing Evelyn's spectacle. Evelyn flung the lid into the fireplace and chugged the bottle deeply. She took a seat next to Rose with her back to the group.

Rose's mystified expression spread into a wide smile.

"I like Ms. Fox," Rose slurred.

"Call me Evelyn."

Just in front of the pair, Amelia Rutger raised a blanket between the guests and Dr. Rutger. She cleared her throat and jerked her head to the side as she glared at Omario. He moved from Alice's side.

"Those clothes will need to be cut off, dear. I thought I would give her some privacy so that she could maintain a shred of dignity," Amelia explained.

Omario nodded and heard the tearing of fabric behind the makeshift curtain. A moment later, a ball of wet clothing was tossed toward the fireplace. Everything had been wrapped in her blouse, but it was clear to see that Alice was going to be quite exposed for the time being. Amelia draped the blanket over her and tucked it under Alice's hips and shoulders as though she were swaddling a baby. Alice was a pale shade of blue. Her soaked chestnut hair looked black in the roaring firelight. Dr. Rutger placed the back of his palm against her forehead and shoulders consecutively.

"She will need to lay here for a few hours at the minimum. If we were lucky, we caught her before the onset of any serious nerve damage. There is no way to know without medical equipment."

"What happened to her?" Mark lunged forward toward her lifeless body. He had not seen her since the start of the whole ordeal. He didn't know she was the one they had called for help about.

His movement was stopped by Winston who stepped between them.

"Not so fast there, lover boy. I believe we have a bit more to talk about," Winston growled. "*Mark*, why don't you tell us what you were researching here? I'm sure the revelation would be positively enlightening."

Mark explained his assignment as best he could. The story that would have seemed outlandish at first was entirely plausible now. People had been disappearing. First it was just ordinals, then more prominent persons. The common thread Mark had been able to deduce was the tight-lipped status of anyone who *did* return from the Arbor. Something was happening at the mysterious abode. He knew that going in was the only way to find out the truth. The first to object to his mission was Omario.

"So, if you knew this place was dangerous, why didn't you

warn anyone? We could have gotten out of here or avoided coming at all!"

"I had expended a great amount of effort in arriving as under the radar as I could. I tried to remain incognito—"

Rose chortled from her seat without looking at him.

"I was undercover," Mark clarified.

"Sure, glad you didn't warn us, mate. Having a lovely time so far. Hope your story is going well," Omario seethed.

"You think it doesn't need to be told?" Mark barked back. "Look around at what's happening! I had no idea that people were going to die. There is no way this is a one-time thing. Look at the complex traps that have been set for us. It's impossible to think the killer has never done this before. I think the more pressing question is, how did he do it under Alexis Fox's nose?"

"You *must* have lost your mind, Mr. Reese!" Evelyn spat as she hopped up from her seat. "My father was an industrious man. He was a brilliant man. He was even sometimes an opportunistic man, but he was *no* killer. If you would like to continue your assertion, I have other ways to express my point." Evelyn kneeled in her chair with her hands gripping the leather tightly. She held so fiercely onto the seat that her nails dug into the material.

"I am not saying he did it!" Mark shot back. "I am saying that *someone* with access to this home modified it tremendously. Who would have had access to the property while your father was not around?"

"I have no idea," Evelyn answered. "He invites many people to the home. I really couldn't tell you."

"Can we abandon the bullshit of this place ever being a home?" Winston retorted. "All the modifications to the *home* make it obvious. It was built like this. There is no way they snuck these renovations in, so how about you tell us what The Arbor really is!"

Evelyn drew her lips together in a dissatisfied grimace. "You want the truth? Fine. None of us ever lived here. Satisfied? It is an investment. The cave was already here after the mining, so my father determined it would be a fantastic place to drain funds from those overly saturated with money. We did visit occasionally, but you are right. It is a glorified hotel. For the low price of $45,000 in credits per night, anyone could indulge. It was easier to sell the concept of being invited to Alexis Fox's mansion than staying at a ridiculously overpriced hotel. The letters with certificates for free stays were a publicity stunt, I suppose. I'm not sure about that."

Omario thought it all through in his head. It didn't add up.

"Maybe the letters weren't sent by Blue Life. With one or two inside men, it wouldn't be challenging to get people here that you wanted dead. Maybe this is some sort of elaborate plan to lure us all here."

William stood and joined the group after ensuring Alice's proper care.

"I do believe Mr. Richards may be on to something," he said. "Perhaps there is some common thread connecting all of us. Figuring this out may lead to evidence as to the killer's identity."

Rose spat her drink slightly as she sloshed out a reply. "Well, you know the thread connecting the three of us!" Her hand wildly pointed between herself, Evelyn, and Alice. "We've all been fucked, and *fucked over*, by that poor excuse for a gentleman!"

She waved with her fingers at Mark as she sipped with her other hand. Evelyn rolled her eyes but didn't dispute Rose's claim.

"A lead to be sure," Amelia admitted as she finished fixing Alice's swaddling of blankets. "But it doesn't explain why the rest of us are here. I think it would be best if we all discussed possible connections. Perhaps Mr. Reese could keep track?"

Mark nodded and retrieved a pen from his pocket. Over the next hour, the prisoners went person by person, all of them sharing every relevant detail they could imagine.

It had to be assumed that Mark's presence was not part of the killer's plan. He'd wanted Jonathan Hulsey, a name that was unfamiliar to everyone present. William and Amelia had been invited by an old friend of theirs but supposed that the letter had been forged to get them there. They resided on Mars in retirement. William still taught online classes out of boredom, not necessity. They provided a list of acquaintances all of whom sounded equally as foreign to the group as Jonathan Hulsey.

Omario Richard's letter had come from the Major League Soccer association. Its authenticity was also questioned. He lived on Earth and had never been off planet. None of his circle of influence came close to intersecting with the others. Evelyn begrudgingly provided minimal information and ran down a list of who she knew and in what capacity. She noted that plenty of people wanted her dead, but she was a *damned fool* who'd trapped herself at the mansion.

Eleanor and James provided names for who they knew and did their best with the people in Alice's life as their aunt slept beside the fire. No one wanted to wake her, for she certainly needed the rest.

Winston was basic. He had friends from school, fraternity brothers mostly, and coworkers. His position was hardly one of stature in terms of power. Winston's wealth was a direct result of his inheritance. He tried to make his life sound more exciting than it was.

The group looked across at each other in frustration. They'd combed their past to no effect.

"Right where we started." William slammed his fist against a side table in frustration. "Either many of us are hiding secrets, which is entirely probable, or our field of search is misguided."

"I believe you all have managed to forget me once again!" Rose stumbled forward to join the crowd. "Shameful, really. Isn't it obvious? *I* am the killer. Cuff me, please! Pull my hair while you're at it!" she laughed, giving her long locks a rough tug to the right.

"I know your all family, and I already had them written down," Mark answered. "I didn't think you were exactly in a position to be of service to the group."

"Marky-Mark, that hurts!" Rose giggled. "I have *many* friends you have probably never heard of. Not that you ever listened, anyway."

"Ms. Grayson!" Amelia faced the drunkard and grabbed her firmly by the shoulders. "Help our investigation or get out. We have neither time nor patience for useless inebriation."

Rose dropped her mouth open in false shock to mock the elderly woman. "Well, that being the case, love, I will take my leave."

Rose steadied herself against various pieces of furniture as she wobbled from the room. Her feet could be heard stomping angrily up the staircase a moment later.

"We should re-group, look at our supplies and prepare before getting some rest." William broke the ensuing silence first. "If last night's chiming was any indication, we should have approximately twelve hours before the next—event."

The group dispersed, staying in small groups for safety. Omario stayed beside the children. Some ate, others made themselves busy doing menial tasks like cleanup. A few of the men covered Peter's body and carried it to his room. There was little fanfare over his death. He was known by no one.

The Arbor was much quieter than it had been the first night. While previously they had thought of all the ways they might be able to defend themselves, now many simply focused on surviving. They had been led around like test subjects in a maze. They were playing his game, there was no doubt now.

Mark scoured his list of people and details while he stood

guard alongside a sleeping Alice Trudeau. There were such varied backgrounds. There was no reason to it. There were no commonalities of culture or social circles. Although they were mostly well-off, some of the group came from poorer families. What could possibly have drawn them together?

As to the killer's identity, almost everyone was part of one group or another at the time of Alice's ensnaring. Unless they'd convinced the others to lie for them, they would not have been able to trigger Alice's trap or ultimately kill Peter. Nothing made sense. He checked his watch. It was just before 4 PM. Peter had died around 9AM. This meant he had five hours to try and get some sleep.

Against his better judgement, he made a pile of pillows on the couch beside Alice. She was still sleeping so peacefully. He wanted a soft bed. He wanted more comfort. He just couldn't leave Alice alone. It didn't feel right for her to wake in a dimly lit room with no one to care for her.

He closed his eyes for what felt like a second.

He was awakened by a light coughing. Mark opened his eyes and saw Alice sitting up. Her back was to him, and she held the blankets tightly around herself, but her alabaster shoulders reflected the flickering firelight.

Mark smiled as he thought back on how he used to count the freckles on her chest. He remembered that slight curve of her hips. He adored the way her neck flowed so gracefully from her shoulders. He wished he had met her first.

Mark stirred slightly, and Alice jumped. Her hair flipped as she looked over her shoulder at him. She blushed without thinking before regaining her senses.

"Mark!" she chastised as he turned away instinctually.

"I wasn't trying to—"

"I'm sure you weren't," Alice griped as she reached for her

clothes beside the fireplace. Much to her displeasure, they were hardly in any condition to wear. "Did they cut these off me?"

"Yes, they had to. You were in that water, and if you had stayed in those clothes, I'm afraid you would have been taken by hypothermia."

Alice grumbled to herself. "Well, clearly, I am in no position to get myself dry clothing. Do be a dear and fetch me some, please?"

"Sure, Alice," Mark answered as he stood up. He opened his eyes to find his way around the couch and got another peripheral glance at her. She was positively elegant. She looked more like a princess being painted for a portrait than a city planner. He dared not steal a second glance as he reached the door.

Eleanor almost bumped into him as she met him in the hall.

"What are you still doing here?" she asked.

"Oh well, I was going over my list and then—"

Eleanor's eyes quickly caught Alice's statuesque silhouette in the firelight.

"You have *got* to be kidding me," she hissed.

"I sent him to get clothes!" Alice yelled. "He was just watching over me while I slept."

Eleanor wrinkled her nose and looked at Mark. "How very innocent of you. Not to worry, I have it from here."

Mark protested with his eyes, but Eleanor redoubled her resolve with a dismissive brushing gesture with her hand. Mark wondered at the girl who might have been Alice's clone in another life. Eleanor wasn't her daughter, but she could have been.

Mark shrugged as he moved down the hall. Again, he checked his watch.

"About 5," he mumbled to himself. "At least I got an hour's rest."

Beside him in the entryway, the grandfather clock continued

to tick away the seconds. It might as well have been a drumbeat leading them to the gallows. He turned away before hearing mechanical whirring.

A colossal twang filled the hall. The clock rang out the first bell of the hour. The color drained from Mark's face. He took long strides as he sprinted down the hallway back to the common room. He spilled through the open door as Alice hooked her brassiere. Eleanor was already halfway out of the room.

"Mark!" Alice screamed. "Go with Eleanor and get James! Keep him safe. I will meet up with you as soon as I can. She has her—"

The lights in the room dimmed to blackness, and the fire extinguished itself to glowing rods of iron as the gas stopped. The bells were finished. The hunt was on.

TEN

E LEANOR LIT HER FLASHLIGHT AS SHE FLEW FROM THE room. Mark did as he was instructed and followed closely. Alice, meanwhile, was alone. Her breaths were short as she searched around the fireplace for her phone. They must have left her the phone with her clothes, she hoped.

She searched in vain. Alice knew she hadn't seen it before the lights went out. She did recall seeing a table full of supplies at the head of the room. She remembered seeing a lighter atop the pile. It wasn't much, but it would have to suffice. She hadn't time to put on her blouse before the chimes, so she resigned herself to the slight chill offered by partial exposure.

She'd groped her way to the couch when she froze. A telltale glow in the hallway was coming through the door. Alice quickly and silently climbed onto the couch and threw the blanket over herself. She covered her mouth with both hands as footsteps entered the common room.

She tried to keep herself steady. Her life depended on it. Everything inside Alice told her to scream as the man got closer to the couch, but she fought the urge. She remembered the doomsday clock. First was a trap. Next was a pair of crosshairs. She guessed this hunt would pass much more quickly than the first.

She kept herself tucked neatly under the blanket and held her breath as the man approached. The thick blanket would hide her heat from the glasses which she assumed had thermal vision. That would make sense for a hunter. With any luck, the still-warm fireplace would distract him enough to ignore the couch.

He stopped just behind her and set something down on the floor with a metallic banging. It was a gun. It had to be a gun, she thought. Her lungs called out for oxygen as the man lingered. She would not be able to deprive herself of air much longer. She remained perfectly still as she shut her eyes tightly. She tried to think of anything but moving, but it began to feel like her breath was going to leap from her swollen cheeks.

Alice didn't hear the intruder pick up the gun, but she assumed he had done so quietly as the footsteps left the room as quickly as they had entered. She let her breath out shakily as she breathed in about a tenth of the oxygen she desired. She dared not rise for a few more seconds.

A deep blasting sound filled the room, and Alice thought her time had come. She didn't move until she heard Amelia scream. Sounds of desperate trampling footfalls filled the reception area as Alice finally moved from her position of relative safety.

She could have stayed. The odds were great that the killer would not re-enter the room. Had she camped there; she would have survived effortlessly. She had no ties to anyone else in the hotel, except her children.

They weren't biological, of course, but her adrenaline spiked as though they were from her own womb. Alice crouched low and felt around for the table she had remembered as another shot rang out.

She would have given anything to know what was happening outside, but there she was, trying to find a tiny firelight. She searched carefully. An object falling from the table would be disastrous, signaling her position to the killer, and could mean death. While they'd freely moved this morning and talked to each other like old friends, this time there was only steps and gunshots.

Alice flicked the lighter and considered going back for her shirt. Her heart was thundering. She felt a burning in her chest. She needed to find them and quickly. She could never forgive herself if—she wouldn't even think it. She would save them or die trying.

James sat in complete darkness upstairs. His breathing was rough and quick. He held his ears, trying not to think of the blasts below. He was always so afraid. He wished he could be brave, but it took everything he had to stop a full-blown gasping panic attack. He imagined that this was what his father heard just before he died. He thought of his poor mother, how she must have begged for his life.

Tears began to streak down his porcelain cheeks.

"Mummy," he whispered. "I need you, Mum. Why can't you just save me? Take me. I don't want to live without you. I *can't*."

He buried his face under pillows and let the heaving sobs take him. He had never been so afraid.

"Dad, I'm not—" he sniffled. "Daddy, I'm not brave like you. I can't do this! I'm going to die. I'm going to be killed—"

His voice crackled as he let a heaving gasp shake through his tears.

"I'm gonna get killed just like you and Mummy. I don't want to die. I don't. Please don't let me die."

His whole body shook as another gunshot sent a shockwave through the house.

"Please, Daddy. Please save me."

The door creaked open to his hotel room.

"Daddy!" he croaked through sobs.

"James, it's me!" Eleanor whispered softly. "It's alright, love. I'm here now."

She pulled James tight to her chest.

"I—don't—want—to die!" he struggled to breathe out. "I don't want to die like Mum and Dad!"

The words crashed over Eleanor. She tried to keep her brave mask, but it shattered at his broken and frightened words. Tears gathered at the slits of her closed eyes as she rocked her brother.

"No, love. I'm here. I'm going to protect you," she cried. "We are going to stay right here, and we are going to pray very hard. We are the only ones upstairs, so that disgraceful thing will just stay downstairs."

Mark had followed Eleanor inside and stood with his back to the door. He held a steak knife tightly. His grip forced the blood from his hand. His jaw was clenched like a bear trap. He worried for Alice. He needed to protect her, but she might have been a hundred miles away with a killer between them. He knew his only job was to keep her niece and nephew safe, and he would do it until his last breath. He just needed her to live. He couldn't bear the thought of them living without her.

He didn't want to live without her.

Seeing her again, talking to her, and watching the blush flood her cheeks, he'd remembered exactly why he'd fallen in love with her. He knew, shameful as it was, that his heart still longed for Alice.

Evelyn and Rose had been talking at the bar when the clock had begun to ring. They'd managed to slip out through the kitchen and into the back yard. Evelyn held her phone tightly to her chest to extinguish most of the light.

"Why did we come out here?" Rose asked at almost conversational volume.

Evelyn pinned her to the wall and placed a hand tightly over her mouth.

"Shut your mouth," Evelyn ordered in an almost silent whisper. "Not another word. I am leading us somewhere safer, and I won't have you getting me killed."

Evelyn released her, and Rose almost grinned.

"Oh, love, you have to order me around me like that later," Rose whispered as she raised a pair of fingers to her lips in a V.

Evelyn shook her head and shut her eyes.

"No more talk. Follow me," she said.

Evelyn led Rose down the yard, moving as quickly as possible without drawing attention to themselves. They hopped over the divider separating the beach from the grass. Evelyn crouched down on the sand.

"Cover yourself," she barked softly as she wiggled her torso to slip under the dunes slightly.

"Are we doing the mermaid thing?" Rose asked with a bit of hope in her voice.

She is dense. Mark was right, Evelyn thought as she shoveled cold sand over her midsection.

"We are reducing heat signatures and waiting this out," Evelyn said.

As the girls fought to make themselves invisible, Omario had a different idea. He was crouched behind the bar with a pair of knives in his hands. The killer had chased Amelia and William into the dining room. There was no way out. Omario had to act quickly, or it would be the end of them. True to form, he heard a massive thudding as the dinner table was flopped to its side.

Old man is making a barricade, he thought to himself.

The killer stopped in the doorway. He laughed lightly. He fired shot after ear-piercing shot into the table, and Omario heard shrieks of fear after they seemed to get closer to the pair.

This was his only chance. He was going to stop whoever it was.

Omario crept from behind the bar and got to a step behind his target as the killer seemed to notice him. Jumping at the vulnerability, he lunged forward with a loud roar. He buried the blades deep in the man's chest. One fell just over his stomach and the other plunged deeply into his heart.

The killer stumbled.

Omario growled again as he waited for the man to fall. Omario's vision blurred as the butt of the killer's rifle met his forehead. He fell against the barstools, knocking them over as the man walked toward him.

"It's not possible. It's not fucking real. You're a *goddamned devil!*" he screamed as the man took aim.

William brought a dining room chair down on the monster just as he fired his weapon. The shot narrowly missed Omario, who quickly scrambled to his feet. The unstoppable man lost his balance but recovered more quickly this time. He was through with games.

The killer drilled the butt of his rifle into Dr. Rutger's throat. A horrible gurgling was heard as his windpipe collapsed in on itself.

William's sight grew dark, and he heard Amelia call his name as the rifle was pointed at him. It was of her he dreamed, even to the last.

The shot staggered Amelia as her husband's blood flew across her chest in an awful spray.

"*No!*" she howled shrilly. The heartbreak filled her voice as her husband of over fifty years slid sideways down the wall. Her hands shook as the gong of the clock rang out three. The murderous juggernaut of a man walked calmly from the dining room.

"No, you don't!" Omario bellowed deeply as he brought a brass barstool down on the devil's neck.

Finally, the demon fell straight to the ground as his rifle clattered across the floor.

Omario raised the stool again and felt a cold hand grip his ankle and sweep his feet from under him. He tightened his fists and pummeled the impossibly strong creature to little effect. The being flipped him over and began pounding its skeletal fists into Omario's face with impossible brutality. Four punches landed before the thing joined its hands and raised them high over its head, as if in preparation for the killing blow. He swung downward as the explosion of a shot reduced the sound of the room to a ringing in Omario's ears.

The creature looked over toward reception to see Alice in a tight black skirt and silver brassiere. The beast looked down and touched a stream of blue liquid flowing from its chest. It glanced back at Alice as she drew the bolt back and returned it to a firing position. She let a second shot fire through its right shoulder as she aimed where its heart should have been.

The creature rose, and Alice rapidly chambered a third round.

"Stay the *fuck* down!" she screamed as she fired a third shot directly through the being's goggles. Metal sprayed out behind it, and the creature finally fell flat. Alice looked on in horror at the almost unstoppable monster as she stepped closer.

Omario moved beside it to remove the mask.

"Not yet," Alice fumed as she chambered a fourth round.

She fired another shot into the side of the creature's head before dropping the long rifle to the ground. Her hands trembled. She had never killed anyone before.

Omario removed the night vision headset and drew back slightly. Timothy's white dome-like face was shattered and facing the ceiling. It revealed the metal superstructure beneath the dome with a host of visual sensors and things he couldn't identify.

He remembered what had happened as he heard Amelia whimpering.

She wiped the blood from William's forehead and placed her handkerchief over the wound. She laid him flat against the floor and brushed her hand over his still open eyes. She swallowed hard and straightened herself.

"Good night, my sweet," her voice shook. She kissed his lips to feel their warmth once more.

Alice knelt beside Amelia and threw an arm across her shoulder in an uncommonly human gesture for her.

"Amelia, I'm so sorry," she choked.

"I owe him my life," Omario squinted, trying to correct his clouded vision. Timothy's four punches had hit him like those of a professional boxer. He slipped closer to Amelia and stood beside William. "He died a hero."

Amelia nodded and sniffed before she cleared her throat.

"It was the same way he lived for seventy-six years. William has always been gallant. He was the product of a bygone era, I'm afraid."

Omario placed a hand over her shoulder. "I don't deserve his sacrifice, but I promise that every action I take here will be to honor him. I'll try to live up to the high bar he set."

Amelia clapped her opposite hand over his.

"I am very sure that would make him happy. This is how he would have wanted to die, not cooped up in some hospital bed with machines extending his suffering. He would be honored to perish saving another."

Evelyn and Rose entered the room a few minutes later. Rose

angrily brushed sand off herself as she paused in the somber chamber.

"We heard the bells," Evelyn half-whispered. "Ms. Rutger, you have my condolences."

Rose looked around the room at the scene. *Oh,* she mouthed as she saw the body.

"I'm sorry too, Amelia. That's really—it's awful. He should have lived longer than some others in this place."

Alice glared at Rose. She pinched her fingers together and drew them in a line across her lips. Rose, usually full of vigor, was considerate enough to nod and comply—this time. Winston left his room just before Eleanor and James emerged from their refuge.

"Where were you, mate?" Omario spoke through gritted teeth. His eyes scrutinized Winston. Mark had an excuse for being absent. Winston didn't.

"What are you trying to say?" Winston asked with impatience.

"I think that we could have killed that thing before William— if you had just been here, we might not be having a funeral," Omario continued, his angry frustration apparent. Winston was hardly patient in the best of situations.

"Or maybe we would have had two. Who's to say another target wouldn't have crossed the line of fire. Maybe whoever shot Timothy would have missed," Winston argued.

Alice spun to face Winston. "I'll have you know that while I haven't been much on guns since Jack's death, I've hunted since I was a girl. My father was always disappointed that Jack had no interest in the sport, so he took me. I don't miss."

"Exactly!" Omario raised his voice in agreement. "She's a crack shot, apparently."

Winston was surprised by the revelation and momentarily tabled his aggression.

"You hunt? Really? I never would have guessed that. You

continue to surprise me, Alice." Winston looked at her a little dif-
ferently. It was as though she had unintentionally proven herself
a woman of worth in his eyes. His eyes traveled up and down her
exposed body, and Alice turned slightly in disgust.

"Can you not?" Alice grumbled. "Look, it doesn't matter. I'm
sure Winston was trying to survive the same as everyone else,
and—"

"Thank you, Alice," Winston spoke over her.

"*And* we took that thing down. What matters now is finding
the other one and figuring out how a servant droid overcame its
non-aggression programming."

Winston continued to stare at Alice, just more subtly.

"You're a fucking pig, mate!" Omario spat. "Got out of your
hole just in time to attend the memorial and ogle the ladies, is that
it?"

Winston closed the distance between them and cracked his
knuckles. Despite Omario's athletic frame, he was confident he
could best him in a fight.

"Boys!" Alice objected, stepping between the two. "We will
not dishonor William like this. Winston get a drink or go for a
swim; it doesn't really matter. Omario, you said some very nice
things to Amelia earlier. Did you mean them?"

Omario was startled by her words. She was right, but he'd
expected an ally.

"Yeah, whatever. He ain't worth it, anyway," Omario took a
step back in surrender.

Winston kept his closeness to Alice. "Will you be joining me
for that drink?"

"Hell, no," she shortly shot the hopeful man down. "We don't
know how long we have until the next bells. We need to figure out
where Silas is. Something tells me he isn't blameless in the grand
scheme of things given his counterpart's *malfunction*."

"Stop calling it that," Amelia vented sullenly. She placed her palms against her knees and rose from her husband's side slowly. Omario advanced to help her, but his hand was swatted as he went to lift her. "I'm quite capable of standing on my own, though the gesture is appreciated."

"You disagree with my assessment?" Alice asked.

"Absolutely," Amelia clarified. "This was no accident. A machine hardcoded to protect humans at all costs doesn't suddenly develop base instincts without influence. Someone, or something, controlled that robot."

Alice suddenly had an epiphany. "Does this house have a Jason?"

Evelyn looked around at the curious faces. "What? You can't be serious."

"Is it that hard to imagine an artificial intelligence turning on its creators?" Alice doubled down.

"Yes. Yes, it is," Evelyn retorted. "Are you really suggesting some malevolent machine is pulling the strings like some old science-fiction novel? These things are limited by hardware. There are physical blocks in place to impede sentience. I might agree that someone controlled Timothy, but to entertain non-biological threats is ludicrous."

Alice let the idea slide, but she couldn't shake her distrust of artificial intelligences. She had seen the way Jason had moved in Lucius's habitation, and it haunted her even now. Even among all the carnage that had been wrought, her mind dwelled on those wicked arms. She knew, indubitably so, that thing was evil.

"In answer to your question . . ." Evelyn went on. "No. This home has central networked connections, but no A.I."

"Regardless." Alice dismissed her words. "We should scour the estate for Silas. Cognizant or not, it is rational to assume he means us harm at the next hunting hour."

The group stayed together a few moments longer to say goodbye to William. Unlike when Peter had passed, many felt bound to speak of his character. There was no place to bury him, nor time to complete the action if there was, so the group carried his body upstairs after Amelia had moved her things from the room. Alice offered to let Amelia stay in her room. Any sleep Alice was going to get from this point on would be in the same room as her niece and nephew.

After the impromptu service had finished, Winston and Mark were tasked with searching the exterior of the grounds. Alice, Eleanor, and James looked for hidden compartments that the android could hide in. Evelyn, Rose, and Omario searched the basement.

Amelia began mixing the chemicals that had been brought upstairs earlier. She knew a fair amount about chemistry. If she was to die, she wanted to do so in a literal inferno, taking as many wrongdoers with her as she could. She was making explosives.

Mark catalogued his experiences in the dining room. It served as a way to compile evidence that the team had gathered and document the situation. If he was to pass on, the story would need to continue without him. Additionally, the location served as a good place to observe the movements of the wicked clock. He would not be caught off-guard again.

The hand moved much faster now. He heard an audible tick every few seconds, where they had been minutes apart before. The hand raced toward that pair of triangles with circular tops.

Some kind of volcano? Mark pondered.

As he considered the possible hazard, Amelia entered the room with a tray of dishes full of something pale.

"I'm assuming that isn't dinner?" Mark inquired.

Amelia shook her head. There didn't seem to be much appreciation for his humor in her countenance. Mark didn't blame her.

She had been through the unimaginable and was still functioning and contributing. That was more than he could guarantee if their situations were reversed.

"I am tired of being caught in the dark," Amelia said. "They are candles. If we light them just before the next, time, we could at least find our way around. It won't be very bright, but it will provide some much-needed visibility."

Mark clapped his hands silently in appreciation. Amelia was invaluable to the group and deserved appreciation.

Amelia felt like she should have smiled but instead simply bowed slightly in acknowledgment of his gesture.

"It's hardly any amazing invention. I worked hard on our offensive explosives, but these are simple butter with a wick. I am not sure how well it will stand when the butter melts. I suppose we will find out."

She placed a few around the room before passing from his company out the same door she had entered. She put one on a hall table before continuing through to the common room. It had been only two hours since her husband had been taken from her. By the look of the clock in the dining room, they were already halfway to the next danger. It would be just after 9:15 at night, if her guess held up.

After she had placed candles around the firelit den, she turned to exit and felt her heart stop. Silas ran a broom along the hall in front of her.

"I have found the *bastard!*" she yelled loud enough for all in the house to hear.

A flurry of pounding feet sounded from all corners of the estate as many people found their way to Amelia. Each seemed to stutter in their stride when they saw the android innocuously sweeping debris from gunshots fired by his mechanical brethren.

Evelyn's face warped in disbelief. Where had he been hiding?

Clearly the group managed to not only fail in locating the robotic monster, but somehow missed its ingress into the living quarters.

"Silas, cease all motor functions," she ordered.

The robot obeyed and flattened itself against the wall.

"I'll grab a barstool," Omario muttered as he disappeared from view.

"Whoa, not so fast!" Winston argued. "I work with peace-keepers. They are all built on the same core-unit. That being the case, what if we reprogrammed him to defend us? We all saw how unstoppable that thing was earlier."

Alice considered it. She had dressed herself in much more sensible attire. A pair of tan khakis and a violet top was much easier to move in than eighty percent of her attire. She had begun to settle into the demanding expectations of their current placement.

"All right, say we did try to reprogram him. Do you know how to do that?" Alice inquired.

Winston rubbed a hand through his hair. He opened his mouth as if to reply but made an uncertain face. "I can definitely get you to the core unit. I know there is a way to change primary drives. I was not, however, on the engineering team."

Omario breathed hard as he jogged back to their location with a metal barstool in hand.

"What are we all standing here for?" He seemed confused. There was no choice in his mind. "Let's kill it."

Evelyn stepped forward. "I know a bit of programming, if we can get him to the access terminal—maybe. The issue is, I know my father was a paranoid man. There are—protections—in place to prevent tampering with their code. If the terminal has administrative rights, we might be able to get around those, though."

"What do you mean, protections?" Alice worriedly breathed.

"Mm, well, he is programmed to self-destruct," Evelyn admitted.

"If I'm clear . . ." Omario paused briefly. "Your father was so terrified of enemies that he programmed a robot to explode in the event of a breach. How ironic that he did that in the *death palace*."

"Enough!" Evelyn snarled. "My father is not the subject of discussion. He is dead. I think we need all the assets we can get. It is worth a try."

Alice thought about her words. There was so little information. How big was the explosion going to be? Were there any other consequences to a hacking attempt? Might it cause instability? It didn't sit well with her.

"No. Stop!" Alice urged loudly. "It is too risky. There is no guarantee that we can get it working, and in fact, the odds are decidedly bad. I'm sorry, Evelyn, but we need to be cautious here."

"All right, then, stay here. All of you keep away. I'll do it myself." Evelyn's frustration was clear. They had no time to waste, and there they stood bickering.

"Evelyn, *stop!*" Alice commanded. "We can't do this. We *won't* be doing this."

The hallway hushed to an entirely silent herd of ewes, looking on helplessly at the titans of character staring each other down.

Evelyn chuckled to herself. "I'm quite certain I misheard you. It sounded like you were telling me, the Chief Operating Officer of my own goddamn company and now-rightful owner of this hotel, what I could or could not do."

"Evelyn," Alice pleaded. "Don't do this. I won't risk you putting everyone in danger. I refuse to let Eleanor and James be put under any added jeopardy because you want an attack droid. Have you ever even reprogrammed something like this before?"

Evelyn's mouth hung open. "I'm not sure that's any of your fucking business, Alice."

"I'm really not trying to undercut any authority you have here, but I am observing the situation for what it is," Alice quarreled. "It is mutually agreed that hacking Silas is a calculated risk. Well, I don't think it's worth it. In fact, the odds of his programming going haywire, even if you succeed, is highly likely."

"You know this from your years of experience programming androids?" Evelyn snipped.

"I know this from living a life full of technical bugs and glitches. The first attempt at things often leads to unexpected errors and malfunctions. We can't afford those when we are fighting for our lives."

Evelyn stood like a bull, ready to charge. She breathed deeply and clearly weighed her options.

"I'm sorry, Alice," she grunted. "Silas, follow me to the coat closet."

Alice felt heat flash across her chest. Her eyes twitched with rage. She was not about to let that bitch put her family in danger. Evelyn had forgotten that she had given Alice administrative privileges with Silas after the poisoned dinner in the dining room. Her plan was going to be ugly.

Alice took a deep breath before running up to catch the android. Evelyn rounded the corner out of the hall before she saw Alice's actions.

"Admin command—remove core control unit with your hand," Alice whispered.

Silas turned to face her.

"Doing so will result in catastrophic unit failure, continue?"

She glanced back at the onlookers. There would be no taking this back.

"Understood, proceed."

Without flinching, Silas cranked his arm behind his back. He forced his fingers into a pointed shape and plunged the hand into the rear of his skull. The robot staggered to the wall as the metal warped.

"Alice!" Evelyn's voice blasted down the hallway. *"What did you do?"*

As her words finished, Silas completed the command. He tore a tangled cube from the innermost parts of his head with a smooth motion. Wiring and circuit board chips flew out as his final action posed him in eternal stillness.

Alice tightened her eyes shut and swallowed hard. She had decided. Now she needed to live with the consequences. James still stood frozen, watching the scene. Eleanor looked on with a smile stretching wide.

Well done, Aunt Alice. Now, I'm proud of you, she thought. *That took balls.*

Evelyn stormed toward Alice with determination. The fire in her eyes should have given away her intention. Mark walked forward. He had a dreadful feeling his intervention would soon be needed. He watched as Evelyn drew back an open hand.

Fine. I deserve that. Alice thought as the hand journeyed forward. She stood firm and resolute. Anything else would be viewed as weakness or over-aggression. She noticed a millisecond before the hand hit her that Evelyn had morphed her open palm into a tight fist. It streaked forward in a perfectly formed hook. Alice tried to put up her guard, entirely too late.

Evelyn had clearly been taught to fight. Her punch landed cleanly and with the force of a hammer. She punched through, not to, Alice's face. Her jaw cocked sideways as her face reverberated. Alice lurched sideways into the wall. Her vision turned bluish at the colossal hit. Blood swirled through her mouth.

"Holy shit." Omario stood dumbstruck as he watched the momentum finally cease.

"All right Evelyn," Alice chuckled. "I deserved that. I can respect your—*passion.*"

She held up a hand in surrender and extended her right hand to Evelyn.

"More professional than I expected, Alice," Evelyn grinned with satisfaction. "Didn't think you had the fight in you, anyway."

Mark quickened his pace. He felt like he was running through molasses. He was just a few steps away. He needed to end this.

"All right, let's—" he began.

As soon as Evelyn's hand met hers, Alice tugged roughly. Evelyn staggered forward. Her cheek was met by Alice's tightly thrown left elbow. Alice rotated her whole torso into the hit. Evelyn wasn't the only girl who'd taken self-defense courses.

Alice had practiced with her rising elbows against heavy bags innumerable times. She saw how she made the 35-kilo bag swing, despite her diminutive stature. She knew it would fucking hurt. Alice was glad.

The elbow streaked sideways across Evelyn's beautiful face. Her skin ripped as her cheekbones tore through against the monumental force provided by Alice's rising strike. The impact rattled the bones of Evelyn's skull as she flew to the left. The crown of her head pounded into the wood paneling, and her body stiffened. Evelyn dropped to the floor, unconscious.

"Oh, my fuck." Rose stood with jaw almost scraping the floor.

"Holy fucking shit," Mark moaned as he reached the mess. He looked at Alice with a commingling of disbelief and amazement.

Alice wiped the blood from her mouth. She straightened herself. Even if it was a sucker-punch, Evelyn deserved it. She briskly cracked her knuckles and stretched her shoulders. She tried to ignore the ringing in her left ear and the awful metallic taste that still flowed across her tongue. How she reacted then would set the tone of the situation. Alice cleared her throat.

"Yes, right," she stammered. "Get her cleaned up. We have work to do. We need to be ready for the next attack."

No one in the hallway moved. They felt their limbs had been paralyzed by shock.

"Need I repeat myself?" Alice spoke more determinedly. "Clean up and ready up. We need a barricade in the bar dining area. Make sure our backs are to the formal dining room. That gives us a side exit if we need it. Omario, can you handle that?"

"Uh . . ." He seemed to snap back to his senses. "Yeah, that won't be a problem."

"So, we aren't going to talk about—" Winston spoke up.

"No, we are not," Alice announced with resolve. "Can you move poor Silas into the dining room, Winston?"

Winston tipped his head to the side and widened his eyes as he took a step forward. "I don't see why the hell not."

The group nervously dispersed to their various duties. They shuffled about uncertainly like cattle. The elephant in the room was there, but Alice had announced that it was not to be mentioned. After her display, who was going to question her?

There was no further debate as to the leader of their group. Alice had proven herself effective, someone whose influence demanded respect. She didn't want it, but she had assumed the role by necessity.

Eleanor couldn't keep the smile from returning to her face constantly. She saw Alice walking toward the bar. As Eleanor trailed her, Alice pushed through the swinging door to the kitchen. Despite the odd choice of location, Eleanor followed again.

She saw Alice crouched in the corner of the room. A single tear rolled down her right cheek. She was trying to breathe slowly like she had been taught. She was failing miserably. Eleanor slipped in quietly and approached her struggling aunt.

"Shit!" Alice covered her face as Eleanor slid down to sit beside her. "Goddamn it, I tried to hold it together, I swear!"

Eleanor didn't respond verbally. She wrapped her arms around Alice and pulled her in for a hug. She didn't wait to be accepted. She simply draped herself over Alice like a cape.

"That was mental. I didn't know you were that much of a renegade," she whispered just inches from her ear.

Alice laughed through her now-freely flowing tears.

"Oh God, my elbow hurts like hell!" she whimpered with a smile.

Eleanor pulled Alice's arm back to inspect it.

"Oh, fuck! That's awful!" Eleanor said as she drew in breath.

The skin on Alice's elbow had split just above the joint and the cut ran a few inches. The tissue around her bone was swollen and bright red.

"That's going to be a big bruise," Eleanor chuckled. "Your face is even worse!"

Alice joined her in laughing and spit out a little blood beside her.

"I thought you were trying to make me feel better!" Alice shoved her niece.

Eleanor looked incredulously at her. "You just beat the shit out of one of the most powerful women on the planet with a *single* hit. Are you kidding? I think I want to be *you* when I grow up."

Alice let a pair of giggles escape her throat before a new set of sobs surfaced.

"Oh my God, it's so good to hear you say that." Her voice cracked. "I thought you hated me. I know I'm not Cara, but I have been trying so hard."

At the mention of her mother, Eleanor looked to the ceiling trying to contain herself. She cleared her throat. "No, you're not. Don't try to be. You're my Aunt Alice and you're ace at just about everything."

Alice brought her lips together tightly. She winced as her ugly cry continued. "Eleanor that's so—oh, it's brilliant." Alice smiled broadly. "I love you and your brother so much. I just want to be good enough for you."

A few small teardrops fell down Eleanor's face. She was surprised by their presence as much as Alice was.

"Well, obviously, James is simply mad for you. He talks about you all the time," Eleanor whispered shakily. "He never leaves you out when he talks about our family, even when I forget."

"It's fine, Eleanor," Alice said. "I know I've not been a big part of your life, what with your school and my career."

Eleanor shook her head and wiped away one of the streaks on her face.

"No, love. Don't you understand?" Eleanor straightened her gaze and looked into Alice's eyes. "I'm trying to say I know how similar we are, and I was frightened by that for a good while. Now, I've gotten to see you in the worst possible situation, and my God, am I proud to be your family."

"Oh, El," Alice melted. She sat up and cleared her throat. "Oh, fuck, I'm sorry. I know you hate when people call you that."

Eleanor tilted her head slightly and rocked it for a moment. "Well," her voice dragged. "James calls me that all the time, no matter how I tell him not to. Mum used to call me that when she was trying to be sweet."

Her face saddened. Eleanor remembered the way her mother would brush her long hair when she was younger. She would always complain about the curls and how they tended to knot up. She would say how she envied Eleanor's beautiful red and how her hair own was so boring and straight.

"El, you're too beautiful for your own good. The world isn't going to know what to do with you," she'd say as she finished. Eleanor remembered how her mother would kiss the top of her head. It was cruel to think she would never talk to that incredible woman again.

Eleanor realized she was daydreaming. She snapped back to reality and continued.

"Anyway, I guess El is a family nickname. You are family, so you're good to call me that. Just don't do it around everyone, right? I don't want them thinking they can get away with it, too."

Alice freed her arms and wrapped them around Eleanor's neck. She kissed her temple and released her.

"Okay, El. I'll be mindful," Alice smiled before she finally stood. She retrieved a napkin from a pile on the stainless-steel counter and wiped away some of the mess that was her face. She tried to catch her reflection in the glass of the oven.

"Oh God! I look awful!" Alice guffawed. She ran some water in a nearby sink and splashed herself. She toweled herself down with more napkins and straightened her hair. "I can't let them see me like that."

Eleanor stood and joined her side. She let her arm fall over Alice's shoulder.

"Yeah, especially now that you're their fearless leader!" she said. "Must maintain your image as the tiny terminator."

Alice stretched her jaw, almost content with her cleanup. It was the best she could do with what she had. The others were just going to have to deal with an unmade face.

"Do I look presentable?" Alice asked, turning to face her niece.

Eleanor moved a stray hair behind her ear. She laughed at the rapidly yellowing bruising on her chin.

"You look like you just took the boxing championship!" Eleanor giggled.

Alice shoved Eleanor with both hands playfully. "Shut it!" She laughed.

"Aunt Alice, you're a tough bitch. You also look stunning. You're more than ready to face your public."

Alice nodded and pulled her shoulders back. She tried to regain the decorum and class that she was accustomed to. She moved to walk out the swinging kitchen door.

"Hey!" Eleanor fussed as she slipped around to head her off. Eleanor pulled Alice into a tight hug before she could escape. "I love you, too, Aunt Alice."

Alice stood on her tiptoes and kissed the top of Eleanor's head.

She was ready for whatever was ahead.

ELEVEN

ALICE CHECKED HER WATCH AS SHE REJOINED OMARIO, who had stacked an array of different-sized tables into a line that cut across the room. It lay flush with the bar, effectively creating a large L that stretched the length and breadth of the area.

"Wow, Omario. This looks great! How'd you do it so fast?" Alice smiled.

"Well, it's definitely not near being ready. Watch," Omario said as he jumped over the short barrier. He gave a swift kick to the table he had vaulted and the whole line buckled a bit. "It's a good start, but I'll need to reinforce it and raise it over the next hour. We should be ready in time, though."

"Excellent to hear!" Amelia exclaimed as she ambled into the room. "I've dressed Evelyn's wounds. I should tell you she's awake and not entirely pleased."

"Ah, well, that is unfortunate," Alice groaned.

Amelia walked behind the bar and patted Alice's shoulder. "Between you and me, Evelyn is an entitled tart who had coming what was delivered to her."

Omario grinned widely. He always loved hearing the elderly curse. It reminded him that they were not always reformed and conservative.

Amelia clicked her tongue as she inspected Alice's face and elbow. "I'll clean that arm up for you. Would you like some ice for the face?"

"Oh, no, thank you," Alice answered. "I do appreciate your help with the elbow, though."

Amelia brought her to a barstool and sat her down. She retrieved a bottle of vodka from the bar. Alice knew it was going to sting.

Back in the common room, Evelyn was stewing. A large white strip of cotton had been plastered across her face by their de facto nurse just before she awoke. She didn't want to look in a mirror. She knew it would only anger her.

Winston shook his head in the chair opposite her.

"What the hell are you laughing at? What's so funny?" Evelyn jeered.

"Just—you. I can't believe she caught you like that. Didn't Daddy raise you to defend yourself?" Winston snickered.

"Why don't you come a bit closer, darling, and see," she whipped back.

Winston stood up and leaned against the fireplace. He lit a cigarette and dropped the hand holding it to his hip.

"This is a mess," he exhaled the words, bringing a cloud of smoke with them. "I feel like I'm all but irrelevant. Now that Alice is in charge, *our* opinions have been filtered to the bottom of the suggestion box."

Evelyn looked around the room. She checked for prying ears.

"Perhaps—" Evelyn began. "No, never mind."

"Do tell, gorgeous," Winston grinned, sauntering to the woman's side.

"Well, someone has to die anyway, right?" Evelyn hinted at her intention.

"Should it be anyone in this room?" Winston traced a finger down the unmangled side of Evelyn's visage.

"Certainly not," Evelyn answered. "Survival of the fittest. Isn't that Darwinism at its best?"

Winston nodded and dragged hard on his cigarette. He lowered the stick and offered Evelyn a puff. She obliged and breathed in deeply as the tip glowed.

"Perhaps . . ." Winston began. "Someone should die who deserves it. How would you feel about the demise of Ms. Trudeau?"

"Ecstatic," Evelyn raised her eyebrows and pulled the tall man in for a kiss. His tongue darted into her mouth and explored it. She moaned under his touch but winced as her face was brushed by the chair. She broke the embrace and lightly tossed him aside. "We will need to be careful, though. If we fail, it would land us both in a very undesirable situation."

Outside in the hall, James slipped as close to the doorframe as he could trying to hear more. He held a hand over his mouth to try to calm himself. He couldn't let them hear him. They wanted to kill Aunt Alice. They would surely kill him, too.

As he took another step closer, the worst happened. His foot caught a spare piece of metal that had exploded from Silas just a half an hour ago. It made a screech as it slid across the slate pieces in the floor.

James gasped and bolted as quickly as his feet could take him down the hallway. He didn't look back as he shot through reception and into the bar. He dipped behind the barricade and grabbed Alice and Eleanor's hands. He dragged them through the kitchen and down into the basement as they protested.

He flicked off the lights and tried to calm himself.

"James, what the bloody hell are you doing?" Eleanor swore.

"They're—they're—" he steadied himself. "They're trying to kill Aunt Alice!"

The words shot through the darkness like a demon. They seemed to echo around the room. Alice felt her throat tighten. Her stomach churned suddenly. Something about his tone let her know that he wasn't mistaken. She didn't question the boy. She simply replied with a single word.

"Who?"

"Evelyn and Winston!" He continued to panic. "They said you put them at the bottom, and they don't like it. You are bad to them, and so they are going to kill you and make it look like an accident during the next hunt."

Alice thought about the dilemma. She wouldn't be able to act on her suspicions publicly until they made some sort of move. Throwing wild accusations around without proof seemed like a rash decision. Instead, she would need to approach this issue with caution. She evaluated ideas in her head before settling on a solution.

Upstairs in the bar, Amelia had begun to wonder about their absence. She stared out over the front yard of the hotel. What the hell had she and her husband done to deserve this treatment? It was inconceivable. Her eyes drifted to the elevator at the back of the lawn. They were mere inches away from freedom. Yet she and her remaining peers were isolated beyond hope. The only other way out would be nigh impossible to use.

She remembered the presentation on the train ride in to the Arbor. She remembered the dramatic sight. She recalled the train exiting the tunnel of ice. She remembered how nothing stood between them and the hundred-foot plummet to the water's edge. It would be impossible for all but the most fit of climbers to scale. There was no point in dwelling on it. Her only hope of survival lay behind the circular lift portal.

Amelia turned to see Omario speaking with Alice. She wasn't sure when the girl had re-emerged, but both parties looked noticeably distraught. She approached the pair.

"Something amiss?" Amelia pried.

"No, uh, nothing like that," Alice lied. "We were just discussing how to shore up defenses against whatever might be coming our way next. He has no more minions to use. That means the chap will have to face us head on. I'm not sure if that's a good thing or a bad thing."

"Well, Ms. Trudeau, I can assure you of this. I do not intend to show mercy to whomever is responsible for this massacre. Promise me this: whatever happens, if one of us three is alive and has the chance—we will snuff them out without hesitation."

Alice was caught off-guard by Amelia's harsh words. They were hardly surprising, given all that had transpired, but she sounded like a woman who had been pushed to the edge and then shoved into oblivion.

"I can't speak for Omario," Alice said. "But I can promise you. I won't flinch. A monster like that isn't deserving of life. I hate to be jury and executioner, but this is an extraordinary circumstance."

Omario cracked his neck.

"I'll kill the fucker with my bare hands if I have the chance."

Amelia crossed her arms.

"It's decided then. We won't allow this brute to pollute our planet any longer. No trial to escape from. Only a swift drop and a sudden stop, metaphorically speaking," Amelia finished.

Eleanor listened to their conversation from the bar. She wasn't asked, but she felt the same way. She had watched enough people die to last two lifetimes. If she had the opportunity to provide frontier justice herself, she would. She even thought of Evelyn and Winston. Alice was too good to kill without provocation, but Eleanor knew she wasn't. She had a thirst for reconciliation. If that meant tripping Evelyn up so her head was on the chopping block, she would.

Rose stumbled her way into the bar and glanced around the room.

"Are we doing a re-enactment of *Les Miserables?* I must play Fantine!" Rose grinned at the thought of singing again. She missed the cheers. She craved the applause. It was no surprise; Rose adored the limelight. *"I dreamed a dream in time gone by!"*

Alice shook her head as she spoke up over Rose's serenade. "On a scale of one to twatted, how smashed are you?"

"Alice, that's offensive! I'm merely a bit sloshed at the moment. Don't worry! I'll be in fit fighting shape!"

Eleanor let out a disapproving heavy sigh. She assisted Omario in completion of the wall. She tucked chairs underneath tables to solidify their position and create a wedge.

Rose walked to her, noticing the groan, and asked what she could do to help.

"Beside a year of sobriety? I couldn't say," Eleanor sarcastically tore into the woman. "Realistically, just stay out of the line of fire and don't run off during the hunt. We can work to keep each other safe as long as our formation is tight."

Rose put a hand over her chest. She found it hard to feel much of anything but loose joy in her inebriated state, but Eleanor's words seemed to cut deeply.

"Ellie, I promise, scout's honor, that I won't have more than one teensy drink for the next hour. How does that sound? You'll have Auntie Rose in peak physical readiness!" She tried to bring comfort with what she viewed as a major concession.

Eleanor dropped the chair she was carrying and balled her hands in anger.

"How can you—" Eleanor fought to form words. "How can

you just drink your life away in uselessness while the rest of us fight for our lives? What gives you the right, hmm? How do you justify your ineptitude in this time of extreme trial?"

Rose was stunned. She knew Ellie had grown up. She looked like a proper woman now. Her vitriol burned deeply into Rose's alcoholic armor. Rose stuttered. She tried to speak, but only nonsense came out.

"About what I figured," Eleanor spewed. "Useless as ever."

Rose fought back tears. She mumbled wordlessly as the girl lowered to grasp the chair that she'd previously abandoned. She knew what to say, but she couldn't say it. How could Rose tell her?

"Have you ever regretted a decision?" Rose muttered.

"What?" Eleanor dropped the chair again in plain frustration.

"Have you ever done something truly vile?" Rose whispered.

"Rose, what are you talking about?" Eleanor whipped. She had a touch of worry in her voice.

"We have five minutes, people! Let's talk tactics!" Alice ordered as she gathered the residents, including Mark who had found his way over to them. Evelyn and Winston were curiously absent. Rose stood stoic as a statue. Eleanor looked on in morbid curiosity. Something about her shaken cadence seemed real.

"Ellie, I've done something dreadful. I drink because—I need to," Rose admitted.

Eleanor's concern was more obvious now.

"What do you mean, you need to?" Eleanor asked.

"Ellie it's all my fault. It's—"

"Rose, Eleanor, are you planning to join us?" Alice barked.

"Yes, sorry!" Rose apologized. "We can talk more later, Ellie, dear!"

Rose flitted away before Eleanor could object. Something

about what Rose said deeply shook Eleanor. She wanted to know more, but their allotment of time had diminished to almost nothing. The group needed to focus and guard against both the killer and the possible malfeasances of Winston and Evelyn.

They talked strategy. They prepared and spread out their pile of explosives. They knew their escape route. The candles were lit, and Omario had built a pyre in reception to cast additional light. It slowly climbed to a roaring flame as the first bell tolled on the clock. It was 9 pm.

As the bells finished, Alice drew back the firing pin on her rifle. She had five shots remaining in the clip. She needed to use them wisely. The electric lights fizzled out, but the group was bathed in a golden glow.

Thundering of foot strides were heard outside the bar window. They sounded urgent and viscerally rapid. Whatever raced through the yard was clearly not human. Alice twitched as the front door slowly drifted open. She took aim at the opening.

A pair of wolves rushed through into reception and snarled at the hidden survivors. Their eyes were green and luminescent. Even as they crept through the shadows, they were easy to spot from their awful gaze.

"They're hybrids," Alice announced, not moving from her ready stance. "They aren't going to go down in one hit. Keep that in mind!"

Mark spun a large metallic meat tenderizer in his right hand. These automaton beasts were going to be relatively impervious to knife attacks. They would need to be crushed.

The wolves snapped their powerful jaws as they entered the designed kill box. Amelia held a palm high in the air. She watched as the first animal passed a small red X in the carpet. She looked to the right and closed her fist.

Omario gave a slight bob of his head and tugged on a cord

that ran to the chandelier in the center of the room. Everyone ducked behind the wooden shield of the barricade.

The string led to a 2.5L wine bottle nested in the light fixture. All the metallic scraps the group could find including silverware, bits from Silas and Timothy, and even jewelry sat in a tight wrapping along the base directly over the head of the beasts.

The explosive was a two-component mixture separated by a fragile membrane. The rope led to a small sharp plunger which tore through the membranous material as it yanked back. The volatile chemicals commingled and built pressure.

This chain reaction occurred in less than half of a second. The explosion was larger than Amelia had expected. Her hearing was deafened as the sonic shockwave filled the room. This was immediately followed by a rapid pattering tapping noise. She knew that the shrapnel would have embedded itself into every surface in direct line of sight from the bomb.

Dust flowed overhead as the room darkened slightly. The explosion had extinguished many of the candles in their proximity. Mark shook his mallet and popped his head over the barricade as the first soul brave enough to check the damages.

His eyes were pulled to a spoon embedded sideways in the tabletop he hid behind. It had been propelled through the hardwood. The silver tip flashed at him as he rose. The velocity of debris must have been positively devastating. As he looked up, he noticed a wolf limping from the room. One of its legs was clearly non-functional and metal bits left large holes in its superstructure.

In the center of the room, one of the canines lay dead. Pearlescent blue hydraulic fluid puddled beneath it. James lifted his head and saw the aftermath next. He raised his hands in the air and let out a surprisingly intimidating battle cry.

Alice smiled. It was hardly the entire fight, but the kill was a victory nonetheless.

"Mark, Omario," she called. "Go pulverize the other one. Be careful."

The men climbed carefully over the tall stack of chairs and tables. They tried to avoid sharp bits of metal digging into their skin but struggled to do so in an expedient manner. James stood atop the pile and studied the room as the men reached the floor.

"It's like one of those party ball things threw up in here!"

"You mean a disco ball?" Alice amended.

James looked at her with puzzled eyes. "What's disco?"

Suddenly, Alice felt her age. She had loved listening to old-time music from the mid-20th century since she was a girl. While most her age were obsessing over the latest boy and girl groups, Alice had played old-fashioned CDs of Earth, Wind, and Fire and the BeeGees. Keeping her CD player running was always a good amount of effort. There were no parts for the specific antique anymore, so its diodes and motors had to be meticulously maintained. She'd cared for it with heartfelt devotion. Luckily for her interests and tastes, boxes of physical media were easy to come by. Perhaps she could educate James on the finer points of the grooviest era in history. For the first time, with one predator down, that seemed like a not-entirely-impossible scenario.

The wolf had clawed its way to the bonfire in the middle of the lobby. The fire still roared and made the trail of lubricant snaking behind the cursed thing glisten. The beast trembled violently, trying to pull itself along. Omario lifted the most effective hand-to-hand combat weapon in their arsenal and the brass stool glinted in the jarring heat of the flames. He pummeled the paralyzed creature at the bridge of its nose and the face folded inward.

Some of the circuitry revealed a spinning gyroscope inside. The whirling slowed to a stop and the body's quaking death throes came to an end. Omario patted the tip of his increasingly weathered implement and turned to face Mark.

"I'll leave you the next one, mate," Omario smiled.

The men knew more challenges had to be around the corner, but this was definitely a boon for the survivors. They returned to join the others but were halted a few feet away from the cyborg. It gave a slight whimper.

"Should have hit it twice," Mark grinned as he spun about to finish the job that Mr. Richards had started.

The beast stirred and increased the volume of its whimper as its front paws lifted the head. An awful noise emanated from the wolf's suffering form. It filled the house with the volume of a bullhorn. It was a howl, but one unlike he had ever heard before. Mark thought it sounded like a roar from the pit of a sewer drain. Omario thought it was closer to how he'd always imagined a duppy would cry out.

His mama would tell stories of the duppies that haunted their coffee fields. She said they were restless spirits. She'd say when that he felt the heat burn deep in his chest, "*dat men a duppy round ya, pickney.*" He knew it was a lie to keep curious seven-year-olds from exploring places they shouldn't, but hearing that awful screech brought him back to the most tremendous fear of his youth. Suddenly the hotness in his torso seemed ethereal and ominous.

The cacophony echoed endlessly at insufferable volume and continued even through the first two hits of Mark's hammer. It finally ceased on the third slam. He cautiously began to back toward the barricade and dreaded what he feared was next. He knew wolves were pack animals.

A pair of howls pierced through the walls from the front yard and joined a chorus that picked up inside the house. Mark and Omario broke into a sprint just as the wolves from the front yard crashed against the mostly open front door. There was no slow approach this time. The wolves charged at full speed toward the fleeing men.

The first caught Omario in his right calf with its paw. The claw extended and buried itself into his boot. He let out a yelp as the pain began to shoot up his leg. The horrible beast held him there as the second reared back to pounce.

The two-pronged response was executed with clairvoyant precision. Alice fired her hunting rifle just as the wolf prepared to jump. The shot tore through the wolf's metal jaw and out the topside of its face. Its steel maw hung open because of the shattered torsion point, and all attention was suddenly on her. As the wolf who had pinned Omario moved to change targets, Mark caught it in the teeth with a haymaker of an inside strike. Titanium teeth skittered across the floor as its jaw was driven inward. The hammer plunged deep into the creature's mouth.

Unfortunately, after his display of force, the computerized canine seemed none too eager to return his weapon. It bit down with its remaining teeth and snapped the narrow handle off the head.

With Omario freed, the men rounded the closest corner. Mark was the first to scramble over the top of the barricade. His instinct was to pull the bleeding Omario over with him. The wolves scratched against the wooden tables and the one without a functioning mouth tried to bite his ankle. The teeth scraped but did not grab as the wolf fell back down the steep incline.

As soon as Omario was over the wall, Amelia chucked the grenade she had been holding just behind the wolves, hoping to damage their barricade as little as possible.

"Down!" Amelia shouted as the smaller explosive hit the ground.

The table wine bottle shattered, and bits of glass were propelled in every direction as the charge detonated. The wolves yelped, but the blast was much smaller than the first. As Rose peered over, one of the wolves now limped but the other galloped toward the first person its saw.

"Fuck!" she exclaimed as the beast slammed the barricade.

It dug in its claws and began to climb. Rose looked over her left shoulder in a panic. "Alice!"

Alice leaned out over the barricade and put a shot directly through the side of the wolf's head at close range. Its head sparked as the slug passed through the control unit. The creature froze where it was, held motionless by its titanium claws.

Another down. Alice thought as she reloaded. The remaining wolf with a broken jaw paced the room for a moment before letting out a shrill cry for help. Apparently already having been on their way, four more monstrosities skidded around the bonfire and charged. Alice knew they could climb now.

There were too many.

The narrow corridors behind the barricade would become a tomb as wolves scaled the wall. She only had three shots. In an absolute best-case scenario, one would get over. She had no doubt in her mind that the wolf with titanium claws and teeth would have no trouble ripping its unlucky victim to shreds before they were able to help, especially with no room to swing their weapons.

"Kitchen!" Alice ordered. "Amelia, give our friends a few parting gifts!"

James slid to Amelia's side and grabbed a pair of wine bottles. The older woman had her doubts about allowing help, but she did not have much for alternatives.

"Good hard throw, chap!" she instructed as her first two wine bottles flew over the top blindly. A pair of explosions were followed by pained yelps.

James flattened his usual smile into a war-face and scurried up the chairs toward the top of the pile.

"James! Throw from here!" Amelia called.

Alice caught her with a hooked arm and pulled her toward the newly reinforced kitchen door. "James! Let's go!"

His eyes were met by a wolf at the foot of the barricade who had just began to climb. He jumped back but remembered his marching orders clearly.

"Good hard throw," he whispered to himself and threw both wine bottles toward the floor. He hopped down just as the explosions sent the wolf's mangled body shooting through the barricade and partially collapsing a section. Despite the good hits, the beasts now had a way to get through easily.

As James passed through the door, Omario slid the top and bottom locks into place. A moment later, the door rattled furiously. A crazed and bloodthirsty face barked mechanically at the kitchen door window and dug its claws into the surrounding rubber. They pierced the plexiglass and gasket as though they weren't even there and pulled hard against the metal frame.

The wolf cocked its head to the side with an unbreakable stare. Over the barking it was hard to hear, but somewhere in the house another creature howled in pain. All the dogs raced toward the call, but the wolf who attacked the door seemed to be stuck by his claws. It yelped in frustration before bracing its back paws against the door, which buckled accordingly, and forcibly tore them outward. The titanium blades ripped through the door paneling and left a trio of tear marks in the metal which could be clearly looked through.

"Bloody fuckin' hell!" Omario muttered as he stuck a finger through one of the canyon-like tears.

"They will be back, and with God knows how many friends!" Alice called. "Let's get this stove in front of the door!"

"That one?" Mark said, pointing across the large kitchen to an appliance he had no eagerness to relocate.

"Yes! We can't very well block the doors with something that has bloody wheels now, can we?" Alice justified.

Mark raised his hands and waved over an unexcited Omario. The oven screeched as it dragged across the stone tiling. James held his hands to his ears as the scraping continued. Eleanor kept an eye on the kitchen door in case the beasts returned. She heard a slight hissing. Almost like someone was trying to get her attention.

"Eleanor," Evelyn whispered, peering one eye through the crevasse. "Quick, let me in before they get back!"

Eleanor reached up to unlatch the first lock and held there. She considered it. She mulled it over in her mind.

"Eleanor, now!" Evelyn urgently breathed. "They will be coming back any second!"

Eleanor's palm rested against the metal slide. She knew letting Evelyn in was the right thing to do. Leaving her to die would be awful. Eleanor would be no better than Evelyn if she didn't oblige. The stove's journey across the room was still enough to hush Evelyn's desperate pleas. The decision was going to be Eleanor's, and hers alone. Was it considered murder if the deed was accomplished by inaction?

"El, I know what you're thinking. It is true, I said some things I should not have said about Alice, but Winston disappeared after we managed to paralyze one of those things. I'm all alone!"

Eleanor lowered herself to Evelyn's level as the appliance neared the doorframe.

"Good. No one to see this."

Her palm flew from the still locked door as she helped the men push the stove into place over the doorway. She heard Evelyn softly shriek and pound the door.

"What is that?" Alice asked.

"Stove. We had to bang it into place," Eleanor flatly lied.

Mark listened as he stopped moving the appliance.

"No, I hear it too. It's like a knocking."

Realization spread over Alice like a terrible wave.

"El, what did you do?" She mouthed as everyone began to focus on listening for the knocking. Alice shot her gaze sideways at the men as the desperate pounding became apparent.

"Mark!" She shouted, pointing at the stove.

"Fuck! On it!" he returned without having to be asked.

Mark pushed his back to the wall and pressed with all his strength against the now locked in stove. He tried to free it but found that it had wedged itself in the doorway.

"Shit!" Omario yelled as he pulled against the top. "You push from the bottom; I'll pull from the top. Ready? Do it!"

The men alternated forces and the stove tipped forward and slammed into the kitchen floor.

"No!" Eleanor screamed. "How are we going to get it back in there?"

"We can't, El," Alice groaned in disappointment. She shook her head slowly and caused a cloud of shame to fall over Eleanor.

Eleanor covered her mouth. She wasn't like the psychopath tormenting them. She didn't really mean to do it directly. She wasn't a killer on the inside, was she?

As the door opened slightly, Omario saw one beast hungrily eyeing Evelyn. He pulled her inside and over the stove as it rammed into the door. He slid the bottom lock into place, but saw that even with the first ram, the screws pulled slightly from their nesting. The door would not survive many more hits.

"Where do we go?" James shouted as a second dog came to assist the first.

"Either to the basement, or we circle the house," Amelia said as the men braced the door with their bodies.

"Basement!" Evelyn shouted over heaving breaths. "There is no way we can outrun those things on open ground."

The group began to file toward the basement door and one by one moved downstairs. The top lock popped off the door as three wolves hungrily dug at the metal paneling. Another set of cuts moved across the midline of the metal.

"Listen mate," Omario started to Mark as he continued to brace the door. "We need to make a promise. It's gonna be one of us, yeah? Whoever makes it to the door better toss a grenade at these fuckers. I don't fancy being ripped apart by some goddamn demon. Don't you let me go out like that. I want to leave ashes, not a cut-up hunk of meat."

"Omario, we can both—"

"We have to go! On three!"

"One!" Omario yelled as a pair of angry green eyes darted back and forth between its menu choices for the next meal.

"Two!" He shouted as both men lifted a leg up onto the stove. They would need to push off and sprint diagonally across the room around the prep table in the center to reach the basement door.

"Three!"

The moments passed in a blur for Mark. The outside world seemed to shut itself out as the snarling barks grew louder. He heard the pinging of a lock bursting from the door and something small slide beside him. The wolves were in. He heard rabid stamping of paw into stone as they closed behind him. The door was so close now. He had to get there.

He felt the first claw dig into his back just a pair of steps away from his destination. The powerful beast pushed into his torso as he crashed to the floor.

"Mark!" Omario called as he zoomed around the other side, helplessly far from the doomed man.

Omario knew it was useless as he hurled the stool at the wolf pinning Mark. He watched as the second claw ripped into Mark's shoulder. The man screamed as tiny bits of bone were scraped off by the much harder saber-like nail.

The shot rang out in the boxed room, and Mark tensed instinctively. The wolf pinning him rolled sideways as it fell from his back. He wasted no time. He sprang to his feet and scrambled into the basement, bumping past his savior Alice who wore a satisfied grin.

She turned the gun toward Omario and saw the wolf clamp its jaw down around his wrist that he had used to steady himself on the table. The teeth sunk into his bone and snapped it effortlessly. He howled as he tumbled from the dragging strike. Alice put a bullet between the wolf's eyes, but its grip remained. The second wolf caught Omario in the leg and ripped off flesh as it tore with its awful jaws. The claw pinned him to the ground as a third wolf pounced onto his back. Alice had one shot. She looked between the three beasts, utterly incapable of removing all threats.

She looked away as his pleading eyes met hers. She dropped her rifle and moved to the basement. Mark flew around her. He had promised.

Omario looked almost thankful through his pained yelps as he saw a trio of projectiles flying toward him and his attackers. The explosion ripped through the kitchen floor. Debris fell slowly into the basement followed immediately by a mutilated beast. It had only two legs, and the right half of its face was missing, but it still tried to snap its jaws at Eleanor. She backed away as it barked angrily. Over the furious chomping of the wolf, four loud bells were heard echoing even down into the basement.

TWELVE

"**F**UCK!" ALICE SCREAMED. "WE HAD IT. WE COULD have fucking had it!"

"Alice, don't." Mark sighed. "Who is to say that after we killed those three, another ten wouldn't have dropped from wherever it is they came from. We can't blame each other. We will go mad!"

"We know who would have died without you," Evelyn said, looking in Mark's direction. "I owe you my life."

Mark gave a momentary smile before he remembered his situation. Evelyn walked toward him with open arms.

"I'd be dead without you, Alice," she finished as she passed by Mark and wrapped her arms around a silently stunned Ms. Trudeau.

"What?" Mark asked, stupefied.

"What?" Alice seemed equally confused.

"I heard you call for the men to remove the stove. Even if they'd wanted to, they never would have done it without your order. I see that they all respect you. After the show of strength I just witnessed, I can't say I could disagree with their assessment."

"Evelyn, thank you, but you understand why I'm finding it hard to—empathize—with your sentiment?" Alice slipped from the embrace.

"Of course. Let me describe things from my perspective. You were a cunt to me. I punched you. You reminded me that my actions have consequences. Despite the original transgression, I think we can agree who won that fight," Evelyn tapped the bandage on her face before continuing.

"Then let's talk of my good. . .friend. . . Winston." Evelyn's words dropped out slowly and deliberately. "We bashed the living hell out of one of those things, and it called for its brothers. When the backup arrived, we both ran as fast as we could. I ran to the bar, and Winston noticed the wolves seemed to be following me. He broke off and left me to die. I hid behind the bonfire and was lucky enough that the wolves ran into the common room. I saw the trail of corpses even as I approached the bar. One beast dead in reception, three dead in the bar itself, and you killed another while it tried to mangle poor Marky-boy."

Evelyn slapped her ex-lover's cheek lightly before finishing her explanation.

"I am a leader. There is no question about that. I do not like to follow orders. That said, I can respect that you are the 'wartime general' in this situation. Would I trust you to run my company? Never! Do I trust your killing potential and leadership? I suppose I'd be a fool not to. So again, I say, thank you."

Alice nodded. She thought about her words before she said them. How would a good leader respond? What would her mother say?

"Ms. Fox, I appreciate the compliments. I do say we did a bang-up job in routing those devils, but I must take your words with a grain of salt. I want to publicly acknowledge something Eleanor said earlier as I believe it must be addressed. It was overheard that you and Winston had been plotting to make sure my death was the next. What can you say to this?"

Evelyn was floored. She knew Alice had gusto, but she was not expecting an outright and public accusation. She scratched her head. There were two ways to play this, and she decided on the lesser of two evils. She took a large breath and released it with her answer.

"Yes, I did, or we did. Obviously, I cannot speak for Winston. Things change very quickly around here now. I made a rash decision when I had just woken up from the most embarrassing fight of my life. What I can say is that the choice was made in haste and the heat of passion. Winston brought it up when he was standing between my legs. I think with my preexisting feelings toward you and desire to have that gorgeous man on top of me, I might have said almost anything."

"Ugh!" Eleanor contorted her face at the thought.

"Eleanor, enough," Alice hushed her niece.

"As you can imagine, both of those feelings have dramatically changed," Evelyn said. "I can assure you of this. I will respect your leadership from this point on, but at the same time, I will not be some lemming. Ultimately, I know this place and am its sole owner. I do wish to retain some control, but in the heat of battle or an emergency—your orders will be gospel to me."

Alice offered her hand to Evelyn. The woman seemed reluctant to accept it.

"I'll behave. You have my word," Alice smirked.

Finally, the two women shook hands. An alliance had been made, despite its shaky foundation. Alice knew she couldn't trust Evelyn, but it was nice not to have a fellow survivor in open defiance. She would test Evelyn's willingness to follow orders soon enough.

If the rapidly increasing speed of their doom was consistent, the group would have a mere two hours before the next hazard. It looked to strike at midnight. There was a lot of cleanup to tend to.

Amelia marched to the library to patch up Mark's deep wounds on the remnants of the library benches. Eleanor and James walked to the bar to reconstruct the barricade that had been so wantonly demolished by the explosion. Alice, Evelyn, and Rose draped some bed sheets over the remnants of Omario. Alice said a few words in his memory.

She'd really cared for Omario. He had a true sense of determination and fighting spirit that would be sorely missed. She mentioned the heartbreak his native soccer club would soon feel at the news. She said that in a perfect world, he seemed just the man she could have seen herself with.

Rose mumbled something about wishing she could have had a sample of dark chocolate. The other women at the vigil tried to ignore her.

"He was truly a gentleman," Evelyn added. "There aren't many of those left."

"We should say a prayer for him, yes?" Rose asked hopefully.

"Uh," Alice stretched her words. "Sure?"

Neither Evelyn or Alice were good Christian girls, nor had they become particularly acquainted with any other common deities for that matter. Despite this fact, Alice bowed her head out of respect for the dead.

The girls stood in silence. Alice knew prayer was often done in this matter, so she didn't think much of it.

"Should I say it, then?" Rose opened her eyes and rotated her torso to look at Evelyn and Alice.

Alice gave an approving gesture and Rose clapped her hands together. She cleared her throat and stood a bit taller.

"*Oh Lord, we thank you that your servant Omario is now a member of your heavenly kingdom. We ask that you accept him gracefully and let him live in your glory forever. May we all join him someday, but not too soon. In Christ's name, amen.*"

"Short and to the point," Evelyn chuckled. "I suppose I should be grateful."

"I've always been a churchgoing girl," Rose explained. "I even sang in my choir before I got signed by Union records. I haven't gotten much time to get back, but if I make it out of this—I think I'll make a day of it."

Alice pondered the irony of Rose calling herself a "churchgoing girl" as she went to check on Eleanor and James.

"Aunt Alice!" James called. "This is the one I got, see!"

James jumped atop a wolf carcass which let out metallic rattling as he jumped on its back.

"Be careful, love. We don't know if those things regenerate or something wicked like that. Best if we use caution," Alice said, draining the wind from James' sails. She noticed and decided to cheer him up. "But that's really cool. I reckon you'll be able to impress all the girls at school with that story. We should have Mark take a picture for his article."

"You **mean it?**" James jumped again at the possibility. "Would I be in the Mars news, then?"

Alice shook her head. James frowned.

"You'd probably make into the solar system feed with a story like that," Alice smiled.

For just a brief few seconds, James' pure joy had lifted her from the darkness that pervaded every segment of her being. Her only focus was survival now. Everything else had faded away. She did see a distinct and new possibility now, however.

James and Eleanor had awakened a new sense of purpose inside her that had not been there before. She had lived a perfectly happy life. She had a fantastic job. She had a great family, before all of it fell to pieces. She didn't feel like her life was missing anything.

Now that Alice was the guardian of two young and impressionable people, she always felt their observation of her life and choices . She wanted to be an example to them. This was not a change she consciously made; Alice just seemed to imagine James' two bright eyes looking up at her before weighing her options. She had to consider more than herself now. It was equal parts horrifying and magnificent.

Alice rustled a hand across James hair. She reached down and kissed his forehead.

"I love you so much, James! Never change."

"Thanks, Aunt Alice, I love you, too, but I'm growing up now! Can't you see? I'm becoming a *big man!*" James stretched his arms across his kill and pretended to lift it over his head.

"Your ego is certainly expanding!" Eleanor quipped from the other side of the barricade.

"Thanks, El!" James yelled back obliviously. He seemed to poke around at his muscles, looking for his ego.

Alice had another Wortz sibling to talk to. She climbed over the rubble and saw the stunning Eleanor stretching upward to lift a tabletop back into place. She approached from behind and helped push the barrier into position.

"Thanks, Aunt Alice," Eleanor said with sincerity, flashing a beautifully sincere smile.

How could someone so innocent in some ways do what she did, Alice wondered.

"El, can we have a quick chat?" Alice asked.

"Fuck," Eleanor whispered quiet enough so James wouldn't hear. Alice hadn't announced what Eleanor did to the rest of the group. James was oblivious to her sinister role in the "rescue" of Evelyn Fox. "Yeah, can we go to the common room?"

"Sure, let me just—" Alice stretched herself over the barrier. "Rose!"

"Yes, yes?" she answered, poking her head out of the mangled kitchen doorway.

"Could you come help James with the barricade? I have to go do an errand with Eleanor," Alice explained.

"Oh, come on," James groaned softly out of sight.

"Of course, I can watch my *favorite boy*! He won't leave my sight, I promise. Not a *single* drink while I'm watching him, I swear on my mother's grave!"

"Isn't your mum alive?" Alice asked.

"Yes!" Rose retorted. "Why?"

Alice had no response. She waved as she thanked Rose and accompanied Eleanor to the common room. Eleanor slouched as a woman walking to the executioner.

"Look, I know what you're going to say," Eleanor spoke first as she plopped into one of the comfortable leather chairs before the fire.

"And what is that?" Alice answered as she lay back onto the sofa to face Eleanor in a reclining position.

"You'll say 'El, we can't let ourselves get dragged into the ugly business of murder." Eleanor tried her best to impersonate her aunt.

"Do I really sound like that?" Alice whined.

"You'll say, 'Doing that makes us no better than the evil people who started this whole place. If I ever catch you doing that again, I'll tell everyone!"

Alice did not expect such self-deprecating words to escape from Eleanor's lips. She knew Eleanor would feel guilty for what she did, she was a good girl, but she never expected such a mature attitude about the event. She certainly did not expect Eleanor to worry about humiliation at Alice's hand.

"El," Alice softly spoke.

Hearing the word made Eleanor break down. She leaned forward and rested her forearms on her knees. She immediately began to cry. Alice had never seen Eleanor have such a blatant emotional response to something, even when Jack had died. Was Eleanor more in touch with her feelings now, or was she finally starting to trust Alice?

"Hey, sweetheart, look at me!" Alice hopped from her seat and dropped to her knees in front of Eleanor so she could look in her eyes. Unmitigated woe flashed over the young woman's face. She avoided Alice's gaze. "Babe, it's okay. Listen to me, it's all right!"

"No!" Eleanor moaned. "No, it's not. I'm not innocent here. I fucking got down and told her I was glad she was about to be torn to bits. I'm a—I'm a monster! You always think that you'd say something like that to your worst enemy, but the way you looked at me when you figured it out. Oh God. I knew I'd done it. I was broken inside."

"Hey, no! Come here!" Alice was dismayed by her words. An eighteen-year-old should not have been having an existential crisis of this magnitude. Eleanor had seen too much for a girl her age. Alice pulled Eleanor's hands, and the girl eased herself to the floor without any further request. She huddled close to Alice and buried her face in her aunt's embrace. Alice felt tears running quickly down her bosom that were not her own.

"God, it was so easy," Eleanor whispered. "Everyone always says killing someone is so hard your first time, but I was willing to do it with prejudice. I just wanted her gone so badly. I thought she was going to ruin everything. She isn't a good person, and I feel like I'm the only one who sees it!"

"Ok, stop," Alice ordered. "First of all, you're entirely wrong about what I was going to tell you. I would have said, 'I know why you did what you did. I would have done the same thing. I would have been wrong, too."

"Don't lie. I know you wouldn't have let her die. You didn't!"

"If Evelyn had threatened to kill you, I would have. I could have shot her myself, and I would have felt as little guilt as you did," Alice explained.

"So what? Is that supposed to make me feel better? You're just trying to say we are both flawed at heart?"

"No," Alice continued. "You didn't lock her out because you're twisted. It was not because you have lost all humanity. It was because *she* was threatening to kill *me*."

"Oh, and what, I'm your bodyguard now?" Eleanor scoffed.

"No, my dear," Alice brought her chin up to look in her face. "It's because you love me just as dearly as I love you. El, I would kill a thousand bastards before I let you die. It doesn't make it right, but it's true. You aren't broken. You were just trying to protect your family."

Eleanor wrapped herself around Alice. She wrapped her arms tightly in a constricting embrace and felt no desire to leave it, even after a respectable amount of time had passed.

"I can't lose you, too!" Eleanor cried.

Alice bit her lip. She fought back tears and only partially succeeded.

"You won't, darling, I'm not going anywhere." Alice returned Eleanor's embrace wholeheartedly. "We will protect each other."

Eleanor sniffed as she released Alice.

"I promise I won't try to murder anyone anymore," she half-joked.

"You're too kind, El," Alice smiled. "I understand your motives, but I think living with her blood on your hands would have proven quite a burden for you."

"Do you really think Evelyn's turned over a new leaf?"

"Probably not." Alice frowned. "But unfortunately, until she gives me reason to believe otherwise, I have to treat her as an ally."

Eleanor sat up on her own again. She stared into the fire. She brooded over the quandary as the tongues of flame were reflected in her eyes. Alice looked into herself through the girl's eyes. She wished to take all the pain in the world away. She wanted to give Eleanor a privileged life.

Despite Alice's most strenuous effort, Eleanor would always be different from girls her age. How could she not? The inauspicious teenager had been forged in flames so hot that she would either snap prematurely or remain as sharp as a razor's edge until she died at a ripe old age. If the girl could survive this, she would weather any tempest that might beat against her.

"You are so entirely beautiful, El." Alice lightly rested her fingers on Eleanor's cheek. "I'm not talking about your looks, you know. Everyone pays attention to that, but your mind is complex. Your heart is faithful. Your care for James is transparently steadfast. You are so much more secure with yourself than I ever was with myself."

"I don't see why," Eleanor admitted. "You have just as much to be proud of as me. Don't you see it? You constantly say how similar we are to each other, and yet you choose to only see flaws in yourself. Everything you just said to me could be mirrored back without exaggeration. If you are going to lead these people, you need to understand your own worth, too."

"You're right, my lovely. I do," Alice agreed. "I think that's a very good personal goal for myself."

Alice leaned on Eleanor as they both paused a moment more. In a short while, the world would be plunged back into the pits of hell. For now, they cherished each other's company. Both had found a confidant that they would never have guessed mere days ago.

⋖◌◯◌⋗

In the bar, James and Rose struggled to lift the heavy furniture back to the tops of their respective piles.

"How on Earth did Omario do this so easily?" Rose groaned as her arms buckled under the weight of the solid wood dining chair being held over her head.

James pulled as hard as he could from the top of the pile and twisted the legs so that they would slide into a pair of preexisting holes in the gnarled home decor. The chair supports scored their finish off as they slipped into the placement that seemed like it was made for them. There was no wiggle-room, and when James checked the tightness of the fit, he was unable to lift the chair even an inch. It was quite locked into place.

"Good, my boy!" Rose clapped. "Now get down here so we can have a—nice cold glass of water."

James wasn't sure whether he should believe her as he carefully scrambled down the pile. Rose sat on the bar and helped pull James up to her when she grabbed the fountain soda gun. True to her word, she poured herself a fizzy glass of seltzer and held the nozzle over James' cup.

"Looks like they have orange juice, seltzer, plain water, cola—" she said.

"Plain water is fine," James stopped her.

"Suit yourself!" she laughed as she dispensed the clear chilled liquid into his brandy glass.

The two sipped their drinks in relative silence for a few awkward minutes. They looked at the repaired wall with satisfaction before Rose got an idea.

"Oh! When adults are particularly happy with something, they clink their glasses together and say cheers. We should do that!"

"You mean like a toast?" James asked.

"I don't have any speech prepared, dear. Let's say cheers to a lot of hard work and a magnificent finished product! Cheers!"

James tapped his glass to hers with relative certainty that what they had just done was still called a toast. He was content, however, that the unmindful woman was sober enough to sit up straight.

"Can I ask you a question, Rose?" James prodded.

"Of course, dear!" Rose cheerfully returned.

"Well—" He halted and thought for a tick before continuing. "Why did you stay an extra week at the Arbor? Evelyn said it was quite expensive. Did you have the free week like we did?"

Rose eyed the gin on the shelf behind her. She flipped the idea of chugging the bottle around in her head. Ultimately, she cared for James too much to set that sort of an example, despite her previous actions. Rose laughed lightly and turned back to face him.

"Well, don't be ridiculous, I just got another coupon! Yes, someone gave me a certificate the first time, and I just was lucky enough to acquire a second!" Rose nervously laughed.

"You got two?" James sounded doubtful. "Who gave you the first one?"

"Hah!" Rose nervously let out a giggle. She again craved the alcohol that brought her comfort and bravery when she was naturally lacking both. "Who gave me the ticket? Well, that's a bit of a complicated question, I suppose."

"Why?" James innocently stared at Rose with his bold blue eyes.

Rose turned away. She did not care to look back at his sweet face. She dared not to.

"Well, because it was two people of course, and they wanted to stay very secret," Rose explained.

"Why was it a secret?" James continued to prod.

"*God*," Rose whispered as she continued to shun the boy with her body language. "It was a secret because—well the people did not want to be found out obviously. They wanted to keep their *charity* hidden. These were very rich people, you see. They had so much to lose. They did not consider anyone but themselves, I'm afraid."

James was intuitive. He was far too clever for his own good. He was incredibly skilled at reading between the lines and noticing details almost anyone else would have missed in the face of concealed intent. He could always catch peer-magicians in his class with their second-rate sleight of hand. Distraction was useless against him. James pierced to the heart of her words.

"*Were?*"

"What did you say?" Rose snapped.

"You just said, 'they **were** rich people.' Are they not anymore? Did they lose their money because of the charity?"

"Time to go!" Rose jumped from the counter. "I've got to get you back to your Aunt Alice right now! You see, I need to be somewhere very important, and unfortunately I'm late."

"Late?" James fussed as he was dragged from the counter by the suddenly panicked woman. "But we have been talking for ages."

"Yes, and you are such a charming lad that I got distracted. Shame on you, James! You're going to be a lady killer one day."

Lady killer. Her words stuck to his brain as though they had been welded irreversibly. She dragged him almost painfully from the bar, and he suddenly wished he'd grabbed his glass. His mouth felt dry.

"Aunt Rose?" James said worriedly, as they walked by the still-smoldering pyre in the lobby. "Did you mean they were rich, or—were alive?"

"No, no, no! We must go now. I'm dreadfully sorry to be out of time to spend with such a dashing lad!" Rose almost shouted as she walked into the common room and circled the perimeter to drop the boy off.

She tossed James to his family with a particularly crazed look. The child rubbed his wrist as he looked back at her. Rose appeared manic because she was more scared than she had ever been. She had almost avoided the matter. She was so close to escaping damnation for her actions. How ironic that she was to be undermined by the least of them.

Alice and Eleanor stared at Rose with great concern.

"Rose, what's wrong?" Alice wondered.

"Oh, nothing, love! We had a brilliant time, but I'm afraid I have to go now. Don't look for me at dinner!" Rose announced.

"Dinner?" Alice seemed confused. They hadn't had a proper dinner in days. Everyone had provided sustenance for themselves by snacking whenever they had a free second. A perennial hunger sat deep in the survivors' stomachs. She doubted that was about to change, unless Rose knew otherwise. "What dinner?"

"OH, Alice! Don't be such a kidder! You know the old saying, 'don't look for me at dinner!'" Rose was all muddled up in her lies now. She kept herself drunk out of self-preservation. Rose was simply awful under pressure.

"I have literally never heard that," Eleanor flatly scorned.

"Hah! What a little minx you are, Ellie!" Rose neurotically spat. "Anyway, ta for now! I'll see if I can't find Winston!"

Rose alighted from the room like a bat running from the burning sunrise before anyone in the room could address her nonsensical rambling.

"That was *really* weird," James groaned.

"What the bloody hell happened, James?" Eleanor sprung to her question before Alice could think.

James explained the situation blow-by-blow. He recounted every detail with painstaking accuracy as he gave the girls a rundown of his experience. He tried to describe Rose's tone. He quoted her responses word-for-word. Alice couldn't help thinking what an incredible detective the boy would make one day.

"She's definitely hiding something," Alice obviously stated. "I want to know more about these people who invited her. That seems particularly critical to the mystery."

"I think I have an idea what happened to them," Eleanor whispered as the fire continued to flash hot against her face. "They're dead."

"You think it was the killer?" Alice questioned.

"I'm quite sure of it now," Eleanor concluded. "Rose feels guilty because she wasn't just a bystander to this whole thing—she was its orchestrator. Rose is the murderer loose in The Arbor."

"But that doesn't entirely make sense—" Alice was interrupted by a sinister chiming.

"Fuck!" She screamed. "We should have another half an hour! Get behind the barricade before it—"

There was something distinct about these bells. Rather than being a repetitive chime signaling the number of the hours, this was a little tune. The melody reminded Alice of her early childhood. The melodic rise and fall of the bells seemed familiar. She tried to remember its name. It was—a doxology?

Alice had never really believed what she heard in church, but her parents pulled her along, nonetheless. She didn't remember much but the songs. The Anglican church her family attended had an order to their service that was followed every Sunday. It brought a sense of consistency to a turbulent world. Despite anything that happened in the week, there would always be three scripture readings. The priest would always lift the Bible high when he read from the gospel. There was the Lord's Prayer. Then, there was this lovely little tune that Alice especially liked after the offering.

They would carry the plates of money back up through the aisles while everyone jumped to their feet. *"Praise God from whom all blessings flow,"* the first stanza declared. She did not sing along with every hymn, but she loved that song. It was called the doxology, and it was playing from the clock that had signaled nothing but doom for three days now. The irony was not lost on her.

Suddenly, a scent began to waft toward their nostrils. It was beyond tempting. It was intoxicating. The smell of grilled meat drifted into their nose and danced across their palate. It seemed to be accompanied by notes of garlic and asparagus. The smell alone hit the starving individuals like a syringe of heroin blasting into a needy addict's veins.

Mark, who had finished up his time with Amelia and a nasty dose of disinfectant, found his feet dragging toward the source of the smell. He passed through the kitchen and tried not to look at the pile in the corner of the room that had been covered. He knew who was under it, and the guilt bit at his soul.

Amelia knew it could not be anything good, but she was drawn to it all the same. She resolved that if it were an attempt on their life, she would want to be with the rest of the survivors anyway. If it were her time to die, she would see her love again. The thought warmed her now-frigid heart.

The unwilling residents of The Arbor found themselves gathered at the head of the dining room. They could hardly believe their eyes. A full set of dinner courses were displayed before them. Seven plates full of deliciously moist bone-in ribeye were set out next to piles of asparagus. In the center of the table were two large bowls of mixed greens. Blue cheese and some kind of berries sat atop the verdant pile and James was hardly alone in his admiration of the meal set before them.

Much to the guests' surprise, Winston sleepily wobbled down the stairs behind them. He looked well rested, for the first time in days, and was the only one of the damned who looked almost put-together.

"What did I miss?" He yawned as he joined the group.

Evelyn turned and slapped him roughly across the face. It sounded almost like a thunderclap as she unwound from her strike.

"Where the *fuck* did you go?" she spoke through narrow lips.

Winston rubbed his face as the blow reddened immediately.

"I don't know what you want me to say, Evelyn! I thought we would have a better chance by separating. The wolves did follow me for a bit before they returned to you and by that point the others had let you into the kitchen. I don't know what you expected me to do against a trio of killer robots while unarmed!"

"I thought you might try to distract them, or at least help once they had broken in!" Evelyn angrily retorted.

"Again, with what? My colossal ego?" Winston repeated. "I don't mean to be upsetting, but there is a delicious meal here, and you are being hysterical."

"*Excuse me?*" Evelyn roared.

A slight microphone feedback chirp filled the bar from speakers that could not be found. The noise seemed to emanate from the walls.

"If you would all be so kind as to join me in the dining room. I have prepared a gift for you."

THIRTEEN

CURIOSITY AND VISCERAL HUNGER ENTANGLED TO DRAW James into the dining room. Eleanor called for him, but he turned his head to reply after he sat down.

"What's the point in ignoring it?" James whined. "It hasn't made a difference so far, and if I'm going to die, I want to do it with a full belly."

Winston shrugged and followed James. Eventually, the resolve of each survivor dropped away until just Alice remained. She decided that she would be more able to defend her family from inside the room, since sticking together meant strength.

Alice felt saliva flood her mouth as she looked down at her dinner. She eyed the choice slab of meat and was quite sure it looked to be the most magnificent steak she had ever seen. The crust was perfect. The asparagus was thick and bathed in butter and garlic. She agreed with James' assessment. They were unlikely to be poisoned twice, and if she avoided the dinner altogether, the next death might have been her own.

Surprisingly, Eleanor was the first to cut into her dinner. She usually liked her meat a bit more done than medium rare, but she was hardly about to refuse the delicacy. The shipping cost of beef from Earth made cuts of real steak prohibitively expensive. The buttery taste exploded in her mouth as herbs and real protein flooded her palate for the first time in months.

"Oh my God," Eleanor moaned in pleasure.

Her feelings were echoed by the other individuals at the table. For a brief few moments, they forgot where they were and who prepared the meal. They laughed together. The girls tried to eat politely, but quickly shook away their inhibitions and proper manners. They ate rapidly, unaware of what was to come.

As the guests finished their food one by one, a pair of arms jutted from the ceiling and pulled their plates into some unknown location. This answered one question for Alice, as to how the plates were delivered in the first place.

Just as the first guests were about to leave the table, the arms dropped covered platters to their seats. James was still picking at his salad, but it was pulled away. He and Eleanor were the only two who were not provided a dish.

"What the hell?" Winston grumbled as he lifted the silver cover. It was not food; it was a manila file folder with the initials W.G. in the label box. He hesitantly flipped it open and was greeted by an image of his mother. She was encircled by crosshairs. The other dining patrons gasped in disgust as they unfolded their "gifts."

Amelia saw her granddaughter with her great-grandchild in arms. Evelyn saw her little cousins, innocently running about their schoolyard on Earth. Mark saw his parents on their porch-swing in one of the few bastions of nature remaining on the planet— sunny Canada.

There were short bulleted biographies of all the friends, family, and loved ones of every adult at the table. It became more and more unsettling as they viewed the daily schedule of anyone worth anything to them. Alice saw her children, James and Eleanor. Their exact schedules including hobbies, intermediate school for James, and even Eleanor's secret rendezvous with various paramours, were detailed precisely. After they had been provided a few minutes to gawk and recoil at the invasion of personal privacy, the voice resumed.

"You are to be provided a choice. Each one of you has a note at the back of your packet."

A lone piece of paper sat with three lines.

Name:

Reason:

Signature:

"This sheet of paper is your painful reprieve." The deep voice paused. "If all of you provide me a name on that paper, you will be granted clemency. List a person who is—undeserving of life. It can be a criminal. It can be an enemy. The listed reason is irrelevant, but the invitation will be extended to them. Once they arrive, you will all be free to leave."

The gears spun in Alice's mind. She felt sick. She knew the implications of this decision. She even knew some prisoners' names she could use. More importantly, she now knew why they were there. It was not an act of kindness.

"They will be provided a one-week's stay at our magnificent Arbor and will remain none the wiser of who has condemned them to this fate. Just as you have been kept innocently oblivious of your executioner's identity."

Most of the room had already begun to place the pieces of the puzzle together, but the revelation was understandably nauseating.

"Who would have chosen us?" Amelia growled.

"I was invited by no one!" Evelyn announced. "This is all a load of nonsense! It's bullshit if I've ever heard it."

"It's true," Alice muttered.

A hush spread through the room as every eye trained itself squarely on her.

"Don't you see," she groaned. "Rose."

"Fuck," Eleanor dropped her face into her hands.

"I betrayed her trust," Alice continued. "I fucked Mark. I shagged my best friend's husband because someone *finally* showed an attraction to me. She did nothing wrong, beside minimizing my romantic struggles, but she complained about him so much. I loved him from the start."

Mark stared at her with clueless eyes. He knew little of the situation, other than the obvious part he had played.

"It was the last straw when she told me she just wanted to get fucked by a stranger on her next vacation. I knew she had cheated on him. I couldn't stand it. He didn't deserve that. He deserved someone who loved him, like I did."

James hung his mouth open. He had not heard a whisper of this. Now with all the ugly details being brought to light, he did not want to believe it.

"It's my fault," Alice murmured. "I've killed Eleanor and James!"

Without hesitation, Alice sprang from her chair. She wanted to vomit. She stormed from the dining room and heard the voice continue behind her.

"You will have 24 hours to choose. Rest well. All must agree to this decision, or all light will be entirely extinguished within these halls."

Alice moved from earshot. Her feet pounded against the stairs as she ran from her culpability. She wanted to escape her life. The only shoulders on which blame could be placed were her own.

Alice was being bombarded by emotion as she entered her

room. She was furious, and the circle of blame seemed to expand in her mind. Rose didn't think. Of course, she didn't. Rose never thought her actions through. She did whatever came naturally, or whatever felt good.

"God!" She screamed, trying to find the right words. "Fuck!"

Alice paced back and forth across her suite. Her rage grew. She understood, of course, why Rose had condemned her.

"Maybe if she'd been true to Mark, he would have been loyal to her!" She muttered, trying to talk through her frustration. *Why couldn't I have been the one to meet him?* Alice thought.

"Why can't I get him out of my *fucking* head!" she steamed. Despite all their past, all their history, and all the reasons she knew he was a bad choice for her—he was Mark. That was all he ever had to be for her.

There would be no tears this time. Anger began to boil deep inside her.

"Have I not suffered enough?" Alice groused. "First my mum, then my brother, now I have two kids, and I lost my best friends in the process."

There was a pounding at her door. Alice stomped to answer the non-verbal request.

"What?" She barked.

"It's El!" A meek voice returned.

Alice opened the door as her chest continued to heave.

"You need to get back down there," Eleanor ordered softly. "They're voting on the proposition, and Evelyn has gotten most of the people to her side. They're really thinking of pushing this nightmare off on someone else!"

Alice cracked her neck sideways in an attempt to release pressure. It failed, but certainly made her feel a degree of relief as it made an awful clicking snap. Eleanor made a disgusted grimace as Alice returned her head to its normal resting position.

"All right," Alice breathed. "Let's go."

The spirited voices of the guests downstairs could be heard as Alice and Eleanor approached the dining room. The women re-entered the room as Mark angrily waved his fist.

"—it feels! Every one of us was invited here by someone who wanted us dead! How could we live with ourselves if we all voted to do a similar horror to the next poor crop of innocents."

"Listen, Boy Scout," Evelyn snapped. "Perhaps you are ready to die for the good of humanity, but I am not. Of course, if we pass this on to the next group, we would inform the authorities upon our exit. That's our only shot at making sure this monster gets justice."

"No, it is not!" Alice contributed. "Evelyn, didn't you see the folder of people who are close to us? That wasn't coincidence. It was a warning. If we tell, those are the loved ones who will die, or worse. We can't tell about it once we get to the surface unless that bastard is dead."

"So what?" Winston shook his head. "You don't have anyone who would be better off dead? I could list any dozens of thieves I have caught. If we all named one, the undeserving would get their just desserts."

"Amelia, is this what William would have wanted?" Eleanor took a low shot at the older woman.

"That's not fair," Evelyn objected. "How dare you? We are all adults, and should all be allowed our own decision."

"Eleanor is right. He would not have condemned another," Amelia agreed. "I'd decided upon a lieutenant who committed vicious atrocities during the war, but it's been almost fifty years. Who am I to pass judgement on what happened a lifetime ago? I am not a murderer."

"Amelia!" Evelyn screamed. "It's all or none! You can't make this decision for all of us."

"And the way I figure it," Alice interjected. "I'm never going to condone something that awful, and neither is Mark. So, if you're ready to kill off at least five more people, then—"

Alice grabbed a steak knife and motored toward Evelyn. She had a look of determination. She was steadfast. Evelyn had the first genuine glance of fear on her face the group had seen. She might not have believed Alice would do it a few days ago, but now anything seemed possible. Evelyn looked to Winston for help. He jolted to intervene but thought better of it when Alice held the blade in his direction.

Alice reached Evelyn and placed an open palm against her chest. She shoved her to the wall roughly and Evelyn raised her hands in defense. Alice touched the blade tip to Evelyn's midriff that had been exposed in their struggle. She trailed the cold steel along her olive skin.

"Alice!" Mark called.

"Shut the fuck up, Mark!" Alice roared. "Now, Evelyn, you seem so keen on murdering five unsuspecting souls, yes?"

Evelyn looked away. She mulled over fighting back, but her father always taught her that the only predictable thing in a knife fight is someone being disemboweled. She held her tongue and waited for the trouble to end. She begged with pleading eyes for Winston to assist, but he began to look almost intrigued by the whole affair.

"Answer me!" Alice ordered as she pushed the steel directly in her bellybutton. Evelyn held her breath to stop the knife from plunging into her gut. "You want to write the letters, don't you? You want those people to die in your place?"

"Yes," Evelyn murmured.

"I didn't catch that, love! Say it like you mean it!" Alice boomed.

"Yes!" Evelyn carefully yelled, trying her best to keep her stomach tight.

"Good. So, you want to take a life?" Alice simmered. Suddenly she roughly grabbed Evelyn's hand. She forced the palm open and stuffed the knife inside. Then Alice dragged the blade to her own throat. "Then fucking do it. Swing the sword. Don't hide behind pen and paper. I would sooner die than condemn someone else. So fucking kill me. End me!"

"Alice, I don't believe you understand what I'm—"

Alice dragged the knife into her skin against Evelyn pulling away. The steel ripped her throat, and she gasped.

"You think I give a damn?" Alice said. "Fucking kill me, or you're probably going to die. Just know you'll have to kill Mark next. You're just like a goddamned politician. I bet it's a hell of a lot easier to sign the order than it is to slit someone else's throat. So, do it. Cross that bridge. Kill me, then kill Mark, and then you're home free."

Evelyn honestly considered it. She was infuriated with Alice, but it was a good gambit. Evelyn highly doubted the others would look at her the same after a pair of murders. Alice had guaranteed her success. Evelyn shook her head and ripped the knife away from Alice's neck.

"I'm getting a goddamn drink and then I think I shall sleep for the next twelve hours," Evelyn angrily whispered. "If you need me, you can kiss my ass and wait."

Evelyn exited the hall. Winston followed just afterward. Mark suddenly saw the line of red dripping down Alice's chest. He waved for Amelia and stood by her side as she tended to Alice's wound.

"Thanks, Amelia," Alice smiled as she absently rubbed the bandage.

"Thank you," Amelia returned. "I'm afraid I quite lost myself back there. I'm pleased you were around to be my conscience. I have not been the same for the past few days."

Alice broke with proper English tradition and suddenly pulled Amelia into an embrace.

"I can't even imagine," Alice whispered. "Seeing my brother that way was challenging enough. I don't think I can fathom what you must be going through."

Amelia did not return the embrace, but she enjoyed it. She was not an emotional woman, but Alice seemed sincere. She patted Alice on the back and released herself from the hold.

"Thank you, dear." Amelia gave a warm half-smile. "I dare say I might have needed that."

Alice squeezed the aged woman's shoulder as Amelia stuffed the medical equipment back in her satchel. She exited the dining room without a word.

"All right come on then," Mark grabbed Alice by the arm and pulled upward. "We are going to the common room and warming up with hot chocolate. All of us."

Eleanor looked at James, who shrugged in response.

"We should be preparing for the next attack or sleeping," Alice weakly protested. She hated to admit just how good a moment of relaxation sounded.

"We will prepare—later," Mark assured. "We have twenty-four hours. That's like an eternity compared to what we have been allotted before."

Mark was right. The barricade had been rebuilt before dinner. They had readied for an assault and were still as prepared as they had been earlier. She turned naturally to the children.

"Are you both all right with that?" Alice asked.

Eleanor wanted to kick Mark. She hated him, but he had Alice's back when no one else did. She owed him a moment of acquiescence.

"Fine with me." Eleanor grinned.

Alice turned her head to James who had bit down on his lips in anticipation. He nodded silently.

The quartet of emotionally worn individuals wandered their way to the familiar warm fire that offered a small degree of comfort. Mark announced he was going to make the cocoa and dashed back in the direction they'd come from. Alice sat in the middle of the couch and was flanked by her adopted charges. She threw her arms around the niece and nephew she'd hardly taken the time to really know before this mess. She gave a light kiss to James on his forehead.

Alice had an epiphany. The children whose existence she had recently viewed as a burden were now the two foremost things keeping her sane.

"I love you both so much," Alice said. "I'm sorry it took all this for me to realize what I'd been given."

James set a small trio of fingers over her mouth and shushed her.

"For someone who never had kids, I think you're a brilliant parent."

The children sat contentedly. The eye of the storm was passing overhead, and they had been provided a brief relief from the battering torment of The Arbor. They rested for several minutes with no warm beverages in their hands. After some more time had passed, Alice looked back toward the kitchen. She sat up a bit and heard nothing, not that she should have.

"I'm going to go make sure he doesn't need any help," she announced as she stood from her warm and comfortable position. "Don't go anywhere. I'll be right back!"

James bobbed his head and rested his eyes as he leaned against one of the throw pillows. Alice shuffled past the black pile in the center of reception and pushed her way into the shredded kitchen door. Mark stood over a sauce-pot and stirred with a long spoon. He smiled at Alice but returned to his duty immediately.

"I burned the cream the first time. This is batch two. Sorry to be standoffish, but I'm not to be responsible for a second spoiled batch of cocoa."

"Far be it from me to stand in the way of a scrumptious beverage," Alice chuckled. She felt a peculiar kind of relaxation. She knew the trouble was eons away from reaching its end, but something about the unexpected infusion of time made her feel like this was the intermission in an awful performance that would not end.

Alice tapped her fingers against the countertop. She leaned over it, unsure of herself.

"Can I do anything to help?" Alice asked.

"Hah! I would say you've done a great deal of that already," Mark smiled. "I knew you had a spark in you, my dear, but your leadership has been extraordinary. No, I would say making cocoa would be an excellent contribution I am quite able to handle on my own."

Alice felt her face warm at the compliment. She was confident in her career skills but still was quite incapable of accepting praise without the urge to vehemently deny it out of reflex. She had to consciously remind herself that someone was telling her nice things and that the polite thing to do was to say "thank you" without repudiating their assessment.

"Thank you," Alice trimmed her retort. "I don't think I see myself the way you do, but I appreciate the kind words nonetheless."

Mark flicked the gas burner to the off position and stirred the pot as he turned around.

"Obviously not, or you'd be walking around a like a football star."

Alice tilted her head ever so slightly. Her eyes narrowed, and she cast a doubting glance over Mark.

"And what is that supposed to mean?" she wondered.

"Just that." Mark broke off to collect his thoughts. "You are so damn wonderful. You seem to be outstanding at everything you put your hand to. I am a bit jealous in truth. I remember when I first met you back in college. You were learning to play the violin because you loved its romantic sound. I realized after a few months of watching you improve that you hadn't been taking lessons. It boggled my brain that you could just pick up an instrument and figure it out like that."

Alice opened her mouth but couldn't articulate the way she felt. She let her head wobble a bit before she offered him an open and unashamed smile.

"All right, that's enough." She rolled her eyes. "I'm not good at everything. That's not fair."

Mark turned back around and grabbed a bottle of vanilla that he had set aside for the recipe. He poured a little into the cap and dumped it into the brew.

"Fine, I'll bite. What is it Alice Trudeau has struggled with?" Mark mused.

"Well," Alice pondered. "For one thing, I have positively awful anxiety, a pretty poor self-image, and I tend toward impulsive decisions when my feelings are involved." She drifted away. She was easily able to list her faults and dwell on far more than what she was telling Mark. She was condescending, a perfectionist, overly critical of those around her, she had a bad sense of direction, and she was hardly modest about her intelligence. There was more.

"I'm depressed," she admitted.

"About what?" Mark shot back.

"No." Alice looked at the ceiling. "I really struggle with depression, like clinically. It's quite awful."

Alice hated even saying that word. She thought verbalizing it would make the wave crash over her again. Her depression had been particularly insidious since her mother's death, but it had haunted her for almost as long as she could remember.

It always came and went like an assassin. She would realize that her mood was imbalanced suddenly as she was chewing out a family member for something completely innocuous. For the longest time, Alice had kept it to herself. She'd lay in bed feeling more and more guilty about her inaction from day to day. When she finally was able to rouse, she beat herself up about the time she'd wasted lying about. Finally, she'd sought help.

For Alice, working with her psychiatrist was the right choice. She paired medical intervention with counseling from a psychologist and clawed her way out of the despair that had begun to so entirely swallow her life and joy.

"I'm sorry, Alice," Mark reassured. "I had no idea. My mum had something similar, and it really wreaked havoc on her life."

"It's fine. I've got it under control now," Alice explained. "I appreciate that you didn't say 'oh, I get depressed all the time, too,' like being sad is somehow the same thing as a medical condition."

Mark nodded. "I think people get uncomfortable when you tell them something like that. They want so desperately to relate that they make connections that aren't necessarily the same situation."

"I'm not trying to be preachy," Alice apologized. "I just—I was careful with my words when I said my mood was within control now. It still *tries* to gallop away from me on a monthly basis. There isn't a day that goes by where I don't wonder if a stressful situation is manufactured by my anxious mind, or if it is really an issue."

Mark set down four mugs onto the counter in front of Alice. He looked about the kitchen while trying to listen earnestly. Finally, his eyes searched out the tool he needed.

"Alice, darling, could you get me that funnel?" he asked. Alice obliged and reached over her shoulder to grab the funnel that hung on the wall behind her. She brought it to the first mug and held it in place while Mark poured the finished product from the pan into its destination. He cleared his throat. "Sorry, you were saying?"

"Right." Alice looked up slightly at him. He was closer than she would have liked now. Her pulse quickened the way it always did when she was near him. "I'm just trying to say it's a part of me. I am never going to be rid of it, and really, that's okay. Everyone has things they need to work through, and this is mine."

Mark finished pouring the last mug of chocolate and ran some water in the pan. He was more than a little disappointed that there were no marshmallows to finish the delicious dish. He loaded the mugs onto a small serving tray and felt content with the finished product.

"Shall we go?" Alice asked.

Her face was so close to his now. The dramatic curve of Alice's cheek was just as striking as it had always been. Her shimmering teal eyes were in stark contrast to the dark brunette hair Mark had always found so mesmerizing.

Alice was not someone likely to be featured as a centerfold in a gentleman's quarterly. She wasn't going to be a cover girl for a makeup ad, but she was completely unforgettable. Her beauty was timeless, with her perfectly symmetrical features and her almost royal carriage. She was elegance incarnate and would have been intimidating to the common man. Mark was far from ubiquitous himself.

He grasped the sides of her face. Instinct had taken over now. Her proximity was too intense. She burned into him like a star. Mark drew her in. Alice put up no resistance.

"We should go," she softly protested as she wrapped her arm around his neck.

Their lips met with trepidation at first. They brushed each other like estranged friends. Then Alice placed a second hand to his chest. She felt the hard frame of the man she'd loved since the day they met. She took in a deep gasp as his arm pulled against the small of her back and closed the already narrow gap between them.

Outside the kitchen, Eleanor had come to check up on her Aunt Alice. She pushed into the room to assist but backpedaled before the otherwise-engaged pair had seen her. Eleanor was disgusted by Mark. He was a liar, a cheat, and often manipulative. But she also forced herself to remember how he was the only one who held the line at dinner just a few moments before. She recalled his unfaltering loyalty and willingness to protect her and James when Alice was unable to.

Alice was simply dreadful in her sense of timing, but Eleanor decided to give her the benefit of the doubt in this case. She waited until she heard some chuckling in the room to push through the kitchen door.

"Oh God, El!" Alice exclaimed. "So sorry we took so long. The cocoa is on its way!"

Alice hoisted the tray without saying a word to Mark. She thanked Eleanor as she passed through the kitchen door, and Mark walked blissfully behind her. Alice was so delirious she didn't hear Eleanor's hand slap its way into the doorframe to block Mark. He almost ran into her as he came back into reality.

"I don't like you," Eleanor stated coldly.

"Oh, I'm sorry, Eleanor. Did I do something to—"

"Shh," she continued. "Alice does. Anything with anyone else is over now, yes?"

Mark suddenly understood her meaning.

"Definitely," Mark replied.

"You'll not toy with her or use her. If I see anything but gentleman-like behavior, I'll make my feelings known to Alice, and the whole thing will be over. We are her family. You may audition. I hope I'm clear."

"Crystalline." Mark nodded.

"Good." Eleanor straightened her frown into an indetermi-nate line across her face. "You seem to make her happy, even if I don't understand why. If you ever do anything to the contrary, the killer will be the least of your concerns."

"I understand, and I'll do my best."

"No." Eleanor lightly tapped her hand to his. "You'll do better, because that's exactly what she deserves. You can't know what a wonderful woman she is or how much she means to James and me."

"I've got an idea." Mark grinned as he looked past Eleanor to see Alice wandering to the common room.

"I hope so, because the worst is yet to come. Your strength of character will be put to the fire along with everyone else." Eleanor backed a few steps out of the door before jogging back to Alice.

"You didn't have to do that, you know," Alice spoke without turning her head as they entered the common room. "But it was really sweet."

"You know me." Eleanor winked. "I'm positively confectionary."

Eleanor nudged James as she returned to the couch. The boy had been getting a head-start on his sleep, but he'd obviously cho-sen to interrupt this for his long-awaited beverage. The four social-ized and drank as though nothing were wrong. They commented on the richness of the cocoa, the obvious absence of whipped cream and marshmallows, and how right it felt to sit before the fire.

While they wove a fantasy, Rose wandered by the happy gathering. She wanted no part of it. She wished to be swallowed by her guilt. Rose still hadn't succumbed to her tendency for alcoholic relief, but her deep and bitter dissatisfaction at life haunted her.

Rose knew Alice loathed her. Any goodwill she had earned was null and void. She wished for the darkness offered by a hunt.

She thought the twenty-four hours of light might be more insufferable than the infusions of darkness. She needed one now.

She staggered to the coat closet, and shutting herself inside, she let tears that she'd been a stranger to escape their ocular prison. She just wanted the dark to swallow her. She felt the same pull she had felt a week ago, when she'd signed Alice Trudeau's name to that paper. Rose always knew the darkness was inside her. She liked to hide it behind shiny trinkets and massive men, but it lingered. Like a shadow that grew ever closer, she became more and more tempted toward larger misdeeds.

It was easy to disguise the malice. Rose felt good doing bad things. It was cathartic to scribble her enemy's moniker there on the invitation to The Arbor. She'd felt a rush of pleasure, knowing that Alice would die for what she'd done to her. Her vindictive streak was massive. Rose had managed to justify cheating on Mark because of what he'd said one night or another, but her logic was flimsy at best. She enjoyed causing pain.

Rose loved to steal things that weren't hers while she guarded her own possessions ferociously. People thought she was unintelligent. It was probably better that way. She sat in the silence only a padded room could offer and beat against the shadow that ate at her soul. Wicked ideas slithered their way into her consciousness. Rose felt as though she was being divided in two as she argued with herself and her mood swung widely. She became so angry at the littlest of things.

Why wouldn't she just let herself drink? Why couldn't she find happiness apart from this evil side of herself? What had she done to deserve these demons? What was that infernal beeping noise?

She stuffed a few items of clothing against the wall where it originated from at the back of her hideaway. Why would the bloody console be beeping anyway? Whatever it was, it could wait.

FOURTEEN

THE HOURS PASSED IDLY. NO ONE WANTED TO acknowledge that their respite from combat would be ending soon. No one wished for another death. Evelyn wandered her way to the basement. The cool moist air licked her skin as she stood in dim light.

A man with a lit cigarette stood in the corner. His silhouette stood out against the stark white light flooding in through the hole in the basement ceiling.

"You're late," he grunted.

"You'll be patient, because I'm worth it," Evelyn smirked.

"Debatably," Winston growled as he stamped his cancer-stick out in the clay of the basement floor.

"Listen, if you're here to apologize—"

"I'm not," he whipped back.

Evelyn tilted her head and examined the stoic demeanor of Winston. He wasn't quite acting like himself. Something was different. Something was wrong. She was offended. She was just so angry with him. She was curious.

"You've got about a minute before I walk away," she snapped.

Winston laughed heartily as he moved to the center of the room and into the white spotlight.

"Ms. Fox is curious, is she?" he teased.

"Less so by the second," Evelyn griped. "Get to it."

"Yes, right," Winston shrugged. "What I gave you this evening was plausible deniability. Our plan had been found out by the boy; you see. The others were watching you."

"I suppose. But regardless of any enmity I held toward Alice before, she did save my life. How will her dying benefit me now?"

"Only that." Winston closed the space between them. "We would stand a great chance of escaping this thing scott-free if Alice, and those who think like her, were eliminated."

Evelyn tasted his scent now. Winston was so close to her.

"If we went with your plan . . ." Evelyn mused. "Would the killer accept our letters luring others here?"

"He would probably enjoy the show. I hardly view him as one to stand on tradition. The least we could do is try."

"Yes," Evelyn agreed, feeling a warmth from between her legs. "We could do a great many things, couldn't we? Do you think the whole thing is being recorded? Even down here?"

Winston grabbed Evelyn's hips and spun her to face the wooden wall holding the earth back. He lifted her skirt and kissed down her back.

"Would it bother you, if he was watching us even now?" Winston breathed the words against her arched spine.

Evelyn groaned and dug her fingers into his scalp. She pressed his head farther down her slender curves and then braced herself against the harsh unfinished wood. She let out a low sigh that almost resembled a purr as she rolled her eyes.

"I don't think it would. We definitely shouldn't be doing this. It's so *wrong*. There's a mangled corpse not four feet above our heads. God, you're fucking sick. You dis—" Evelyn gasped deeply.

She clapped a hand over her mouth. "You *disgust* me. You're a fucking coward. You're worse, a damned pervert."

"Am I?" He stopped.

Evelyn moaned in frustration. She looked over her shoulder and saw a hand rushing at her neck. He forced her bandaged face against the wall as he entered her from behind. She was powerless against his strength. Not that she had any desire to escape her punishment.

Suddenly, the kitchen door swung loudly upstairs. Evelyn braced her hand against his hips as the unknown person wandered about. She placed a finger to her lips as the refrigerator was pulled open.

Winston fought against her pleading hand and slowly continued. He tugged hard against her tank top and freed her from any inhibiting clothes as he grabbed the reins of loose garments that hung around her midriff. He continued, and Evelyn bit down hard against her lower lip. She tried desperately not to let a sound escape her panting mouth.

Amelia absently exited the kitchen with a loaf of bread and various cuts of meat and cheese. She had resolved to make the group sandwiches for the next day so that lunch wouldn't have to be a consideration. She felt like she needed to keep busy. The sadness would take her if she sat still, and she wouldn't allow herself to become a burden to the group.

She ran through a list of what needed to be accomplished in her head. *Refill candles, rebuild pyre, use ashes to minimize odors around those who have passed. What else needed to be done?* She wondered.

The sneaking thoughts tore at her relentlessly, like she was forgetting something. It bothered her so much. What was she forgetting? She considered herself a very independent woman, and yet she missed William so much. He'd helped to keep her often-scattered mind on track, even if it only needed a nudge in the right direction. They'd compensated for each other's weaknesses. William was often rash and failed to think of little things in an everyday situation, while Amelia was often overly cautious and concerned with being perfectly prepared, sometimes to an extreme degree.

She tried to imagine William telling her to let it go and begin on her list. Usually, once she started working, she would remember the lesser thing she'd forgotten. She needed to remind herself now. Rose came out of the coat closet to join her.

"Can I help?" she asked, eyeing the loaves of bread.

Amelia nodded, and the women made an assembly line of sorts. Rose spread condiments on the bread and passed the open halves to Amelia. The moment was disturbingly normal to her. For a little while, they weren't trapped in a nightmarish hell which threatened their lives; they were just preparing food. It was calming to Rose. She suddenly thought back to the happy days of her childhood.

"I used to help my mum like this, you know. Whatever we were making, she would find some way to let me assist." Rose thought back. "She was a kind woman. Everyone always compared her to me after she passed."

Amelia frowned and placed a hand on Rose's knee.

"So sorry to hear that, dear. What was her name?"

"Kelly," Rose answered. "But everyone called her Kel. She didn't have a mean bone in her body. Everyone looked up to her. She was a real paragon of our community. She died when I was fourteen."

"I can't imagine how I would have grown up without my mother," Amelia sighed. "It's a testament to your resilience, my dear."

"Oh, I don't think so." She rolled her lips together. "When

she died, I faked it as best I could, but people saw through me. I wasn't good like her. My father saw it, too. He saw what was in me. He hated it."

"What do you mean?" Amelia asked. "What did he do?"

"Well," Rose sighed. "First it was just comments like, 'all the good women in my life are dead now,' and 'Quite sure you can come to church with me? Wouldn't want you to burst into flames.' Then he started drinking."

Amelia watched the way she discussed the emotional abuse like it was normal. The girl had suffered more than Amelia had realized at a very formative age.

"He'd come home plastered and drone on about how it should have been me who died. He said I had the devil in me. He'd beat me senseless. I didn't spend much time at home after that. His mind was pretty much gone after a few years."

Amelia reeled at the casual revelation. She was not sure how to approach the trauma. On the one hand, Rose had done a terrible thing drawing Alice and her children to this place. On the other, Rose was still a person, detestable as her actions were. She'd undergone something terrible and was still deserving of pity.

"Rose, that's dreadful to hear. No one deserves that," Amelia comforted.

"Not even me, you mean?" Rose saw through her carefully chosen words. Amelia looked away in embarrassment.

"Rose, I did not mean for it to come out that way," Amelia apologized. "We have all made errors in judgement. What is important is that you work past those and begin bettering the lives of people around you. I have not seen you pick up a drink in a day or so. That is progress."

"It's the least I can do, I'm sure," Rose shrugged. "Who knows what this psychopath might have in store for us next? I just want to be an asset instead of a liability."

"It's a start down the path, love." Amelia shook Rose's knee before withdrawing her hand.

The two continued their work in relative silence. Neither one was quite sure where to take the conversation from where they left it. Rather than putting forth a futile effort, they sat in a positively English quiet for the remainder of their time together.

Around three in the morning, the lights had all but disappeared in the Arbor. For the first time in what seemed like ages, the residents were tucked neatly in their bedrooms. Alice looked over on a sleeping pair of heads in the king-sized bed as she brushed her teeth. She considered joining them, but restlessness stormed her mind. It raced over the events that clouded what should have been a calming release.

For the last few days, Alice had been a leader. There was no doubting that. She had kept many people alive but doubted her overall effectiveness in the long run. Someone had still died at each hunt. The killer had gotten his way. Perhaps her efficacy was manufactured by her own mind and by others' opinions. She spat out toothpaste and splashed her face. No, Alice wasn't ready for bed at all. She should have been. She felt exhausted. She wondered if a light snack before bed might make her feel better.

She quietly tiptoed out of the room and locked the door behind her. She turned toward the exit of the stairwell but saw light peeking from under room two on her way by. Straightaway, she was sure of what she wanted.

Alice rapped lightly on the door. She shook her head impatiently and tapped her foot. She started turning back round to go to her room as light from the door flooded the darkened hallway. Mark's tired face squinted to see who it was in the darkness.

"Alice, it's late. Is everything all right?" he asked, cinching his robe tighter and tying the cord into a small bow.

"Yeah, it's fine." Alice shifted her foot uncomfortably. "I am just having a bit of trouble sleeping. Can I come in?"

"I—um, yeah, of course," Mark struggled to sound neutral. "Come right in, and I'll make us a cuppa with chamomile and lemon. Hopefully that will solve our insomnia problem."

"That sounds lovely." Alice smiled as she followed him inside.

His room was much the same as the ones on the other side of the hotel, but it had a small fireplace tucked into the corner by the window. The cylindrical stone construction ran up to the ceiling and appeared to run on gas like the one downstairs.

"Make yourself comfortable," Mark said lightly. "I'm going to put the pot on, and then change into something more appropriate for company."

Alice rubbed her hands together and felt her muscles relax as the warmth of the hearth began to flood over her. She dragged a pillow down from the bed and plopped herself in front of the source of heat. She rolled her shoulders back and heard the typical crackling of tense joints.

When Mark emerged from the bathroom, he was clothed in a light tank and long pajama pants. Alice was dressed much the same, but her outfit was lavender-colored and had frills on the edges of its satin and tiny delicate straps holding up the camisole.

He took a blanket from one of the armchairs in the room and grabbed a throw pillow. He laid the pillow down first and then leaned back against the bed as the pair stared toward the tiny roaring fire.

"So—" Alice began.

"Should I—" Mark started at the same time.

The two laughed, and Mark held his palm out toward his conversation partner.

"You first."

"All right," Alice resumed. "I was going to say, we need to talk about what happened earlier—in the kitchen."

Mark drew in a deep breath. He opened his mouth but closed it again.

"I have been racking my brain to come up with a way to say that I'm sorry for that," he muttered. "This is—the most awful situation anyone could imagine. I know now is hardly the right time to consider any feelings that might have been laying beneath the surface. It wasn't fair of me to—"

"Mark, stop," Alice ordered. She shook her head and leaned forward on her palms to place a kiss over his lips. "I would not have come here at our only time of rest to berate you about situationally appropriate behaviors. You are right. It's not a good time. Unfortunately, it is our only time."

Alice hopped to her feet before Mark could stop her. She unplugged the small kettle and poured piping hot water into a pair of mugs. She dropped the tea infusers into their cups and turned back to where he still sat.

Alice set a tray full of saucers with cups of hot tea, milk, sugar, and napkins on the stone floor in front of them. She tipped a tiny bit of milk into hers and offered the same to Mark. Mark dropped a cube of sugar into his tea but did not offer one to Alice.

"Not trying to be rude, but I know how you like it," Mark said.

"Do you, Mark?" Alice smirked.

Mark's heart thumped as Alice took his words for more than he meant them. He thought of correcting her but realized that it would certainly be wiser to remain quiet in this occasion. He stirred his cup and sipped.

"Delightful," he sighed with satisfaction. "Just—perfect."

He looked down at Alice's slender calves peeking out from under her pants. They were ivory-colored and had none of the spotting her chest and shoulders shared. Her skin reflected the firelight like a mirror. It was so bright and radiant.

Alice felt her chest warm. She could let him enjoy the view for hours. The way his eyes surveyed her body made her feel desired. She knew she was pretty at times, but Mark could make her feel beautiful with a single glance.

She hadn't come for tea, after all.

"Mark, you should know, I don't see how it would ever work with us—in the future," Alice yanked him back toward reality.

"Why is that?" Mark was taken aback

"We just—" Alice waved her hand about in little circles while she tried to summon the right words. "We have so much baggage between us. Could I ever be more than someone who broke up my best friend's marriage? What would it be like starting a relationship based on cheating?"

Mark huffed. He felt the wind drop from his sails as he leaned back into the bed.

"I don't know, Alice. I really hadn't thought that far ahead."

Alice saw the effect she was having. This was not the intention at the start of the conversation.

"Wait, I think that came out wrong. Let me start over." Alice cleared her throat. "I don't know what the future holds for us, but I know what I want—now. You've always made me so happy, and I know I did the same for you. I just want to enjoy that."

A bewildered expression stretched across Mark's visage. One moment he was discouraged, and the next he was apparently beloved. Raising his gaze from the floor to Alice, he saw that she'd moved several feet closer to him.

"You mean?" Mark let his question hang, sounding cautiously optimistic.

"Sex, Mark. Companionship. I want you to hold me until I forget that I'm surrounded by death and damnation. I've always loved you, and I don't know what will happen if or when we get out, but I know that I want to let go of my over-calculating side and just enjoy life while I have it."

The dumbest of grins spread uncontrollably across Mark's face.

"Are you sure?" Mark clarified. "I have so much respect for you, and I know we made some rash decisions in the past."

"Is that it?" Alice lifted her shoulders.

"What?"

"Is that your one gentlemanly protest?" she clarified.

Mark gulped down another swallow of tea and set the cup on its saucer. He slid the tray out of arms' reach and sat up. Without exerting much effort, he scooped up Alice under her shoulders and knees. She wrapped her arms around his neck and giggled lightly as she allowed herself to be hoisted.

He didn't rush with her. Alice was like a fine wine among light beers. Mark savored her scent. He let his hand drift under her shirt and up her spine. Alice breathed in as he brushed the small of her back. She pulled herself up to his lips and pecked kisses down his jaw and onto his neck.

Alice melted as he ran his other hand down the back of her thighs. She eagerly kissed his lips again and pushed her tongue into his mouth. Suddenly, she broke the embrace and pushed off from his body.

Mark looked with confusion to her for a moment. Wondering if he'd done something wrong. Alice stared longingly toward Mark as she reached toward the base of her top and lifted it over her head.

Mark let his eyes linger. Her breathing quickened as he looked up and down her body. His fingers danced at her waistband as he delicately pulled while dropping kisses down her chest.

The two had little trouble staying warm the rest of the night.

Alice snapped awake in the morning. She grabbed Mark's watch from the nightstand.

"Shit!" she cursed. "Oh, goddammit, I just know Eleanor will be up by now. I can't believe I overslept. Fuck!"

Alice scrambled around the room snatching up what limited

articles of clothing she'd entered with. Mark watched with a sly grin as he tossed her bottoms to her waiting grip.

"Would it be so bad if anyone knew you had spent some time with me?" Mark sighed.

Alice raised an eyebrow. "Let's say they did. Suddenly I'm the slut who couldn't keep it in her pants while everyone is getting murdered around her."

"Well, that's not fair. What's to say I didn't seduce you?" Mark smirked and puffed out his chest. "Maybe it wouldn't be viewed as your fault."

Alice rolled her eyes. She let out a frustrated huff of air as she looked around for her other slipper. "Mark, I'm glad you don't see the one-sided prejudices that rule the public eye, but I can assure you—that's not the way it would happen." Alice pulled her brows together at the injustice of it all. "You'd probably have a receiving line of high-fives while they adhered my scarlet letter."

Mark was wiser than he used to be. Rather than debate the flustered woman, he dropped to the opposite side of the bed and peeped under in search of her missing shoe.

Alice looked at the watch again. It was almost 9 am now. She groaned and resigned herself to an Oedipal lopsided exit. She turned the door handle but was intercepted by Mark who turned her face for a quick peck on the lips.

"No matter what happens . . ." Mark trailed off. "You have my heart. You know that, don't you?"

Alice groaned. A pained expression changed to one of love and flip-flopped again.

"Jesus, Mark." Alice struggled. "You know I've always—well, we have been great, but I just don't think now is the right time. I'd be willing—that is, if you wanted to—to start fresh as friends back at Villanova. We'd need to be more than just, what happened last night. I'd have to—"

"Shh." Mark placed a finger to her lips. "I'm patient. You're worth it. Last night was great, but I'm not going ring shopping yet."

Alice noticed the "yet" at the end of Mark's sentence. She didn't have the luxury of being able to consider it further. She patted his chest as she unevenly walked back into the hallway. It was dead quiet. There was some activity downstairs, but she was alone and able to sneak back into her room successfully.

Alice unlocked, opened, and shut, their door with swiftness. The bedroom was still dark. She slid the lock closed behind her and tiptoed to the bathroom. She flattened her hair a bit and made it look like she had just woken up.

When she got back to the bed, she saw the children sleeping peacefully. Alice breathed a sigh of relief as Eleanor rolled over.

"You finally up?" Eleanor stretched skyward.

"Yes, I just had to use the bathroom," Alice told the truth, but only just.

"Mmmhmm." Eleanor gave a slightly sarcastic nod. "How was the bed? Did you have enough room?"

Alice had to be careful there. She didn't want to lie to Eleanor, but she also had no desire to advertise her behavior or sleeping arrangements from the night before.

"Oh, I actually had a lot of trouble getting to sleep, so I decided not to crowd you children and went—"

Eleanor wore a teasing expression. She drooped a pointing finger down to Alice's one bare foot.

"I suppose I should clarify." She clucked with a cracking voice. "Did you have enough room in *Mark's* bed?"

Alice stifled a chuckle and felt a swell of pink overwhelm both cheeks. She looked away and rubbed her eyes.

"Oh God, it's that obvious?" Alice groaned.

"To me," Eleanor replied. "And I should add that your secret is safe. As much as I might disapprove of your choices and timing. You must do what makes you happy. You deserve that much."

Alice smiled at Eleanor. She mouthed a thank you.

"You're just amazing, you know that?" Alice complimented her niece. She grabbed clothes for the day and washed her face. They had a few scant hours left to burn before the revolving horror began again.

Downstairs, Amelia was placing the finishing touches on her breakfast for her fellow survivors. Rose assisted, contributing all that she could to the meal. Rose was putting in a real effort. She had caused so much damage. She suppressed her urges. Real guilt was pressing down on her soul, and the force was strong enough to hold back the wicked desires within her.

Amelia was thankful for the company, even if it was Rose. Despite Rose's awful past, she seemed repentant. It might have all been a deception, but Amelia had no patience for holding grudges now.

Alice burst through the door with a smile, then her eyes met Rose's uncertain stare.

"I was going to see if you needed any assistance, but I see you have help." Alice's morning perkiness was spoiled at the sight of the woman who'd sentenced her to death.

"Well, no, it's fine," Rose mumbled. "I'll just take my plate out, and you can do whatever you like."

Amelia tapped her nails against the countertop. It was like listening to a passive aggressive verbal war.

"Stop!" Amelia shouted, slapping a flat hand to the cutting board beside her. "You two need to work this dilemma out. Now. I don't mind staying to mediate, but I will not have a second set of people exchanging verbal blows and remaining incapable of standing in the same room. Alice, state your piece and do it quickly."

The women stood in stunned silence. Neither wanted to talk

about what had to be discussed, but there was not much getting around it with a lady as determined as Amelia forcing the issue.

"Well," Alice began with reluctance. "Despite your recent change of heart, there is no getting around the obvious. You are responsible for bringing me here, and by proxy, you have now put Eleanor and James in grave danger. How do we come back from that?"

Rose steepled her fingers together. She rolled them along her chin as she thought about Alice's words.

"I don't think we can," Rose admitted. "There are no words I can say to make up for my actions, just like what happened with Mark. Despite that, I think we can move past it with time. What happened is done. Nothing can change that. I can't ask forgiveness. I can just—show you that I am making choices that you'd be proud of."

Alice shook her head from side to side. There was anger brewing inside her. Comparing a death sentence to cheating sounded a bit too Old Testament for her. When she'd been in Sunday school, she'd found the extreme punishments of the Bible's first half almost laughable.

"Rose." Alice held her tongue back from lashing out. "While I can really appreciate your words, you understand why I have a hard time reconciling the inequity of it all, don't you?"

Inequity? Rose thought. It was so like Alice to toss about large words indicating just how superior her position was to Rose's. It was typical, storybook Alice.

"Yes, I will admit the two are not alike," Rose conceded. "I was just saying the situations were similar. I know forgiveness is out of reach for you, just as it was for me when you had sex with my husband. The situation is ugly and—"

"Completely different!" Alice interrupted. "I'm sorry. I fucked Mark. That is true. Shall we discuss the number of times you went to the pub and left with a stranger while he was working on his stories?"

Rose ground her teeth together. She maintained control, even as Alice was beginning to lose it.

"I know you don't mean that the way it sounds. It makes me—frustrated—when you see fit to criticize my marriage post-mortem. You're not an archaeologist, dear. Stop digging in the past. I'm trying to move through our current situation, and it seems like you are working to blame shift on what is ancient history!"

Who was this woman standing before Alice? Rose was a flibbertigibbet. She was light-hearted and about as mighty as a mouse with verbal arguments. Her use of proper psychological terms really threw Alice for a loop. Worse, her argument was sound. Alice struggled to bite back with a reply.

"Rose!" Alice huffed. She breathed angrily through her nose in deep inhales and exhales. She needed to say something, anything! "You . . . you are right. Shit, you're right."

Amelia grinned at the admission as she continued to listen. Perhaps the only thing harder than admitting fault is doing so when a person so wants to be in the right.

"It was an excuse," Alice agreed. "You had what, who, I wanted so forlornly. God, I loved him, Rose. It killed me to see you just— I'm doing it again. I'm sorry. He was your husband. I was your best friend. Nothing I can say will make what I did okay. I'm going to stop trying now."

Rose was floored. She'd almost never seen Alice lose an argument, much less one with her. Rose didn't quite know what to say.

"Thank you, Alice," Rose breathed mournfully. "We aren't even. I know that. What I did was so much worse. I know that. You shouldn't have to endure the calamity that I've wrought upon your family, but it's done. All I can do is swear to you, I'll protect those children until my dying breath."

Alice gave a reluctant nod. That was one thing they could do for each other. Despite their differences, Rose and Alice could agree that the children needed to be protected above everything else.

Satisfied that nothing could top Rose's words, Alice approached Rose with an outstretched hand. Rose saw her gesture and touched a palm to her heart. As Alice approached, Rose spread her arms wide for a hug.

Alice stopped dead in her tracks.

"We aren't there yet, Rose."

Rose pouted slightly in protest but accepted the handshake.

Amelia allowed no time for awkward pauses. She handed each of the girls a platter of steaming breakfast food. The scent billowed to Alice's waiting nose and caused her mouth do drop open in anticipation of the second most enjoyable activity of her morning.

The women delivered the trays to a waiting table of residents. The guests had almost become used to eating like kings over the past twelve hours. It would be equal parts disappointing and unsatisfying to return to a life of snacking and scrounging for survival.

No one was entirely sure how far apart the next hazards would be, but their approach was inexorable. It marched forward like an awful tide of calamity. The survivors could construct defenses. They could fight. They could band together, but they were all still playing his game. Alice speculated as to how they could change that.

She wasn't able to reflect in peace for long.

Alice had told herself that Mark meant nothing. Last night was for fun. There was a zero percent chance of their affair having a long-term shelf life. All those truths aside, her heart thumped as his exhausted gaze met her eyes. She was cognizant of exactly *why* those eyes were tired, and Alice felt her chest flush and present itself like a cardinal in heat.

"Mark!" She greeted him with a touch of overzealousness as he pulled out a chair beside her. "Hey! Good morning! How'd you sleep?"

Mark turned away from the others and raised an eyebrow.

James and Eleanor sat across from the pair. The boy looked on with a blissful ignorance. He chomped on diced potatoes and onions while cutting into a sausage patty. Eleanor lacked the delight of ignorance. She groaned obviously while retrieving a healthy portion of bacon with her fork. Eleanor repeatedly stabbed with more force each stroke, picking up an excess of bacon as she tried to subtly grab Alice's attention.

"Jeez, El!" James exclaimed, utterly wowed by her gratuitous portions. "You're gonna be sick!"

"I already feel a bit queasy, James," Eleanor grunted. She slid the strips of delicious pork from her fork by sliding a butter knife down the tines. The blade scraped down the silver with an awful scratch and clattered against the plate with a bit of force.

Finally, Eleanor had managed to wrest away Alice's attention from her dreamy bliss.

"Oh my, Amelia!" Alice kept up her pep to avoid suspicion. "You have truthfully excelled this morning. I don't even want to consider how early you had to rise to prepare this extensive array of heaven."

"Probably three in the morning at the latest, right?" Eleanor chuckled but addressed her question to Amelia.

Mark coughed up a bite of egg.

"Oh, not that early, love," Amelia returned. "An experienced cook can prepare a meal like this in a pair of hours at most. I believe I started the cook around seven in the morning?"

"Well, you are a woman of remarkable gifts," Eleanor cajoled. "I hope I've a degree of your exceptionality when I've reached—your measure of experience."

"Measure of experience?" Amelia repeated. "That's a flowery way of saying old, darling, but you're right. I was 'experienced' thirty years ago. Now I'm borderline geriatric."

"If more grandparents cooked like this, assisted living facilities would go bankrupt," Mark added with a grin.

"Well here's to the elimination of granddaddy daycares!" Winston declared, raising his glass of juice like a spire.

"*Enough!*"

The abyssal voice thundered, and the cheery room froze. No one wanted to acknowledge the furious announcement. They sat in bewilderment as the voice continued.

"You were provided an absolution, and you tossed my kindness back like an unwanted plaything! I am *not* a fool! My gracious spirit has been taken advantage of, and it ends *now!*"

"What's happening?" James screeched. "I thought we were safe!"

Never safe, Alice thought with surrender.

"That's it, then," Alice announced. "We can't win his game, so we must break it. There is a boiler in the basement isn't there, Evelyn?"

"What?" she replied. "What do you mean to do?"

"It's geothermal, I'm sure," Alice declared. "If we can't win. We will demolish the stadium and bring the whole complex down. We'll fire it to full heat, then blow our remaining fertilizer around its base. The central placement should bring the whole house down in flames at minimum. It'll collapse the whole cave system if we're lucky. Geothermal generators have a nasty proclivity to cause earthquakes in the event of catastrophic failure."

"Have you lost your mind, Alice?" Winston barked. "You'll kill us all, Eleanor and James too!"

"Don't you get it, Winston?" Alice roared. "We are already dead! We died the moment this awful game began!"

The crowd was speechless. No one challenged her. Her authority was absolute, her words too severe to stomach.

"He thinks it's a game?" Evelyn finally agreed. "Well, let's flip the board and send the pieces flying."

FIFTEEN

A S SOON AS EVELYN ANNOUNCED THEIR INTENT TO DISRUPT the killer's plan, a twanging chime filled the room. The hand of the doom clock slid forward in a large single tick.

Alice wasted no time.

"Barricade! Go!" she shouted mid-stride out of the room.

As the clock finished its ringing, the house was plunged into darkness. They had not gotten the chance to light the newly distributed candles. Amelia took the opportunity to rectify that with the limited number of lights she could reach from behind the mountain of furniture.

A light clicking sound was heard along the walls.

Alice looked toward the ceiling, trying to find the source of the noise. She leaned close to the source and heard something awful— a sinister hissing.

"I'd planned this one for later, but I cannot have you ruining my sport so soon," the despicable voice said filling the room like a specter. "You are currently breathing in a custom blend of lysergic acid diethylamide and some other particularly destabilizing drugs.

"LSD?" Evelyn wondered aloud. "I've had a bad trip before."

"Perhaps fear is not the right word. The gas dispersal will continue pumping the entire complex full of my little experiment until one of you suffers a fatal overdose. I'll be sure to slow the spray as we approach that point. I want you to suffer."

The broadcast clicked off, and Eleanor looked at Alice with wide eyes.

"Take James upstairs now!" Alice screeched. "I'm going to lock you in."

"What?" Eleanor whipped back. "No!"

Alice gathered her family in her arms and bulldozed them up the stairway as fast as she could. Eleanor fought her aunt loudly, but Alice was assisted by a straight shot of adrenaline and the desire to keep her kids safe.

"Bring me James' knife and anything else you could use as weapons. Your view on reality is about to be dramatically shifted, and I won't have you two hurt each other. Lock him in the bathroom."

"Aunt Alice, what about you?" Eleanor cried. She was frightened, truly terrified, of facing a mental threat.

Eleanor was proud of her mind. She was sharp. She loved being just a touch faster than her classmates at almost anything academic. The thought of her own brain betraying her scared Eleanor more than any boogeyman ever could.

"I'll be fine, love," Alice said with too much obvious worry in her tone for Eleanor to buy it. "Do what I said! Now! The drug will be taking effect soon."

Eleanor passed the items and pulled Alice in for a tight hug.

"I'm scared," Eleanor admitted.

"Me, too, El," Alice said as she closed the door.

Downstairs, Mark saw something strange. A man walked through the front door of the hotel lobby and moved to the stairwell. He wore a long black trench coat. Something metal gleamed in his right hand.

"Alice!" Mark screamed. "There's someone after you!"

Mark climbed the makeshift parapet and slid down the faces of the tables on the other side. His world sloshed around like it was on roller skates. The drug had begun to take effect.

"Not now!" he groaned. Silver forks and knives began to flow down the tabletops where they had been embedded. The shrapnel from the explosion pooled near the base of the furniture and elongated into an awful metallic snake. Mark tried to tell himself it wasn't real. He trudged through the lobby and found his clothes weighing him down as though they weighed a ton. He watched helplessly as the unknown stranger distanced himself up the stairs.

"I'm coming, Alice! Watch out!" Mark screeched. He unbuttoned his shirt and removed it as it had begun to encumber his movement beyond reconciliation. His pants seemed to melt away as he struggled to give chase to who he assumed was the killer.

He heard a woman's wailing screech from above him.

Downstairs, Amelia fought hard against what she knew was coming. She steeled her mind. It was critical to stay sharp. In the corner, Rose swatted against something unknown while flailing her legs about to kick at nothing. Amelia tried to step and help her.

She couldn't move.

Amelia again tried to lift her leg, but only managed to raise it an inch or so off the floor. She felt her muscles slowly losing their ability to function and began to lower to the ground. This was a hallucination. She was sure of it. Why could she still think so clearly, but remain unable to move?

Her bottom reached the floor softly, and despite her most sincere efforts, she began to wither lower to the carpet like a toy automaton whose batteries had been exhausted. She tried to yell for help. Her mouth wouldn't open.

She finally reached a stop flat on her back. Amelia lay paralyzed but fully cognizant of everything happening around her. She had always worried about this. She never wanted to be someone who needed to rely on others for her care.

Amelia had been independent all her life. The oldest of four siblings, she was like a third parent to the younger children. Her early life was filled with rational thought and sensible decision-making that led her to captain any educational group or club she was a part of. William always respected that about her. She was far more bullish than any of her classmates, male or female, and dominated her foray into higher education with a rigid schedule and unmatched work ethic. Then the bombs had dropped.

In the mansion now, Amelia fought to lift a finger. She could see a steak knife that she'd carried from the dinner table sitting beside her. She wanted a way to defend herself if needed. Her mind wandered back to the war. She had worked as a nurse in the same company as her husband. The deployment had been ideal, to put it mildly. A few years into the conflict, William had gone into the field. She was alone in the trauma ward.

She couldn't see the men who'd grabbed her and forced her over the workstation, but she heard them, heard their jeers and snickering as they forced themselves upon her. The men were so incredibly strong. She felt during the war as she did at The Arbor with her back against the floor. She stared up at the ceiling and wept. Tears streamed down her cheeks as she begged for her body to respond.

When Mark finally reached the upstairs hall, there was no one around. Had Alice somehow escaped? He banged against room doors shouting her name but heard no answer. The silver snake slithered its way up the stairs behind him. The scales gleamed against the light from the torch he carried. Mark didn't remember grabbing a torch.

The grayish beast reared up to strike, and Mark blocked with his arms. He felt a bit ridiculous. There was no way this imagined demon could hurt him.

It snapped over his wrist and bit down hard. Mark let out a cry of pain as he slammed his arm against the door to knock the serpent away. Even if the hallucination was not real, the agony of the bite was tangible and excruciating.

He felt the hot venom shoot into his muscle. It burned as it moved up his arm. Finally, the serpent released when he touched the torch to it. He kicked hard against the room door he was backed against and the lock gave way. The room was empty. He pressed his back against the wooden door and held it shut as the snake struck against it.

He tried to blink away the blistering heat emanating from his arm, but the suffering flowed up his veins. He was terrified to think what might happen when it reached his heart.

In her room, Eleanor was huddled with a blanket tight around her body. She understood that what was happening wasn't real, but sounds seemed to fade. The already dark room was swallowed into nothingness. She saw an eerie black scene as even her phone's light was swallowed.

The floor disappeared. Her blanket was gone. She felt around for something, anything, but found herself drifting into an empty abyss instead. Eleanor tried to scream, but her lips were being drawn closer together. She couldn't breathe now.

Her nostrils zipped themselves shut, and her panic escalated into a full-scale meltdown. Her perception of the world was completely wrong. She couldn't think. Why couldn't she breathe? How could she not scream?

Eleanor brought her hands to her mouth and felt around a

smooth cheek down to where her lips should have been. She had
no mouth. Her fingers seemed to feel around her body for any
tether to the outside world, but she found none.

Eleanor was alone. She always knew it would be this way.

Alice was lost. She wandered halls of what no longer looked
like The Arbor. She chased her brother. Alice was so small. How
was she back in England now? Had the whole thing been an awful
dream?

She flew as quickly as her short legs could carry her. She felt
almost happy. It wasn't real, but it was such a thorough deception.
The high-ceilings of their London home were always so palatial
to her. She ran her hand along the lily-white lace curtains and
pushed through them as she followed her sibling.

Her mother's blue-stockinged legs strode in front of her.
Alice came to a screeching halt.

"Mummy?" her voice squeaked.

Her mother's face was there, wise and knowing as it ever had
been. She smiled down at her daughter and lowered herself to
crouch at eye level.

"Are you having fun with Jack?" her mother inquired.

"Oh yes, Mummy," Alice responded. "We are playing chase!"

"I know you are, my love." Her mother's head drooped. "You
must know it wasn't random."

Alice took a step back. She glanced at her hands. They were
her own, but older. Was she not a child anymore? What was happening? She had a reason for being here.

"What do you mean, Mum?" Alice queried in her adult voice
now. She stretched upward, reaching higher in the hallway and
forcing her mother to stand.

"We both know it," her mother sighed. "They took nothing
but the platinum and even that was probably for show. What
other reason could there have been for his death?"

Alice glanced up in awful horror as her now-grown sibling lay dead on the floor behind her mother. She choked back vomit as she spun away from the carnage.

"Mummy, I don't know!" Alice screamed. "You don't think I've gone through it a thousand, ten thousand, times in my head? He was so good! He didn't have enemies. I know it seems like there's more to it, but I just don't know what it could be!"

"Jack was in construction, wasn't he?" her mother hinted. "Who did he work for?"

"Well, it—there were contracts with all the major firms on Mars. Everything was on the up and up. I checked it over so many times."

"Everything?" Her mother's words pierced her. "Did you check transaction amounts?"

"Well, they had all paid him," Alice returned. "There were no missing balances or suspicious sources."

"Your brother's work was predictable. Some jobs paid for a hundred hours, others a thousand. Volume discounts included, it should be consistent, shouldn't it?"

"I never thought of it like that, but yes—I suppose that is right," Alice agreed.

"Do any of these look out of place, my love?"

An array of open file-folders stretched down the hallway in the opposite direction of her brother's corpse. Alice began searching the ledgers. If there was something here, she would remember it.

Back at the Arbor, Mark grew impatient. He needed to make sure Alice was all right.

He took a deep breath and flung open the door to his room. The quicksilver monstrosity was hurled inside, and Mark shut the door to seal him in. The lock was missing, so he was sure the serpent would find its way out eventually, but it seemed safe for the moment.

He journeyed down the hall, pounding on door after door. Mark felt odd doing this in his underpants, but he had to get to Alice in time. He had to save her.

Finally, he threw open door four. A small form lay lifelessly in the middle of the floor. There was a slim athame protruding from the corpse's spine. He recognized the beautiful brown hair immediately. It was Alice, his Alice. He slid to her side and felt around helplessly at the blade sticking from her back. He rolled her onto her side and wept mournfully at the sight of her empty eyes. He dropped a kiss on her cold forehead and returned the body to its stomach. He'd failed her.

The athame was gone.

He looked around the room by his torchlight and saw no sign of where it could have disappeared to. Then he heard it, a light hissing from behind him. A tiny snake coiled itself to strike. The coloring was the same as the steel blade that had been embedded in Alice. He slammed his flame against the creature, but it wrapped around the handle and slithered up to his palm. It reared back and bit into his hand.

Mark swatted his palm to the flame, and the tiny serpent wailed. Rather than retreat, it dove under his skin. Mark's torment dialed up in its intensity, and he roared for the awful torture to end.

In another world, Evelyn, like Alice, found herself transported somewhere else entirely. She sat on the left-hand side of a large leather-bound throne. A mahogany conference-table stretched out before it and many men with shadowed faces and pinstripe-grey suits sat judging her.

"Ms. Fox," one spoke up. "Are we to understand that you not only allowed your father's death but also now wish to take up his place as chief executive?"

Evelyn swallowed her anxiety and straightened her back.

"I allowed nothing, sir," Evelyn corrected. "We were attacked by an unknown assailant who—"

"You don't even know who the attacker was?" another angry man growled.

"We are working with authorities to determine motives to learn the killer's identity," Evelyn nervously returned. "Now, I want to mention our handling of the news. We must control flow of information or share price may begin to—"

"You are nothing more than an advisor to this board, Ms. Fox!" the man at the opposite end of the table spat. "We find it quite convenient that your father's untimely death resulted in what might be a spectacular windfall for you."

"I loved my father!" Evelyn shouted now. "He taught me everything I know. He—groomed me for this. Now you will recognize what is rightfully mine!"

"Is it, Ms. Fox?"

They couldn't know. Her brother hated the family business. He wanted nothing to do with it. What right had he to preside over a trillion-dollar company because he was born a few years earlier than she had been?

"Yes," she doubled down. "It is mine. I won't have a group of jealous executives talk me into submission!"

"Have you looked at the will, Ms. Fox?" a man sitting across from her asked. "It mentions that his child should gain control of his shares. We happen to know that despite Mr. Fox's efforts to conceal it, you have a brother."

"Not only that," another man continued. "But he is older, and without specificity in the last will and testament, that makes him the acting agent in control of Jones Computing and Networking."

"No," Evelyn groaned. "You can't do that!"

"We already have, Ms. Fox," the executive across from her said flatly.

The leather-bound seat shot out of her arm's reach. She struggled to grab after it, but without success.

Evelyn had failed her company, she'd failed the other survivors, and worst of all-she had failed her father.

Meanwhile, Alice continued to scour what must have been her own memories for something that stuck out about Jack's contracts. She knew obvious impropriety would be scrubbed, but her mother was right. When looking for suspicious actions, follow the money.

Finally, her calculations made one file stick out. Jack was paid three times his usual rate for a job done a couple of months before his death. The client was not listed. The location was also unknown, but definitely outside Villanova.

Alice was not sure what this told her, but it was a lead. If they ever got out of the mess they were in, she would have something to go on.

Alice stood. She turned to face her mother with hesitation. She knew it wasn't real. She understood the abstraction was spun from herself.

Alice did not want to see her brother laying there anymore, but her mother before her was a much more palatable illusion. Victoria Wortz towered as statuesque and intimidating as she always had.

Alice knew her mother was a facade constructed by the painful dust Alice had tried to leave behind, but she so wished for another minute to linger.

"You were always so remarkable, in every sense of the word," Victoria said softly as she managed to turn one corner of her mouth slightly upward. "Not to lay undue pressure on you, but the fate of our family now lays in your hands. You must be their matriarch. Lead them through the insurmountable darkness. Know that even in the lonesome stillness, their eyes will be fixed upon you."

"Mum," Alice struggled. "I can't take this. You know that I've never had the stomach or desire to govern."

"Alice, my sweet, that is why you must."

Victoria placed a palm against Alice's now-moist cheek. She moved to kiss her but paused as she was interrupted by a booming shot.

Alice stared as a deep maroon began to spread outward on her mother's yellow pastel blouse. Victoria shook her head and breathed in shakily. It almost looked as though she knew of the inevitability of their reunion's end but was just as unprepared as Alice had been to part.

Alice screamed as her mother fell sideways and slid down the hall of her childhood home. A bright red spray covered the sea of manila papering the floor. She collapsed to her mother's side and wept. Alice was so exhausted by watching family die. She was content to part with the sensation permanently and would do everything in her power to see it through to conclusion.

"Grandma?" A familiar young voice piped up from behind her.

Alice jumped as though she'd been shocked by a bolt of lightning. Her head snapped up to see James looking on at his murdered father and grandmother. By instinct, her head whipped back in the opposite direction to see a mysterious man with an obscured face.

"Who are you?" she screeched. Alice hoped in vain that her mind would help piece together the evidence to discover the murderer's identity. His arms raised to an all-too-familiar position as she saw something shine in his hands. "James ru—"

Her exclamation was interrupted by another hammering blast from the killer's rifle.

"*James!*" she howled in utter brokenness.

The youngest Wortz reached up to touch a bubbling wound

in his neck. He coughed and sputtered blood across the floor before him. He collapsed straight down as though his muscles had all given up at once.

"No, no, sweetie, please!" she begged hopelessly. She dashed to his side and scooped up his limp form into her arms.

His breathing was erratic and bubbled around the hole in his windpipe. Alice sobbed as she wiped the spurting blood from her face.

Alice hardly noticed the man standing over her now. She closed her eyes and wished for the pain to subside.

"Not yet," the recognizable voice laughed a mischievous cackle as he slammed his rifle into the back of her head.

Back at the bar downstairs, Amelia focused all her efforts into extending her fingers around the knife at her side.

She stretched hopefully but gasped as the wooden handle slipped away from her. Amelia heard something beside her. It was the rustling of clothing. Someone was down on the floor with her, just out of sight.

Amelia wanted so badly to move her head. Her breathing changed and became rough. Why had her body betrayed her? Why couldn't she be strong enough to get up?

She saw a flash of black cross the periphery of her vision. It looked to be human. It crawled on all fours. She thought she heard it whispering to itself.

"First cut must—" it murmured lightly. "And then we peel the skin. We could split her down the side. Yes, now that is a plan."

Amelia tried, but she could not recognize the voice. It sounded familiar and light. Whoever it was sounded positively giddy at their upcoming task.

She felt a cold hand lift her blouse from her hip, revealing the skin. The dull edge of the same knife she had tried to grab slid up her hip.

The killer had done good work. Helplessness was Amelia's biggest fear. She closed her eyes and wished for the hallucination to pass.

"No! Stay awake!" the being whispered like an angry troll.

Amelia closed her eyes tighter. She was still so lucid. It almost felt real. The pain was genuine and palpable as the icy steel slit up the side of her hips. She wished to cry out but was only able to show her protest in wild dancing eyes and slight squeaks. A single tear dropped down the side of her right cheek. It was all too awful to bear.

To make matters worse, she felt hot breath by her hip a moment later. The disgusting degenerate sniffed at her wound. She felt a tongue run up the sliced-open skin. Amelia winced as much as she could.

The blade dragged its edge across her stomach and chest. It came to rest above her heart.

"No, no," the fiend breathed. "Like this."

The creature angled the knife almost flat with her skin and moved it back so that they would be able to stuff the entirety of it into her chest cavity before reaching her heart.

Amelia gasped as the knife plunged into her. It ran between her ribs and scraped along her bones as it journeyed deeper. She was grateful at least that the paralysis seemed to slightly numb her. It hurt but not unbearably so.

She felt her heart flutter as the blade finished its journey. Her vision darkened. For the first time, she realized that the assassin might not be imagined.

Thank God. She would get to see William again.

◦◦◦◁◉▷◦◦◦

Upstairs, Winston was yanked from a hallucination to the sound of the clock ringing out a set of five bells. It seemed so soon.

Winston was no stranger to LSD. He handled the bad trip better than most, but all around him, the walls continued to melt into a pool around his feet.

Water was what terrified him most. He closed his eyes tightly and tried to stay afloat in the marsh of his melted furniture. Winston took comfort in the fact that he knew, for now at least, that this morning's death wouldn't be his own.

Winston had thalassophobia, a fear of deep water and more specifically, what might lay beneath the surface. He was unafraid of showers and pools, but when he was unable to see the bottom of whatever body of water he entered, Winston started to feel anxious.

The real irony of his phobia was Winston's affinity for the beach and walking around without a shirt. He adored the warm sand. Winston loved the attention he received from men and women. It didn't really matter to him from whence his affection came, as long as he did, too.

The worst of it was, he'd only been successful in one of his romantic attempts this trip. Alice had proved to be a bit too upstanding for his taste, the young Wortz girl was nubile and delicious—but too squeamish. The only other woman who really fulfilled him was Evelyn, and she had a host of issues of her own.

This was not the way he'd wanted his vacation to go, to put it mildly. Despite doing a relatively good job at surviving, and even getting his rocks off in the process, Winston knew that his odds weren't good.

Something inside him gave way to a new fear. Even if he hadn't died during this day's hunt, who was to say it wouldn't happen during the next? Winston wasn't ready to give up the ghost yet. He was here to relax, not to fight for his life. Winston was a security guard, but his crew stuck together for the most-part. His day-to-day risk was actually quite low. He didn't have the constitution to endure stress of this magnitude long-term.

He leaned back to float in a reclining position. If nothing else, now that the drug flow had stopped, he'd sleep it off. The other survivors rode down from their highs in a similar manner.

The entire situation was stuffed so full of sordid intentions. Winston felt that he and the others were really getting to the meat of the ordeal now. Each person's personalities had been laid bare. Their attitude was one of madness. The survivors' decision-making had grown more manic to ensure their lives' continuance. Where there had once been twelve souls at this detestable retreat, now there were seven.

SIXTEEN

MARK'S HEAD THROBBED AS HE AWOKE IN THE LIBRARY. *How did I get here?* He moaned as he forced his body to sit upright. The question ripped at his brain. He had been upstairs—or at least he thought he had been. It was possible that the whole thing was imagined. There wasn't likely to be a colossal silvery serpent patrolling the halls.

Mark looked down at his arms. They were stained dark maroon. He remembered. Mark was sure he'd heard the tolling of bells indicating the death of another soul. The rusty scent hit his nostrils, triggering an awful realization. His hands were doused in the blood of the dearly departed.

He shivered as the subarctic air wafted through the demolished wall at the rear of the house. He sat in boxer shorts. At least some parts of his memory were accurate. Mark's face fell as he looked toward the side kitchen door. Just inside the swinging doorway was a blade covered in dried sanguine sludge. The situation grew more dire for Mr. Reese.

"Oh, no. Oh, that's very bad," he mumbled.

In the absence of other evidence, Mark appeared quite

culpable indeed of the murder of whomever had recently died. Worse yet, Mark began to worry about his own innocence in the matter. Hallucinogenic drugs pushed what might have been un-thinkable just a few days ago into the realm of distinct possibility.

Mark heard voices a few rooms away. Some of the others were up. He needed to figure out his story. He had to determine just how to prove his innocence. Mark delicately pressed the kitchen door until he could get a more distinct ear for the conversation going on by the barricade.

". . .but Amelia didn't deserve this."

"I just don't understand. Didn't the murderer say the killing would be through overdose? He is breaking with his own set of paradigms," a different voice answered.

"Yes, let's start analyzing the maniac's choices in murder methodology," Evelyn groaned. "I'm certain that is the most un-usual event of the week thus far."

"You know what I mean, Evelyn," Alice returned.

"Is Mark still not up yet?" Eleanor broke in. "Have we checked on him?"

Mark gasped and tiptoed back through the kitchen. He had no idea how to proceed. Winging it seemed the best solution as his acquaintances scoured the facility looking for him. He lay back down and awaited his own discovery by the search party.

As she searched upstairs, Eleanor was shaken to say the least. She had not bothered to reapply makeup today. It didn't seem relevant to her anymore. For some reason, Amelia's death hit her so much harder than everyone else's had. She'd become a kind of den mother to the crew. She was their heart, a moral compass of sorts. Now Eleanor worried that the group would begin to drift aimlessly.

She knocked on Mark's door but found it unlocked. Inside there was no one. Eleanor was hardly surprised. She somehow knew he wouldn't be there. When it came to sleeping arrangements, he never was where he should have been.

She returned to the hallway and leaned out over the bannister. "He's not in bed!"

She plodded downstairs, frustrated with the injustice. Amelia had almost certainly been the best of them, and she'd expired in one of the most awful ways Eleanor had yet seen. Why had her life been filled with so much suffering? The sheer volume of deaths Eleanor had been a witness to outnumbered the amount many would see in their lifetime. She was eighteen. Eleanor had never even driven a car. Now, she thought about funerary plans for Amelia because everyone else would likely be too busy or preoccupied with themselves to care.

She investigated the common room to see Rose staring out the window. Rose looked almost as empty as she felt. Despite the active manhunt, Eleanor felt compelled to pay her a visit. She pulled out a chair at the tiny but ornate bistro table and looked out onto the lawn with her.

The scene was so deceptively peaceful. Breathtaking sheets of cool blue ice served as the backdrop for the most picturesque lawn Eleanor had seen since the days of her childhood on Earth. It was immaculately kept and stretched out toward the shimmering still water which surrounded the estate. There were no trees. That bothered Eleanor. She really felt like there should have been trees, but there was probably some architectural reason they'd chosen not to include them. Instead, the blue-green grass would serve as the only living decoration for the yard. There, in the background, sat the awful circle of nickel which separated them from the outside world.

"Such a little thing, isn't it?" Rose sighed, noticing Eleanor's gaze. "It's cruel. I think the designer made the elevator stick out on purpose. It sits there like a gleaming beacon of hope taunting those cast so far from it."

Eleanor looked at Rose. There was a depth to her that she'd never seen in all the years she had known her. The bifurcation of Rose from the technology she had held so dearly allowed a vision of the woman who had been obscured from public eye while her digital substitute soaked in the spotlight. How could someone surrounded by so many friends seem so—isolated?

"I am becoming more tempted to claw my way up the walls to the train tracks above it as the hours tick by," Eleanor admitted. "But I know it would be fruitless. Even if I could grip into the solid outward-sloping surface, I haven't done more than a few pull-ups in years. That ice-wall would give an experienced climber a run for their money."

"No," Rose admitted. "I don't think that will offer an escape to anyone but Winston, and even he would need climbing spikes and boots to do so at an outward slope of what appears to be at least seven degrees at the base, and twenty or more near the top. It would be a climb that would constantly increase in difficulty. You'd have to be superhuman, and even then, it would be a herculean effort."

Eleanor glanced over her shoulder at the people madly scouring the home. She felt she should join them but just couldn't bring herself to do it. She knew why she was lethargic, but it seemed inane that her body seemed to be on vacation while her mind spun wildly. Eleanor felt the urge to ask a question but was not sure she wanted to know the answer.

"Rose," El began. "Why did you stay once we arrived? Everyone else who lur—made someone come, left. You remained. I can't believe I didn't think of it until now."

Rose lowered her gaze to the floor. She breathed in and let the hot exhale flow quickly from her mouth. Her cheeks puffed slightly as she pondered the right words to say.

"What was I supposed to do, Ellie?" Rose asked without raising her head. "I don't claim it was right, but obviously I decided I could stomach Alice's death. When she showed up with you two, something changed. It was like the weight of my actions crashed into me like a runaway tractor-trailer. When I saw James, I hadn't even realized who he was. It wasn't until I saw you standing next to Alice that I realized what I'd done."

"So you—" Eleanor started.

"So, I stayed. I drank. I imbibed until the world around me flowed into a river of guiltless grey. I hoped that I would be able to drown my crushing guilt under a sea of spirits. All my usual escapes were gone here. I had no support network. There was nowhere I could post a picture and fish for compliments to lift my mood. I was alone. I'm quite sure I will die alone as well."

Eleanor couldn't bring herself to feel sympathy for the woman who might have condemned her to death, but pity was manifesting inside her. Despite Rose's choices, she was a product of her environment. Eleanor wondered how much of it was nature over nurture. Another emotion swelled within Eleanor: suspicion. Despite all this, all the remorse, Rose still hadn't thought to apologize to Eleanor or James. This struck Eleanor as a note of the subsistent narcissism that lurked beneath Rose's sincerity.

"Well," Eleanor let her words drag. "I'd better get back to the search. Why don't you do the same? It's probably better than sitting here and letting ourselves wallow."

Rose agreed and stood up to follow Eleanor into the bar. The women went around the side of the barricade, and Rose split off into the kitchen while Eleanor continued on to the dining room. Eleanor had decided that she should figure out how much time they had before the next killing hour. She guessed that Amelia had died an hour or so after breakfast. Eleanor had woken up from her stupor around 4 PM, which would have been approximately five hours after Amelia's death. It was 5:15 PM now, she saw, checking her phone as she searched.

She did some math in her head, examined how close the hand was to the next hazard, and guessed they had just under an hour until it was time again to hide. She heard a screech from just beyond the kitchen and dashed in to see the source of the commotion. Rose stood a few feet back from Mark, looking down at the bloody mess.

"What have you done, Mark?" Rose howled.

"Listen to me, Rose," Mark defended. "I know this looks dreadful, but I know I didn't do this."

"How do you know?" Rose retorted. "How can you be so absolutely sure it wasn't you with the damning evidence surrounding the situation."

Eleanor examined the whole situation. It seemed a bit too perfect. Mark, much as she disliked him, didn't seem the type to murder anyone. She had been wrong about people before, but Eleanor liked to think of herself as having good instincts. She had a distinctly bad feeling about Rose.

"What if he was set up?" Eleanor asked.

"Are we making random guesses?" Rose spat back.

"Look at the situation." Eleanor changed modes and analyzed the scene. "Look at his position there. Blood is on the topsides of his arms, but not underneath."

"That could have been caused by the spray!" Rose argued.

"Yes," Eleanor agreed. Alice finally pushed into the room and saw the horrible scene of survivors accusing each other of horrific acts. Eleanor continued without flinching. "But I see two things that give me pause. The blood droplets appear to have been smeared. It's possible Mark was running his hands up and down his forearms, but it looks to me to be the work of someone rubbing in the blood that they placed there. Not only that, look at this pattern of blood on the floor."

Eleanor pointed down at a pooling of blood that cut in an

inverted V. The lines were crisp on the interior edges and uneven on the exterior ones. Evelyn entered the room as the group observed the patterning of red on the forest-carpeted library floor.

"Mark was laying here for quite some time," Eleanor continued. "Then he got up and moved to his current location. This means he chose to be discovered. An interesting choice to be sure, but not one I would expect a guilty man to make."

"Well, listen to Detective Wortz." Evelyn brusquely chuckled. "That's all very well and good, madam, but it does nothing to explain away the obvious evidence. Mark was found with a blade and bloodied hands while everyone else awoke from their stupors and had nothing compromising to be seen."

"I think it's high time we search rooms to be sure no one has anything to hide," Alice spoke up and stepped between the feuding women.

"Mark is literally found with blood on his hands, and you want to search *everyone else?*" Evelyn groaned.

"I'm saying . . ." Alice collected herself for a moment. "We will search everything in the estate. We probably should have done that ages ago, but at least we thought to do it now. Mark will be locked in the basement for the duration of the search, and Rose will stand guard."

"*What?*" Mark and Rose simultaneously growled.

"You both will, and I won't hear another word. This search must happen if we are to retain our sanity and have a modicum of trust between each other. We must determine the killer's identity and whether he is one of us," Alice finished.

"Or she," Eleanor softly spoke.

"What did you say, girl?" Evelyn turned to face the young woman with anger painted across her face.

"The killer could be a woman." Eleanor confirmed her point. "We can't rule out anything. Every death has been indirect beside this one. Nothing has been done that would require any strength. Androids can be controlled. Poison is so often called a woman's weapon in history books."

Evelyn cleared her throat and breathed in through her nose. "You must, however, understand the implication of your words. I take it you don't suspect your loving aunt, which means. . .you think it could be one of us?"

Evelyn gestured between herself and Rose wildly. She was trying to give Eleanor a chance to retract her words, even though she was seething just beneath the surface.

Eleanor looked up to the ceiling to compose herself before lowering her gaze once more. She stared directly into Evelyn's eyes as she continued.

"Yes."

The concealed displeasure on Evelyn's face ripped free of its bindings, and she closed a pair of fists in front of her face. Evelyn cast them down in a shrill huff and let her rage bubble to the surface.

"You must be out of your goddamn mind if you think—"

"*We are done here!*" Alice burst out.

"The hell we—" Evelyn argued.

"*We are!*" Alice reiterated. "Now, go lock up Mark and let's get on with it. Eleanor, grab the rest of the room keys from reception. We have a search to get underway."

Mark walked willingly to his dusky prison. He stepped inside and heard the lock click behind him. He descended the staircase and approached the light seeping into the room from the hole in the ceiling above. Rose stood by the door with her arms crossed in obvious frustration. He was not about to be the one to make small talk.

Eleanor did as she was asked and ran to the battered reception desk. She reached underneath and retrieved the keys.

Something grabbed her attention. Were her ears ringing? She swore she could hear something coming from one of the rooms behind her. It was a beeping, coming from the coat room.

"Eleanor, let's move!" Alice's voice pulled Eleanor from her curiosity. She passed the keys to Alice and protested when her aunt demanded that she remain at reception with James. After a short argument, the crew approached the main stairwell. Winston joined the women and marched up with them.

"What are we doing?" he asked.

"Some foolhardy search of the rooms," Evelyn returned. "As though the killer would hide incriminating evidence where any search could find it."

Alice ignored her rival's jabs and walked into the same cavernous hallway she had entered just a few days before. It had seemed so much more inviting then.

"Give me key number one," Alice ordered.

Evelyn obliged, and they opened the door to the room of the late Peter Corgrave. The room smelled foul. Evelyn showed no desire to follow Alice, despite her curiosity. The bed was caked in rancid sludge that had bubbled through the sheet covering the body. Alice lifted her blouse to cover her nose as she searched the drawers. It hardly helped the malodorous invasion of her senses.

Despite a thorough look-around of the belongings, nothing was found but clothes and a few bottles of pills. Alice grabbed them just to be sure poison wasn't left sitting about. The search of rooms two and three were easier than the first. No belongings meant a more expedient null result.

Mark's room was left almost exactly as it was when Alice had left it just the night before. The teapot sat by the fireplace. A pair of saucers and cups were neatly placed on the mantle, still full of the tea that had been poured while awkward silence passed. As Alice searched the room, she noticed a slim white slipper leaning against the protruding left side of the fireplace, just out of sight. A brief smile spread across her lips before she recalled the reason for their search.

Alice knew rooms four and six had nothing to conceal, although she still grabbed James' knife from his room to be consistent. Evelyn seemed to take great pleasure in rifling through Alice's things and leaving them in piles across the floor of her room. She seemed content after removing every item in her closet from their hangars and tossing them haphazardly across the room. Alice settled on letting it slide, despite the obvious disrespect of her personal space and things.

Winston's room held an abundance of prophylactics, liquor, and fine clothing. Nothing seemed out of the ordinary other than an extremely old book. "Of Mice and Men" sat on his nightstand. Alice was struck by the fact that Winston hardly seemed like a Steinbeck man, and more so wondered about his knowledgebase of classic literature. The struggles of migrant workers seemed hardly likely to cause a blip on his radar. Despite this, there the aged book sat.

"Have you read it?" Alice asked, leafing through the ancient pages. She smiled at the well-preserved illustration on the front cover. This book had been carefully preserved.

"God, no!" Winston laughed. A moment later, he changed his jovial demeanor slightly and continued. "I should say, I have just started it, so obviously I have not had as much time to read as of late."

Alice returned the book to its proper place, if it was to be called that, on Winston's nightstand. She shrugged his reaction off as typical Winston, but something about it troubled her sensibilities. He hardly seemed the literary type.

Rose's room held several emptied bottles of liquor and an unkempt bed. Her clothes were neatly placed in all of the dresser drawers, and other than the bottles, one could almost call it tidy. Omario's room was starkly empty beside the one suitcase that sat still full of clothes in the center of the floor.

Room six had a single bag tucked away in the corner. It didn't look familiar. Alice fumbled around the suitcase and found nothing but elegant men's clothing. The apparel seemed old, or at least made to look old, and she decided the most likely owner must have been one of the previous guests. She didn't imagine they cared much for non-essentials when it came to be time to leave.

The room of Dr. and Mrs. Rutger held the corpse of the late William Rutger on the bed before them. It didn't smell quite as badly as Peter's room, but it was close. Once again, Evelyn refrained from entering. The fruitless search ended much the same as the analysis of Peter Corgrave's room. Alice and Winston exited the room with makeshift masks covering their faces and looking decidedly pale.

Door number eight stood before the trio. Evelyn grimaced as Alice unlocked the door to her room.

"I'm sorry to ask, but would you mind staying—" Alice tried to be polite.

"I'll be here," Evelyn finished. "Don't break anything."

It was markedly bigger than the rest and well-kept. Her clothes were stacked neatly, and her closet was stuffed with beautiful dresses that sparkled in the light. Evelyn's room had several more unique items of furniture and a chess board pushed up beside the fireplace.

There seemed to be a distinct lack of personal effects, despite her unique decorating choices. There were no paintings or pictures on the walls. Evelyn's things were all expensive. Her furnishings were exquisite, but it all seemed so impersonal. The room didn't feel lived-in.

"I didn't find anything suspicious," Alice admitted as she exited the room.

"Praised be! Now I can live my life in peace," Evelyn chortled. "The worry of being found guilty by you was really keeping me up at night."

Alice rotated slightly to push past Evelyn. She stood before the double French doors at the end of the hall.

"I don't have a key for this one," Alice said.

"Neither do I," Evelyn added. "So, what do we do now?"

Alice tapped her lips with her forefinger. Evelyn was not going to like her answer.

"Winston, can you kick it down?" Alice asked.

"Break down the door to my father's master suite?" Evelyn clarified, disgusted with what she'd heard. "I believe Timothy and Silas carried his body back inside after he passed, which means the stench of my rotting father will fill this hallway for the rest of our stay."

Alice shrugged and tried to seem less than uncaring.

"We can pull the doors shut again by tying the knobs together," Alice sighed. "I'm sorry, but I think we have to do it."

Evelyn let out a tiny chirp of frustration through her gritted teeth.

"I'm not going to be a part of this!" she almost shouted. "Plunder it your damn selves."

Evelyn disappeared back down the hallway without another word. She stomped with every heaving breath. Just after she began to shrink out of sight, Winston looked to Alice for approval and positioned himself in front of the doors.

"Do it," Alice ordered.

French doors were notoriously easy to break into. A single well-placed kick to the central support was almost always enough to smash even the most expensive of doorways. This assumed, of course, that the installer did not place a crossbeam to bar the opening. Luckily for Alice, the doorway security appeared mostly ornamental.

They both poured into the room almost on top of each other. If Evelyn's room was nice, this one was resplendent. The multi-room suite sprawled out into several smaller gathering spots. They stood in the circular hub which connected each room to the next. The domed ceiling looked to be hand-painted and had an incomplete version of the Michelangelo's "Creation of Adam" adorning the half-sphere.

Incomplete was not the right word. Adam seemed to float toward heaven of his own accord. He was not reaching for God's hand like in the original. He seemed to be stretching toward the sky on his own merit. The hubris and gall of the painting were not lost on Alice. Here was a man who thought he could do anything. Now he was dead.

A projection like the one on the train blasted into existence in front of them. He was seven feet high and fuming.

"Who breaks into my sanctum to pilfer what is left of my earthly belongings? The same ones who murdered me, I must wonder?"

A pair silvery fixtures on the wall rotated to face Alice and Winston. The light in the room glinted off their barrels. They appeared to be autocannons of some sort. They whirred to life and followed the specter's piercing stare.

"Whoa, stop! Disarm! It's me, your security chief!" Winston held his hands out begging for mercy.

"Well." Alexis Fox's projection turned to face Winston. "This is an unusual surprise."

The barrels of the turrets retreated as they snapped shut. Without the guns, they looked to be little more than questionable decorative choices as bright shiny domes in the midst of a classically decorated turn of the century master suite.

"Thank you very much, Mr. Fox," Alice replied.

His enormous form rotated to analyze her. The towering man looked downward like a parent staring at a petulant child.

"And who might you be?" Mr. Fox queried posthumously. "A yokel come to loot my earthly treasures?"

Even in death, Alice found the man remarkable. It was easy to see how he amassed such a colossal fortune. The way he spoke, with such power and determination, was exerting enormous pressure on Alice to respond with haste.

"No, sir. We are looking for something that might give us a clue as to who is killing people at the mansion. Winston and I were hoping for some sort of clue, but you are—different. Can you tell us anything about the people in the mansion?"

Alexis' left eye gave a slight twitch as he pondered her statement. The illusion turned from the pair and sat at a massively tall leather throne at the head of the room. Despite its size, his form managed to fill it perfectly.

"I'm afraid I don't have an answer for you there," Alexis sighed. "The shadow you see before you is but a veneer of who I really was. It is severely limited in its understanding and neurological pathing. You are going to have to ask more specifically if you want a useful answer."

Winston thought for just a second before firing back a response.

"Who has entered the suite this week?

Alexis did not hesitate in providing an answer.

"The androids and the body are the only individuals to enter this room before your unceremonious invasion."

If the killer wasn't one of us, Alice pondered, *where would he or she be hiding if not here.*

"Can you provide us a list of the occupants who have come and gone from the Arbor for the past few months?" Asked Alice.

"This phantasm does not have access to that information,"

Alexis responded. "I am a local sentry and nothing more. My databases are limited at best."

"Okay," Alice tapped her foot as she searched her mind for the right information. "What weapons are in the suite?"

"Beside the turrets, there is a bow hanging on the wall in the den—but no arrows, there is a non-functioning Remington .308 rifle mounted in the bathroom, my sabre is nested in its sheath in the master bedroom, and there are two spearcaster rounds in the den beside the fireplace."

"What is a spearcaster?" Alice asked instinctively.

"I'm sorry, but the weapon is not here. I don't have any information on it. The ammunition is on my manifest, but simply as a line-item."

"I'll go grab the sword," Winston whispered as he headed to the door on their immediate right.

"Ah, the looting has finally begun," Alexis chuckled. "I'm thrilled that my ornamental trinkets will prove to be of such use to you. What valor you have showcased in this incursion against your betters."

"We are fighting for survival here," Alice justified the thievery. After she paced a moment more, another question came to her mind. "Can you provide a list of authorized users to this room? Who are the friendly targets?"

"This action requires privileges that you do not have," the hologram smirked.

"Alexis, tell her what she wants to know," Winston ordered as he re-entered the room with sword in hand.

"There is Mr. Graham, Evelyn Fox, Alexis Fox, Silas, Timothy, Jack Wortz, Rudy Fl—"

"What did you just say?" Alice interrupted.

"I was answering your question. Is that not what you just asked me to—"

"Repeat it!" Alice barked.

"Hmm," Alexis growled. Even this vision of him did not like being bossed around. "Winston Graham, Evelyn Fox, Alexis Fox, Silas, Timothy, Jack Wortz, Rudy Flynn, and Constance Williams."

This was some sort of game. It had to be. Alice shook her head with increasing urgency.

"What the *fuck* do you mean, Jack Wortz?" she screeched.

SEVENTEEN

WINSTON FINALLY PUT THE NAME TO HIS KNOWN ASSOCIATION. "Jack Wortz—Wortz, Eleanor and James?" he mumbled unbelievingly.

"You're lying!" Alice shouted at the machine. "Why would you say that?"

"Ms. Trudeau," Alexis grunted, rising from his seat. "I cannot lie to you once privileges have been given from an administrator. They have been provided by Mr. Graham, and he *is* a system psuedo-user. There are no errors in my programming. There cannot be. My database has not been tampered with. I believe it was Jack Wortz you had doubts about. Allow me to read that user's data entry. 'Jack Wortz, construction director, ID last active here six months ago.' Is this him?"

A projection of Alice's brother was cast in unmistakable three-dimensional still in the center of the room. He wore a typical stupid grin. Seeing him in such vivid detail caused her to bring a palm to her mouth in shock. It was Jack. There was no questioning it. She felt her insides twist and turn in her gut. The story had become so much more convoluted now.

"What the hell is he talking about, Alice?" Winston turned on his compatriot. "Your brother built this fucking thing? And now you are here by *sheer* coincidence? That is the most outrageous farce I've ever heard."

"I don't know! He wouldn't have done that," Alice stammered. "He *couldn't have* done that."

Alice began to slide the puzzle together.

"Maybe he . . ." she paused. "Maybe he didn't know what he was building. I've seen his work. It's entirely possible that while the structure was made by him, the innards were—"

"Structurally critical in many places. They sure as shit don't seem like an afterthought to me!" Winston boomed. "He wouldn't have been made an administrator to the system unless he was here *while* the system was active."

Jack, what the hell did you do? Alice thought. Her brother was so kind. He was such a superb father. It was impossible that he could have been a part of this. Wasn't it?

"Mr. Fox, play system logs surrounding all users. I don't care if it's video, audio, or text. Tell us what you know!" Winston ordered.

"Those records have been purged from my system," Alexis returned flatly.

"By whom?" Alice whipped instinctively.

"The system does not provide information of that depth," the construct replied. "Information permanently deleted by an administrator is simply—gone. No backup copies are kept if the intention was to purposely obfuscate their discovery."

"Shit!" Winston aimed a clenched fist at the gilt cream stucco wall. The plaster chipped as his knuckles scraped against the unforgiving surface. Winston shook his hand after the impact. "Fuck! This is solid stone!"

"What did you think it was made of?" Alice asked in a bemused tone.

"Is there anything else you need?" Alexis broke in. "My time is valuable, and I tire of frittering it away on churlish folk who seek only to plunder what information and possessions I have. Did you not get enough from my office?"

Alice turned back to the holoprojection. Her mouth fell open slightly as she analyzed his statement.

"What do you mean by that?" Alice sought clarification.

"Playing coy, Ms. Trudeau?" he replied.

"*We have maybe five minutes!*" Evelyn called from downstairs. "*Could be less! It's time to finish up!*"

"What are you talking about?" Winston posed the same question. "Your office is locked behind a plate steel door. No one has been in or out of it since you passed."

"Well." Mr. Fox thought over his objection. "That isn't quite the whole truth for several reasons. The door was opened once a week ago, and it has remained unlocked since the parasite, Mr. Corgrave, successfully hacked the system seventeen hours ago. In fact, it was just opened a moment ago by Ms. Wortz."

Seventeen hours ago? The door is unlocked. Eleanor! Alice thought.

She spun on her heels and raced downstairs.

"And will one of you worthless simpletons get that body out of my bedroom!" the hologram called as Alice flew out the door.

A few minutes prior to this, Eleanor had been left alone downstairs, much to her own chagrin.

"What do you mean I'm not coming?" she objected.

"Thank you for the keys, but we can't take the risk of putting you in harm's way," Alice explained. "Besides, we are likely to find some very unpleasant things, and you have seen more than your share of ugliness. More than that, someone must keep James safe."

Eleanor huffed but could not repudiate her logic. James looked fragile enough after coming down from his high on LSD.

No child should have to endure that, and she could only imagine the things he saw. The boy seemed less than eager to divulge exactly what horrors he had been presented with. If they were anything like the terrors that haunted Eleanor, she was sure that the imagery would stick with him for quite some time.

"Fine, go. I'll babysit," Eleanor capitulated.

As Eleanor watched the crew march up the stairs with determination, she wondered exactly when she would be treated like a contributing member of society and less like a glorified governess. It wasn't Alice's fault. She wanted to keep them safe. But Eleanor was a woman now. She had her own opinions and skills to contribute. She tapped her palm against the beautiful but mangled reception desk.

"It's utter bullshit," she mumbled quietly.

Eleanor watched James wander the lobby. He took long wobbling steps and forced air through his closed lips to make a motoring sound. She was astounded by him. He was so normal despite a set of scarring circumstances. Eleanor wondered about his mental resilience. The only way she could imagine his carefree attitude was a tremendous amount of compartmentalization. The boy had to have a recess of his mind that held the most twisted and vile sections of his memory. *Note to self*, she thought. *Get him into therapy ASAP upon return to the mainland.*

"Maybe I should get back into it, as well," she breathed.

"*What?*" James called from the center of the room in front of her. "I didn't hear you!"

"I wasn't talking to you, James!" she replied tersely.

"Well, then, who *were* you talking to?"

Eleanor let out a deep sigh and pulled over a high-backed chair that had been resting against the wall. It looked like the chair could have belonged in the dining room, but the design was just slightly different. The cherry wood curled toward the top and sloped downward toward a lavish royal blue cushion. It looked surprisingly comfortable even without padding on the backside.

Eleanor plopped down and rested her feet on the reception desk. James seemed to take the unrefined nature of her action as a cry for help and strolled over lazily making strange noises with his mouth along the way.

"Oh. My. God. I'm so *bored!*" He enunciated with each step.

"You know what I always say," Eleanor quipped. "Bored people are boring."

James wore a mocking look of shock on his face as he took a step back.

"My goodness!" he exclaimed with a smile. "I just came over to you to have a good time, and I'm honestly feeling so attacked right now."

Eleanor flipped up her middle finger at her brother.

"I'm sure you'll get over it," she chuckled. "Now, go and find yourself something to do!"

Not wanting to upset Eleanor or continue to have his mood further harshed by her unconstructive criticism, James wandered behind the reception desk and into the coat closet. He rifled through the colorful garments of all shapes and sizes. James wondered if these clothes all belonged to the people who had died before him.

He shook off this thought and pulled down a beige safari-hat from an organizer that sat just beside the entry to the dark room. A pair of gilded initials were sewn in raised-gold type inside the brim.

WG

Content with his discovery, he placed the oversized fabric crown over his head and giggled as the brim drooped well over his forehead. Venturing farther into the room, he spied a tanned leather duster that he felt would serve as perfect accoutrement to his new rugged look. The coat provided a gratuitous amount of warmth in a rapidly chilling home. Cold air poured through from the kitchen. It slowly fought a winning battle against the home's central heating system.

As he reveled in self-satisfaction with his matching coat and hat, his attention was grabbed by what several others before him had overlooked. He was curious about the beeping emanating from behind the pile of clothing in the back of the closet. James ripped away at the heap, sending deep maroon garments flying over his head and priceless fur coats careening into the flanking walls. Finally, he was face-to-face with the panel of wood that concealed the console. He grabbed the nickel handle and slid it out of the way. On the screen before him was an old user interface. It wasn't a three-dimensional hologram, but instead seemed to be a simple touchscreen.

The look was boxy and had many buttons on-screen including fire suppression, security, food service maintenance, personnel, and lighting control Even in his current state of blissful curiosity, James knew the security tab would be extremely important. He clicked it and saw surveillance feeds, door control, and emergency transponder flip onto the screen.

James gasped and tapped the transponder. The words *transponder active, proceed to emergency broadcaster* flashed across the screen in a pop-up before returning to the previous button options. He tapped the surveillance feeds and saw a screen full of camera feeds fill the screen. Most of the rooms made sense and were empty, but his gaze was drawn to the bottom right square.

Containment

His slim finger tentatively reached for the tempting square and the pitch-black feed filled the screen. He couldn't see anything but found himself trembling, nonetheless. Despite a lack of visual stimuli, he could *hear* something. A low menacing growl cycled repeatedly. The rumbling was paced by a sort of clicking just before the pattern repeated. If only he could see the menacing thing.

Almost answering his request, whatever it was noticed him. He couldn't see it, but the eyes caught the infrared lighting of the security camera and flashed green. They were gigantic. It seemed to be an error in the feed. He was sure of it. It wasn't until they began to approach the camera that James repelled from the screen and slammed the tiny red x in the top of the feed.

"What the bloody hell?" His breath came quick and raggedly. The camera was playing tricks. It had to have been.

He tried to shake off the momentary terror, but he continued to tremble. He had not been prepared for that. With any luck, he'd never get to meet whatever was being contained.

"James what the hell was—" Eleanor walked into the closet, and her mouth dropped open. "Oh my God, you got it!"

The girl slid down beside her brother and flipped the page over to door locks. She tapped the door immediately to their right and the wall hissed beside them.

"You're amazing, little brother! How did you get it?" Eleanor smiled.

"I, uh . . ." James paused. "I'm just that good!"

Eleanor shook her head and ran a hand across his tangled dirty-blonde locks before continuing.

"Come on, James. Let's go get rescued!" Eleanor said with the first degree of hope she'd had in a while.

The pair of siblings cautiously moved from the coat closet to the office beside it. The room was long like the library had been, but on a smaller scale. At the end of the room, an Ebony-Wood titanic desk sat with a pair of black leather armchairs were before it. The burlwood leather chair behind the desk was expertly crafted to be sure. The structure curved outward as the cushion fanned out toward the top. Beautifully stained accents left little doubt as to whom the chair belonged.

Despite the ornate gold and green wallpaper, and the undoubtedly priceless collection of antiquities, their attention snapped to the lit radio in the middle of an end table beside the couch in the middle of the room. They both raced over to it with haste. Eleanor reached it first and pressed in the transmit button while James tried to hop directly over the extremely padded dark maroon couch. He got hung up on the cushions and had to fight his way to her side as she began speaking.

"This is Eleanor Wortz. We are locked in the Arbor and need immediate rescue!"

There was an awful silence as she awaited a response. She repeated her call. Again, she tried the phrase. After a few minutes, no one had answered.

"El, look!" James said as he pointed to the top of the radio.

A two-digit channel indicator sat in the middle of the grey box.

"Shit," Eleanor fussed. She pressed the up arrow beside the display and the 01 switched to 02.

"This is Eleanor Wortz. We are at the Arbor and in need of immediate rescue!"

"This could take a while," James whispered. He let out a sigh and rested his head on the armrest of the comfortable couch. *There's got to be something else*, he thought. He groaned and slowly began to roll off. Somehow, James managed to land on his feet and wandered over to the mammoth desk that sat a few feet in front of them. The desktop stood almost as high as his neck. He knew if he wanted to see its contents, he would need to get higher.

James approached the large leather armchair at the rear of the desk. He clambered up into the seat and sat up on his knees to observe the documents. His eyes drifted over several folders full of paperwork. Most notably, he remembered a name that he saw.

Wade Gomez—personnel

James remembered that was the name of man Peter had been looking for. As he reached for the red cardstock folder, he felt as though he were standing on the precipice of revelation. Suddenly his relaxed attitude was gone. Between the creature in containment and this mysterious man, he wished for a time before The Arbor. He wanted to forget. The reality of the situation cascaded down around him. He was probably going to die, just like everyone else he had once loved.

His tiny fingers grasped the information and opened the paperwork to its first page. There was a picture of a tanned Hispanic man paperclipped to a bio sheet. His vitals were laid out in detail. Wade was six foot three, two hundred and ten pounds, married, claimed twenty years acting experience, and hailed from New York City—Earth.

He flipped up the page to reveal the next.

Correspondence from his employer was laid out in a text thread.

I'm so very excited to come aboard. I know you will not regret hiring me. What are the job requirements? I can ship out right away.
WG

The job requires nothing that we won't be providing. Your presence is enough. Prepare by familiarizing yourself with twentieth century period mannerisms, literature, and practice your Mid-Atlantic accent. You will be expected to be an utterly flawless interpretation. Anything less will result in your immediate termination.
AF

Mr. Fox, you can understand why I would be nervous about this whole thing. I'm en-route now, but I can't imagine travelling all the way to Mars to simply be fired and turned away. I've been studying those recordings and I truly feel I've nailed the impression, but isn't there some kind of reassurance you can provide me?

WG

If you require coddling, I would suggest you search elsewhere, Mr. Gomez. I've no time for nascent boors who seek an ironclad guarantee of success. You will either complete the task or you will not. If you cannot appropriately perform your duties as a man of the stage, I will find someone who can.

AF

My apologies Mr. Fox. I am ready, and God knows I need the work. I will see you shortly.

WG

As the boy reached the end of the page, he instinctively flipped it again and read through what seemed to be a medical chart. It was hard to make out for someone unfamiliar with the terminology, but he clearly saw the words *reconstructive, malar implants, rhinoplasty, extensive trauma, reinnervation of bronchi, laryngeal electro-morphography, complete upper torso lightening with hydroquinone.* What had they done to the poor man?

As though reading a horror story, he continued onward. The next page was filled with the Gomez's immediate and extended family. The page had several crinkled marks from where teardrops had fallen onto it. James was disturbed that he could recognize the telltale signs so easily. As his family had gone over his grandmother's estate paperwork, and that of his parents, he'd become increasingly familiar with the sight of someone crying over documents.

He flipped the sheet to the back and saw an agreement of nondisclosure signed by Mr. Gomez. He was not to talk about the performance with anyone before, during, or after production. It outlined exactly what assets could be seized from himself and his family were he to break the agreement. He wasn't even to be allowed to call home until completion of the assignment.

As James turned the page, he was upset to see nothing behind it. He had reached the end of Wade's tale, at least for now. To his immediate right, he spotted another file just as Alice and the others burst through the door.

Arbor Construction Logs.

"Oh, my God!" Alice screamed with delight. "You got the radio working, El. That's brilliant!"

"Not quite enough, though," Eleanor complained. "I've tried twenty-three channels and no response. We are almost out of time. There's maybe a minute until the next hunt."

"Channel sixty-five!" Evelyn shouted as she dashed to the side of the radio.

Eleanor changed the frequency and pressed the transmit button hopefully.

"This is Eleanor Wortz. We are trapped at The Arbor with a killer. We need immediate rescue!"

The group stood hovering around the box hoping, and praying, for an answer.

"Eleanor Wortz?" the speaker called out. "Who the hell are you?"

Evelyn snatched the communicator from the girl and slammed her finger onto the transmit button.

"This is Evelyn Fox. Send transport now. This is not a drill!"

James silently slipped beside Alice and tugged on her blouse.

"Yes, sweetheart, just a minute," she dismissed, trying to hear the response.

"Right away, Ms. Fox, but the train is on its way back to us now. We have at least three hours until it gets here, and then another six to reach you. Just hold tight until we—"

The sound of the first clock chimes filled the large office.

"Shit!" Evelyn screamed into the microphone. "Hurry, we are about to lose power!"

James yanked hard on Alice's shirt this time and made her lean slightly to the side. He forced the file he was holding into her hand beside him.

"*Now!*" he harshly whispered.

Alice frowned, but pulled her attention away from the radio and ringing of the bells for a moment before the power could flash off. She opened the file. Inside was a basic synopsis of the Arbor's final days before completion.

Est.Completion date: November 12, 2102

Chief Architect: Alexis Fox

Construction Manager: Jack Wortz

Onsite Security Chief: Winston Graham

The rest of the paper faded to black as she focused keenly on the last name she'd read. Knowing that Alexis Fox designed the place was a big enough shock, but to see Winston in black and white beneath her brother's name could mean only one thing.

He'd been here for six months. Everything he had told her up to this point had been a lie. Every detail, from the robotics factory, to his feigned shock at seeing the resort for the first time, was all fake.

Her heart hammered in her chest as her breathing shortened. She flipped her head around like a cannon and fired her gaze at the man standing just a few feet behind her.

Winston stood statuesque, staring at the radio station. He noticed her rapid movement and his eyes snapped to her alarmed stare. Slowly, he turned his head so that he could return her glare.

His mouth was stretched into a perfectly flat line as the eighth bell rang out. Somehow, inside himself, he knew beyond a shadow of a doubt what the expression on her face meant. Winston took cool air deeply into his lungs before the last bell could chime. As the ringing tolled, the right side of his mouth jumped up only slightly.

It was time to indulge his dark craving once again.

EIGHTEEN

H<small>E'D KNOWN THIS DAY WOULD COME. HE'D BEEN</small> preparing for months. Truly, he'd longed for that look. The knowing glance felt like a hit of cocaine. What was he to do with it now? There was little point in extending the game farther. The others would all know soon enough. The timetable would need to be moved up. With rescue coming, everyone would need to die in the next ten hours, or he would be found out.

As the room filled with an eerie darkness, adrenaline coursed through his veins. He felt almost aroused at the thought of killing again. There was something so sensual about watching life drain from another's eyes. He was hungry for that particular high once more.

He had waited his whole life for this place.

Ever since he was a boy, Winston had been excited by death and pain. His mother looked on with such disgust as he would catch lizards around their home and snap their heads sideways like the tips of bean pods.

"Winston, love, please don't," she would say. "Just think of the

He never cared, though. Sometimes he used death like a pleasurable punishment for those who crossed him. One of his neighbors once called him a freak in front of his family. Winston was twelve years old when he snuck into their backyard. He injected rat poison into a steak and tossed it toward the doghouse of the Fleming family's St. Bernard.

He looked on with excitement as the happy dog stretched out the door of the blue-pastel enclosure. The canine drooled as it approached the slab of meat and took several ripping bites. After just under an hour, the poor unfortunate mutt lay dead in the midst of the Fleming's lawn. Winston was far from finished. He carved up the dead animal and flung the scraps about the yard.

After he'd come back home, Winston had hesitantly washed the blood from his hands and thrown his clothes into a garbage bag. He hated to throw away such a canvas of perfection, but his desires needed to be kept hidden, at least for now.

The next day, a very angry Jacob Fleming came knocking on his parents' door. He screamed profanities and called Winston all sorts of derogatory names, but Winston's father stood firm. His father asked what proof the family had of their theory that his son had done it. Winston had been cautious; he knew there was none. The dog passed quietly, with only a few miserable whimpers as it succumbed to the poison. They certainly hadn't seen him at the time, or they would have cried out bloody murder.

"You must know it was him!" Jacob howled.

Winston's father had stood tall like a statue. His features were stoic as the man raged on. He told Mr. Fleming to come back with proof of Winston's guilt and not to bother them again until that time.

Todd Fleming cornered Winston the next day after school. Winston got off the bus from his private school and was tossed into the retaining wall of the retention pond behind the stop by a furious preteen.

"You better watch out, freak!" he seethed. "Me and my friends are going to make your life a living hell."

Winston brushed off his clothes as the boy reared back for a right hook. The punch caught him in the jaw and was respectably strong for a prepubescent boy. Winston tasted a hint of blood and spat to the side as he turned back toward the boy.

"That was one," he flatly said.

"One what?" Todd replied.

"One for the thing I took from you," Winston informed. "Should you touch me again, I'll be forced to even the score."

The boy had looked at Winston with confusion. These weren't the words of a stable twelve-year-old. Winston sounded more like a megalomaniacal super villain in that moment than a child. He took a step toward Todd and began to whisper.

"I wonder what I would cut out next?" Winston purred softly. "Your sister, your mother, your father . . . do you have any other pets you'd be willing to part with? Maybe. . ."

Winston had inched even closer to his rival so that his breath flowed over the child's face.

". . .maybe I could take you instead," Winston said with subdued excitement. He flipped open a pocketknife and dragged the flat edge of the blade up the boy's trousers. "Maybe I could just slice a piece or two. Would you terribly miss your right ear, or your pinky toe, or even something more critical?"

The knife stopped just above Todd's crotch. The traumatized boy was frozen in place, listening to Winston's verbal assault. Dark streaks appeared in the boy's blue jeans as his courage failed along with his bladder. He dropped to his knees and began to sob quietly.

"Please—" Todd shook his head with his hidden face buried

in his palms. "Please don't hurt me. I don't want. . . I will leave you alone, I swear! Just don't hurt my family!"

Winston folded the slim blade calmly back into its grip. He looked down with positive revulsion at the weak child kneeling before him.

"Pathetic," Winston grumbled. He left the blubbering boy there and walked home without saying anything else.

Mr. Fleming once again visited Winston's father that night. The two had a heated argument for almost thirty minutes on Winston's front porch. He listened from his room upstairs.

". . .and it seems awfully convenient that your son, who has an obvious grudge against mine, Mr. Fleming, is the only one who witnessed this incident. I'll have none of it and bid you goodnight!"

Winston heard a door slam downstairs and then silence.

He remembered how his father came up with such serenity. There was no pretense of misunderstanding about what Winston had been doing. Winston was told he needed to find an outlet. They began hunting together the following week.

This placated him for a time, but he still snuck out for the thrill of killing that which was thought safe. Winston began to take more precautions. He wore shoe covers, leather gloves, long pants tucked into his boots, and even shaved his arms and legs to avoid dropping body hair that could be traced back to him, not that police regularly used DNA evidence to track down pet murderers.

When he was nineteen, Winston had crept into the home of a young professor. This woman had unfairly graded his papers, saying that his societal ideas were sick and hardly to be promoted. He'd gotten a C in that class despite expertly crafted essays. She had gone on about her prized parakeet in class. Winston's next target seemed clear.

He'd slithered around her apartment and slowly approached the covered cage. Killing the bird quietly would be challenging, but he had thought of a way. He'd brought a canister of carbon monoxide with him that could easily choke out the life from her innocent feathered friend. Winston slipped the tube underneath the cloth and turned the valve on the top of his cylinder. The gas ran out for a minute or two before rattling began to fill the cage. He had heard that gassing would be a silent death, for humans perhaps. The parakeet let out a loud pair of dying howls before falling from his perch and thudding against the bottom of the cage. Winston spun around and saw a shadowy figure rising from the bed. She began to tiptoe out into the living room and Winston was forced to think fast.

He'd crouched behind a burgundy-cloth reclining armchair and watched as his professor dizzily shuffled to the cage

"What's wrong, baby?" The woman whispered as she lifted the cloth from her pet's enclosure. Shock washed over the thirty-something woman as she recognized the lifeless form of her parakeet on the bottom of the cage. "Oh my God, Maisie! Shit!"

She had reached inside and plucked the bird from its resting place. She ran to her granite kitchen counter and began giving the tiny animal CPR. Winston tried to suppress a laugh as she wrapped her lips over the bird's beak and blew air into its lungs. He failed. A slight and brief chortle rose over the alarmed hyperventilating of his professor.

Her head snapped toward his position, and Winston sunk lower. The woman grabbed a carving knife from her butcher block. The blade shook wildly as she began to realize that her pet's death might not have been an accident. Winston pulled his ski-mask down over his face. He'd hoped to avoid its use, but desperate times called for barbaric measures.

If the bitch would have discovered the bird in the morning, it would have been untraceable. Autopsies aren't usually performed on furry or feathered friends, so its cause of death might have been ambiguous. Unfortunately, the connections would be far from challenging in this case. Winston had been seen to be furious with her during office hours. Even if he escaped, it wouldn't have been a stretch to connect him to the conspiracy. There might have been a piece of evidence he missed. His history might have been obvious to outside observers. Winston couldn't let her report this.

He sprang from his hiding place and hammered his knuckle against the backside of her wrist, which sent the blade flying sideways into the drywall. The knife buried itself deeply into the sheetrock. The woman had been caught unaware. She tried to fight, but Winston at the peak of young health wrapped her into a tight bear hug from behind. His powerful arms began to constrict around her like a serpent. The professor tried to claw at his massive arms, but she was severely outmatched in both strength and endurance.

He'd slipped his right arm around her neck and yanked back so her spine lay flush with his sternum. She tried to thrash her skull against his jaw, but only managed to cause a slight bleed on the inside of his cheek, as though he'd bitten into a sandwich wrong. It was hardly enough stopping power to abate his bloodlust. She choked and gasped to find breath but let out only hapless squeaks as the world began to fade.

Her hands fumbled around his face, searching for anything that could stop him. Finally, her fingers found his right eye. She pushed her middle knuckle forward and drove it into his eyeball. Unlike her useless attempts, this assault made Winston yelp in pain. His grip loosened ever so slightly and allowed the woman enough space to sink her teeth deeply into his tricep. She snapped down like her life depended on it and resembled more of a dog than a human as she clenched her jaw ever harder.

Winston shook her off and tossed her to the floor. The woman was stunned for a moment but managed to roll out of the way of a pounding jab. His fist pummeled the hardwood floor and not only cracked the board but tore through his thin skin as well. Rage flared in Winston's eyes as he turned back toward the professor.

"Please," she begged, "Just leave. I won't tell a soul. I just—I think you need help!"

Winston saw the blade that had been sandwiched by drywall was missing. He looked closely and saw a hand tucked behind her back. She was lying, just like the rest of the women in his life who had always deceived him. He rested his left foot on the woman's oak coffee table and with a powerful kick sent it hurtling toward her shins. The professor tried to jump over it, but the table caught her right leg just under the knee. She toppled forward and her head slammed into the surface of the piece of furniture. She looked to be out cold. The knife clattered to the ground beneath her.

Winston looked down at his arm. Red blood flowed down the sleeve and pooled in his glove. Luckily, he had chosen to wear long sleeves. The wound appeared to be well contained within his clothes—almost. He looked over at his professor's unconscious frame. She had made him. His identity would hardly be a secret . . . were she to wake. Worse yet, she had bitten him. He had read crime novels. He knew that as carefully as he might clean out her mouth, there was no way he could be sure a tiny scrap of flesh hadn't nestled itself between teeth. He'd need to take the evidence with him.

Winston retrieved the long blade from the floor and thrust it deeply into the back of her neck. The woman gurgled slightly but didn't cough. He was almost sure she felt no pain in the process. With a rough sawing motion, he disconnected her head from the rest of her body. He tried to make sure none of the blood got on his clothes. Despite the fact he would surely dispose of them at the end of this ordeal, he needed to get home without being suspected.

He stuffed the head into a doubled-up trash bag. He removed the fingers that had clawed his eyes as well and threw them in beside the empty gazeless face of the innocent woman. Winston spent the next hour scouring the place for any evidence that could lead back to him. When fully confident he had covered his tracks, Winston exited through the door he had entered, key in hand. He relocked the apartment and pulled his mask back up to reveal his face. One person saw him a couple streets over from the murder scene. They looked at him with a bit of suspicion, but Winston kept his wits about him.

He waved to the onlooker with a jovial smile. The observer's look changed to one of amusement.

"Bit late for a stroll around the neighborhood!" he called to Winston.

Without missing a beat, Winston replied.

"Bit early, you mean. I've got the AM shift. I'm on in an hour."

"Hoo boy," the man groaned. "Better you than me! Good luck, my man!"

With a grinning nod, Winston caught his breath again. It seemed like the nosy man had bought his excuse. It was a cold New York morning. His apparel fit the expectation. He'd even seen joggers carry spare clothes in trash bags before, so that wasn't entirely out of the ordinary.

Winston had the distinct advantage of being a handsome, well-off, white male. By his nature, he was not to be expected of crime or misdeeds. That was a thing for those of a lower class than him. He had gotten away with it. He knew it even then. Thing was, over eighty percent of murders in the United States were committed by friends, neighbors, family, and most often by the spouse or lover of the victim. Winston was none of that to his professor. He had even delayed the murder until the semester after his class, just barely, so he wouldn't be on her current roster of students.

It wasn't planned, per se. He'd meant to cause her pain by extinguishing her beloved pet, but it felt far more pleasing than anything he had ever done before. From his first kill, Winston was hooked. He disposed of the evidence of his deed by burning it in the backyard along with some old tires. The smell of rubber was enough to disguise the searing flesh being consumed by the massive flame.

His father was able to put together the pieces when the news story finally broke about his son's poor professor. He enrolled Winston in a paramilitary group defending transports and freighters from both land and sea-based pirates. The problem had grown over the years as more desperate people sought to plunder the massive wealth floating by their countries on a daily basis. He still, of course, went on hunts monthly with his family.

Winston's first critical error was several years later when his estranged mother came to visit. He was suspicious of her from the moment she walked through the door. People don't tend to come into the wealthy's lives just to socialize.

Sure enough, Isabella was broke and entirely starving for funds. He listened upstairs as she begged his father for money. His interest was particularly piqued when she screamed out a curious and doubtful revelation.

"He's not even yours!" she hissed. "I fucked Bill every night when you would work late."

"Isabella," his father sighed with resignation. "Why would you be telling me this now?"

"Because," she laughed. "You beat it out of me!"

The crazed woman took her fist and repeatedly slammed it into her nose until Winston heard cartilage crunch. She rotated punches around her middle-aged face, seemingly immune to the pain she had to be causing herself.

"You'll give me the fucking money because—" Isabella threw herself to the ground and then dragged bloodied hands across the sofa in their living room and over several other pieces of furniture. "I know you are on the board. Your company is going public Friday, right? Sure, you could fight the charges, maybe even win, but your *impropriety* will cost the company millions, maybe even billions."

Winston saw his father throw up his hands.

"You want some money, you'll have it," he finally concurred. "But after this, I want you out of our lives for good. We are leaving after the offering, and I don't expect to ever see you again."

"You won't, Brer, believe me." Isabella had smiled through bloodied teeth.

His father retrieved a bundle of cash a moment later and shoved it into her greedy hands. It looked to be at least fifty thousand in untraceable bills. He'd escorted her from the home without a word.

This just didn't sit right with Winston. If she had done it once, what was to stop her from doing it again? He didn't want to leave that up to chance. He just couldn't. One more killing before their move wouldn't be too much. Winston rapidly suited up and slid down the side of the roof to catch his mother. She hadn't brought a car. It was dangerous to walk through town after midnight all alone. Anything could happen.

He stalked her along the foggy street. She stumbled along as though she were high or drunk, or a mix of both. Winston knocked her into the drainage ditch beside the road and brought a weathered two-by-four down across her face. She screamed in agony after the first hit. He almost moaned as his mother's terrified eyes recognized him. She was permanently silenced after the second crushed her skull.

It had been over a year since he had killed someone at such an intimate distance. Killing pirates who didn't even speak his language was just not as fulfilling as murdering someone who did not expect it. He dropped the board and walked up from the crime scene to see a Greyhound stopped at the cross street. By the ghastly look on the driver's face, he knew that he was in trouble. Winston sprinted away and took side streets in case anyone tried to follow him, but the illusion had been shattered. He was sloppy.

The murder was televised the next morning.

Isabella Graham found dead. Witnesses say suspect was wearing all black and sprinted down Magnolia away from the scene. Police are questioning the onlookers to learn more.

His father was furious. Although he had an alibi being home with his children, the cameras on property had caught Winston sneaking out. His father paid a reliable family friend in the media business handsomely to edit out his son's appearance on the footage.

The irony was that the very damage that Winston had tried to avoid was compounded upon news of the woman's murder. Although the connection was not made the first morning, by the day of the initial public offering the association with the victim and Winston's father was everywhere.

It took many years for Winston to live down the shame that he'd brought upon his family, even though there was only one man who knew it. He finally was granted the job as head of security to the Mars JCN production facility due to all his family's remaining clout being spent. Against all odds, he flourished. But the hunger remained.

Lucky for him, killing Ordinals was so much easier than

citizens in a politically aware and watchful Earth. Mars more closely resembled The Wild West than high society, despite the simply ridiculous sums of cash being tossed about like party favors. People were separated from each other. The walkways were closed off. The streets were patrolled by soulless automatons empowered to be judge, jury, and executioner for crimes that were considered "clear cut." Luckily for those with means and ability, it was easy enough to construct a crime scene to fit any need.

The Arbor was simply the next natural step. It sounded like a fantasy as Winston made the plan. What more perfect place was there to deliver death and despair than at an isolated resort buried underneath more than a mile of ice. The only thing left to do was to get himself into a position of authority over the project. Strings were pulled. Favors were called in. Winston Graham became the security director over the facility.

The actual changing of the plans was almost effortless as a worker on the project. As contractors came in, he would switch out the blueprints for his own before delivering them to the work crews. The use of many subcontractors meant that no one talked to each other. Despite suspicious looking rooms and devices, the workers had no desire to miss out on what might prove to be nothing. Worse yet, many people on Mars who dared to ask questions had been blacklisted by members of the Mars oligopoly on high-paying jobs. Loss of a career above a certain level meant dropping to the lowly ordinals and serving as maids and manservants to an ungrateful and unforgiving populace.

The entire construction process was truly facile. Almost all of Winston's modifications were invisible to the naked eye when not activated. A spare pipe here could be chalked up to worker error. An extra-thick ceiling panel could be attributed to poor measurement leading to cover up of the mess. Any inconsistencies could be swept away as the all-too-real errors common within the business of construction. *What the customer doesn't know won't hurt them,* would be his reply when the local managers asked about discrepancies from the original plans.

Jack Wortz had visited very infrequently during the actual construction process. He was busy acquiring materials necessary for The Arbor's completion, which proved a challenging task due to the parts required by its choosy owner. The issues crept up when he began residing at The Arbor for the finishing stages of the build. Winston had done an excellent job hiding his modifications from the untrained eye, but Jack was far from a pliable imbecile. Winston remembered the turning point of the whole affair well.

"You're telling me one thing, Winston, but my contractors are telling me another. Now which is it? Did three separate foreman fuck this up in *substantial* ways, or is there something that I'm missing, because I've spent the last four goddamn days on the phone trying to figure out how the bloody hell this happened!" Jack fumed.

"You know what they say, Jack. *Good help is hard to find!*" Winston had said with a toothy grin.

"Don't bullshit me, Winston!" Jack had shouted. "One of the workers took a picture of his plans because he could hardly believe it. Look at this!"

Jack pulled up a three-dimensional shot of the blueprint on his phone. The entire Arbor stretched in blue and white above the display. He spread his pinched fingers apart over the moat surrounding the peninsula.

"Look here," Jack insisted. "These overflow pumps are installed backward. They are supposed to suck water *out* in case of a flood, but these would do the opposite. They could *pull* from the reservoir of water sitting a hundred meters east of here, and you know as well as I do what that would mean."

"That is why safety switches exist, Mr. Wortz," Winston had chided. "If they have been installed backward, then we must simply call the contractor, and have it reversed. If it would make you feel better, we could even install a few pumps in the interim that could take all the water out in the event of a catastrophic malfunction."

Jack ran his hands through his sandy blonde hair as he exhaled.

"Winston, if this failed—a few pumps wouldn't be enough. Theoretically, water could fill above the mansion's roof in fifteen minutes. These pumps are over ten times the size I indicated in the blueprint. Combined, the twelve pumps could manage—"

Jack pulled a calculator from his pocket and typed away, despite holding what was almost a supercomputer in the palm of his hand.

"Fifty-eight thousand cubic meters of water per minute! Look at this goddamn wiring and tell me it wasn't purposeful! The pathing of circuitry had to be changed all along the line in order to accommodate the higher-gauge electric wire. Now tell me again that the contractor not only ordered the wrong thing but covered his tracks by increasing materials cost by 10,000 percent."

Winston had underestimated Jack. He was no sheep to be led. Jack wasn't a machine-man like the rest of his underlings. He had opinions and the knowledge to back them up. In this case, it seemed that he had caught Winston in a lie.

"Perhaps," Winston stammered for the first time. "Perhaps it was an oversight in blueprint conversion to physical plan? I don't know what to tell you, Jack. It is truly beyond me."

Jack snapped the panels of his phone shut and stuffed the tablet back into the pocket of his worn jeans. His expression seemed to shift from one of frustration, to one of concern.

"That's the thing, Winston. If I'm to blame the conversion—I suppose I need to blame the converter," Jack's thundering grey eyes seemed to pass judgement on Winston in that moment. "You're either criminally incompetent, or a different type of something altogether. You see, when I look at all the mistakes as modifications—it seems like they tell a different story."

"I'm going to give you a chance to walk that back, Mr. W—"

"I wasn't finished," Jack interrupted. "You see, the pumps being larger could be advantageous if your *intent* was to flood the Arbor. That also begs the question, why were the foundation supports drilled a hundred meters down? Why were the walls changed from plaster to stone? Why were the shelves all built with— Jesus bloody Christ. It's designed to be reset. You *made* it like this."

Winston spun from Jack to hide the panic in his visage. This was exactly what he didn't need. Witnesses were what ruined him on Earth. He couldn't start the same cycle over with a new and set of eyes and minds.

"You don't know what you are talking about, Mr. Wortz. I'm afraid I will have to ask you to—"

"No—" Jack mumbled as the puzzle pieces fell together. "No, it makes perfect sense if you don't view the flubs as errors but as changed plans. They were—precautions. What the hell are you building, Mr. Graham?"

Rage swept over Winston's face as he entered the elevator to the train platform. He felt a gnawing, ripping, desire within him. It was like the beast was about to tear violently from his chest and consume the arrogant Jack Wortz in a boiling thrash of fury.

As the doors closed behind Jack, Winston drew a firearm from behind his back and pinned Mr. Wortz to the cold steel wall.

"Listen closely," Winston seethed as he pressed the pistol to Jack's temple. "When we get out of this elevator, you are going to resign, effective immediately, and tell no one why. You won't get your things. You won't make a scene. You are just going to leave. If you do anything different than this, I'll kill you, your wife, your daughter and son, and just about everyone else I can think of. There are plenty of backups I have, too, so if you seriously think police could stop me—just try telling them and I'll be laughing as I post bail during your son's funeral. Am I perfectly, crystal, clear?"

Jack nodded just as the doors retreated. Winston holstered his gun in view of the ordinal who had worked on the train for its entire existence. He wouldn't tell a soul. He valued his position too much. Jack looked as though he'd seen a ghost as he moved silently up the steps to the train and walked inside.

Winston used his influence to listen to the audio feeds from Jack's home on a nightly basis. For several months, he managed to keep it under wraps. Then one fateful afternoon, his wife found him crying in their bedroom. He told her everything. Winston was glad. It had been past time to feed the animal within him again.

He waited until the children had left the house that night. Winston paid for Jack's door to be unlocked. He'd sat on Eleanor's bed as he lay in wait for his prey. The couple entered the house around eight in the evening. He listened to their small talk while they put away their keys and unwound. It wasn't until they reached the master bedroom that Winston moved to strike.

He had a pair of pistols that night. One for each person he'd planned to kill. He wanted to tell them exactly why they were going to die before doing the deed. Winston made Jack kneel in front of him, something he'd wanted to do since he met the entitled bastard. He executed him at point-blank range and showered the floor with the man's insides. Cara's incessant screaming was irritating. He told her to stay put or there would be trouble as he walked from the room. Somehow, inside himself, he knew she wouldn't be able to just let him leave. She dashed for her dresser and Winston assumed there must have been some sort of weapon inside. He shot her through the neck, and she tried to crawl toward her husband. He had no stomach for the suffering of someone who he had no quarrel with. He shot her through the head as a showing of mercy. Winston thought he owed her that much.

To cover his tracks, he looked around the room for valuables. *What might be the most likely place to hide expensive things?* He thought. The mattress was the first place he looked, and sure enough, a minimally secure safe held what turned out to be a respectable amount of money in untraceable platinum bullion.

Winston was sure Jack hadn't told anyone else. Over the years, Winston had learned how to leave no trace. He disappeared from the Wortz home, content to never hear that name again. How surprising it was when he heard Alice talk about her dead brother. It seemed like kismet. He had never killed an entire family line before.

For that matter, killing a child seemed like it should have felt wrong, at least in theory. Despite that, Winston was more cavalier now. He was on his own home field. It didn't matter that Alice knew his identity now. It was useless for her to tell the others. He had many places to hide. After the next trap, at least one more would be dead. The only question that remained was: who?

How long did the others think they could survive his assaults? They would fall like the rest. The "survivors" would perish along with everyone else who had ever crossed Winston Graham. He stared right back into Alice's wild eyes as the bells finished their warning gongs. This quarry would be more exciting, it seemed.

This prey would fight back.

NINETEEN

A S THE POWER CUT AND THE LIGHTS WENT OFF, JAMES screamed.

Alice dropped the folder she had been holding and shook her phone to activate the flashlight. She swung the beam around at the other people in the room, but saw no innocent eyes staring up at her. There was no light pattering of steps in the dark. James was gone.

"Where the *fuck* are you, sick freak?" Alice roared.

"James? Where did James go?" Eleanor asked nervously, unaware of the non-verbal exchange that had occurred between Winston and Alice.

"That disgusting piece of shit took him!" Alice spewed angrily. "It's Winston! He planned this whole thing. He designed it!"

"What do you mean, *designed* it?" Evelyn asked doubtfully. "My father—"

"He must have changed the construction orders or something!" Alice growled as she searched every corner of the room. "Look in that file I dropped. He was the security chief over the construction of *this* facility, and he said he'd never been here before. I highly doubt he sat back and watched someone build a murder palace."

Evelyn hesitantly reached for the file Alice had dropped on the floor. It couldn't be true. His name wouldn't be there. She liked him. She *fucked* him. He couldn't be printed on some document that implicated his guilt, could he?

"My God," Evelyn groaned. "There he is. Now he has taken James. This has just gone from bad to worse, hasn't it?"

A dreadful groaning hum began to rise over their conversation. It seemed their next obstacle was coming to meet them. A moment later, the sound of water rushing from all sides and pounding into the building made a screaming crash. Rose peeked out from the office and saw what began as a puddle of water forming under the kitchen door turn to an invading force to be reckoned with.

"The flow is coming this way!" Rose warned. "We need to hurry!"

"Go get Mark!" Alice ordered.

Rose darted out toward the kitchen and left the others standing about, unsure what their next step would be. Alice needed to think quickly. Content that James was probably not sharing the room they were in any longer, she exited the office. As she stepped slightly down, she was met by water that already washed over her toes.

It's flowing so fast. All right, think. Where would he go? Alice wondered to herself as she looked around the first floor. Rose re-entered the room with Mark in her wake and breathed heavily as the water gathered around her shoes.

"Who can swim well?" Alice asked, turning around to face her peers.

"I hesitate to say this, but me," Mark sighed. He looked and saw Rose's hand lifted high beside him.

"Great," Rose mumbled. "Looks like we're a team again."

Alice looked to Evelyn. "Is there any way onto the roof?"

"Not sure what good it'll do us, but yes," Evelyn said. "Through my father's suite."

"Good," Alice nodded. "You two—"

"We'll look for James and Winston down here," Rose agreed. "You three sweep the upstairs."

Alice appreciated her friend again for the first time. She had always been very straightforward, and her willingness to explore a rapidly filling aquarium for a nephew that wasn't hers, with a murderer in the house, could almost be construed as brave.

"Thank you, Rose." Alice hugged her before beginning the slog through now ankle-deep water toward the staircase. Alice had half the keys to the rooms, and it hardly seemed likely Winston would flee there, but she had to check.

Downstairs, Rose used Eleanor's phone to find her way around. There was no more absolute measure of trust for a teenager than the act of lending her phone to someone else. Rose felt sort of privileged in that way. By the time they'd finished searching the common room to the best of their ability, the water was waist high.

"Did I ever tell you I was a lifeguard, Mark?" Rose asked as they made their way to the next room.

"No," Mark answered. "I'm surprised you didn't let me know, if I'm honest. You tend to—inform people of your skills."

Rose cast a side-eye glance his direction as they investigated the coat closet. Nothing. The frigid flow was even more chilled than pools she used to patrol in London. It seemed to suck the energy from her every time it washed up over a new body part. She guessed it was just over forty degrees, which meant they didn't have much time before their bodies gave out entirely.

"I really did love you," Rose informed him as she swam under with the phone. The light barely cast a beam two feet in front of them as they circled the dining room. Rose briefly came back up for oxygen before re-entering the room with the now-bobbing barricade. Furniture cracked and smashed into each other, presenting an unforgiving environment to swim through. She faced Mark's slightly pale face as she looked toward the kitchen door, with water now licking the underside of the top doorframe. "Get around this furniture while you can. I'm going to check the kitchen briefly, and I'll be right behind you."

"Rose I—" he began. What was he to do with the revelation she presented him with? "I'm sorry."

"Not important," Rose sighed. "Get around the barricade and head upstairs, now!"

Rose plunged back under and pushed her way through the swinging door. She had always been adept at holding her breath. Doing so in water that was only slightly above freezing was a new stress test for her. Despite a thorough searching, she found nothing. It was only on her way out that she noticed the bubbling from the ceiling. Why hadn't she thought of that before? The hotel rooms seemed to stretch in one direction from the top of the stairs, but the kitchen was slightly offset from the rest of the floorplan. There had to be a room above it. She could hazard a guess as to whose room might harbor an entrance. She took note of this and pushed back through the kitchen door.

Her muscles began to ache as her body craved oxygen. She noticed a tiny pocket of air at the corner of the dining room and pushed chairs and tables aside to reach it. She streaked upward until her lips found the familiar chill of air after being underwater. She knew the flow wouldn't abate, and she would soon be trapped. Rose made her way back toward the stairway and the others.

After the survivors had poked their way around the rooms they could search, they headed back to Mr. Fox's suite. As they pushed open the unsecured door, Alexis Fox's hologram flashed on before them.

"It wasn't enough to take everything I owned in life," he snapped. "Now you feel the particular compulsion to flood it as well?"

"What can we say, Father?" Evelyn said as she entered behind Alice. "We felt like a swim, and this seemed the most effective and sensible way to accomplish that."

"Always one for the theater, Eve," the ghost of Mr. Fox returned.

Something about the way he'd said her name struck Evelyn. It was the most inconvenient time for her psyche to give weight to his death, but here it was happening, regardless. She bit down hard on her lower lip and pushed past the illusion, trying not to think about who it represented.

Water began to flow into the room at the same time Mark rushed in. His breathing was rapid as he gasped for air and warmth.

"Rose, coming, checked kitchen, told me to go. Said I'd slow her down."

Against all odds, Alice thought she actually understood Mark's message that had been sent through chattering teeth. Mark was soaked from head to toe. She knew that getting him out of his wet clothes could be a priority later, but for now they had to avoid the rapidly rising tide.

As Mark finished his announcement, Evelyn made her way to her father's master bedroom. The scent of the body flooded her senses immediately. She felt ill. Despite the offending situation, Evelyn pushed through to his closet and more specifically the panel in the ceiling. She retrieved a long rod from the right side of the closet door and pressed it up into the opening. Eleanor watched as she turned a locknut on the panel and the hatch came swinging down.

"This will get us into the attic," Evelyn explained. "From there we will have to cross the studs to reach the roof exit. We are going to need to move fast, it seems."

As Evelyn continued to speak with Eleanor, the water rose more rapidly. Alice speculated that this was due to the shape of the dome. The bottom half would take longer to fill than the top. Unfortunately for them, the water had filled the entire base of the cavern and now crawled rapidly upward.

One by one, the survivors scrambled up into the refreshingly warm attic. Surprisingly, it looked much like any other attic—just taller. Flooring had been placed along the entire surface and numerous suitcases had been tossed hither and yon. It seemed Winston wasn't fond of waste. Crossing the mostly empty room was easy enough, although its length was surprising. The attic stretched over all the living quarters of the Arbor, and the roof ladder sat just above the center of the room.

Water started to bubble through the still-open closet hatch as Evelyn pulled the roof-access down. The unrelenting flood was rising beyond quickly now. As Evelyn reached and unlocked the hatch, the waves licked at Eleanor's knees.

"Hurry!" Alice encouraged. As she climbed the ladder to temporary safety, she did not particularly want to think about what would happen once they reached the roof. More importantly, she tried not to focus on where James might be. She couldn't stand it. If she let her mind drift in that direction, there would be no functioning because of the paralytic worry it would bring about. Alice felt the near-frozen air brush against her soaked legs and thought about how insufferable it would be for Mark and Rose whose whole bodies had been stewed in icy broth. Evelyn offered her hand to help Alice crawl through the narrow opening and onto the uneven roof.

"Not sure where we go from here," Evelyn sighed. She

looked out over the veritable sea of water now surrounding the mansion with concern. This situation seemed truly dire. The water would sap the strength of anyone caught in it. The problem of sinking against the flow wasn't their main issue; exhaustion was.

"Wait," Rose muttered as she joined the others at the Arbor's highest point. "The tunnel!"

Rose pointed at the train passage that still sat over a hundred feet above them. There seemed to be a small glimmer of hope in her eyes.

"What if we let the water raise us up to the tracks and then we made our escape?" Rose continued.

Evelyn shuffled her feet slightly.

"I can't really—swim," she admitted.

"You can't *swim?*" Rose asked in disbelief.

"It just wasn't—I can tread water, but if I had to go that far? There's just . . . it wouldn't happen."

"Oh my God, James!" Eleanor screamed.

She had wandered a bit from the group and looked down over the colossal skylight that let illumination bathe the lobby when the lights were on. Eleanor shone her recently regained light down onto the half-sphere of thick glass. There, desperately treading water in the center of the mass, was James.

"Oh no, sweetheart, no!" Alice let out a plaintive cry. "Evelyn, where is the maintenance hatch?"

Evelyn stared dumbfounded at the boy struggling for his life. His face contorted as he gasped at the rapidly shrinking bubble in the dome.

"How do we get in there?" Alice changed her tone and shouted at the befuddled woman.

"You—" Evelyn paused. "You can't. The ventilation holes are small and along the periphery. There aren't any—"

"I can do it," Rose mumbled, nodding her head in solid

resolve. She seemed to be almost convincing herself as her skull continued to bob. "I will save him. I have to."

Rose sprinted back toward the attic hatch which was already being swallowed by rapidly rising waves. She tore at her shirt buttons along the way. After the blouse dropped to the ground, she slipped from her trousers.

"I'm going to be squeezing through some tight spaces. I can't afford a snag," she explained.

"Rose, you can't," Alice muttered. "It's at least a hundred meters underwater. It's suicide. You'll di—"

Rose turned to face Alice and placed a finger over her mouth.

"It's what I have to do."

Without offering time for rebuttal, Rose disappeared under the rising waters. She sped through the current like a torpedo. Alice hadn't even noticed her phone slipping from her hand as Rose grabbed it.

It's all right, Rose thought. *She'll have it back soon enough.*

The waters stripped heat from her like an ice box. Rose contorted her smooth and toned body to fit through the tiny opening in the floor of the attic. As she passed through the second hatch into Mr. Fox's bedroom, she let out a slight amount of air to scream in silence. Her muscles started to whine in protest. Luckily, the goal couldn't have been more than fifty meters ahead. She wouldn't last much longer than that. She hadn't planned to.

As she entered the main hall of rooms, Rose kicked her feet into high gear. She thrust her limbs against the water madly. She watched as the bubbling boy dropped into her vision. He was struggling to stay afloat and looked to be quickly losing the battle. Rose swirled her arms so quickly that they almost seemed to blur. She wondered if that was her speed, or her senses failing.

She reached James about ten feet beneath the surface and

wrapped him into her arms. The boy was hardly conscious and completely spent.

It's all right, James, she thought. *Your favorite aunt's got you.*

She rotated toward the top of the ceiling and watched Alice just above the glass as she ascended in the water.

Alice had swum downward to view them as the water continued to flood. She shook her head as she saw her friend swimming up, and not out. She slammed a fist into the glass and mouthed Rose's name.

Rose's plan hadn't been to rescue James by getting him out. Rose just needed him to last longer than she would. She forced his head back into the warm bubble of air and felt relief on her palms as she kept her torso underwater. This wasn't a deliverance; it was a sacrifice.

She struggled to kick as she felt her lungs begin to burn. Icy liquid flowed into her body like embalming fluid. It strained every instinct Rose had within her to stay just beneath the surface. Finally realizing what she was doing, James began to tug at her shoulders and hair in vain.

Alice watched his pained sobs as he pulled for her to rise in vain. Alice was running out of air. She propelled herself from the glass with her feet and swam much farther than she had come initially to reach the surface. All the others were treading water thirty feet above the roof now. Eleanor grabbed Alice to help her stay afloat.

"Where's James?" she asked in a panic.

"With Rose," Alice sobbed.

"And where's she?" Eleanor spat impatiently.

"Saving him." Alice sniffed before taking another breath. "By sacrificing herself."

Evelyn floated over, grasping her pants in front of her arms. They'd been inflated and tied off at the ends presumably before the water fully engulfed the roof.

"Take off your pants!" she insisted.

Eleanor looked at her with confusion before seeing what she held.

"I'll help you tie off the ends," she said, with a roll of her eyes.

"No!" Eleanor replied.

"Eleanor, do it!" Alice chastised. "I need to go back down. James needs to know to float on his back."

Alice took a heaving breath before disappearing back beneath the waves. Suddenly, she heard the pumps stop. *Rose,* she thought, fiercely propelling herself downward. Luckily, the pumps made a different sound now. She assumed they had flipped into reverse after Rose—she didn't even want to think about it.

Finally, she met James at the dome, pressure squeezing around her like a vise. She motioned for him to lay back and tried fruitlessly to ignore her friend's corpse sinking beside him. He finally understood her message and rotated onto his back. As soon as he did so, Alice was forced to resurface. The water level was receding, albeit slower than it had come in.

"Is James all right?" Eleanor screeched as she positioned herself over the roof in preparation of finding her footing. When she heard the speakers blast the gong from overhead, she'd feared the worst.

"He should be," Alice answered as she gasped for breath. Her feet met roof tile as her strength gave out.

"I'll get James," Mark sighed as he ran back toward the opening in the roof. It was the least he could do, to swim down to him as Rose had. She'd done so much more for him, though. Mark couldn't help thinking it should have been him. Perhaps he could have saved the both of them.

It was nonsense. As he journeyed lower into the home, lights blinked on as the water sunk beneath their fixtures. The impressive design of the place was enough to almost make him forget its evil purpose. He swam more rapidly as he watched James sink

across his line of vision. Mark reached James and swept the boy
into his arms as he returned to the surface. He transported the
now-unconscious boy over to the top of the stairs which had just
revealed themselves. He wasn't breathing.

The Wortz child felt like a sack of ice in his arms. Mark
flipped the body down onto the soaked carpet and immediately
took a huge breath of air and forced it into the child's lungs.
Eleanor screamed as she entered the scene from Alexis Fox's suite.

"Get over here! You're on breaths!" he insisted.

Eleanor had no intention of waiting for a second insistence.
She sprinted down the squelching carpet and slid down beside
James, her knees slamming into Mark with her momentum. She
felt the urge to apologize, but she was so entirely overcome with
worry that she could do nothing more than stare as Mark leaned
repeatedly into her motionless brother.

"Wake up, love!" she demanded. "Don't you dare do this to
me! We're a team, remember?"

"Now!" Mark shouted as he pointed toward James' mouth.

Normally Eleanor would have objected to kissing her brother
on the mouth, but she leapt into action with fervor. She tilted the
frozen head back and pinched his nose. Eleanor expelled all the
oxygen she had into her brother's lungs.

"No, no!" Alice muttered as she watched Mark resume compressions. "Please, James! Mark, do you need me to take over?"

"Not yet!" he replied curtly without breaking stride.

Mark hummed the Macarena to himself as he continued.
The old catchy tune had proved itself to be an effective melody
to time compressions. Mark fought his emotions as he pumped
roughly.

It's all right to break a rib if it means saving the life, he told
himself. "Fuck, come on, James. Don't do this to Alice. You can't
do this to me!"

"James, baby, you have to wake up for me. I can't lose you, too," Alice sobbed.

"First Rose, and now James." Evelyn shook her head sadly.

"Don't you say that!" Alice barked. "He's not—we are not giving up yet! I refuse to!"

"Well, let's at least get him in front of the fire!" Evelyn argued. "If the boy is to survive, there's no way he can do it without warming first!"

Evelyn was right. Mark picked up James and carefully made his way back downstairs. In the several minutes they had been performing CPR, the building had completely drained. Against all his expectations, the fire was roaring just as it should have been. It seemed the entire house was planned to survive the purposeful flooding. He placed James gently before the blaze and continued pumping away after giving him another breath.

Fifteen minutes elapsed and their worry turned to hopelessness.

"Alice, how long are you going to drag it out?" Evelyn asked.

"Until he wakes up!" she fired back with a broken intonation.

"I—" Evelyn trailed off. "I can't watch this anymore. Mark has broken at least two ribs while I've been watching, and he looks like he's knocking on death's door himself."

Evelyn observed what the few other survivors had failed to notice before she left the room. Mark was dripping sweat from every pore in his body. He seemed to shiver and overheat at the same time. Crimson lines ran down his arms from muscular exhaustion. He'd swam for so long and continued to deliver life-saving aid for over fifteen minutes. He clearly needed a break.

"Mark, I'm taking over," Alice said flatly.

"No, I can do this!" he protested. "I have to save James!"

Alice placed a hand over his shoulder and felt his rock-hard muscles bulging through his shirt after their overexertion.

"You can't do that if you're dead. Now rest."

"Fine," he grunted through compressions. "We'll switch at the next breath. Eleanor, go in three, two, one."

Eleanor breathed fresh oxygen into James and Mark flipped sideways out of Alice's way so she could continue with chest compressions. There was still plenty of fight in her. Admittedly, the amount was decreasing by the minute. At some point, she would have to face the inevitable.

She matched the motion Mark had set and looked over her shoulder. In the thirty seconds since he had moved from James, Mark passed out behind the crew and lay sprawled out across the common room floor.

"I guess his body really had done enough," Eleanor said with what would have been a smile, if she could have conjured one.

Alice felt the same exhaustion Mark did ten minutes after she had taken over. Their efforts would need to end soon. She just didn't know how to stop. How could she let James go? Her compressions paused while she stared at the wall. James—was dead.

"No, I can't give up yet," she whimpered and resumed her CPR techniques.

"Alice, it's been over a half of an hour now," Eleanor sniffled. "How long are we going to—how do we call it?"

"We don't," Alice answered as though it should have been obvious. "I won't."

Eleanor looked at Alice and saw some of the same shaking that Mark had before he passed out. "Well, you have done your part. Let me take over compressions, and you do breaths for a while. Your arms are going to give out."

Alice nodded. "After the next breath."

A brief countdown led Eleanor to shoot another breath of hot air down her brother's lungs. The two women rotated in a dance, and Eleanor pressed at approximately the same pace she'd seen her other pseudo-medical companions set.

"You'll wake up, yes?" she grunted in James' direction. "I'll kick your bloody arse if you don't. You know how bad it is when I'm mad at you, yeah? Imagine that times a thousand if you don't come back. I'll wallop you good as soon as I step through the pearly gates. I'll be sent to hell. You wouldn't want your only sister to go to hell, would you? Well, that's why you need to get up now."

Alice averted her gaze as tears flowed freely again. Eleanor was wholly dedicated to her brother. Alice couldn't imagine what her life would be like without him. She didn't want to. It wasn't right that their little family had just started coming together— only to be ripped apart by tragedy again. There would be nothing left inside Eleanor. For that matter, Alice would be quite empty as well.

"Wake up, you silly little bastard!" Eleanor cussed.

"El, maybe we should—" Alice tried.

"On breath!" Eleanor commanded with a point. "Now!"

Alice obeyed and filled his lungs. She sat back and watched Eleanor relentlessly slam her brother's chest.

"You're a little shit, you know that?" Eleanor fussed. "I wasn't lying! We are a team! We *were* a team! Now you've left, and expect me to carry on?"

She didn't compress anymore, she more punched into his sternum with increasing force.

"Don't you get what you've done to me?" Eleanor openly wailed as she continued to beat on her brother's corpse. "Mum and Dad are dead. Grandma's dead. All of these people are dead. Soon, I'll be dead, too, and it's your fault!"

Eleanor brought her fists together and slammed down onto the corpse, sobbing as she did. The cracking of another rib made Alice wince. A few droplets of water bubbled from the boy's lips.

The little flow caught the corner of Alice's vision. She touched the icy liquid that sputtered from his mouth. It hadn't come from James' stomach.

"Do it again," Alice commanded.

"What?" Eleanor squeaked back.

"Slam his chest again, harder!" she demanded.

"Aunt Alic—"

"*Now, girl!*" Alice roared.

Eleanor reached her hands upward a second time and beads of sweat poured downward into her already wet shirt. She flung her arms down wildly with such force the whole child buckled.

More water flew from his mouth this time, but nothing else.

"Again!" Alice ordered.

"Aunt Alice—"

"Fucking do it!" Alice roared.

Eleanor reared back for a third strike. She clasped her fists together again and even said a slight prayer. Not that it would make any difference. With even more anger and venom, she hurled her entire torso downward and spread the entirety of her weight over James. His body jumped and sprayed water a third time. Then it jolted again, expelling still more water.

"Did you see that?" Alice wondered. "The second time?"

Eleanor shook her head. She placed her ear low to the boy's chest to watch for a rise. The body didn't move. As she leaned even closer though, a slight rumbling was audible. She pushed her whole head over his heart and heard a slow, weak, thumping.

"Heartbeat!" she screamed in ecstasy. "There's a heartbeat!"

She continued listening to the erratic, uneven, thudding, and it was more beautiful than the most profound symphony. Its rhythmic hammering was mightier than the guns of Navarrone to her. She reveled in hearing its sweet music but was worried by the lack of independent breathing. Eleanor closed her lips over his and pressed new oxygen into his lungs. As she breathed out, the boy coughed hard and sprayed the remaining contents of his lungs onto her face.

"Oh my God!" She recoiled and grabbed a throw pillow to wipe her face with.

Alice laughed hysterically and hugged James tightly.

"Oh, honey, you're back. We were so worried!" she smiled.

James wasn't conscious yet, but he was breathing on his own now. His hands were ever so slightly warmer than when they had begun the life-saving procedures. Alice laid herself down beside the boy and caressed his mostly dry hair. Eleanor followed suit and stretched herself across the rug, using his calves as a pillow. She held his hand tightly and squeezed it twice.

"I knew you wouldn't desert our team."

TWENTY

THE TIGHTLY KNIT CREW SLEPT FOR WHAT FELT LIKE DAYS. No one had bothered to check the clock before going to bed, but Eleanor was the first to wake. It was one, but light outside. She quickly determined that it was not one in the morning, but in the afternoon. Could she really have slept almost an entire day away?

James' body was still pale, but she wasn't sure how much of that was a result of being British and how much was contributed by his near-death experience. Alice slept soundly with a thin smile painted across her face. Mark had hardly moved from his frozen and mildly embarrassing contorted position.

Eleanor needed to check on the doom clock. If they'd been asleep for this long, it was entirely likely that the next hazard would be coming soon. If she could catch a glimpse, at least she would have an idea of how urgent their waking would be.

Eleanor shuffled her bare feet across the frigid stone floor and shivered. The air was warmer than it had felt since the wall blowout. As she crossed the lobby, she heard the ventilation system running in what sounded like overdrive. It made sense. If the killer designed the home to be reset, he'd need to dry out the building to prevent mold from forming in what was supposed to be a luxury resort.

She saw the fruits of their labor entirely destroyed in the bar. The barricade of chairs, tables, and other bits of furniture was in an untidy pile in the center of the room. Eleanor decided to make herself breakfast, and so she climbed around the newly dropped obstacle course with care. She was about to enter the kitchen when she saw Evelyn sitting in the dining room chomping on something. It smelled delicious.

Inside the now-messy dining room, Evelyn was downing a strip of crisp bacon inelegantly. A massive bowl sat before her, along with a serving tray full of sweet rolls. She noticed Eleanor's presence and scoffed through her full mouth.

"I made breakfast, but I'm no Amelia. I microwaved a shit-ton of bacon and Hawaiian rolls from the pantry. Merry Christmas, I guess."

It was July.

Despite the unorthodox presentation, Eleanor shrugged and joined Evelyn at the table in the seat opposite her. She took a small plate and loaded it with bacon and bread before hauling the load back to consume. The gesture was appreciated, even if it were a bit less grand than when Amelia had cared for the family.

"Thanks, Eve," Eleanor breathed between bites, not really thinking of her words. She liked the nickname for Evelyn. It made her seem a bit more approachable.

Evelyn thought of biting back at the teenage girl. She wanted to, but it seemed so pointless now. The cards were going to fall as they had to. The odds were good that she'd be caught in the bloodbath to follow. Why take out frustration on Eleanor, who only sought to make light of a frightfully bad situation?

"It's nothing, dear." Evelyn softened ever so slightly. "I threw raw bacon onto a plate and waited a few minutes. It isn't like I cooked an elaborate feast."

Something about Eleanor struck Eve as familiar. Her mental prowess was exceptional. She was intuitive and unencumbered by the same rigid moral mooring that her aunt had been tethered to. Eleanor was a *tabula rasa*. She sat before Evelyn as a wealth of possibilities.

"So, El, how do you feel about what Rose decided to do?" Evelyn wondered aloud.

Eleanor couldn't exactly begrudge Evelyn for addressing her colloquially.

"I feel that she's a heroine," Eleanor answered. "Without her, there is no way my brother could have survived in there. He owes his life to her."

"Curious." Eve sipped an uncommonly clear glass of orange juice that had obviously been cut with liquor of some sort. "You see, I would have had no such feelings in your shoes. It is my understanding that Rose was the one responsible for your invitation to this terribly bloody soiree. How are you able to divorce the devious action from its natural end? Maybe you're just better at overlooking flaws than I am, though attempted murder seems a rather damning offense. Honestly, we've yet to see if it is a foiled attempt at assassination. I'm crossing my fingers to be sure."

Evelyn was unapologetic in her condemnation of the recently deceased. Eleanor, of course, felt the same horror as she did about Rose's awful act, but she'd surely redeemed herself by carrying out such a selfless act. Hadn't she? There was no way Rose could have known that Alice would have brought the two of them to The Arbor as guests, but it wasn't a terribly long stretch. Rose had known of Jack Wortz' death. Eleanor winced as she thought back to the event. She rolled her lips together. Suddenly, she wasn't entirely sure she did feel sympathy for Rose.

Alice yawned widely as she entered the room.

"Oh Jesus Christ, I thought I smelled bacon." Alice's words dripped from her salivating mouth. "Was this you, Evelyn?"

Evelyn nodded and raised her glass to Alice. "Nothing at all, Alice," Evelyn returned. "If you want one of these, the pitcher is in the kitchen. It's great for a—relaxing breakfast. For that matter, El, you're of age now. Do you want to get another round for us three girls?"

Eleanor considered the proposal but was cut off by Alice's quick response.

"You're too kind, but I'm afraid I'll have to decline," Alice said with a smile.

Eleanor sighed. She hardly wanted to go against her aunt's example now, but she'd wondered exactly what the concoction was brewed with. Rather than ask and cause a scene, she decided to change the subject.

"I think I'm going to bring a plate to James," Eleanor said, trying to take her mind off things.

"He's not likely to wake so soon," Alice answered, replying to an unasked question. "I just don't want you to get your hopes up, love."

Eleanor shrugged as she loaded the tiny plate down with a mountain of bacon and carbohydrates. She knew it was improbable, but something just told her to obey her impulse.

"I don't know," Eleanor sighed. "The aroma was enough to rouse you, wasn't it?"

Alice raised an eyebrow and rolled her lips into a closed smile. She pointed a finger at Eleanor before touching her own nose with it.

"Touché, sweetie," Alice agreed. "Let me know if he wakes, yes?"

"I think you'll hear my excited screeching first," Eleanor laughed as she walked back to the common room.

Alice sat diagonally to Evelyn in a small square of chairs after Eleanor's departure. She looked over her shoulder at the clock in curiosity. Alice wanted to know how much time they had to relax before things really heated up.

What could Winston possibly do to top the awful fear of a rushing and inescapable flood of frozen water? Alice wondered, not having any desire to have the answer revealed any time soon.

"It's stopped," Evelyn informed her shortly.

"Stopped?" Alice repeated in disbelief.

"I didn't really understand it myself," Evelyn admitted. "It's been sitting at the same point since I've been awake. It hasn't moved a millimeter."

"I doubt he's done," Alice mumbled with clear disgust.

"True," Evelyn grunted, sipping her cocktail. "I fear we are entering the endgame now. There's no sport in hunting children, so the game is unlikely to continue once we are gone. There is only one clock space left. You understand that, right?"

Alice had not really thought of it being a continuous circle. Winston was unlikely to be entertained by reruns, so this hunt would probably be his last with their crew. That meant that with three adults and two children left, the last round was intended to be a final slaughter.

"He's going to kill all of us, you know," Evelyn breathed.

"I'm not as sure," Alice replied. "We know Winston."

"Some of us better than others, unfortunately," Evelyn grunted.

Alice raised an eyebrow.

"You two?"

"Yes."

"When?" Alice asked.

"After the break. You know, when *everyone else* was fucking?" Evelyn chuckled and held knowing eye contact with Alice for a moment to confirm her allusion.

Alice felt a heat in her cheeks.

"I thought Eleanor was the only one who figured that out." Alice nervously smiled.

"I had my suspicions: both of you woke late, seemed uncommonly happy, and made eyes at each other all through breakfast, though I guess that has been happening the whole trip."

"Shit." Alice coughed up a bite of bacon as Evelyn's final tidbit of information was shared. "The whole time? I thought—I mean, I wasn't even sure how I felt until that night."

"Well, apparently your body had a hypothesis by the way you would swing your hips and throw your hair around him." Evelyn grinned before gulping down the remainder of her powerfully strong mimosa. "—hardly relevant now, anyway. I hate to say it, Alice, but I think I'm beginning to admire you. Most white knights of righteousness are ineffective boors who manage to get themselves and others around them killed, but you are a different kind of leader. You're selfish at times."

Alice recoiled slightly at Evelyn's backhanded compliment, if it was to be called that.

"Thank you?" Alice answered with trepidation.

"No, it's a good thing!" Evelyn quickly clarified. "That is where most noble leaders meet their downfall. You see, every once in a blue moon, they are faced with a no-win scenario. It is at that time leaders are tested. Do they try to save everyone? Do they make the self-serving choice? That doesn't hinder you, Alice. When the shit hits the fan, you are decisive. Sure, people may die, but the unit will survive. Your single-minded and unapologetic style of rule is commendable. I was wrong to doubt you."

Evelyn finished her statement and tapped the still-raw stitches on the side of her face.

"You keep people tightly reined in." Evelyn smiled. "Even those who have never been told what to do by anyone."

Alice grinned as she ran a palm over the bruise on her jaw. Evelyn was entirely different than she was, but somehow, they'd managed to bond, or at least foster mutual respect, in their awful situation.

"He's awake!" Eleanor screamed excitedly from across the house. "James is up!"

Alice gave a smile and nod to Evelyn as she stuffed one more bite of sweet roll into her mouth and jogged across the warm building. James was sitting up by the fire, and Mark was wiping his eyes groggily.

"James is up, and now so am I," he teased Eleanor.

Eleanor ignored Mark, mesmerized by James' tired eyes as she wrapped up his head tightly into an embrace.

"You're suffocating me, El!" he whined through squashed lips.

"Too bad." She wept happy tears and kissed the top of his head. "Not stopping!"

Alice smiled and tapped Mark on the shoulder as she passed.

"You all right, dear? James would have been gone for sure if you hadn't been brave enough to save him."

The room felt so many kinds of warm to Mark. He wrapped an arm around Alice's waist without pausing to ask. Alice wanted to pull away from his grip, but she felt held together by sticks and twine at that moment. Human contact was welcomed and refreshing, especially from Mark.

"Of course, I'm fine," Mark fibbed. He knew Winston wasn't done. This was hardly likely to be a perfectly happy ending. While Mark was sure Winston held some sort of an ace up his sleeve, he intended to do everything possible to make sure Alice and the children stayed alive long enough to be rescued. He would do anything to keep her safe. Alice glanced down and noticed his far-off stare even at what should have been a happy moment.

"What's wrong, Mark?" she asked.

"Nothing, just—thinking. I can't believe James pulled through. He never would have made it without you two, you know. I fished him out, right, but it was his family's determination that helped him pull through."

As Eleanor continued holding her brother, he shifted a bit and let out a yelp.

"Oh God, why does my chest hurt so badly? It—hurts to breathe!" he moaned.

"A couple of your ribs cracked while we were resuscitating you, it was—oh shit!" Eleanor was interrupted as the boy lifted his shirt. Red and blue petechiae snaked from the center of his chest where she had beaten on him the day before. James breathed in deeply at the sight of it, which made another swell of pain crash over him.

"Oh, it hurts, El!" he winced.

Guilt slapped Eleanor as she stood. "I'll grab some ice for you, baby brother," she whispered before darting from the room.

"Mark, make sure he eats that breakfast. I'm going to go—help Eleanor," Alice murmured.

Alice chased after her niece and heard her sniffling as she pushed into the kitchen. The young woman stood loading ice from the freezer into a quart storage bag as a makeshift ice pack.

"You did what you had to, El," Alice comforted.

"I know that!" Eleanor bit back harshly. "I'm not crying because of that. I'm crying because—" Eleanor flattened her back to the refrigerator upon closing it and slid down to the floor. "—because this is it. This is the last time we are all going to be together and happy. Let's not pretend. Even if all of us don't—well, some of us are going to—I mean let's look at what's happened! We've fought back, and for what? Every time he's set out to kill someone, he did it. Now there's just us. We all know who he is. There's no way he can let *any* of us leave! Don't you see? He'd be ruined. All

the money in the world wouldn't save him! He's going to kill us all.
What the *fuck* does it matter that we saved James once? He's dead
anyway."

Alice moved to her niece and met her on the floor. "I can't
help but smile," Alice said in a low tone. "I was in a similar place
just a few days ago, and it was you playing psychologist."

Eleanor let out a little laugh but hardly felt elevated as she
leaned into her aunt and nestled her head under Alice's chin.

"Look here, Eleanor," Alice began. "We are going to do everything we can do. We will fight with all we have inside us. I will do
the whole lot of what I possibly can to keep you and James safe.
Rescue is on its way. We just need to get up the elevator to that
train platform."

"But how?" Eleanor fussed. "It wasn't an option on the console. That means that it is still locked!"

"Either way, darling," Alice rubbed Eleanor's shoulders. "We
need to keep our heads clear. We have one shot left in the rifle,
and that seems enough for Winston. Just—keep the faith for now.
That's all we have to work with. I need you at your best. We are
undoubtedly going to have to scramble soon. The rescue will be
here shortly."

That was just it. There had been no rumblings of what
Winston was planning. The survivors would be going in blind.

"You're right," Eleanor said, wiping her face. "There's no point
worrying about it. We have to be strong now, for James."

". . . and for you, love." Alice smiled and squeezed Eleanor's
hand as she pulled her up from her funk.

The women left the kitchen together feeling much more prepared. They had tackled everything at the Arbor thus far, together.
They would handle the next challenge in the same manner. It was
while they walked through the lobby back to the warmth of the
fire that Mr. Graham made himself known.

"Good afternoon, friends," Winston's unmasked voice spoke from the same sound system that the distorted one originally had broadcasted from. "I've got a bit of an opportunity for you all."

Evelyn joined the others in the common room, listening to the voice from above. Everyone huddled together, both out of fear and a desire for security.

"I feel that there has been little sport in the past few days, and I am sorry about that. A hunt with prey in a cage is hardly fair. Without risk, how can there be any reward? That is why— I've unlocked the elevator for you. All you need do now is ride it to the train platform to await rescue. I feel it's a real kindness, don't you?"

"No way," Evelyn whispered. "It's a trap."

"Obviously," Alice returned. "Not sure what choice we have at the moment, though. Our little plan to blow the geothermal core has been ruined by the flooding. The explosives are saturated. Our only option at this point is that train."

"You all have been such excellent players. I truly mean it when I say, I never expected my game to last until the end. Everyone always sold out, but not you! You even managed to call for a rescue. All of you have been so resourceful. I'm actually quite proud. I should mention, if you are coming to the lift, please do so quickly. I'm only leaving it open for fifteen minutes. Good luck!"

As the speakers cut out, Alice nodded her head.

"So, this is it, then?" she murmured. "The final test. Everyone grab some kind of a weapon. I'm thinking we are going to face Winston himself."

"Is he going to be in the elevator?" James asked as he stood slowly.

"It's possible," Alice said. "Only one way to find out."

The friends gathered what they could spare. They loaded the

last of the now-moist bandages into a satchel and left everything else behind. Alice knew their belongings would only slow them down at a time when she guessed they would need a lot of speed.

The five remaining survivors wrapped themselves in coats. Alice wondered whether Winston would be waiting at the train platform or the elevator. Either way, she had a bullet with his name on it and a carving knife eager to get a slice of the action.

"Ready?" Alice asked to the group piled behind the entrance door.

"Oh, but I am going to miss this place so much," Evelyn sighed.

"Really?" Eleanor hissed.

"Of course not," Evelyn returned. "My father died here. My valuables have been inundated by floodwaters. I'm content never to darken this doorway again. Ready when you are, Alice."

Cool air whipped across the five remaining guests of The Arbor as Alice opened the door. It was strange to move together as a unit in the light. She had almost become used to the darkness when danger was afoot. Despite this, every survivor had their lights at the ready. It seemed hardly likely that a ticker tape parade was awaiting them at the icy port of exit.

The lawn felt so familiar now. Alice recalled where she had been dragged by a rope into the icy moat. She remembered walking about with Omario. She'd never gotten to play tennis with Rose. They'd walked along the same path William and Amelia had just under a week ago. She even remembered Peter. Without him, they never would have been able to call for help. Despite having been lost so soon, he was as much a part of their survival as everyone else had been.

Finally, there was the late Mr. Fox. This whole place had been his design, but it had been contorted so malevolently. It was designed to be a shining beacon of the past. It was supposed to

remind guests of the grandeur of days gone by. Instead, it had
been twisted into little more than a murderer's playground. It was
beautiful, but wrong. It was tranquil, but turbulent just beneath
the surface. The shallow exterior was a facade. It was a ruse to distract from The Arbor's true purpose.

Alice recognized the irony as they approached the silver set of
doors. The retreat was built as a place to indulge in carnal desires.
It was, indeed. The Arbor was supposed to fundamentally change
all who stayed there. It did. The place was posited as a retreat to
truly get to know the kind of person one's self was. Alice could say
with certainty, she did. As the group pulled within twenty feet of
their exit, Alice held up a fist.

"You all stay back. If it's an explosive, I'll trigger it. There is
no need for all of us to die in one sweep."

"Like hell you will," Evelyn grunted. She took a few large
steps forward against Alice's wishes.

"Evelyn—" Alice protested.

"You have a child." Evelyn grinned and stared back at Mark.
"And your family to protect. The world will hardly miss me if I do
die here. Let me do this."

She allowed no time for thinking as she sauntered up to the
bright nickel doors. There was no button. Was she to press the
doors themselves? Evelyn finally rapped lightly on the plate metal.
On command, they began to slowly rotate. Evelyn turned back to
the others and raised a palm like a proud gameshow host. By the
time she'd turned back, the doors had slid apart.

Evelyn suddenly wished she hadn't volunteered for the task.

She wasn't even sure how to describe what she saw. The inky
black mass made no sense to her eyes. The light seemed to just
disappear into what appeared to be fur. The beast was elegant but
so dark that it resembled a black pile of sludge on the floor before
her. The lights in the elevator were off, so she could hardly make

out the thing's approximate size. Her vision was drawn instead to the man standing before it. Winston stood in a tan canvas shirt and burnished leather pants. His shimmering black boots caught what little light flowed into the elevator. He gave a sarcastic wave and placed a finger to his mouth.

"Shh!" he quietly cautioned.

Apparently, the others couldn't make out what she saw. They could see Winston but not the *massive* creature behind him.

"You piece of shit!" Eleanor cried out.

Evelyn spun backward with amazing speed and wildly flailed her hands in a shushing motion. She hushed the group but offered no explanation as to why. She knew that if whatever it was awoke, she would be the first devoured.

"So nice to see all of you again," Winston grinned as he walked with swagger from the elevator.

Alice took aim with her rifle between his eyes.

"I wouldn't do that, Ms. Trudeau," Winston cautioned. "You see, I have a sleepy friend, and I'm quite sure that even if you killed me—he would get a rude awakening. Trust me, you don't want Rudy mad at you."

"*Rudy?*" Evelyn mouthed in confusion.

"All this to say . . ." Winston smiled and drew his rifle from his back. "I am going to count back from ten before I fire a shot. I will definitely be out of the way before I fire. I would recommend you do the same. You see Rudy here is—perfect. He is the greatest killing machine ever manufactured. He's fast, deadly, and armored beyond reason. Frankly, I had to remove some of his protections and scanning features, or there would be no fun in this at all. He will be hunting all of us. I can't imagine many will survive it, even myself, but there is no greater thrill than hunting prey which can kill you."

"You're fucking insane!" Mark whispered harshly.

"Probably," Winston agreed as he turned his back to the group and marched like a toy soldier. "Ten, nine—"

"Back to the house, now!" Alice's voice cracked as she made the decision. The elevator was so close, but it held something powerful enough to kill everyone left alive. They needed to lose it first. Mark, who was the first to reach the doors, flung them open as Winston finished counting and aimed at the sky.

"One!" Winston shouted, excitement filling his voice. The hammering bang echoed throughout the dome several times. Everyone froze. It was hard to make out, but something inside the elevator stirred. As it took a step forward, the lights went out in The Arbor for a final time.

James was the last one inside. He ran as quickly as his legs could carry him but worried it wasn't fast enough. Whatever chased them thundered behind like a grizzly bear. Its slamming footsteps were smooth and galloping. It crossed the yard like a shooting star in the same time it took the others to close the door. They ducked behind the bar just as the creature reached the entryway. Alice managed to turn her light off just before the colossal beast crashed through the panels of solid oak reinforced with iron ribbing. She saw nothing but heard wood and metal splinter across the floor as the creature entered The Arbor.

Its footfalls were slow and deliberate. The beast sniffed at the air and walked toward the common room. It was impossible to tell exactly where the beast roamed, but everyone heard a tearing of fabric that they assumed was the couch. Evelyn relit her phone but placed a finger over the flashlight. A tiny amount of light flowed in front of her. She motioned for the rest to follow her and slowly pressed through the kitchen door.

"It's got quite the appetite," the speakers blared. From the common room, the creature must have lunged at one of the sources of the voice. Metal tore and stone crumbled. From the sound of it, the wall and electronics had been bested by the assault. "You know, it's not quite dramatic enough. I've wanted to use this thunderstorm program for a while. It will give you all some cover to move, at least."

True to his word, a bolt of lightning flashed through the tiny kitchen window and was followed immediately by thunder. The pitter-patter of raindrops falling on the tennis court could be heard through the open wall of the library.

"It's actually raining?" Eleanor whispered. "I assumed he meant it like a simulation!"

Alice waved her hand downward to encourage silence. The deep thumping was getting closer. Just on the other side of the wall, everyone flinched as something tore across the wooden bar. The footsteps sounded different on top of furniture. Had the bar not been made of such sturdy wood, it could never have supported the gargantuan amount of weight. Even with a strong superstructure, the supports creaked with each movement. The beast must have had claws, for as it moved there was a thud followed immediately by a light clink of metal.

James was the first to notice the actual beast as it passed the kitchen window. His heart seemed to stop for a second time as the green eyes reflected back a bolt of lightning that flashed. Somehow it hadn't seen him, but James couldn't claim the same. He shivered at the size of the monstrosity. It was too large for what it was. There was no way.

Alice noticed the pallor in James' countenance as she looked around the room from her crouched hiding place. He sat opposite her and looked as though he'd seen a ghost. The reality was much worse than she could have imagined.

"*You okay?*" Alice mouthed.

The boy wordlessly shook his head back and forth. A second flash of lightning let him make out a tail whipping about as the colossal cat slipped past the window. James was a nature buff. He loved reading about the flora and creatures on Earth. There wasn't a nature documentary that he hadn't absorbed. He was familiar with predatory cats. They didn't grow much over four feet high. Whatever this was looked to be at least six feet tall from the angle he was viewing. Its tail looked three feet long and had a pointed spike at its tip. The ebony beast whipped it into the door as he passed and sliced into the metal easily. The sound finally grabbed everyone's attention.

"*What is it?*" Eleanor mouthed so slowly that James could understand her.

"It's too big," he returned almost silently. "Can't be."

Eleanor wasn't sure what it was, but James' grim assessment wasn't exactly encouraging. She stood slowly and craned her neck to get a better look. It was nothing but black in the other room, but she stared in the general direction of the noises. She slipped slightly closer and waited for a strike of surging electricity to illuminate their man-eater. She didn't have to wait long.

A moment later, a bolt of lightning crashed in the front yard. A coat of black fur sat mere inches from her face. The black beauty had doubled back. What was in front of her seemed to be the forelegs of something truly massive. The sharp, almost pyramidal, shoulders of the beast gave way to a neck of trunk-like thickness. Past that was a set of ears that were a little larger than Eleanor's palms. She managed to hold in a gasp as the beast raised its head to peer into the porthole. As it moved up, Eleanor made her body flat beside the door. She couldn't see the enormous predatory cat anymore, but she could hear it.

The panther, if the engineered monstrosity was to be called that, took deep curious sniffs at the door. Evelyn pointed to the tangled mess of carnage in the corner. If it was beginning to rely on its sense of smell, the rotting gore might provide gruesome

cover for their distinctly living scent. Alice was quick to agree,
much to the bewilderment of Mark. The three scurried quietly
toward the bloodied cover while Eleanor stood in silence. Just as
James made a face and ducked underneath, the sable panther began to curiously paw at the door. Alice was the last to pull under
as the hulking feline stepped into the kitchen. The door pushed
open to conceal Eleanor's hiding spot. She held one hand over her
mouth and clutched her chest with the other. Her mind screeched
in terror, and her eyes were beyond wide, but as the door began
to slip shut—Eleanor pushed a finger into the handle to keep it
open.

A bolt illuminated the kitchen through the open door. The
panther's shadow was cast in ferocious detail on the back wall of
the kitchen across pots and pans. Its size was truly difficult for
Eleanor's mind to fathom as she viewed it through the slashes in
the kitchen door. Its back rose above her eyeline. Were it to stand
on its back legs, it would have surely towered five meters high.
Rudy's tail swung wildly as a low cycling snarl clicked through the
air.

The other survivors were huddled in a slippery mess of tangled metal and blood. They remained perfectly still, using the recently deceased to hinder the creature's search. The titanium tip
of its tail slashed with horrible speed and cleaved bottles of spices
on nearby shelves in half, scattering their contents across the floor.
The beast looked terribly annoyed by the noise and let out a chirp-
ing hiss at the source from whence it had originated. The warning
call sent a shiver up Alice's spine.

Eleanor knew that with the panther headed in Alice's direction, she needed to create a distraction. As quickly and quietly as
she could, Eleanor slipped around to the front side of the kitchen
door and dashed silently from the room. She walked quickly to
the common room and spread herself over the same couch Alice

had hidden on several days earlier. She covered all but her face with a blanket before taking a deep breath in preparation.

"Hey, you daft fucking twat, I'm out here!" she screamed. Eleanor covered her face with the blanket and tried her best to sit in absolute silence as the monster tore back through the kitchen.

As Rudy bashed through the swinging doorway, he let out another deep growl. The door finally bent and snapped at the claw marks that had damaged it earlier. The top half of the steel door went flying into the bar while the bottom half remained attached and simply hung flaccidly in a permanently open position.

As the ebony panther made his way toward Eleanor, Alice slipped out from under her hiding space. A drip of dark and partially coagulated blood ran down her cheek. It wasn't her own. The thought of hiding there among the shredded bits of Omario disgusted Alice, and she wanted to be out from underneath that stinking mess immediately upon the cat's exit.

She was followed by Mark and James shortly. Evelyn didn't look too eager to give up a relatively camouflaged spot but did so begrudgingly.

"We distract it from Eleanor!" Alice whispered harshly.

Mark pointed to the library, and Alice nodded just as James made his way out from underneath the wicked sludge, a little paler than he'd entered. The four made their way into the hall of knowledge, and Evelyn's face slightly sunk. The books she'd loved so much were mostly ruined. It was bad enough that Winston had put *her* into mortal danger, but to punish innocent texts seemed inconceivable.

The room was still saturated with water. Evelyn guessed that this was because the heating system would have been fighting against an open wall, and so would have been unable to dry out the space. This wetness was hardly lessened by the pouring rainfall scattering into the room from the outside. As they entered the library, a lightning bolt struck one of the support poles for the tennis court net. Electricity coursed across the cloth and melted the plastic along the top. Sparks scattered down the pole and skipped across the soaked clay court.

Alice knew that traveling outside with frequent strikes of several million volts would be tantamount to suicide. Any movements would have to be timed between strikes, and even then, only when absolutely necessary. Alice checked her watch. If Winston was to be believed, the elevator would be locked in just over eight minutes. They would need to get out quickly or lose any ability to do so in perpetuity.

Back inside the common room, Eleanor tried not to quiver. There was no way she could see the creature from underneath her blanket, and so she was forced to utilize only her sense of hearing to determine its location. Each step reverberated through the couch like something out of a nightmare.

Rudy stopped behind the couch and remained still for a few seconds. Eleanor had to let a miniscule amount of air escape her lips so that she could draw fresh breath. A quick but menacing trill filled the air as the panther sniffed curiously at the back of the furniture. He opened his mouth and snapped his jaws shut in what sounded like a yawn. The engineered animal was bored by the pursuit.

The beast took a few strides away from the couch and moved toward the front of the room. A lightning strike in the front yard filled the area with light. In the illuminated scene, she watched the big cat walk up the wall beside the couch with its front paws. It dug its claws into the wood beside the fireplace and stripped through it as if it were butter. The shredded remnants of molding fell in a clattering to the floor. It had been about a minute since Eleanor last drew breath. She would need to do so in short order. She bit her lower lip so hard that she tasted blood.

Rudy raised his head and took in the smell at the center of the room. The beast knew prey was nearby. He howled wickedly in a shrill call. He was growing impatient. The cat pawed at the pile of blankets on the floor that James had been wrapped in only a few minutes prior. Not wanting to leave any stone unturned, the massive claws ripped at the vacant cloth. Eleanor would be found soon enough. If she was to die, at least her death would likely be quick.

In the library, Alice had the idea to draw Rudy into the backyard between strikes. He almost certainly had a metal skeleton and would be the highest object in the yard. The beast was built tough, but was he hardy enough to stand a bolt of lightning? That remained to be seen. Alice had a plan, but she was sure almost everyone would think it insane.

"The hall beside the common room, where Peter lost—where Peter was trapped. I could draw him through that way and then run around the house. By the time I make it back inside, he'll likely be struck."

"You're daft," Mark sighed. "What's to say that lightning won't strike you in the process?"

"That's a risk I'm willing to take for Eleanor!" she hissed back. "What's your idea, then? If you have a better one, then I'm all ears."

Evelyn considered her words and tapped a shoe against the carpet with a repeating squish.

"I—" Mark dropped off in his words.

"You can't, Aunt Alice!" James whispered. "It's too dangerous."

Alice felt pierced by James' words of concern. How much longer could all of them cheat death?

"Your right, dear," Alice comforted, lowering herself to James' level. "I'll have to be very quick, but it's for Eleanor, yes? I have to save her."

"The boy is right," Evelyn snapped. "It's far too risky. Even if you aren't struck by a billion volts, Rudy will tear you to bits."

"Evelyn, I hear—" Alice began.

"I'm doing it," Evelyn nodded as she softly jogged to the back of the room.

"Evelyn, you just said it was impossible!" Mark protested.

"That's why it has to be me. You all would just mess it up." She was tired of their protests. She hopped in place until the familiar crack of a thunderbolt filled the air from the front yard. As the light flashed, she dashed into the maelstrom. The shattered window of the Arbor's back door was a few steps to the left of the hole blown in the side of the library. She nodded her head a few times to convince herself to do the unthinkable. She raised a pair of fingers to her lips and blew an ear-piercing whistle. Over the roar of the storm, she couldn't hear if her distraction had its desired effect, so she prepared to blow again.

As she raised her hand, her keen eyes caught the glint of Rudy's furious visage mid-charge just fifteen feet down the hall.

"Oh, fuck," she whispered as her torso rotated right and began the sprint back around the house.

She'd barely taken two steps before the juggernaut burst through the ballistic glass in a single pounce without breaking momentum. Its head whipped back and forth looking for Evelyn. Unfortunately, her loud sprinting steps caused the panther's now-slick ears to twitch. The menacing claws dug into the clay as he turned and followed the heiress.

Evelyn was halfway around the house when Rudy caught her within his sights. She ran with everything inside her, but of course it wasn't enough. Rudy was almost on her when she felt a tingling in her soaked hair.

He was too close. Even if her plan was successful now, she'd be caught in the arc of the lightning. Evelyn hated her only solution. At that moment, she pushed hard into the soil and spun on her front foot. Evelyn knew that she had a lot less mass to stop than her pursuer. Isaac Newton's laws applied even on Mars. She twisted her body and shoved hard on her back leg. Her movement switched from a forward sprint to a reversed run.

Rudy shot past her and had a hard time resisting prey. He reached out with a paw and extended his paw in a swipe. He caught Evelyn in the meat of her shoulder with a claw. It was enough to rip through to the bone of her shoulder-blade. Evelyn let out a scream as warmth ran down her back.

Because it chose to attack her instead of focusing on stopping, Rudy slid across the soaked ground. When the burning in Evelyn's hair began to tug at the base of her soaked locks, she dropped to the ground.

The flash was blinding at that distance. A millisecond later, the crackling boom filled her skull as lightning pounded into Rudy as though called by Thor himself. Sparks scattered all around the strike, and Evelyn watched in horror as the aftershocks arced to her fingertips. She felt her entire body seize as the electricity burned through her veins. It ran up her right arm and she felt sparks fly from her cheek to the wet ground. She blacked out for a moment.

When she awoke, the lights in the compound had returned. The storm was over. Rudy lay in a tangled mess of burnt fur and steel thirty feet from her. He looked to be down for the count. She stood and used her left arm to feel for the claw mark along her back. She felt bubbled skin from where the electricity had coursed through her. Evelyn's nerves were numbed by the strike. She ran her finger along the edge of the gash and felt nothing but pressure.

She jumped a moment later as a gunshot echoed through the Arbor and flew into the wall beside her.

"Oh, come *on!*" she screamed to Winston as she resumed a sprint alongside the house. A second shot whistled past her as she rounded the corner to run into the opening that Rudy had left in the front door. Eleanor stared dumbly at Evelyn as she saw her in the light.

"What is it?" Evelyn barked. "Winston is right behind me!"

"You—" Eleanor stammered as she followed Evelyn into the kitchen. "Your face—"

Evelyn got a good look at herself in the glass of the oven. Bright-red fractals scattered across her right cheek in a tree-like pattern. She had been lucky that the power traveled in a short arc across her body, but it had certainly left its mark.

"Oh my God, Evelyn!" Alice smiled. "You made it!"

Evelyn rolled her eyes as dramatically as she could and paired it with a sarcastic gasp.

"Let's fawn over my bravery *after* we kill this fuck," she said dismissively.

"Or you'll drop your weapon," Winston ordered loudly from the bar.

Alice saw the rifle pointed in her general direction through the kitchen doorway and went to pull her own gun from her back.

"I wouldn't, Ms. Trudeau!" he called. "It's not you I have in my sights at the moment!"

Eleanor stood just beside Alice. She should have known. Winston was too cowardly to target an actual threat. He went for the emotional blackmail instead. Alice raised her hands in surrender. She slowly slipped the leather strap from her shoulder.

"Alice!" Eleanor spat angrily. "Kill him!"

As the strap dropped into the crook of her elbow, Alice was tempted to do just that. She could kick the rifle up from that position in little more than a second and put a bullet right between the eyes of Mr. Graham. But then, there was Eleanor. She could certainly save James, Mark, and Evelyn—but the prospect was restrictively expensive. She would never be able to live with herself if Eleanor died.

The rifle clattered to the ground, and Eleanor's eyes dropped. "Damnit, Alice," she breathed.

"That's a good girl," Winston smiled. "Not as much fight when your family's threatened, is there?"

"Where's Mark?" James asked worriedly.

"You see, I figured you out the moment you arrived with those little—darlings," he said, centering his gaze on Eleanor in particular as he walked closer. "Your delicious little darlings."

Eleanor felt a chill run down her spine at the attention of the handsome, but entirely incurable, man.

"Only in your fantasies, you bastard!" Eleanor whipped.

Winston grinned wickedly. "Oh, how right you are, love. You're the first to turn me down in quite some time. I can't lie. I've been—tempted—to have my way with you regardless of your feelings on the matter."

"So, you're talking about raping a child now, Winston? That's a new low—even for you," Evelyn scorched with her words.

"Is it, now?" Winston growled. "I feel that some of our actions have been of a more lascivious nature. Don't you? Tell me you didn't enjoy being pinned against the basement wall while I pounded into you. You see, you're a bit of a deviant, too. You're like me."

Evelyn's nostrils flared in disgust. "Whatever might have happened between the two of us was a mistake, and never to be repeated."

"How right you are, Eve," Winston clucked. He pulled the slide back on the rifle and loaded a round into the chamber.

Alice huffed. She could have shot him before he loaded the round if she would have thought quickly enough. Unfortunately, she'd no idea the gun hadn't been loaded. Alice wouldn't be caught unprepared like that again. Unlike Winston, Alice was ready to fire at a moment's notice. Only idiots saved reloading for dramatic effect.

"It's me, then?" Evelyn stepped closer to Winston. "I'm the one you're choosing to kill first?"

"Is that a problem?" he said as he narrowed his gaze down the sights at her.

"Hah," Evelyn chuckled. "I bet you didn't even notice."

"Notice what?" he asked.

"Mark."

On cue, Winston spun with his rifle to face the charging man. Mark had approached from behind the killer and ducked under his first shot. Winston reloaded and raised his rifle a moment too slowly. Mark slapped the rifle away, which discharged its payload into a nearby wall. He tackled Winston to the floor and began pummeling the pretty man's face. Mark hammered with everything inside of him. Winston raised his arms to guard his vitals, which led Mark to punch the man in the gut as he knelt over the killer. Alice raised her rifle and waited for a clear shot.

"Mark, move!" she screamed.

He did as he was told, but Winston rolled along for a body's length, keeping Mark between himself and Alice. Winston grabbed at his belt and retrieved a short-staved spear. At the press of a button, it extended two feet into a small javelin. The blade forced its way into Mark's kneecap, and the man let out a howl as he dropped to the ground. Winston wrapped his arm around Mark's neck from behind as the collapsed man lay grasping madly at his kneecap, trying to remove the spear.

Winston hoisted Mark into his lap and yanked the weapon free of Mark's knee with his free hand.

"Stand now, boy!" he commanded. "Do it on your other leg."

With Winston's help, Mark was forced to his feet. Winston held the spear behind Mark's back just out of Alice's sights.

"Beautiful!" Winston shouted through bloodied teeth. "Oh,

what a marvelous play! The man almost had me! Oh, I was so sloppy, Eve, you were right. Don't worry, it won't happen again!"

"Put him down, Winston!" Alice demanded.

"Must be more careful with your choice of words, Alice," Winston cackled. "As you wish."

Alice watched with a blank expression as the titanium rod forced its way through Mark's torso and out the side of his rib-cage. As the head emerged, Mark coughed up a mouthful of blood and his good leg buckled.

"*No!*" Alice screeched, letting her shot fly at Winston's head. Mark's falling body dragged Winston down along with it, and for the first time—Alice's shot missed its target. She wailed in a mixture of sadness and frustration as Winston hopped to his feet and retrieved the rifle. He aimed the sizable gun with one arm as he pulled the spear from Mark's failing body.

"It was a good shot, Alice, I'll give you that! Better luck next time!"

Winston lowered his gun as he ran for the open door of the lobby. He disappeared through it without stopping to gloat.

"Mark!" Alice yelped as she ran to his side and slid to her knees. "No! You aren't doing this to me!"

Mark coughed and sputtered a crimson spray as he let out a pained laugh.

"Alice, my sweet, I don't think even you are going to stop this."

"No, but I can't beat him on my own!" Alice moaned. "I'm not strong enough to go on without you!"

"Now that," Mark's speech began to crack. "—is a lie. You keep saying you are weak, but you're the most resilient one here. If anyone is going to blow this place open, it's you. Take my story. Make sure word gets out. The files are all here."

Mark pushed a small recording device into her palm.

"I will, Mark. I love you. You know that, right? I always have."

He stared back into her eyes. His gaze wasn't focused.

"Mark?" Alice whispered through tears. "Tell me you heard me, ple—"

Her words were interrupted by the ringing of the clock from behind them. Mark was gone.

TWENTY-ONE

ALICE STOOD WITH AN EMPTINESS IN HER COUNTENANCE. Eleanor knelt where she had been a moment before and slipped a hand over Mark's eyes to shut them. He'd done everything he possibly could to save them, but it wasn't enough. The remaining survivors were on their own now. Three women and one boy against a sociopath with unlimited resources and weaponry on his own turf.

Evelyn looked at her phone. The group had three minutes. They needed to move or be trapped in the icy tomb forever.

"I know what to do," she mumbled.

"And what is that?" Eleanor wondered aloud.

"I'll run out the front of the house first," Evelyn elucidated. "I'm a sprinter, you know. I'm faster than you all can be towing James' wounded body. You sneak around the back and make a run for the elevator while I have Winston's attention. He's clearly a piss-poor shot. I'll make a loop and meet you at the elevator."

"That's mad!" Alice replied. "You're going to what, dodge bullets the whole time?"

"*Alice! Listen for once in your goddamn life!*" Evelyn shouted.

"I'm doing this *for* you. You have kids. You have the story needed to bring justice to my father's killer. You have a future! Now shut the fuck up and do what I say for once."

Alice breathed in deeply.

"Thank you."

"It's not for you, goodie-girl," Evelyn corrected. "It's for my father. Now go!"

As Evelyn watched the family make their way to the kitchen, she prepared to run one last time. Evelyn had been through hell and back. She was tired of being passive. It was time to take the fight to Winston. She slipped a trio of kitchen knives into her left palm and held a fourth in her right hand. She was ready, if needed, to die.

She darted from the home at full speed. Winston's large rifle flashed from the right side of the house. The shot whirred past her as she turned to run straight for his position. He stood at least a hundred and fifty feet ahead of her. As he loaded a second shot and took aim, Evelyn darted left. His shot missed her widely. Out of the corner of her eye, she saw the Wortz children and Alice running down the path.

Good for you, she thought. *There is such a thing as sensible selfishness.*

She was about fifty feet from Winston when he noticed Alice and the kids. Evelyn lowered her stance and poured all remaining energy into her speed. She flipped the knife in her right hand and cocked her arm back. She felt the injury in her shoulder and was sure she would regret the charge later, but she had a job to do. She hurled the blade slightly high and it soared just over Winston's head.

Winston spun with his rifle and aimed for Evelyn's torso. He fired again and Evelyn dove right. She sprang to her feet before Winston could reload.

"What are you doing?" he howled. "You're ruining *everything!*"

Evelyn tossed a second knife his way and forced Winston to dodge for the first time.

"Unbelievable!" he screamed.

Winston aimed for her leg in frustration and pulled the trigger. Evelyn's lithe form twisted around the shot and threw another blade at Winston's chest. She was so close now that she only narrowly missed. Had her arm have been in top shape, her aim would have been true.

"They're getting away!" Winston screeched with a cracking whine. *"How dare you?"*

Evelyn saw Alice and the others enter the elevator and smiled.

"Winston, you should know by now that I do whatever I want!"

Evelyn stabbed high. Winston went to grab her arm, but she dropped into a feint and thrust the steak knife into his calf. Hearing him yelp in pain, she sprang off her back leg and tore into a full sprint for the elevator. She weaved through the lawn, dodging shots from her injured rival. He was inaccurate to begin with. Without a second leg to steady him, his shots sprayed wildly.

"You'll pay for this!" he shouted. "Your precious train isn't even here yet!"

Evelyn stopped a few steps from the elevator. Winston was right.

"Eve! Get in here!" Eleanor urged. "Hurry!"

"The train isn't here," Evelyn repeated. "He's going to catch up."

"Well, then let's go!" Alice said plaintively.

"No, I'm afraid not," Evelyn sighed.

She slammed the raised panel on the door and the pieces began to slide together.

"I'll stall hi—"

Alice dropped her mouth open as the lift began to hum in silence. Evelyn, of all people, had saved the day.

"Why did she?" Eleanor struggled for words. "Why would she do that? We would stand a better chance fighting together."

"I guess Eve thought maybe she could kill him?" Alice hypothesized. "I really don't have a good answer. I just know she bought us some time. I'm grateful. Let's hope the train comes quickly, because I don't know how long she can hold him off."

"Maybe she'll meet us here after she kills him?" James smiled.

"Maybe, love," Alice rubbed his head. She knew it wasn't going to happen. It was a miracle Evelyn had managed to dodge so many shots when she had a bevy of knives to toss. Her distraction would be temporary at best. She hoped for a quick arrival of their overdue ride.

As the doors rotated open, the scene was one of eerie placidity. It felt like a tableau Alice had once dreamed. The four projected gateways lit as they had when the three remaining survivors had arrived. Whoever had designed this portion even had a different message for those leaving.

"The Arbor"
"Will linger within"
"Until . . ."
"You return again"

No one could comment on the palpable irony of those words. They were beyond tired. They had reached the point of such mental and physical exhaustion that the three simply walked to the end of the carpet and collapsed together.

They held each other in silence, hoping the train would arrive before their pursuer. Alice felt tears welling in the corner of her eyes as she held her children. She rolled her lips together and held her eyes shut. Alice pulled their heads tightly to her breast. She kissed each of them and smiled through her sadness.

"You are everything."

"What?" James rotated his head to look at her face.

"I promise, from this day until my last, you are everything to me. You are mine. Do you hear me? I'm never letting go. I will never waver in my resolve. You are my children, and I will always be here for you."

"Thanks, Aunt Alice," Eleanor smiled. "I love you so much. No matter what happens, I promise it's true."

Eleanor stretched her neck up and kissed Alice on the cheek before returning to her tightly entangled position with her brother. Their family wasn't out of the woods, but they could see the edge of the tree line now.

The three sat for several minutes, praying for the train to arrive. Their hearts jumped at the sound of metal scraping. James looked down the tracks, but Alice looked behind them. The elevator door turned. Alice felt her stomach jump into her throat.

There, waiting in the sterile room, was a bloody and limping Winston Graham. He no longer smiled as he had at the beginning of his game. His face was a twisted scowl. It seemed as though Evelyn had sapped some of the enjoyment from his sport.

"Nine fucking kills," Winston groaned. "Nine kills, and you sorry lot are all that's left. A pair of children and a woman who only survived by her command of others."

"And what do you mean by that?" Eleanor stalled.

"What do I mean?" Winston laughed as he dragged his right leg along the red carpet, dripping blood onto the already ruby-colored surface. "She never stopped me! Every single assault she has made on me failed."

"I sure gave those wolves hell!" Alice smiled. "And let's not forget Silas and Timothy!"

"Oh, right, so you are perfectly capable of 'killing' androids and cyborgs. Let's all give a big round of applause for Alice Trudeau, slayer of the unliving!"

James jumped as he heard a crashing of ice down the tunnel. *The train?* he wondered. *Let's keep him talking.*

"You talk about my Aunt Alice being ineffective," James fired back like an angry kitten. "What about your precious little cat? He didn't kill anyone! How many million credits did he cost?"

"Billions, when you include R&D," Winston answered. "But he's worth every penny, I assure you. He's going to make the company very rich. The form is perfect. He has so many tricks hidden up his sleeve that you don't even know about."

"Just don't throw him into a rainstorm!" Eleanor taunted.

"Oh, I'm not so sure," Winston grinned widely. "But don't take my word for it!"

The killer pointed behind the trio toward the tracks.

"It can't be," Alice muttered hopelessly.

Rudy, a bit worse for the wear, was making his way down the tracks toward them. He eyed each of the people on the platform above him suspiciously as he snarled and snapped his jaws over and over. His stride was almost lazy, like a jungle cat who'd had a long day but was considering dessert.

The torso behind his forelegs had been stripped of fur. The lightning had clearly damaged some of his armor plating, but the superstructure under fur looked mostly undamaged. He leapt the ten feet to the ice platform like a child jumping rope. Winston was right about one thing; Rudy looked to be a near-perfect killing machine. And by the looks of things, he seemed almost invincible.

The panther's head swayed back and forth looking between the survivors as though he were picking a favorite chocolate. Finally, his stare rested on Winston. Rudy opened his mouth wide and cried out in a hissing snarl.

"Rudy, deactivate friendly fire protocol," Winston ordered. "Reacquire targets from non-familiar personnel."

The big cat began to rotate around the icy terminal,

continuing his low clicking growl that had haunted James from the first moment he heard it over the monitor.

"Rudy!" Winston ordered. "Deactivate all motor functions! Admin code 3-2-3-1-4"

The beast had circled to the point where he was almost parallel with the carpet. He extended his claws into the ice and lowered his stance.

"Rudy! Activate emergency self-destruct protocol! Admin code 3-2-3-1-4!" Winston's voice sounded increasingly panicked as the creature silenced itself.

As the predator leapt from his stance, he shredded ice into a spray behind himself. He strode across the ice with all the grace of a hunter in his prime. The chamber shook as he pulverized the station with each footfall. His claws tore through ice as he zipped toward Winston at blinding speed. Not only was he several magnitudes larger than his earthbound cousin, he appeared faster as well. The whole scene played out in slow motion, but Rudy was on Winston a few seconds after he began the charge. He sunk his forelegs into the athletic man's fleshy torso, and titanium sliced through Winston like he wasn't even there. His spear went skittering across the ice and slid to a stop at James' feet.

The late Mr. Graham was dead at the first half of the strike, but with deadly efficiency, Rudy stooped down and crushed Winston's skull with a single snap of its powerful jaws.

"Jesus fucking Christ!" Eleanor exclaimed.

Rudy's ears twitched.

"Oh, shit," Eleanor whispered.

Coated in mulched up bits of Winston, Rudy turned his wicked eyes toward James. Almost instinctively, the boy picked up the spear at his feet.

"Whatever happens," Eleanor said through rapid breaths. "Know how much I love both of you!"

Alice looked down at the shimmering rod in James' hands as the beast lowered for another pounce.

Her mind snapped back to something Alexis Fox's hologram had said.

Spearcaster.

"James!" Alice screamed as the creature pushed off. "Spear!"

The boy fumbled to hand Alice the weapon and closed his eyes tightly as the colossal cat thundered toward them. Alice looked madly for a button or a trigger of some sort as the creature closed on their position. Finally, she rotated the base of the lance.

A pair of tiny fins ejected from the midsection of the spearcaster. Alice instinctively raised the weapon and tucked it under her shoulder. The front section blasted off with a minimal hissing and shot toward Rudy. The tip pierced the front section of his left foreleg, and it was almost as though nothing had hit him. The panther charged with increased vigor.

Alice held her children tight and dropped the useless section of the spearcaster to the ice. A small switch at the base of the handle pressed inward as it impacted the frigid but stable surface.

A tiny yellow dot at the point of impact on Rudy swelled outward slightly before imploding. The following explosion knocked the three on their backs. Their ears rang as they felt the panther crash and slide just beside them. The ice ripped up and shattered as the massive cyborg tumbled end over end before crashing into the ice wall almost twenty feet behind them.

"Holy shit!" James exclaimed with a raised arm. On their other side, just before the train platform dropped off, was one of Rudy's legs.

Eleanor stretched her jaw open as she tried to stand through her dizziness.

"It's a missile launcher?" she chuckled.

"So, it would seem," Alice grinned before tucking the base into the back of her waistband.

"Where is Ms. Fox?" a voice called from behind them.

The three survivors turned around to see the railcar that had arrived while their hearing was impaired.

"She's—down there!" Alice pointed to the elevator. "We should at least gather her—"

A furious growl filled the cavern.

"Never mind, we need to go," Alice revised. "We need to go right fucking now."

Rudy clawed his way out of the crater he had made in the ice slowly. It was clear that he was trying to adjust to moving with three legs. He stumbled slightly as his familiar but awful low cycling growl started again.

"Ma'am, get on the train!" The uniformed security officer ordered as he took aim. Four more soldiers poured out of the armored railcar as Alice and the children found their way inside.

"Open fire!" a different gruff man ordered in a lower voice. Small arms didn't even seem to bother the beast. Five fully automatic rifles emptied their clips into the panther without effect. Rudy started running toward the soldier closest to him at a slower, but still deadly, pace.

"We need to *leave!*" Eleanor stressed. "He's going to kill everyone!"

"Gunner!" The commander called.

A turret at the front of the train rotated as a soldier popped out the top. Large caliber weaponry had evolved over the years, but the same premise remained. The dual-barreled gun lowered to fire on the beast who had just pounced on the first soldier. The deep thump-thump-thump was much louder than the already deafening machine guns. Unlike the soldiers' weapons, Rudy seemed to take notice of the larger turret. The heavy slugs ripped into its armor plating and sent bits of fur flying along with some shards of metal.

Rudy let out a pained yelp and roared at the turret. He lowered his stance and tanked the shots for a moment before raising his head to the turret. Alice watched helplessly as the panther fired a shell from his mouth and sent bits of soldier flying onto the ceiling of the tunnel.

"Good God," the commander mumbled, awestruck. "Get back on the fucking train, ASAP! We are getting the hell out of here!"

Rudy managed to catch another two of the men before they could board and dispatched them both with deadly efficiency before turning his attention on the train.

"He's not going to stop," Eleanor muttered before running to the front of the train as it began to roll.

She looked up and saw a small hatch with a rotating handle. She climbed toward the round doorway via the ladder mounted underneath and spun the handle. As the metal cover lifted, blood flowed down Eleanor's back. They had come this far, and disgusted as she was, there was something more important to do. She pushed aside the torso of the recently departed soldier in the turret nest and grabbed the controls.

She aimed the guns at Rudy who was tearing at the recently closed entry door on the train. Eleanor hoped guns were as easy as they looked. She centered the crosshairs over the hulking beast and pulled both triggers. The thump of the guns kicked against her arms and pierced her eardrums. Rudy yelped and fell from the train as it gained speed. Eleanor looked to her left and had her breath taken away.

There was the same view she had seen on their way into the Arbor. She saw a mangled building, hardly recognizable from the paradise she had been promised just under a week ago. There were black charred bits all across the lawn from where lightning had ravaged the landscape. The wall was blown out of the library. There was a large hole in the back of the house where Rudy had charged out of after Evelyn.

Evelyn.

Eleanor crouched and shut her eyes. They owed so much to her. Without her sacrifice, they would never have had a fighting chance. *Hope you finally have peace*, she thought.

But she wasn't given much time to reflect more than that. Rudy roared and spit a large explosive round over her head.

"Holy bloody Jesus, are you kidding me?"

She stood in the turret and saw Rudy keeping pace with the train.

"Hey! Girl!" A man's voice called from below. Eleanor leaned over and looked down. The commander was looking up at her. "I don't know who you are, but you need to keep fire on that fucker until we get through the blast doors, or it'll follow us all the way back to the station. I don't know about you, but I don't see us surviving that!"

Eleanor took a deep breath and nodded. "Yes, sir!"

As she crawled back to the guns, she could hear her aunt's fervent protests to the CO's decision, but they didn't deter her. The train couldn't be more than thirty seconds from the airlock. *How hard could it be to fire for thirty seconds?*

She peppered a multitude of shots into the creature but to little effect. Every time she would fire a burst, Eleanor would be forced to duck again as the monster took aim for returning fire.

"Go for the eyes, girl!" The commander called from below.

Eyes, she thought.

Eleanor aimed at the creature's maw blindly from below. She would have one shot at this. The doors were approaching fast.

"This is for everyone we've lost," she breathed before checking her aim and firing a final long burst.

The car sailed through the blast doors as Eleanor lay on her back. She was suddenly surprised by the lack of oxygen. She had to check first, though. She stood up one last time and saw the closed doors. Rudy wasn't following them. She'd done it.

Now she needed air.

Eleanor scrambled back through the hatch and the commander slammed it shut behind her. She took a gasping breath and tried to talk fruitlessly.

"Did you get it?" James wondered, wide-eyed.

"Yes!" she replied hoarsely.

A large bellowing laugh shot from the surprisingly endearing southern man beside them.

"Well, hot-damn, girl. I got to say, I'm impressed. What's your name?"

"Eleanor Wortz," she said.

"Well, Eleanor, if you ever think you wanna get some combat training, I could help you out. If you're this deadly as an amateur, I'd love to see you go pro. That is, if your mother is all right with it."

The man's two statements caught Eleanor off-guard. She'd never really thought about what she wanted to do with her life, but law enforcement did sound intriguing, considering all the ugliness she had seen. Then there was the other thing he said.

"Oh, she's not—" Alice began.

"I think I could do some good, Mum," Eleanor meekly replied.

Alice and James both felt their mouths drop open.

"We'll talk about it, mister . . .?" Eleanor added, glancing at the man.

"Cobb," the gruff man answered. "Simon Cobb. Pleasure to meet you. Now, does someone want to tell me what the ever-living hell happened down there?"

"We'd better sit down," Alice suggested.

As her aunt moved to a booth to talk with Cobb, Eleanor followed them into the next room. She felt a tug on her arm. Whipping her head sideways, she saw the same ordinal who'd seen them off on the trip into The Arbor. The steward had a far-away look in his eyes.

"Is he dead?" the aged man asked.

"You—knew?" Eleanor curiously stared. "And you didn't—"

"Is—He—Dead?" the man roughly repeated, squeezing her arm tighter.

"Yes, Jesus, yes! All right?"

"The girl, too?" the man wondered.

"The—girl?"

"Ms. Fox." he answered.

"What do you mean? Why would you ask that?" Eleanor wondered, worry painted across her face.

"I mean, is she dead? Just answer me that."

"Yes," Eleanor hesitantly answered.

"Thank God. I can finally rest."

The man released her arm. He walked calmly to the exit door and slid the handle to the open position. He shoved the door hard, and it flew open. Air rushed from the cabin rapidly and sent paperwork flying. The ordinal was sucked from the train and into the emptiness of the cavern they passed over.

Red cabin lights flashed, and the door shut and locked itself. The papers that had been tossed about gradually wafted their way back down to the floor. Eleanor stood in frozen silence. Her eyes were crazed and wide. Her hands shook. She could still feel the spot on her arm where the man had so roughly grabbed her.

He lumped Winston and Evelyn together. Why would he do that? Eleanor wondered, already knowing the answer.

"She—and he—but that means—" Eleanor muttered in abject horror.

"Eleanor!" Alice called, seeing the room in disarray. "We heard the cabin decompress! What the hell happened?"

Eleanor couldn't find the words. She couldn't speak. She couldn't move. She hadn't budged an inch since that poor nameless ordinal had jumped to his death. It wasn't—Eleanor couldn't imagine it. The thoughts wouldn't assemble in her mind. It was like staring at an optical illusion and not quite believing one's senses.

"Eleanor!" Alice repeated. "Say something!"

"He—was killed," she muttered.

"What?" Alice almost exploded. "Who? What do you mean?"

Eleanor didn't reply. She was still staring at the place from where he had been pulled.

"Who killed him?" Alice screamed.

EPILOGUE

VELYN.

E I watched the doors spin shut. I'd come so far. I'd been through so much. The death of my father was—insufferable. He'd raised me and my brother since our mother was such a complete failure.

I had been saddled with responsibility since I was a little girl. In the absence of a functioning family unit, I took care of many of the duties my mother should have attended to. My father was always so busy constructing his business empire, the kingdom which would one day be mine, that I was tasked with keeping the house, bills, social contacts, and even my brother, in order.

Isabella Fox couldn't take the pressure of living with a husband like my father. She was manic depressive and struggled to cope with day-to-day events without a bottle of liquor glued to her grip. These problems were exacerbated by the emotional toll of having a criminally unstable son. My mother divorced my father when I was eighteen. Of course, both children made the decision to stay with him, and not the psychotic woman who had almost ruined us. Isabella took back her maiden name after divorcing my father, naturally. I always wondered if she just wanted no part of our family anymore, or if she was simply spiteful toward him. Isabella Fox was a powerful name. Isabella Graham sounded almost as weak as she was.

"Evelyn!" Winston screamed. "What the hell did you think you were doing? You fucking stabbed me!"

Winston raised his rifle to my face as though he was going to hurt me. It was as ridiculous as it ever had been as a threat. Winston liked to play the tough man, but he'd always been weak. He had a feeble constitution, minimal impulse control, and always required *me* to clean up after *his* messes.

I pushed the barrel aside and took a step closer.

"Winston, love, do be a dear and give me the benefit of the doubt. Have I ever steered our family wrong?"

He melted slightly as I placed my palm gently against his face. I'd always had a way with him. He was like putty in my hands. My brother possessed a sick mind. Ever since I was a little girl, he'd always tell me how beautiful I was. Honestly, I didn't mind the attention. Winston was handsome and intelligent, and I hardly ever found boys my age who could even hold a candle to my impressive mind.

My father had once said, "*As breathtaking as everyone says you are, don't forget your most magnificent asset—your Fox brain.*"

"No," Winston sighed. "You're right. I know you had to put up a convincing show for the others, but why couldn't we just kill them now? What's the point of extending the charade?"

"Think about it, Winston. Baby, you get a joy out of killing that I just—don't. I've presented them on a platter for you now. So, take your gun and your spear—"

I grabbed the enormous member in Winston's pants and gave an encouraging squeeze along with a raised eyebrow.

"—and go get your dinner, so you can come back for dessert."

"Oh, Evey," he crooned. "I'll be back soon. Don't start without me. You take such good care of me and that was so considerate. What did I do to deserve you?"

I stared at my brother's naive face. It was almost pitiable.

"I don't know, babe," I smiled. "Now hurry back."

He walked into the elevator with the stupidest smile on his face, convinced he was having his wildest fantasies fulfilled when really, I was. The silvery doors slid closed, and I let out the breath I'd been holding to push out my chest. He was so malleable when it came to sex. It was effortless.

"Jason," I called. "What's Ruby's status?"

A speaker hidden beside the elevator chirped on.

"Hello, Ms. Fox," Jason replied. "Now that the others are gone, should I fully re-enable voice commands?"

"Please, Jason. Thank you."

"In that case," he replied. "Ruby has several blown capacitors in her main circuitry. It's nothing that redundant materials couldn't cover, though. Ruby is built with survivability in mind."

"I know," I smiled. "I designed her, Jason."

"Of course, Ms. Fox. Would you like me to pull up replacement procedures for you?"

"No, Jason, thank you. That won't be necessary. I can remember it," I answered as I began to walk toward my downed creation.

How hadn't I accounted for overvolting? The thing had electromagnetic shielding, but that wouldn't do a damned bit of good if lightning struck the sensor pod. When I got around to a redesign, that would be fixed.

I spread myself over Ruby's poor charred frame and lifted from the nape of her neck to reveal the maintenance panel. I'd designed Ruby from the ground up because I was always fascinated with apex predators. It was Winston's stupid fucking idea to name her Rudy because, "*he looked like a boy.*"

As I began swapping circuitry for her spares, I considered my time with Winston.

He had never shown any interest in the company for his entire life until "The Arbor." My father was a man of wisdom, but I never understood his placating of Winston's childish desires. He deemed the boy unworthy of carrying our family name, called it protection for him, and yet he was willing to constantly risk everything for my childish older brother. His desires were basic, barbaric, and yet my father acquiesced to his desire to kill and maim. Rather than shape Winston's behaviors, he invited them through inaction.

What really bothered me, though, wasn't Winston's inability to manage his impulses; it was his selfish nature. I remembered the first time he told me that he had an interest in JCN. I was helping Winston construct his little carnal playground and he said, "I think I might like having a bigger part of running the company."

How convenient. I'd served on the board for six years, but my older brother, who'd never so much as managed a pancake house, thought he would like to come in at the executive level and ruin the empire my father and I had built.

"Oh, poor girl," I muttered as I pulled the singed supercapacitor from her circuit board. "I must add a secondary repair suite in the mark two. Can't have an independent thing like you breaking down on the go."

I stroked Ruby's slick fur as I pushed the replacement part into the blackened socket. Luckily, I'd always loved the A-10 Warthog. I was inspired in my design by the stalwart resiliency of the close-combat fighter. My father used to speak accolades of the plane with his war stories. He romanticized it, and for good reason.

The aircraft had a history of surviving impossible

circumstances. It remained unchanged through almost eighty years of service. I wanted Ruby to gain the same reputation. As I tugged against her central processing unit, its heat sink was still warm to the touch.

"All right and just one more—push!" I said with a grunt as I snapped the replacement CPU into position. I heard the gyro spin up. I flipped the maintenance flap down and took a step back.

Ruby's eyes flitted open.

"Enter safe mode, Ruby. Admin authorization, Evelyn Fox."

Ruby stood frozen in place, awaiting new commands.

"Jason," I called. "Erase all other users but myself from her programming. Also, remove the restrictions Winston placed on her abilities. I want Ruby at her best."

"Of course, ma'am," Jason returned from an indeterminate location. "It's done. She is awaiting your command."

"Hey, baby," I cooed with a smile as I rubbed the underside of her jaw. "I want you to climb that ice wall and take the train platform. Your primary target is Winston Graham. After he is dead, kill the rest."

The cyborg brushed against my hand before giving an affirmative chirp. She was a beast of action. She leapt forward and shook the earth under my feet as she dashed for the ice. Ruby flew from the lawn to the wall without touching water. The leap looked to be at least fifty feet. After she caught her grip on the wall, she ran upward at a pace that rivaled her speed on flat ground. I turned to head back inside as she reached the tracks.

I looked around the lobby of my mangled property. Everything had gone exactly as I'd planned it.

Winston hadn't lived with Father and me for several years. He hadn't seen the once-titanic man's decline. Over the last fourteen months, his condition had worsened. Father had taken a turn for the worse ten months before the Arbor had opened its doors. He'd passed of an internal hemorrhage overnight. I was—devastated.

Despite this, I knew that I would need to tread carefully. The board would be in shambles without his powerful leadership. He hadn't dared to have a meeting with them after he took ill and so had resorted to teleconferencing. My powerful influence was what held JCN together, working as though nothing had changed. My brother, who no one on Mars knew existed, didn't know of his death. I wasn't eager to tell him.

So, I saw opportunity. I allowed the construction to finish on my father's foolhardy dream of The Arbor, and even provided guidance to the architects as him with the assistance of a voice changer.

The question of how to broach my father's death was answered one night while I re-read Shakespeare's "The Tempest." I would manufacture a storm of sorts. I hired poor Wade Gomez under the guise of an acting job and made a few—modifications. I shaped his body into my father's. I snatched his voice away. I broke his mind and threatened his family until he agreed to my terms and expectations of absolute perfection.

The easiest part, ironically enough, was to bait Winston into killing his own father—or the illusion of it. I needed only talk of how he was holding back "our love," and how he would become CEO when our father was gone.

I chuckled at the possibility.

Poor misguided Winston. He was so intelligent but had all the wisdom of a third grader. The man-child was clay in my hands as I sculpted a vision of perfection. With the trap set, all I needed to do was allow Winston to do what he did best.

I'd killed Amelia Rutger on a whim. While living my own personal nightmare, I'd felt the urge to cause pain. I hated to admit it, but as I'd slipped the blade into the widow's chest, I felt a hint of the same excitement my brother felt when he took life.

All good things in moderation, Evelyn, I thought to myself.

"Jason," I called as I climbed the stairs. "Two things. One, draw me a bath in my suite. Two, send out a distress call using my voiceprint in about—three hours? Make me sound absolutely panicked. Urge them to get here quickly. Come up with some excuse for why I'm not dead. Artist's choice."

"Yes, Ms. Fox," Jason replied. I walked in silence for a moment before he chimed back in. "Do you feel relief? Things seem to have worked out just the way you had wanted them to. I must ask, why did you kill your brother? I'm sure there was a reason, but I'm missing the logic."

"Because, Jason," I mused. "Without him, I'm finally free. JCN is mine without a question of ascendancy. I can be free of his childish urges. I can live my life any way I want."

I grabbed my book "Of Mice and Men" from Winston's room before heading back to my own. I'd stayed with him during The Arbor's construction. How did the saying go? Keep your friends close, but your adversaries as bedmates?

"And—" Jason trailed off. "What exactly do you want, miss?"

I re-entered my suite and stripped off my shirt. Letting my skin breathe after being restricted underneath sopping wet clothing felt delightful in the roaring glow of my fireplace. I walked across the large room into the bathroom and let out a sigh of relief.

I stopped and admired my new look in the mirror. The lightning scar curled beautifully like a rough paisley but had all the might and power that I felt within myself. I grinned widely. I'd fought for so long, and now I was glad to rest for a moment. I'd shred all the paperwork in the morning and use my contacts to erase all records of my actions.

I brushed my bruised hand against my marred face and saw nothing but elegance, brilliance, and ferocity staring back at me.

"What do I want, Jason?" I mused as I responded to his question.

"Everything."

How did all this happen? Subscribe to learn more!

Get your free copy of "Virulence," here!

ALSO BY GREG PRADO

Unnatural Selection

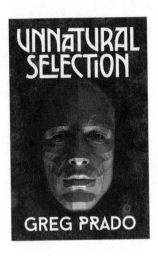

After journeying back to the Gratitude Bio-Mechanical research station, Paul Freeman finds out that his ex-girlfriend's team has discovered intelligent life in the solar system. It's completely contained and is not hostile, yet.

This intense thrill-ride follows our hero as the situation escalates and unfolds in dramatic and unexpected fashion.

Can Paul save his friends? Will the alien life escape containment and wreak havoc on Gratitude? Read "Unnatural Selection" to find out!

Something evil has been born aboard the Shensheng fuel processing facility. The question isn't, "Can it be killed," it's, "Can Sergeant Quintero survive the process?"

After two months of radio silence, the Chinese government has asked the US Army for assistance in a rescue operation aboard the Shensheng fuel processing facility. Upon arrival, Sergeant Dominic Quintero and his joint-operation squad are greeted by an unfriendly welcoming committee who thrusts them headlong into the fray. The descent into madness is peppered with hellbeasts whose true nature remains suspiciously mysterious. Is there more going on than meets the eye? Read *Virulence* to find out!

ABOUT THE AUTHOR

After almost a decade, Greg Prado is extremely pleased to offer his stories to the public. He enjoys writing anything related to Sci-fi, the future, and especially mystery. Greg lives in Apopka, Florida with his wife, daughter, and two mischievous cats. He's a bit of a space junkie and is unafraid to discuss it with anyone willing to listen!

Subscribe and read *Virulence*, a chilling tale of a super-bug gone horribly wrong. You might also learn a bit more about the Fox family . . . !

Made in the USA
San Bernardino, CA
05 April 2020